William Shakespeare, Karl Warnke, Ludwig Proescholdt

Pseudo-Shakespearian Plays

William Shakespeare, Karl Warnke, Ludwig Proescholdt

Pseudo-Shakespearian Plays

ISBN/EAN: 9783741186509

Manufactured in Europe, USA, Canada, Australia, Japa

Cover: Foto ©Andreas Hilbeck / pixelio.de

Manufactured and distributed by brebook publishing software
(www.brebook.com)

William Shakespeare, Karl Warnke, Ludwig Proescholdt

Pseudo-Shakespearian Plays

PSEUDO-SHAKESPEARIAN PLAYS.

EDITED

BY

KARL WARNKE, PH. D.

AND

LUDWIG PROESCHOLDT, PH. D.

I. FAIRE EM.

HALLE:

MAX NIEMEYER.

1883.

THE COMEDIE OF FAIRE EM

REVISED AND EDITED

WITH INTRODUCTION AND NOTES

BY

KARL WARNKE, PH. D.

AND

LUDWIG PROESCHOLDT, PH. D.

HALLE:

MAX NIEMEYER.

1883.

The comedy of Faire Em has been handed down to us in two quarto editions, the one published in 1631 (A), the other without a date (B). Of the former, three copies are preserved in the British Museum (643. c. 14, $\frac{\text{b. 21. c}}{\text{b}}$, 161. a. 26); of the latter, only one copy is known to be extant.[1]) The edition of 1631 is entitled: 'A Pleasant Comedie of Faire Em, The Millers Daughter of Manchester. With the Love of William the Conqueror. As it was sundry times publiquely acted in the Honourable Citie of London, by the right Honourable the Lord Strange his Seruants. London, Printed for John Wright, and are to be sold at his shop at the signe of the Bible in Guilt-spur street without Newgate. 1631.' The title of the undated edition agrees with the one just given, except in the imprint, which runs thus: 'Imprinted at London for T. N. and J. W. and are to be solde in S. Dunstones Churchyarde in Fleete-streete.' As little as in the title, the two editions differ in the text of the play itself. In both editions, the critic meets with the same senseless readings; in both, a number of scenes, evidently written as verse by the author, have been corrupted to prose; and in both, these prose-passages have, in the same most arbitrary manner, been printed as verse. It is therefore all but certain that one of the two editions is a mere reprint of the other. And there can be little doubt as to which of them is to be regarded by us as the *Editio princeps* of the play. The spelling in the undated edition is of a more ancient character than in the edition of 1631; cp. the frequent use of *au* (A) for *a* (B) in *Blaunch, straunge* e c., the ending *-es* (A) for *-s* (B) in *ornamentes, cowardes* etc., the use of *y* (A) for *i* (B) in *tylt, Yle, reuyled*; *ashamde* (A) for *asham'd* (B),

---

[1]) The initials E. M. on the fly-leaf of the copy in the Bodleian Library point to Malone as former possessor of it. Two short notes, occasionally written in the margin of the book, were probably made by the same scholar.

uerie (A) for *uery* (B), etc. In some few instances, besides, the edition of 1631 corrects misprints or wrong readings of the undated edition, viz. II. 1. 82 A *true lover*, B *truer love;* III. 1. 15 A *I would*, B *It would;* V. 1. 144 *is* wanting in A, added in B. Moreover, it is not probable that a piece of so little intrinsic value as Faire Em should have been reprinted after the year 1631, i. e. a few years before the Puritan Revolution put a temporary stop to all play-writing.

A third edition of our comedy is mentioned by a certain Chetwood, who, in 1750, published Faire Em together with five other plays. His edition bears the same title as A and B; the imprint is as follows: Dublin: Printed and Sold by the Editor W. R. Chetwood, in the Four-court-marshalsea; Messrs. G. and A. Ewing, P. Wilson, H. Hawker, and S. Price, in Dame-street; G. Faulkner, and A. Long, in Essex-Street; J. Hoey, in Skinner Row, and J. Edall, in Corkhill, Booksellers. MDCCL.. In his short preface, Chetwood imparts to the reader his opinions as to the time, the author and the different editions of our play. 'I cannot learn', he says, 'who is the Author of this Play, but by the Stile, Conduct and Manner, take it to be wrote in the latter End of the Reign of Queen Elizabeth. I have seen three different editions of it, the First without a Date, and not divided into Acts; the second, in 1619, with the Acts divided, and some immaterial Alterations. However I have chose to follow that. The last Edition seems only to be a copy of the first, since no Acts are distinguished.' The 'Last Edition', mentioned by Chetwood, is probably that of 1631; the second, however, which he pretends to have followed, must certainly have been a *rara avis*. No copy of it is known to be extant, and with the exception of Chetwood, no one seems to have mentioned it. It may, therefore, well be doubted whether there ever existed an edition of 1619. And indeed, examining the alterations in Chetwood's text, which are far from being immaterial, we shall easily find that all of them bear the stamp of the age in which Pope edited the works of Shakespeare. The metre has occasionally been smoothed by the omission or the addition of some indifferent word; harsh and vulgar expressions have carefully been expunged; so *chastity*, *God*, *huswife*, *lust*, *slut* have been changed into *honour*, *Heaven*, *madam*, *love*, *maid*. Very often one or more lines have been omitted, and once or twice prose-passages have been turned into verse. At the end of the acts, some rhyme-couplet has generally been added, which, in its rhetorical and bombastic style, widely differs from the rest of the play. We shall, therefore, hardly be mistaken in supposing Chetwood himself to have been the author of the alterations in question. In order to give more credit to his own emendations, he probably thought it expedient to pretend them to have been drawn from an old edition. Steevens, too, occasionally calls Chetwood, who was also the author of a History of the Stage and of a Life of Ben Jonson, 'a blockhead and a measureless and bungling liar.'

In our own time, the Comedy of Faire Em has been twice republished, by Prof. N. Delius and by the late Mr. Simpson. In the introduction to his edition [2]), Prof. Delius discusses Tieck's hypothesis on the author of our play and gives a short account of Chetwood's edition. As to the latter, he arrives at the same conclusion as the present editors who for several of the details given above are indebted to his remarks. As Prof. Delius was not aware of the existence of the undated edition at the Bodleian Library, his text of the play, printed in modern orthography, is on the whole formed from the edition of 1631. In the Introduction, he enumerates some of Chetwood's alterations and some conjectures of his own. That list, however, is far from being exhaustive; for in more than one instance, Prof. Delius has departed from the original text, or has adopted Chetwood's alterations, without giving the reader any notice of it. His edition has certainly the merit of having first called the attention of German scholars to Faire Em, but our notes will sufficiently prove that it cannot stand the test to which we now-a-days usually submit a critical edition.

Mr. Simpson's edition of Faire Em [3]) is superior to that of Delius in many respects. In a number of passages, the English editor has succeeded in restoring the sense and in correcting the metre of the play. In most of these cases, short foot-notes indicate the reading of the quarto-editions. We must however regret that Mr. Simpson was prevented by a premature death from comparing those foot-notes once more with the originals. Many an error

---

[2]) Pseudo-Shaksperesche Dramen. Herausgegeben von Nicolaus Delius. Fünftes Heft: Fair Em. Elberfeld, 1874.

[3]) The School of Shakspere. By Richard Simpson. London, 1878, vol. II, p. 337 seqq.

would, we are convinced, have been corrected, many an addition
would have been made, and many a reading would have been
amended. The editor of Mr. Simpson's posthumous work, Mr.
Gibbs, has been contented with adding some few conjectures or
corrections and with superintending the printing of the book. Such
as it is, Mr. Simpson's edition of Faire Em is only an example
of the ancient, now-a-days superseded eclectic method of editing
the productions of the past.

The greatest interest in our play has been evinced by Prof.
Elze. On different occasions [4]) he has tried to restore the corrupt
text and the defective versification of the play. A number of the
emendations, proposed by that distinguished scholar, are almost in-
contestable; others may be called in question by a more conservative critic; all of them bear testimony to their author's skill and
learning and should certainly not be overlooked either by the editor
or by the reader of Faire Em.

The question as to the author of the Comedy of Faire Em
has been repeatedly taken up; but as conclusive proofs are absolutely wanting, it is not likely ever to be brought to a satisfactory
close, unless new documents are produced.

The German critic-poet, L. Tieck, to whom his countrymen
owe a translation of Faire Em, ascribed the play to no meaner
a poet than to Shakespeare himself.[5]) The evidence by which he
supported this hypothesis is the same as that by which he was
induced to attribute Mucedorus to Shakespeare. In the library of
King Charles II., we are informed, there existed a volume labelled
Shakespeare, vol. I., which contained Mucedorus, The Merry Devil
of Edmonton, and Faire Em. The same remarks which we have
made on this criterion in our Introduction to Mucedorus, apply to
Faire Em. We are entirely ignorant to whom the book originally
belonged, and on whose authority the bookbinder gave it the title
in question. It may be that the original owner of the volume was
guided by some tradition which has long since sunk into oblivion,
or that he ascribed the three plays to Shakespeare only because
they had been represented at the Globe. That, moreover, at the

---

[4]) Notes on Elizabethan Dramatists. Halle, 1880, p. 6 seqq., p. 125 seqq.
— Jahrbuch der Deutschen Shakespeare-Gesellschaft, vol. XV., p. 344 seqq.

[5]) Ludwig Tieck, Shakespeare's Vorschule. Leipzig, 1829, Vol. II,
p. VI seqq.

time the book was bound, Shakespeare was not generally considered as the author of the three comedies, appears from the fact that the editors of the third folio of Shakespeare's works, although admitting seven plays, not contained in Ff AB, did not include in it either Mucedorus, or the Merry Devil of Edmonton, or lastly Faire Em.

Tieck's hypothesis seems not to have met with much approbation: as far as we know, only one critic has taken it up and endeavoured to support it with a number of new arguments. That critic is Mr. Simpson, who in the long and learned Introduction to his edition of our play has carefully pointed out all that can be alleged in favour of Shakespeare being the author of Faire Em. We think it well to lay before the reader the line of argument adopted by the English scholar.

The basis of Mr. Simpson's inquiry is a passage taken from the Introduction to Greene's Farewell to Folly, in which the Comedy of Faire Em and its author appear to have been alluded to. That passage, as far as it is of interest to us, runs thus:[6] 'But, by your leave, gentlemen, some, overcurious, will carp and say, that if I were not beyond I would not be so bold to teach my betters their duty, and to show them the sun that have brighter eyes than myself. Well, Diogenes told Alexander of his folly, and yet he was not a king. Others will flout and over-read every line with a frump, and say 'tis scurvy, when they themselves are such scabbed lads that they are like to die of the *fazion*; but if they come to write, or publish any thing in print, it is either distilled out of ballets[7]), or borrowed of Theological poets, which, for their calling and gravity being loth to have any prophane pamphlets pass under their hand, get some other Batillus to set his name to their verses. Thus is the ass made proud by this underhand brokery. And he that cannot write true English without the help of clerks of parish churches will needs make himself the father of interludes. O 'tis a jolly matter when a man hath a familiar style, and can endite a whole year and never be beholding to art. But to bring Scripture to prove anything he says, and kill it dead with the text in a

---

6) Simpson, l. c., p. 377 seq.

7) 'Part of the plot of Faire Em was probably distilled from the ballad licensed to Henry Carre, March 2, 1580—81, under the title of *The Miller's Daughter of Manchester*.' Simpson, l. c.

as well as the third of Faire Em's suitors, Manuile, are to represent play-writers of the time. As to Mountney and Manuile, Mr. Fleay agrees with Mr. Simpson in identifying them with Marlowe and Greene. Valingford, however, is not Shakespeare, but George Peele.[9]) All three of them try to win the hand of Faire Em. Who is Faire Em? Certainly not the Manchester public, with whom the poets had nothing to do, but the Company of the Queen's players, with whom the poets were seeking connection. Greene, we know, was connected with that company up to the year 1589; Orlando, Friar Bacon and Friar Bungay, and James the Fourth were all written for the Queen's players. In 1589, when Kempe had returned to England, the Queen's company seems, according to our play, to have dissolved its connection with Greene and entered a new engagement with G. Peele. This date coïncides pretty well with what we know about the time in which Faire Em was published (before 1591).

We cannot but acknowledge the skill and sagacity which the English scholar has shown in putting forth and defending his theory. Nevertheless, he has not succeeded in winning us over to his opinion. Mr. Fleay himself must own that the allegory for which he and Mr. Simpson take the fable of the play, lacks consistency. Mountney and Valingford are the managers of the Queen's Company, left in England by W. Kempe, and directly after we are told they are two poets who try to get connected with the Queen's Company, i. e. with the very same managers of it. Then, we have no historical proof whatever as to the relations entertained by Greene and Peele with the Queen's Company. We do not know how it came that Greene ceased writing for that Company, nor are we anywhere informed that Peele was his successor. Lastly, it is not probable that Greene, alluding as he did to the Comedy of Faire Em, should have been content merely with glancing at it, when he himself played such a part in it, as Manuile does. Vindictive, as we know he was, he would certainly have wrought his vengeance in a less gentle manner.

It may well be that the idea of the comedy was prompted to

---

[9]) 'Camden says that *Wallingford* is *Guall-hen* "The old rampire or fort." But an old fort is a Peel, and under this name that of George Peele is as certainly indicated as it is under that of Pyeboard in The Puritan.' Mr. Fleay, l. c., p. 282.

the unknown author of it by W. Kempe's visit at the Danish court. Likewise, it may well be that some of the incidents of the play refer to certain events of the stage. But it seems impossible to find out the clew of these events and to fix the details of them with any degree of probability.

As to the present edition of Faire Em, there remains little to be said. The text, as given in the old copies, seems not to have been derived from the author's manuscript, but from some report taken down in short-hand at the representation of the play. Only thus can we account for the numerous instances of faulty versification; only thus can we explain the fact that several scenes which, to all appearance, were written in verse by the poet, have been handed down to us in prose (printed as irregular verse in Qq). Notwithstanding, we have thought it best to be as conservative as possible in the re-establishment of the text, and to admit emendations only in cases where the sense or the construction decidedly require to be corrected or where the metre may without difficulty be restored. The different readings of the two quarto-editions as well as the conjectures, made by Delius, Simpson, and Elze, have been carefully embodied in the notes, which, we hope, will prove to be more faithful and complete than those of the former editions.

The quarto-editions of our play are not divided into acts and scenes. Chetwood divided the play into five acts, Tieck into eighteen scenes; Delius, combining these two divisions, has five acts and eighteen scenes. Our acts and scenes correspond with those of Delius; but we have followed Simpson in contracting sc. XVII and XVIII (Act V.) into one. Simpson has seventeen scenes, but only three acts, act III., IV., and V. forming one act in his edition.

FAIRE EM,

DRAMATIS PERSONÆ. [a]

WILLIAM THE CONQUEROR.
ZWENO, *King of Denmark.*
DUKE DIROT.
MARQUES LUBECK.
MOUNTNEY.
MANUILE.
VALINGFORD.

ROSILIO. [b]
DEMARCH. [c]
Danish Ambassador.
The Miller of Manchester.
TROTTER, *his man.*
Citizen of Chester.

BLAUNCH [d], *Princess of Denmark.*
MARIANA, *Princess of Swethia.*
FAIRE EM, *the Miller's Daughter.*
ELNER [e], *the Citizen's Daughter.*

English and Danish Nobles.
Soldiers, Countrymen, and Attendants.

a. Wanting in Qq.; first added by Chetwood. — b. *Rocilia* B (III. 5, 25), *Rozilio* Chet. — c. *Dimach* A (I. 1, 74), *Dimarch* Chet. (III. 6, 14). — d. *Blanch* B (passim), *Blannch* A (II. 2, 44). — e. *Eliner* Chet., *Elinor* Del.

A C T I.

SCENE I.

Enter William *the* Conqueror; Marques Lubeck, *with a picture;* Mountney; Manuile; Valingford; *and* Duke Dirot.

    Lub. What meanes faire Britaines mighty Conqueror
So suddenly to cast away his staffe,
And all in passion to forsake the tylt?
    Dir. My Lord, this triumph we solemnise here
Is of meere loue to your increasing ioyes,   5
Only expecting cheerefull lookes for all;
What sudden pangs then moues your maiesty
To dimme the brightnesse of the day with frownes?
    Wm. Ah, good my Lords, misconster not the cause;
At least, suspect not my displeased browes: 10
I amorously do beare to your intent,
For thanks and all that you can wish I yeeld.
But that which makes me blush and shame to tell
Is cause why thus I turne my conquering eyes
To cowardes looks and beaten fantasies.   15
    Mount. Since we are giltlesse, we the lesse dismay
To see this sudden change possess your cheere,
For if it issue from your owne conceits
Bred by suggestion of some enuious thoughts,
Your highnesse wisdome may suppresse it straight.   20
 Yet tell us, good my Lord, what thought it is

Actus Primus. Scæna Prima. Qq. — Stage-direction. *Enter . . . . Marquis of Lubeck, with a picture on his shield, as coming from the tournament, Mountney ..* Chet. — 1. Prefixed *Marques* in Qq (passim), *conqueror*, Del. — 4. For *solémnise* see Abbott, A Shakespearian Grammar, s. 491. Chet. has needlessly altered the line to *My Lord, the triumph, we have here set forth.* — 7. *pang* Del. — 12. *thanks: and* Simp. — 15. *coward looks* Del.

1*

That thus bereaues you of your late content,
That in aduise we may assist your Grace,
Or bend our forces to reuiue your spirits.

25   *Wm.*   Ah, Marques Lubeck, in thy power it lyes
To rid my bosome of these thraled dumps:
And therefore, good my Lords, forbeare a while
That we may parley of these priuate cares,
Whose strength subdues me more than all the world.

30   *Val.*   We goe and wish the priuate conference
Publicke affectes in this accustomed peace.

       [Exit all but WILLIAM *and the* MARQUES.
 Wm.   Now, Marques, must a conquerer at armes
Disclose himselfe thrald to vnarmed thoughts,
And, threatned of a shaddow, yeeld to lust.

35   No sooner had my sparkeling eyes beheld
The flames of beautie blasing on this peece,
But sodenly a sence of myracle,
Imagined on thy louely Maistres face,
Made mee abandon bodily regard,

40   And cast all pleasures on my woonded soule:
Then, gentle Marques, tell me what she is,
That thus thou honourest on thy warlike shield;
And if thy loue and interest be such
As iustly may give place to mine,

45   That if it be, my soule with honors wings
May fly into the bosome of my deere —
If not, close them, and stoope into my graue!
 Lub.   If this be all, renowned conquerer,
Aduance your drooping spirites, and reuiue

50   The wonted courage of your Conquering minde;
For this faire picture painted on my shield
Is the true counterfeit of louely Blaunch,

---

24. *Or bind* Del. — *your joys* Chet. — 26. *To aid my* Del. — *thral-led woes.* Chet. — As for *thraled*, cp. Elze, Notes, XII, p. 6 seq., and Shakesp., Sonnet CXXIV, and Tam. I. 1. 225; for *dump*, see Marlowe's Doctor Faustus and Greene's Friar Bacon and Friar Bungay, ed. A. W. Ward, Note to I. 12 (p. 197). — 30. *thee priuate* Qq, *this private* Del., *the private* Simp. conj. — 31. Del. prints and Simp. explains *Public effects.* — *in thy accustomed* Del. — 34. *yield to love?* Chet.

Princes and daughter to the King of Danes,
Whose beautie and excesse of ornamentes
Deserues another manner of defence,   55
Pompe and high person to attend her state
Then Marques Lubeck any way presents.
Therefore her vertues I resigne to thee,
Alreadie shrinde in thy religious brest,
To be aduanced and honoured to the full;   60
Nor beare I this an argument of loue,
But to renowne faire Blaunch, my Soueraignes Childe,
In euerie place where I by armes may doe it.

   Wm. Ah Marques, thy words bring heauen vnto my soule,
And had I heauen to giue for thy reward,   65
Thou shouldst be thronde in no vnworthy place.
But let my vttermost wealth suffice thy worth,
Which here I vowe, and to aspire the blisse
That hangs on quicke atchiuement of my loue,
Thy selfe and I will trauell in disguise,   70
To bring this Ladie to our Brittaine Court.

   Lub. Let William but bethinke what may auayle,
And let mee die if I denie my ayde.

   Wm. Then thus: The Duke Dirot, and th'erle Demarch,
Will I leaue substitutes to rule my Realme,   75
While mightie loue forbids my being here;
And in the name of Sir Robert of Windsor
Will goe with thee vnto the Danish Court.
Keepe Williams secretes, Marques, if thou loue him.
Bright Blaunch, I come! sweet fortune, fauour me,   80
And I will laud thy name eternally!

                                     [Exeunt.

61. *this, an* Del., *this an* = *this as an* Gibbs (apud Simp.). — 64. *Ah,
friend! thy* Chet. — *heaven into my* Chet. and Del. — 67. *my utmost* Chet.
— 69. *atchievements* Del. — 71. *our royal court.* Chet. — 74. *Dimach* A
(through the rest of the play spelled *Demarch*). — *and earl Dimach,* Chet.
— 77. *And, in the feigned name of Robert Windsor* Chet.; Simp. proposes
to expunge *Sir.* — 80, 81. *sweet fortune, smile on me,* ‖ *And altars shall be
rais'd to worship thee.* Chet.

SCENE II.

Enter the MILLER *and* EM, *his daughter.*

Mil. Come, daughter, we must learne to shake of pompe,
To leaue the state that earst beseemd a Knight
And gentleman of not a meane discent,
To vndertake this homely millers trade:
5 Thus must we maske, to saue our wretched liues,
Threatned by Conquest of this haplesse Yle,
Whose sad inuasions by the Conqueror,
Haue made a number such as we subiect.
Their gentle neckes vnto the stubborne yoke
10 Of drudging labour and base pesantrie.
Sir Thomas Goddard how old Goddard is,
Goddard the Miller of faire Manchester.
Why should not I content me with this state,
As good Sir Edmund Trofferd did the flaile?
15 And thou, sweet Em, must stoope to high estate
To ioyne with mine that thus we may protect
Our harmlesse liues, which, ledd in greater port,
Would be an enuious obiect to our foes,
That seeke to root all Britaines Gentrie
20 From bearing countenance gainst their tyrannie.
  Em. Good Father, let my full resolued thoughts
With setled patiens to support this chaunce
Be some poore comfort to your aged soule;
For therein restes the height of my estate,
25 That you are pleased with this deiection,
And that all toyles my hands may vndertake
May serue to worke your worthines content.
  Mil. Thankes, my deere daughter. These thy plesant words

SCENE II. 3. *of no meane* Qq; the correction as given in our text
was suggested by Simp. — 9. *vnto their stubborne* Qq, corr. by Del. —
11. *Thomas Godard* A (in all other instances spelled *Goddard*). — 14. *Edmund Trostard* Del. — 15. *stoope,* i. e. *submit.* — *stoop thy high* Del. —
Simp. thinks *to high* to be a mistake for *to like; to like estate,* however,
would little agree with the following *to ioyne with mine.* — 19. Simp., over-
looking that *Gentrie* has the quality of a trisyllable here, adds *up* at the
end of the line. — 19, 20. Omitted by Chet. — 20. *against* Qq. — 25. Omitted
by Chet. — 28. *thy pleasing words* Chet.

Transferre my soule into a second heauen:
And in thy setled minde my ioyes consist,   30
My state reuyues, and I'm in former plight.
Although our outward pomp be thus abased,
And thralde to drudging, staylesse of the world,
Let vs retaine those honorable mindes
That lately gouerned our superior state,   35
Wherein true gentrie is the only meane
That makes vs differ from base millers borne.
Though we expect no knightly delicates,
Nor thirst in soule for former soueraigntie,
Yet may our myndes as highly scorne to stoope   40
To base desires of vulgars worldlynes,
As if we were in our presedent way.
And, lonely daughter, since thy youthfull yeares
Must needes admit as yong affections,
And that sweet loue vnpartiall perceiues   45
Her daintie subiects thorough euery part,
In chief receiue these lessons from my lippes,
The true discouerers of a Virgins due,
Now requisite, now that I know thy minde
Something enclynde to fauour Manuils sute,   50
A gentleman, thy Louer in protest;
And that thou maist not be by loue deceiued,
But trye his meaning fit for thy desert,
In pursuit of all amorous desires,
Regard thine honour. Let not vehement sighes,   55
Nor earnest vowes importing feruent loue,
Render thee subiect to the wrath of lust.

31. *reuyued, and I in* Qq; for the reading as given above the present Edd.
are answerable. — 33. Omitted by Chet. — *And thrall to* Del. — 35. *That
lately* A. — 37. *from plebeian birth* Chet. — 38. *Knightly delicates.* Compare *princely delicates* (Marlowe's Doctor Faustus I. 83) and *a prince's delicates* (3 Henry VI., II. 5, 51). — 41. *of vulgar worldliness* Chet. — *word-
liness* Del. (see II. 3, 38). — 44. *admit of young* Chet. — 45. Instead of
perceiues Simp. needlessly proposes to read either *deceives*, or *peruses*, or
pursues, or *perverts.* — 45, 46. Omitted by Chet. — 46. *dainie* B. —
through Qq, *thorough* Del. and Simp. — 47. *In brief* Del. — 54. Omitted
by Chet. — 57. *wrath of love* Chet.

For that, transformed to form of sweet delight,
Will bring thy body and thy soule to shame.
60 Chaste thoughts and modest conuersations,
Of proofe to keepe out all inchaunting vowes,
Vaine sighes, forst teares, and pittifull aspects,
Are they that make deformed Ladies faire,
Poore wretch, and such intycing men,
65 That seeke of all but onely present grace,
Shall in perseuerance of a Virgins due
Prefer the most refusers to the choyce
Of such a soule as yeelded what they thought.
But hoe: where 's Trotter?

> *[Here enters* TROTTER, *the Millers man, to them: and they within call to him for their gryste.*

70   *Trot.* Where's Trotter? why, Trotter is here. Yfaith, you and your daughter go up and downe weeping and wamenting, and keeping of a wamentation, as who should say, the Mill would goe with your wamenting.

        Mil. How now, Trotter? why complainest thou so?

75   *Trot.* Why, yonder is a company of yong men and maydes, keepe such a styr for their gryst, that they would haue it before my stones be readie to grind it. But, yfaith, I would I coulde breake winde enough backward: you should not tarrie for your gryst, I warrant you.

80   *Mil.* Content thee, Trotter, I will go pacifie them.

        Trot. I wis you will when I cannot. Why, looke, you haue a Mill — Why, what's your Mill without mee? Or rather, Mistres, what were I without you?

> *[Here he taketh* EM *about the neck.*

58. *to former* Qq; *to form of* is Simp.'s conjecture. — 63. *deformed bodies fair.* Del. — 64. Simp. proposes to read *And poor ones rich* instead of *Poore wretch.* — 64, 65. By a strange blunder the words *such* and *all* are transposed in Simp.'s edition; but Simp., rightly discerning what the sense of the passage requires, proposes in a foot-note the arrangement of the words as it is found in the old copies. — 66. *Virgin's vow* Simp. conj. — 68. '*Qy: they sought?*' Simp. — The whole speech of the Miller reminds the reader of Polonius' advice to Laertes (Haml. I. 3, 55—81) and of the precepts given to Bertram by the Countess in All's Well I. 1, 69—81. — 69. *where is* Qq, *where's* Simp. — 70—73. As four lines in Qq, divided at *here | weeping | wamentation | wamenting.* — 70. *Trotter's here* Chet. — 80. *I'll go* Simp. — 82. *Ot rather* A. — 83. The stage-direction omitted by Del.

Em. Nay, Trotter, if you fall a chyding, I will giue
you ouer. 85

Trot. I chyde you, dame, to amend you. You are too
fyne to be a Millers daughter; for if you should but stoope
to take vp the tole-dish, you will haue the crampe in your
finger at least ten weekes after.

Mil. Ah, well said, Trotter; teach her to play the good 90
huswife, and thou shalt haue her to thy wife, if thou canst
get her good wil.

Trot. Ah, words! wherein I see Matrimonie come loaden
with kisses to salute me: Now let me alone to pick the mill,
to fill the hopper, to take the tole, to mend the sayles, yea, 95
and to make the mill to go with the verie force of my loue.

      [Here they must call for their gryst within.
I come, I come; yfaith, now you shall haue your gryst, or
else Trotter will trott and amble himselfe to death.

      [They call him againe. Exit.

SCENE III.

Enter KING OF DENMARKE, *with some Attendants,* BLAUNCH *his
daughter,* MARIANA, MARQUES LUBECK, WILLIAM, *disguised.*

King. Lord Marques Lubecke, welcome home.
Welcome, braue Knight, vnto the Denmarke King,
For Williams sake, the noble Norman Duke,
So famous for his fortunes and successe,
That graceth him with name of Conqueror; 5
Right double welcome must thou be to us.

Rob. Wind. And to my Lord the King shall I recount
Your graces courteous entertainment,
That for his sake vouchsafe to honor me,
A simple Knight, attendant on his grace. 10

King. But say, Sir Knight, what may I call your name?

---

84. *yon fall* A. — *you o'er* Del. — 85—88. Printed as five lines in
Qq, ending *amend you | daughter | tole-dish | finger | after.* — 89. *fingers*
Chet. — 90. *to play* omitted by Del. — 96. *Here they call* ... Chet. —
98. *They ... again. Exeunt.* Del.
    SCENE III. Stage-direction: *Enter Zweno, King of Denmark* ... Chet.

 Rob. Wind. Robert Windsor, and like your maiestie.

 King. I tell thee, Robert, I so admire the man

As that I count it haynous guilt in him

15 That honours not Duke William with his heart.

Blaunch, bid this straunger welcome, good my gyrle.

 Blaunch. Sir,

Should I neglect your highnes charge herein,

It might be thought of base discourtesie.

20 Welcome, Sir Knight, to Denmarke, hartelie.

 Rob. Wind. Thanks, gentle Ladie. Lord Marques, what is she?

 Lub. That same is Blaunch, the daughter to the King,

The substance of the shadow that you saw.

 Rob. Wind. May this be shee, for whom I crost the Seas?

25 I am ashamde to think I was so fond,

In whom there's nothing that contents my mynd,

Ill head, worse featurde, vncomly, nothing courtly;

Swart and ill fauored, a Colliers sanguine skin.

I neuer saw a harder fauour'd Slut;

30 Loue her? for what? I can no whit abide her!

 King. Mariana, I haue this day receiued letters

From Swethia, that lets me vnderstand

Your raunsome is collecting there with speed,

And shortly shalbe hither sent to vs.

35 *Mar.* Not that I finde occasion to mislike

---

12. *Robert of Windsor, so please your* Chet., *Robert of Windsor. an't*
Del. Qy: *Robert Windsor, an it* (*Robert* having the quality of a monosyllable)? — 13. Del. reads *Knight* instead of *Robert*. — 14. *famous guilt*
Del. — 15. *in his heart* Del. — 16. *good my child* Chet. — 17. *Sir* omitted
by Del. — 17, 18. Printed as one line in Qq; in placing *Sir* in a separate
line we have followed Simp. Both lines are omitted in Chet. — 18. *therein*
Del. — 20. *to Denmark's royal court* Chet. — 22. *Blaunch, daughter* Qq,
the inserted by Chet. and Simp. Elze prefers to read *Blanch, sole daughter,*
since, lower down (IV. 2, 7), we are informed that Blanch is the king's 'only
daughter' (See Elze, Notes, XIII, p. 7). — 27. *Ill head = Ill-headed?* The
only passage where we have met with the compound *ill-headed,* is in Spenser's
Faerie Queene, bk IV, c. I, st. 3, l. 4; but there it has the sense of 'disturbed in the head'. Simp. and Elze think our passage corrupt; the former
proposes to read *Ill head, worse face,* the latter (Notes, XIV, p. 8) *Ill-shaped,
worse-featured.* — 29. *harder-favour'd maid.* Chet. — 34. *shortly hither
shall be* Del. — 35. *of mislike* Qq, *of misliking* Del., *to mislike* Simp. conj.
— 'Evidently there is something wanting here; Mariana's speech should begin

My entertainment in your graces court,
But that I long to see my natiue home —
 King. And reason haue you, Madam, for the same.
Lord Marques, I commit vnto your charge
The entertainment of Sir Robert here; 40
Let him remaine with you within the Court,
In solace and disport to spend the time.
 Rob. Wind. I thank your highnes, whose bounden I remaine.
  [*Exit* KING OF DENMARKE.
 Blaunch. [*speaketh this secretly at one end of the stage*]
Vnhappie Blaunch, what strange effects are these
That workes within my thoughts confusedly? 45
That still, me thinkes, affection drawes me on,
To take, to like, nay more, to loue this knight.
 Rob. Wind. A modest countenance; no heauie sullen looke;
Not uerie fayer, but ritchly deckt with fauour;
A sweet face, an exceeding daintie hånd; 50
A body were it framed of wax
By all the cunning Artists of the world,
It could not better be proportioned.
 Lub. How now, Sir Robert? in a studie, man?
Here is no tyme for contemplation. 55
 Rob. Wind. My Lord, there is a certain odd conceit
Which on the sudden greatly troubles me.
 Lub. How like you Blaunch? I partly do perceiue
The little boy hath played the wagg with you.
 Rob. Wind. The more I look the more I loue to look. 60
Who seyes that Mariana is not faire?
Ile gage my gauntlet gainst the enuious man
That dares auow there liueth her compare.
 Lub. Sir Robert, you mistake your counterfait,
This is the Lady which you came to see. 65

with a line somewhat to the following effect: *It glads my heart to hear
these joyful tidings'* &c. (Elze, Notes, p. 134). — 37. *But I that I* Del. —
home. Qq, *home* — the pres. Edd. — 38. Omitted by Chet. — 43. *hightness*
A, *highnes* B. — *whose bounden I remain* om. by Chet. -- In Qq the
stage-direction is after l. 42; set right by Del. — 44. [*Aside*] Del. --- 45. *work*
Del. -- 51. *formed all of wax* Del., *framed all of wax* Simp. conj. —
54. *in a study.* Compare *in a brown study*, Friar Bacon and Friar Bungay,
ed. Ward, XIV, 100 (p. 105 and p. 266).

Rob. Wind. Yea, my Lord: She 's counterfait in deed,
For there's the substance that contents me best.
  Lub. That is my loue. Sir Robert, you do wrong me.
  Rob. Wind. The better for you, Sir, she is your Loue —
70 As for the wrong, I see not how it growes.
  Lub. In seeking that which is anothers right.
  Rob. Wind. As who should say your loue were priuileged,
That none might looke vpon her but your selfe.
  Lub. These iarres becomes not our familiaritie,
75 Nor will I stand on termes to moue your patience.
  Rob. Wind. Why, my Lord,
An't I of flesh and bloud as well as you?
Then giue me leaue to loue as well as you.
  Lub. . To loue, Sir Robert? but whom? not she I loue?
80 Nor stands it with the honor of my state
To brooke corriuals with me in my loue.
  Rob. Wind. So, Sir, we are thorough for that L[ady].
Ladies, farewell. Lord Marques, will you go?
He finde a time to speake with her I trow.
85   *Lub.* With all my heart. Come, Ladies, wil you walke?
                [Exit.

SCENE IV.

Enter MANUILE *alone, disguised.*

 Man. Ah, Em! the subiect of my restlesse thoughts,
The Anuyle whereupon my heart doth beat,
Framing thy state to thy desert —

---

66. *Yes, my Lord* Del. — *She is* Qq, *She's* the pres. Edd. — 67. *there is* Qq, *there's* Chet. and Simp. — *that best contents me* Qq; Simp. proposes to read, either, *For there's the substance that doth best content me,* or, *For there's the substance best contenteth me;* our text is regulated according to El.'s suggestion (see Notes, XV, pp. 8 seq.). — 68. *That is my love, Sir Robert; you do me wrong.* Del. — 74. *become* Del. — 76, 77. Printed as one line in Qq, divided by Del. — 77. *Am not I* Qq, *Am I not* Del. — 82. Omitted by Chet. — '*Thorough,* a mistake — perhaps *thwart.* (*So, sir, we're thwart for)'.* Simp. — *for that L.* Qq, *for that.* Del.; we have adopted the reading of Simp. (*So,* at the beginning of the line, being a so-called monosyllabic foot). — 84. Omitted by Chet. — Del. adds [*Aside*]. — *I will finde* Qq, *I'll find* Simp.
 SCENE IV. 3. *Forming thy* Del. — *thy lowly state* Chet.

Full yll this life becomes thy heauenly looke,
Wherein sweet loue and vertue sits enthroned. 5
Bad world! where riches is esteemed aboue them both,
In whose base eyes nought else is bountifull!
A Millers daughter, saies the multitude,
Should not be loued of a gentleman.
But let them breath their soules into the ayre, 10
Yet will I still affect thee as my selfe,
So thou be constant in thy plighted vow.
But here comes one — Ile listen to his talke.

     [MANUILE *staies, hiding himselfe.*

   Enter VALINGFORD *at another dore, disguised.*

Val. Goe, William Conqueror, and seeke thy loue,
Seeke thou a mynion in a forren land, 15
Whilest I draw backe and court my loue at home,
The Millers daughter of faire Manchester
Hath bound my feet to this delightsome soyle,
And from her eyes do dart such golden beames
That holds my harte in her subiection. 20
 Man. He ruminates on my beloued choyce:
God graunt he come not to preuent my hope.
But heres another, him yle listen to.

   Enter MOUNTNEY, *disguised, at another dore.*

Mount. Nature vniust, in vtterance of thy arte,
To grace a pesant with a Princes fame! 25
Pesant am I, so to mis-terme my loue:
Although a Millers daughter by her birth,

---

6. *Bad world where riches are esteemed most* Chet. (and not *is esteemed most,* as Del., p. XI, erroneously states); Simp. proposes *'boue both* for *aboue them both.* — 10. Compare *Here could I breathe my soul into the air,* 2 Henry VI., III. 2, 391 (quoted by Simp.). — 13. *I will* Qq, *I'll* Del. and Simp. — 20. *That hold* Del. — 22. *Heav'n grant* Chet. — 23. *listen too.* Del. — 25. *Princes fame* Qq, *prince's frame* Chet., *princess' fame* Del., *prince's fame* Simp. Elze proposes to read *princess' face,* which, indeed, would better agree with Mountney's subsequent praise of *'her beauties worthynes'* (l. 35). See Notes, XVII, pp. 9 seq. — 26. *Pesant: Am I so to* Chet.

  Yet may her beautie and her vertues well suffice
  To hyde the blemish of her birth in hell,
30 Where neither enuious eyes nor thought can perce,
  But endlesse darknesse euer smother it.
  Goe, William Conqueror, and seeke thy loue,
  Whilest I draw backe and court mine owne the while
  Decking her body with such costly robes
35 As may become her beauties worthynes;
  That so thy labors may be laughed to scorne,
  And she thou seekest in forraine regions
  Be darkned and eclipst when she arriues
  By one that I haue chosen nearer home.
40 *Man.* What! Comes he to, to intercept my loue?
  Then hye thee Manuile to forestall such foes.

          [Exit MANUILE.

  Mount. What now, Lord Valingford, are you behinde?
  The king had chosen you to goe with him.
  Val. So chose he you, therefore I marveile much
45 That both of vs should linger in this sort.
  What may the king imagine of our staye?
  Mount. The king may iustly think we are to blame:
  But I immagined I might well be spared,
  And that no other man had borne my minde.
50 *Val.* The like did I: in frendship then resolue
  What is the cause of your vnlookt for stay?
  Mount. Lord Valingford, I tell thee as a friend:
  Loue is the cause why I haue stayed behinde.
  Val. Loue, my Lord? of whom?
55 *Mount.* Of Em, the millers daughter of Manchester.
  Val. But may this be?
  Mount. Why not, my Lord? I hope full well you know

  28. *and her vertues serve* Chet. — 37. Simp., not being aware that *region* is to be pronounced as a trisyllable here, needlessly adds [*out*] after *seekest* (See Elze, Notes, XVII, p. 10). — 40. *What comes he to,* Qq and Simp., *What comes he too,* Chet., *What! Comes he too* Del. — 43. *hath chosen* Del. and Simp. — 55. *Of* omitted in Qq. We have adopted El.'s emendation (Notes, XVIII, p. 10), which seems to be required both by grammar and metre (*Daughter* must, of course, be pronounced as a monosyllable here).

That loue respects no difference of state,
So beautie̅ serue to stir affection.

    Val. But this it is that makes me wonder most, 60
That you and I should be of one conseite
In such a straunge vnlikly passion.

    Mount. But is that true? My Lord, I hope you do but iest.

    Val. I would I did; then were my griefe the lesse.

    Mount. Nay, neuer grieue; for if the cause be such, 65
To ioyne our thoughts in such a Simpathy,
All enuie set asyde: let vs agree
To yeeld to eythers fortune in this choyce.

    Val. Content, say I: and whatsoere befall,
Shake hands, my Lord, and fortune thriue at all. 70
                            [Exeunt.

A C T II.

SCENE I.

Enter EM, *and* TROTTER, *the Millers man, with a kerchife on his head, and an Vrinall in his hand.*

    Em. Trotter, where haue you beene?

    Trot. Where haue I beene? Why, what signifies this?

    Em. A kerchiefe, doth it not?

    Trot. What call you this, I pray?

    Em. I say it is an Vrinall. 5

    Trot. Then this is mystically to giue you to vnderstand,
I haue beene at the Phismicaries house.

    Em. How long hast thou beene sicke?

    Trot. Yfaith, euen as long as I haue not beene halfe
well, and that hath beene a long time. 10

    Em. A loytering time, I rather immagine.

    Trot. It may bee so: but the Phismicary tels mee that
you can help me.

    Em. Why, anything I can doe for recouerie of thy health
be right well assured of. 15

---

    63. *But is this true?* Del. — Simp. proposes to omit *my Lord.* —
65. *for if thou canst be such* Del. — 70. *thrive o'er all.* Simp. conj.
    SCENE I. 9. *e'en* Simp. — *halfe* om. by Chet.

Trot. Then giue me your hand.

Em. To what end?

Trot. That the ending of an old indenture is the beginning of a new bargaine.

20 *Em.* What bargaine?

Trot. That you promised to doe anything to recouer my helth.

Em. On that condition I giue thee my hand.

Trot. Ah, sweet Em!   *[Here he offers to kisse her.*

25 *Em.* How now, Trot! your maistres daughter?

Trot. Yfaith, I aime at the fairest.   Ah, Em, sweet Em!

        Fresh as the flowre,

        That hath the poure

        To wound my harte,

30   And ease my smart,

        Of me, poore theefe,

        In prison bound —

Em.   So all your ryme

        Lies on 'the ground.

35 But what meanes this?

Trot. Ah, marke the deuise —

        For thee, my loue,

        Full sicke I was,

        In hazard of my life,

40   Thy promise was

        To make me whole,

        And for to be my wife.

        Let me inioy

        Thy loue, my deere,

45   And thou possesse

        Thy Trotter here.

26—34. Printed as six lines in Qq; ending *fairest* | *flowre* | *harte* | *theefe* | *bound* | *ground;* in Del.'s and Simp.'s edd. the lines end at *sweet Em* | *flower* | *power* | *heart* | *smart* | *bound* | *ground.* We have adopted El.'s arrangement (See Jahrbuch der Deutschen Shakespeare-Gesellschaft, vol. XV, p. 345). — 27. *Fresh as a flower* El. conj. — 28. *the* out of Qq, added by Simp. — 37—46. In Qq these lines form only four lines, ending at *life* | *wife* | *deere* | *here.* Del. and Simp. have the same division. Our arrangement is owing to El. (Jahrb. XV, p. 345). — 44. *My loue* Qq, *Thy loue* is El.'s correction. Compare IV. 3. 24, 25.

Em. But I meant no such matter.

Trot. Yes, woos, but you did. Ile goe to our Parson, Sir John, and he shall mumble vp the marriage out of hand.   50

Em. But here comes one that will forbid the Banes.

> [*Here enters* Manuile *to them.*

Trot. Ah, Sir, you come too late.

Man. What remedie, Trotter?

Em. Goe, Trotter, my father calles.

Trot. Would you haue me go in, and leaue you two here? 55

Em. Why, darest thou not trust me?

Trot. Yes, faith, euen as long as I see you.

Em. Goe thy waies, I pray thee hartely.

Trot. That same word 'hartely' is of great force. I will goe. But I pray, sir, beware you; come not too neere the 60 wench.

> [*Exit Trotter.*

Man. I am greatly beholding to you.
Ah, Maistres, somtime I might haue said, my loue,
But time and fortune hath bereued me of that,
And I, an abiect in those gratious eyes,   65
That with remorse earst saw into my griefe,
May sit and sigh the sorrows of my heart.

Em. In deed my Manuile hath some cause to doubt,
When such a swaine is riuall in his loue!

Man. Ah, Em, were he the man that causeth this mistrust, 70
I should esteeme of thee as at the first.

Em. But is my loue in earnest all this while?

Man. Beleeue me, Em, it is not time to iest,
When others ioyes, what lately I possest.

Em. If touching loue my Manuile charge me thus,   75
Vnkindly must I take it at his hands,
For that my conscience cleeres me of offence.

48. *woos* om. by Del. — 55. In two copies of B (Brit. Mus. 643. c. 14 and $\frac{\text{b. 21. c}}{\text{b}}$) *here* has dropped out, while in a third copy (161. a. 26) it is to be found as well as in A. — 57. *e'en* Simp. — 60. *I pray you, sir,* Del. — 65. *I am abiect* Qq; in our text we have adopted the emendation as proposed by Simp. — 71. *at thee first* B. — 74. *others 'joy* Del.

Man.   Ah, impudent and shamlesse in thy ill,
That with thy cunning and defraudfull toung
80   Seeks to delude the honest-meaning minde!
Was neuer heard in Manchester before
Of truer loue then hath been twixt vs twaine:
And for my part how I haue hazarded
Displeasure of my father and my freindes,
85   Thy selfe can witnes.   Yet notwithstanding this,
Two gentlemen attending on Duke William,
Mountney and Valingford, as I heard them named,
Oft times resort to see and to be seene
Walking the street fast by thy fathers dore,
90   Whose glauncing eyes vp to the windowes cast
Giues testies of their Maistres amorous hart.
This, Em, is noted and too much talked on,
Some see 't without mistrust of ill —
Others there are that, scorning, grynne thereat,
95   And saith, ' There goes the Millers daughters wooers'.
Ah me!· whom chiefly and most of all it doth concerne —
To spend my time in griefe and vex my soule,
To thinke my loue should be rewarded thus,
And for thy sake abhorre all womenkind!
100   *Em.*   May not a maiden looke vpon a man
Without suspitious judgement of the world?

80. *seekese* A. — 82. *Of true louer* A. — *betwixt* Qq, *'twixt* Chet.
and Del. — 85. 'Dele *Yet*' Simp. — 86. *genlemen* A. — 87. El. proposes
either to pronounce *Valingford* as a dissyllable, or to contract *Mountney and*
and to begin the verse with two trochees, or to enclose the line in a parenthesis and to expunge *as* (See Notes, XX, pp. 11 seq., and p. 125). — 88. *to
see and to be seene.* Compare Friar Bacon and Friar Bungay, ed. Ward, I.
139 seq., *the troop of all the maids | That come to see and to be seen that
day.* Ward, l. c., p. 204, very aptly quotes a line from Ovid, Ars Amatoria
I. 99: *Spectatum veniunt, veniunt, spectentur ut ipsae.* — 90. *up to windows*
B, *up to the windows* A (and Del.), *up to thy windows* Simp. — 91. *Give*
Del. and Simp. — *Gives witness of* Chet. — 92. Simp. needlessly inserts *is*
between *and* and *too.* — 93. *see it* Qq. Chet. restores a regular blank verse
by adding *plain* after *see it.* Del. has adopted Chet.'s reading. — 95. *go* Del.
— 96. Chet. obtains a blank verse by omitting *and* and *of all;* El. proposes
to expunge *chiefly and.* — 99. *maiden kind* Chet., *women-kind* Simp. —
100. *maid* Qq, *maiden* Del.; *May not a maid* [*then*] *look* Simp.

Man. If sight doe moue offence, 'tis th' better not to see.
But thou didst more, vnconstant as thou art,
For with them thou hadst talke and conference.
   Em. May not a maid talke with a man without mistrust? 105
   Man. Not with such men suspected amorous.
   Em. I grieue to see my Manuiles ielousie.
   Man. Ah, Em, faithfull loue is full of ielousie.
So did I loue thee true and faithfully,
For which I am rewarded most vnthankfully.   110
               [Exit, in a rage. Manet EM.
   Em. And so away? What, in displeasure gone,
And left me such a bitter sweet to gnaw upon?
Ah, Manuile, little wottest thou
How neere this parting goeth to my heart.
Vncourteous loue, whose followers reaps reward   115
Of hate, disdaine, reproach and infamie,
The fruit of franticke, bedlome ielousie!
             [Here enter MOUNTNEY *to* EM.
But here comes one of these suspitious men:
Witnes, my God, without desert of me,
For onely Manuile honor I in harte,   120
Nor shall vnkindnesse cause me from him start!
   Mount. For this good fortune, Venus, be thou blest,
To meet my loue, the mistres of my heart,
Where time and place giues oportunity,

---

102. *it is the better* Qq; *'tis better* Simp. conj. — 108. Simp.'s proposal
to restore a regular blank verse by expunging *Em*, will hardly find favour,
because 'it is customary with our poet to add the name of the person addressed, especially after an interjection which begins the verse'. Cp. II. 1.
70, 113, 164. El. proposes to place *Ah, Em!* in an interjectional line and to
read: *Ah, Em!* | *All faithful love* &c. (Notes, XIX, pp. 10 seq.). — 110. Scan:
For which | *I'm r'wár* | *ded móst* | *unthánk* | *fullý* |. (See El., Jahrb., XV,
p. 345). Whether we read the line in that manner or no, Simp.'s conjecture
So I'm rewarded is at any rate unnecessary. — 111. The prefix *Em.* om. in
Qq. — 112. Simp. proposes to read *on* for *upon*. — 113. Chet. restores the
legitimate number of feet by duplicating *Manuile*. — 115. *reap* Del. —
116. Del. erroneously prints *bate* for *hate*. — 117. *Here enter* .... A. —
119. *Witness, my soul*, Chet. — 121. *from him to start* Qq; the omission
of *to* is Simp.'s conjecture. See Abbott, s. 349. — *Nor shall unkindness
cause my love to start* Chet.

125 At full to let her vnderstand my loue.

       [He turnes to EM *and offers to take her by the hand,*
                             and she goes from him.

Faire mistres, since my fortune sorts so well,
Heare you a word. What meaneth this?
Nay, stay, faire Em.

    Em.   I'm going homewards, Syr.

    Mount. Yet stay, sweet loue, to whom I must disclose

130 The hidden secrets of a louers thoughts,
Not doubting but to finde such kinde remorse
As naturally you are enclyned to.

    Em. The gentleman, your friend, Syr,
I haue not seene him this foure dayes, at th' least.

135   *Mount.* Whats that to mee?
I speake not, sweet, in person of my friend,
But for my selfe, whom, if that loue deserue
To haue regard, being honourable loue,
Not base affects of loose lasciuious loue,

140 Whom youthfull Wantons play and dally With,
But that Vnites in bands of holy rytes,
And knits the sacred Knot that Gods —

                          [Here EM *cuts him off.*

    Em. What meane you, sir, to keepe me here so long?
I cannot vnderstand you by your sygnes;

145 You keepe a pratling with your lippes,
But neuer a word you speake that I can heare.

    Mount. What? is she deafe? a great impediment!
Yet remedies there are for such defects.
Sweet Em, it is no little griefe to mee,

150 To see, where Nature, in her pryde of Art,
Hath wrought perfections ritch and admirable —

    Em. Speake you to me, Sir?

<hr>

128. *I am* Qq. — 133. *The gentleman, your friend, Sir?* Del. —
134. *the least* Qq. — 135, 136. Printed as one line in Qq; we have adopted
the division of Del. and Simp. — 138. *being* used as a monosyllable here. —
139. *loose lascivious lust* El. conj.; cp. I. 2. 57. — 141. *in honourable bands*
Qq; we have expunged *honourable* on the authority of El., who justly remarks that this word is owing to a faulty repetition from l. 138 (See Notes,
p. 13). — 142. *God's* Del.; *Knot that heauen* Chet.

Mount.   To thee, my onely joy.

Em.   I cannot heare you.

Mount. Oh, plague of fortune! Oh, hell without compare!
What boots it vs to gaze and not enioy?   155

    Em.   Fare you Well, Sir.

                      [Exit EM. *Manet* MOUNTNEY.

Mount.   Farewell, my loue, nay, farewell life and all!
Could I procure redresse for this infirmitie,
It might be meanes· shee would regard my suit.
I am acquainted with the Kings Physitions,   160
Amongst the which there's one, mine honest friend,
Seignior Alberto, a very learned man,
His judgment will I haue to help this ill.
Ah, Em, faire Em, if art can make thee whole,
Ile Buy that sense for thee, although it cost me deere.   165
But, Mountney, stay: this may be but deceit,
A matter fained onely to delude thee,
And, not vnlike, perhaps by Valingford.
He loues faire Em as well as I —
As well as I? Ah, no, not halfe so well.   170
Put case: yet may he be thine enimie,
And give her counsell to dissemble thus.
Ile try th' euent and if it fall out so,
Frindship, farewell: Loue makes me now a foe.

                      [Exit MOUNTNEY.

---

154. Simp. proposes to expunge the second *Oh!* — 155. 'Probably
and not to hear? so to rhyme with *compare*'. Simp. — El. doubts whether
we should not read *and not converse,* or whether a line to the following
effect has not dropped out: *and not enjoy | The sweet converse of mutual love
between us.* In our opinion, the reading of the Qq offers no difficulty. —
157. For the shifting accent of *Farewell* compare V. 1. 208. — 163. *His
judgment will I crave* Simp. conj. — 165. *though't cost me dear* Simp.
conj. — 166. *may be yet deceit* Chet. — 169. *loves the lovely Em* Chet. —
171. *Yet he may* Del. — Instead of this line Chet. reads: *Yet he may prove
thy favour'd friend,* which line Del. has inserted in his text between ll. 170
and 171. — 173. *the euent* Qq, *th'event* Chet. and Del. — *if it should be
so* Chet.

SCENE II.

Enter Marques LUBECK *and* MARIANA.

Mar. Trust me, my Lord, I 'm sorry for your hurt.

Lub. Gramercie, Madam; but it is not great:
Onely a thrust, prickt with a Rapier's point.

Mar. How grew the quarrel, my Lord?

5   *Lub.* Sweet Ladie, for thy sake. There was, this last
night, two maskes in one company; my selfe the formost: the
other strangers were: amongst the which, when the Musicke
began to sound the Measures, eche Masker made choice of
his Ladie; and one, more forward then the rest, stept towards
10   thee, which I perceiuing, thrust him aside, and tooke thee my
selfe. But this was taken in so ill part that at my comming
out of the court gate, with iustling together, it was my chaunce
to be thrust into the arme. The doer thereof, because he
was the originall cause of the disorder at that inconuenient
15   time, was presently committed, and is this morning sent for
to aunswer the matter. And I think here he comes.

    [Here enter Sir ROBERT OF WINDSOR *with a Gaylor.*
What, Sir Robert of Windsor, how now?

SCENE II (See Appendix). 1. *I am* Qq, *I'm* Simp. — 2. *I thank you
madam;* Chet. — 5. *Ladie* om. by Chet. — *There was last night* Del. — 6. *in
our company* Simp. conj. — 5—18. The speech of Lubeck is printed as ir-
regular verse in Qq; the lines end at *for thy sake | one company | strangers
were | the Measures | of his Ladie | towards thee | thee my selfe | ill part | iust-
ling together | the arme | disorder | committed | the matter | how now.* — The
same passage has been versified by Chet. as follows: *Last night three mas-
kers in one company | Enter'd the spacious hall. I observed them well; |
Each masker chose his lady in the dance | And one, the foremost, bent his
steps tow'rds thee; | Which I perceiving, thrust myself between, | But this
was taken in so ill a part, | That, when the sports were done, he drew upon
me, | And in the scuffle I receiv'd this hurt. | The peace and quiet of the
place thus broke, | The guards seized on the bold offender, | And in durance
stayed him to answer this |.* — 6, 7. *the others* Del. and El.; the use of
other as a plural pronoun, however, is consistent with ancient use; see Abbott, s. 12. Compare also Marlowe's Edward II., ed. Fleay, I. 4. 415: *Whiles
other walk below.* (Dyce, p. 193[b], Wagner, p. 36, and Tancock, p. 23,
read with the later quartos *While others walk below*). — 9. *steps* Del. —
12. *out at the* Del. — 17. Stage-direction. *Enter William with a Keeper.*
Chet.

Rob. Wind. Ifaith, my Lord, a prisoner: but what ayles
your arme?   20

Lub. Hurt the last 'night by mischaunce.

Rob. Wind. What, not in the Maske at the Court gate?

Lub. Yes, trust me, there.

Rob. Wind. Why then, my Lord, I thank you for my
nights lodging.   25

Lub. And I you for my hurt, if it were so. Keeper,
awaie, I discharge you of your prisoner.   *[Exit the Keeper.*

Rob. Wind. Lord Marques, you offerd me disgrace to
shoulder me.

Lub. Sir, I knew you not, and therefore you must par-   30
don me, and the rather it might be alleaged to me of meare
simplicitie to see another daunce with my Maistris, disguysed,
and I my selfe in presence. But seeing it was our happs to
damnifie each other unwillingly, let vs be content with our
harmes, and lay the fault, where it was, and so become friends.   35

Rob. Wind. Yfaith, I am content with my nights lodging,
if you be content with your hurt.

Lub. Not content that I haue it, but content to forget
how I came by it.

Rob. Wind. My Lord, here comes Ladie Blaunch, lets   40
away.   *[Enter* BLAUNCH.

Lub. With good will. Ladie, you will stay?

[Exit LUBECK *and* SIR ROBERT.

Mar. Madam —

Blaunch. Mariana, as I am grieued with thy presence:
so am I not offended for thy absence; and were it not a   45
breach to modestie, thou shouldest know before I left thee.

---

19. Simp. proposes to omit *my Lord.* — 21. *Hurt last night,* Del. — Chet.
omits *by mischaunce.* — 26, 27. As two lines in Qq, divided at *were so.* —
27. *awaie; discharge* Simp. conj. — 30—35. Instead of these lines Chet.
reads: *Sir, I knew you not, and therefore crave excuse.* | *Come, let us be
contented with our harms,* | *And lay the fault on chance, and become friends.* |
— 30—39. In Qq the lines end at *pardon me* | *me of* | *my Maistris* | *seeing
it* | *unwillingly* | *our harmes* | *become friends* | *lodging* | *hurt* | *but content* |
by it. — 33. 'Qy. read *hap?*' El. (Notes, p. 130). — 40. *Enter Blaunch.*
after l. 38 in Del. — 42. *will you stay?* Del., Simp., El. — 44—48. Ending
in Qq at *presence* | *absence* | *modestie* | *thee* | *madnesse* | *begyn, you* |
scoulding '.

Mar.   How neare is this humour to madnesse! If you hould on as you begyn, you are in a prety way to scoulding.

Blaunch.   To scoulding, huswife?

50   *Mar.*   Maddam, here comes one.

                               [Here enters one with a letter.

Blaunch.   There doth indeed. Fellow, wouldest thou haue any thing with any body here?

Mes.   I haue a letter to deliuer to the Ladie Mariana.

Blaunch.   Giue it me.

55   *Mes.*   There must none but shee haue it.

Blaunch. [snatcheth the letter from him, Et exit Messenger.] Go to, foolish fellow. And therefore, to ease the anger I sustaine, Ile be so bold to open it. Whats here? Sir Robert greets you well? You, Maistries, his loue, his life! Oh amorous man, how he entertaines his new Maistres; and

60   bestowes on Lubeck, his od friend, a horne night capp to keep in his witt.

Mar.   Maddam, though you haue discourteously redd my letter, yet, I pray you, giue it me.

Blaunch.   Then take it, there, and there, and there.

                              [She tears it. Et exit BLAUNCH.

65   *Mar.*   How farr doth this differ from modestie! Yet will I gather vp the peeces, which happelie may shew to me the intent thereof, though not the meaning.

                         [She gathers up the peeces and ioynes them.

'Your seruant and loue, sir Robert of Windsor, Alias William the Conqueror, wisheth long health and happinesse'. Is this

70   William the Conqueror, shrouded vnder the name of sir Robert

---

47, 48. *yon hould* A. — 49. *To scolding, madam!* Chet. — 50. Stage-direction: *Enter a servant with a letter.* Chet. — 51. *would's thou* Simp. — 56—63. In Qq the lines are divided at *fellow | sustaine | What's here? | well? | man | Maistries | friend | witt | discourteously | giue it me |.* — 58. *your Maistries* Qq, *You Mistress* Simp., *You, mistress* Del. — 60. *old friend* Chet. and Del. — 65—67. In Qq ending at *modestie | happelie | thereof | meaning |.* — 68. In the old copies the prefix *Mar.* is repeated at the beginning of this line. — *and lover* Del. For *love = lover* see Al. Schmidt, Shak.-Lex., s. v. *love* (4), p. 672b. — *alius* Qq, corr. by Del. — 68—75. Ending at *Windsor | happinesse | under | Windsor? | world | loue | can | Blaunch | my selfe | may |* in Qq. — 69. *wisheth long life and* Del.

of Windsor? Were he the Monarch of the world he should
not dispossesse Lubeck of his loue. Therefore I will to the
Court, and there, if I can, close to be freinds with Ladie
Blaunch; and thereby keepe Lubeck, my loue, for my selfe,
and further the Ladie Blaunch in her sute, as much as I may. 75
                                                        [Exit.

SCENE III.

Enter EM *sola.*

Em.   Jelousie, that sharps the louers sight,
And makes him conceiue and conster his intent,
Hath so bewitched my louely Manuils sences
That he misdoubts his Em, that loues his soule;
He doth suspect corriuals in his loue,   5
Which, how untrue it is, be iudge, my God!
But now no more — Here commeth Valingford;
Shift him off now, as thou hast done the other.

Enter VALINGFORD.

Val.   See, how Fortune presents me with the hope I lookt
for! Fair Em!   10
    Em. Who is that?
    Val.   I am Valingford, thy loue and friend.
    Em.   I cry you mercie, sir; I thought so by your speach.
    Val.   What ayleth thine eyes?
    Em.   Oh blinde, sir, blind, stricken blinde, by mishap, 15
on a sudden.
    Val.   But is it possible you should be taken on such a
suddain? Infortunate Valingford, to be thus crost in thy
loue! Faire Em, I am not a little sorrie to see this thy hard
hap. Yet neuerthelesse — I am acquainted with a learned 20
Physitian that will do anything for thee, at my request; to
him will I resort, and enquire his iudgement, as concerning
the recouery of so excellent a sence.

71—73. *He should not dispossess my Lubeck's love | Therefore I will
to court; and, if I can* &c. Chet.
    SCENE III. Stage-direction: *Enter Em solus.* Qq. 1. *[Ah,] Jealousy,*
Simp. — 6. *be judge, high heaven,* Chet. — 11. *Who's* Simp. — 12. 'Dele
Valingford' Simp. — 14. *thy eyes* A. — 17. *But it is* Del. — 17—23. In
Qq the lines end at *suddain | loue | hap | Physitian | request | iudgement*

   Em. Oh Lord, sir, and of all things I cannot abide
25 Physicke, the verie name thereof to me is odious.

   Val. No? Not the thing will doe thee so much good?
Sweet Em, hether I came to parley of loue, hoping to haue
found thee in thy woonted prosperity; and haue the gods so
unmercifully thwarted my expectation, by dealing so sinisterly
30 with thee, sweet Em?

   Em. Good sir, no more, it fits not me
To haue respect to such vaine fantasies
As idle loue presents my eares withall,
More reason I should ghostly giue my selfe
35 To sacred prayers, for this my former sinne,
For which this plague is iustly fallen vpon me,
Than t' harken to the vanities of loue.

sence |. Del. and Simp. print them as prose. Elze, taking this passage and
ll. 23 seqq. to be two instances of metrical composition degenerated into prose,
restores the former one in this way (Notes, p. 15): *Infortunate Valingford,
to be thus cross'd | In love! — Fair Em, I'm not a little sorry | To see this
thy hard hap, yet ne'ertheless | I am acquainted with a learn'd physician |
That will do anything for thee | At my request; to him will I resort | And
will require his judgment as concerning | Th'recovery of so excellent a
sense |.* After the third line the same critic thinks a verse to the following
effect to be wanting (Notes, p. 132): *I fairly hope, all will be well again.*
Chet. versifies the passage in this way: *But, is it possible you should be taken
thus? | Unhappy Valingford! to be thus cross'd. | Fair Em, I'm tortured
at thy great mishap. | I have a learn'd physician for my friend, | That will
do anything at my request. |.* — 24. *Ah Lord,* Del. — *and* om. Chet. —
24, 25. Divided at *Physicke* in Qq. — 26—30. Printed as five lines in Qq.
ending *good | loue | prosperity | expectation | sweet Em |.* Del. and Simp.
print the passage as prose. Elze tries to arrange the lines in a twofold
manner; Notes, p. 15: *No? Not the thing will do thee so much good? |
Sweet Em, I hither came to parle of love | Hoping t'have found thee in thy
wonted state; | And have the Gods thwart'd so unmerc'fully | My hope, by
dealing so sinisterly | With thee? Em. Good sir, no more. It fits not me |
To have respect to such vain phantasies | &c.;* p. 133: *Sweet Em, I hither
came to parle of love, | Hoping t'have found thee in thy wont'd prosper'ty; |
And have the Gods | Thwart'd so unmerc'fully my expectation, | By dealing
so sinisterly with thee, | Sweet Em? Em. Good sir, no more; | &c.* Instead
of ll. 26—30 Chet. has only the following two verses: *No! Not the thing
will do thee so much good? | Sweet Em, hither I came to parley love |.* —
34. Simp. erroneously states *giue my life* to be the reading of B. —
35. *pray'rs* Del. — 36. *fall'n* Del. and Simp. — 37. *to harken* Qq, *Than
hearken* Simp. conj.

Val. Yet, sweet Em,
Accept this iewel at my hand, which I
Bestow on thee in token of my loue. 40
    Em. A jewell, sir! what pleasure can I haue
In jewels, treasure, or any worldly thing
That want my sight that should deserne thereof?
Ah, sir, I must leaue you,
The paine of mine eyes is so extreame, 45
    I cannot long stay in a place. I take my leaue. *[Exit* EM.
    Val. Zounds! what a crosse is this to my conceit! But,
Valingford, serch the depth of this deuise. Why may not
this be fained subtiltie, by Mounteney's inuention, to the intent
that I seeing such occasion should leaue off my suit, and not 50
any more persist to solicite her of loue? Ile trie the euent;
if I can, by any meanes, perceaue the effect of this deceyte
to be procured by his meanes, friend Mountney, the one of
vs is like to repent our bargeine. *[Exit.*

38—40. As two lines in Qq, ending *hand* | *loue* |. We have adopted
El.'s arrangement. Simp. and Del. print the passage as prose. Simp., however, proposes to drop *Em*, and thus to restore a regular blank verse. *Yet,
sweetest Em, accept this ring from me,* | *Which I bestow in token of my
love.* Chet. — 42. *worldly* Del., see, above, I. 2. 41. — 43. *mine sight* Simp.
— 45. The metre requires that we pronounce *e* final of *paine*, a trace of the
early English pronunciation. Cp. Abbott, ³. 489. — 46. Instead of this line
Chet. only has *I cannot longer stay.* — 47—54. In Qq the lines end at
conceit | *deuise* | *subtiltie* | *intent* | *suit* | *loue* | *perceaue* | *meanes* | *bargeine* .
El. restores the passage in the following way (Notes, p. 12): '*Zounds! what
a cross is this to my conceit!* | *But Valingford, search the depth of this
device.* | *Why may not this be some feign'd subtlety* | *By Mounteney's in-
vention, to th'intent* | *That I, seeing such occasion, should leave off* | *My
suit, and not persist t' solicit her* | *Of love? I'll try th'event. If I per-
ceive* | *By any means th'effect of this deceit* | *Procurèd by thy means, friend
Mounteney,* | *The one of us is like t'repent our bargain.* |. — 49. Simp. is
mistaken in giving *some feign'd* as the reading of B; *some* is not to be found
in either of the old copies. — 50, 51. *and not . . . . loue?* om. by Chet. —
Simp. is again mistaken, when stating Chet. to have expunged the words
I'll try the event. — 52. *Th'effect of this deceit procured by him,* Chet. —
54. Chet. concludes the scene with the following rhyme-couplet: *Rivals, in
war, create a glorious strife;* | *But hate ensues, when rivals for a wife* |.

A C T   III.

SCENE I.

Enter MARIANA *and* MARQUES LUBECK.

   Lub. Ladie, .

Since that occasion, forward in our good,

Presenteth place and opportunitie,

Let me intreat your woonted kind consent

5 And freindly furtherance in a suit I haue.

   Mar. My Lord, you know you need not to intreat,

But may commaund Mariana to her power,

Be't no impeachment to my honest fame.

   Lub. Free are my thoughts from such base villanie

10 As may in question, Ladie, call your name;

Yet is the matter of such consequence,

Standing vpon my honorable credit,

To be effected with such zeale and secresie

As, should I speake and faile my expectation,

15 It would redound greatly to my preiudice.

   Mar. My Lord, wherein hath Mariana

Giuen you occasion that you should mistrust,

Or else be iealous of my secresie?

   Lub. Mariana, do not misconster of me:

20 I not mistrust thee, nor thy secresie;

Nor let my loue misconster my intent,

Nor thinke thereof but well and honorable.

Thus stands the case:

Thou knowest from England hether came with me

Robert of Windsor, a noble man at Armes,   25
Lustie and valiant, in spring time of his yeares,
No maruell then though he proue amorous.
   Mar.   True, my Lord, he came to see faire Blaunch.
   Lub.   No, Mariana, that 's not it.   His loue to Blaunch
Was then extinct, when first he saw thy face.   30
'Tis thee he loues; yea, thou art onely shee
That's maistres and commaunder of his thoughts.
   Mar.   Well, well, my Lord, I like you; for such drifts
Put silly ladies often to their shifts.
Oft haue I heard you say you loued me well,   35
Yea, sworne the same, and I beleeued you to.
Can this be found an action of good faith
Thus to dissemble where you found true loue?
   Lub.   Mariana, I not dissemble, on mine honor,
Nor failes my faith to thee.   But for my friend,   40
For princely William, by whom thou shalt possesse
The tytle and estate of Maiestie,
Fitting thy loue, and vertues of thy minde —
For him I speake, for him do I intreat,
And, with thy fauour, fully do resigne   45
To him the claime and interest of my loue.
Sweet Mariana, then, denie mee not:
Loue William, loue my friend, and honour me,
Who els is cleane dishonored by thy meanes.
   Mar.   Borne to mishap, my selfe am onely shee   50
On whom the Sunne of fortune neuer shyned:
But Planets rulde by retrograde aspect

29, 30. As three lines in Qq, ending *it* | *extinct* | *face* |; our arrange-
ment is that of Del. — 29. *that is* Qq, *that's* Del. — *non it* A. — *Blnnch*
A. — This line is, in our opinion, to be scanned thus: *No Mãr | ian[a]
thãt's | not it* | &c.   For the dissyllabic pronunciation *Mãrian[a]*, compare,
below, l. 72. — 31. *thou are* B. — Qy. Read, here and below, l. 50, *th'onely she?*   See Abbott, s. 224; the same expression occurs in Henry V., II.
1. 83. — 32. *That is* Qq, *That's* Del. and Simp. — 33, 34. Omitted by
Chet. — 36. *you too* Edd. — 39. *I don 't dissemble* Del. — 41. *by* is to be
slurred; Simp. proposes to print *b'whom.* — 42. *tytte of estate and Maiestie*
Qq; we have followed Del. — 43. Simp. erroneously gives *Fitting the loue*
as the reading of B. — 52. *retrogarde* Qq, *retrograde* Edd. Cp. A Looking-
Glass for London and England, *Retrograde conjunctions of the stars* (quoted by Ward, l. c., p. 162).

Foretold mine yll in my natiuitie!

> *Lub.*   Sweet Ladie, cease, let my intreatie serue

55 To pacifie the passion of thy griefe,

Which, well I know, proceeds of ardent loue.

> *Mar.*   But Lubeck now regards not Mariana.
>
> *Lub.*   Euen as my life, so loue I Mariana.
>
> *Mar.*   Why do you post me to another then?

60 *Lub.*   He is my friend, and I do loue the man.

> *Mar.*   Then will Duke William robb me of my loue?
>
> *Lub.*   No, as his life Mariana he doth loue.
>
> *Mar.*   Speake for your selfe, my Lord, let him alone.
>
> *Lub.*   So do I, Madam, for he and I am one.

65 *Mar.*   Then louing you I do content you both.

> *Lub.*   In louing him, you shall content vs both:

Me, for I craue that fauour at your hands,

Him, for he hopes that comfort at your hands.

> *Mar.*   Leaue of, my Lord, here comes the Ladie Blaunch.

Enter BLAUNCH *to them.*

70 *Lub.*   Hard hap to breake vs of our talke so soone!

Sweet Mariana, doe remember me.   *[Exit* LUBECK.

> *Mar.*   Thy Mariana can't chuse but remember thee.
>
> *Blaunch.*   Mariana, well met. You are verie forward in
> your loue.

75   *Mar.*   Madam, be it in secret spoken to your selfe, if you
will but follow the complot I haue inuented, you will not
thinke me so forward as your selfe shall proue fortunate.

---

54. *seace* A. — 64. Cp. As You Like It, I. 3. 99, *Which teacheth thee
that thou and I am one.* — 67, 68. Omitted by Chet. — 68. *He, for hopes*
Qq, *He for he hopes* Del., *Him, for he hopes* Simp. — 72. Scan: *Thy Már |
ian[a] cán't |* &c. See, above, l. 29. Elze (Notes, p. 127) proposes to ex-
punge *Thy.* — *Thy Mariana never can forget thee* Chet. — 73—101. There
is little doubt that also this passage was originally written in verse. But it
has been handed down in a state so hopelessly corrupt that an attempt to
emend it would certainly not he compatible with the rules of criticism. —
73. *verie* om. by Chet. — Elze (Notes, p. 127) proposes to read: BLAUNCH:
Mariana, | Well met. You're very forward in your love. | MAR.. *Madam, |
Be it in secret spoken to yourself: | If you'll but follow th' complot I've
invented, |* &c. — 75. seqq. In Qq the lines end at *your selfe | inuented |
forward | fortunate | how | you | Windsor* . — 75. *in a secret* Del. — *but*
om. by Chet. — 76. *the plot* Chet.

Blaunch.   As how?

Mar.   Madam, as thus. It is not vnknowen to you that Sir
Robert of Windsor, a man that you do not little esteeme, hath   80
long importuned me of loue; but rather than I will be found
false or vniust to the Marques Lubeck, I will, as did the constant ladie Penelope, vndertake to effect some great taske.

Blaunch.   What of all this?

Mar.   The next tyme that Sir Robert shall come in his   85
woonted sort, to solicit me with loue, I will seeme to agree, and
like of anything that the knight shall demaund, so far foorth as
it be no impeachment to my chastitie.   And, to conclude, poynt
some place for to meet the man, for my conueyance from the
Denmarke Court: which determined vpon, he will appoynt some   90
certaine time for our departure: whereof, you hauing intelligence,
you may soone set downe a plot to were the English Crowne,
and then —

Blaunch.   What then?

Mar.   If Sir Robert proue a King and you his Queene,   95
how then?

Blaunch.   Were I assured of the one, as I am perswaded
of the other, there were some possibilitie in it.   But here
comes the man.

Mar.   Madam, begon, and you shall see I will worke   100
to your desire and my content.   [*Exit* BLAUNCH.

<hr>

79 seqq. *esteeme* | *loue* | *false* | *Lubeck* | *Penelope* | *taske* | Qq. — 79. *It
is well known to you.* Chet. — 80. *not a little* Simp. — 81. *found* om. by
Del. — 85—93. *come* | *loue* | *anything* | *foorth* | *chastitie* | *the man* | *court* |
time | *intelligence* | *crowne* | Qq. Elze arranges this passage as follows (Notes,
p. 127): *The next time that Sir Robert shall come here* | *In's wonted sort
to solicit me with love* | *I'll seem t'agree and like of anything* | *That th'
knight shall demand, so far forth as it be* | *No impeachment to my chastity;
t'conclude,* | *I will appoint some place for t'meet the man,* | *For my convey-
ance from the Denmark court.* — 86. *I'll* Chet. — 88. *to my honour*
Chet. — *appoint* Del. — *appoint some meeting place for my conveyance*
Chet. — 90. *the Danish Court* Chet. — *Which fix'd, he will appoint*
Chet. — 97—101. The lines end at *perswaded* | *in it* | *the man* | *see* | *content* |
in Qq. — 100, 101. *Madam, begone, and you shall see* | *That I will work
to both your souls' content.* | Chet.

Enter W. Conqueror.

Wm.   Sweet Lady, this is well and happily met,
For Fortune hetherto hath been my foe,
And though I haue oft sought to speake with you,
105 Yet stil I haue beene crost with sinister happs.
I cannot, Madam, tell a louing tale,
Or court my Maistres with fabulous discourses,
That am a souldier sworne to follow armes —
But this I bluntly let you vnderstand —
110 I honour you with such religious zeale
As may become an honorable minde.
Nor may I make my loue the siege of Troy,
That am a straunger in this Countrie.
First, what I am I know you are resolued,
115 For that my friend hath let you t'vnderstand,
The Marques Lubeck, to whom I am so bound
That whilest I liue I count me onely his.
   Mar.   Surely you are beholding to the Marques,
For he hath beene an earnest spokesman in your cause.
120   *Wm.*   And yealdes my Ladie then, at his request,
To grace Duke William with her gratious loue?
   Mar.   My Lord,
I am a prisoner, and hard it were
To get me from the Court.
125   *Wm.*   An easie matter, to get you from the Court,

101. *[Enter W. Conq.]* not in Qq; added by Del. — 102. *Lady* Qq, *Sweet
lady* proposed by El. (Notes, p. 127); cp., above, l. 54. — 102—104. Printed as
prose by Del. and Simp. -- 103. *For* added by Simp. — 104. Del. erroneously
prints *often*. — 105. *sinister* to be pronounced as a dissyllable (*sin'ster*). —
106. 'Compare Henry V th's courtship: Henry V., V. 2. 98 et seq.' Simp. —
107. Are we allowed to consider *Maistres* as a monosyllable here?   Or must
we pronounce *Maist(e)res*? The latter pronunciation would involve the admittance of a weak-ending alexandrine.   Chet. reads *with false vows of love;*
Simp. proposes *Or with discourses fabulous court my mistress,* and El. would
regulate the line thus (Jahrb., XV, p. 346): *Or court with fabulous discourse
my mistress.* — 113. *Countrie,* a trisyllable here; cp. Abbott, s. 477. — The
line is omitted in Chet. — 115. *you that to* Qq, corr. by Simp. — *let you
understand* Chet. — 118. Cp. As You Like It, IV. 1. 60, *you are fain to
be beholding to your wives for,* where Pope reads *beholden;* just so in our
passage Chet.; *beholden to that lord.* — 119. *spokes-man for you* Chet. —
122. *My Lord* placed in a separate line by El. (Jahrb., XV, 346).

If case that you will thereto giue consent.

    Mar.   Put case I should, how would you vse me than?

    Wm.   Not otherwise but well and honorably.

I haue at Sea a shipp that doth attend,

Which shall foorthwith conduct vs into England;   130

Where, when we are, I straight will marrie thee.

We may not stay deliberating long,

Least that suspition, enuious of our weale,

Set in a foot to hinder our pretence.

    Mar.   But this I. thinke were most conuenient,   135

To maske my face, the better t'scape vnknowne.

    Wm.   A good deuise: till then, Farwell, faire loue.

    Mar.   But this I must intreat your grace,

You would not seek by lust vnlawfully

To wrong my chaste determinations.   140

    Wm.   I hold that man most shamelesse in his sinne

That seekes to wrong an honest ladies name,

Whom he thinkes worthy of his marriage bed.

    Mar.   In hope your othe is true,

I leaue your grace till the appoynted tyme.   145

                      [Exit MARIANA.

    Wm.   O happie William, blessed in thy loue,

Most fortunate in Marianaes loue!

Well, Lubeck, well, this courtesie of thine

I will requite, if God permit me life.   *[Exit.*

SCENE II.

Enter VALINGFORD *and* MOUNTNEY *at two sundrie dores,*
   looking angerly each on other with Rapiers drawen.

    Mount.   Valingford,

So hardlie I disgest an iniurie

---

127. *What if I should* Chet. — 133. Simp. erroneously reads *conscious of our weal;* both of the old copies have *enuious.* — 134. *to hinder our pretence;* cp. Mucedorus, III. 5. 3: *But other business hind'red my pretence,* and ib., III. 4. 2: *frustrate my pretence.* — 136. *to scape* Qq̄ and Edd. — 146. 'Qy, read, *fortune* for *loue?*' Simp. — 147. Omitted by Chet. — 149. *if heav'n permit* Chet.

    SCENE II. 1—5. Printed as three lines in Qq, ending at *iniurie* | *stands* | *name* |; in the edd. of Del. and Simp. the lines end *proffered me* | *detest* | *name* |. For our arrangement see El., Notes, p. 12 seq.

Thou 'st profered me,
As, were it not that I detest to do
5   What stands not with the honor of my name,
Thy death should paie the ransom of thy fault.
    Val. And, Mountney, had not my reuenging wrath,
Incenst with more than ordinarie loue,
Beene such for to depriue thee of thy life,
10 Thou hadst not liued to braue me as thou doest.
Wretch as thou art,
Wherein hath Valingford offended thee?
That honorable bond which late we did
Confirme in presence of the gods,
15 When with the Conqueror we arriued here,
For my part hath been kept inviolably,
Till, now, too much abused by thy villanie,
I am inforced to cancell all those bands,
By hating him which I so well did loue.
20 *Mount.* Subtill thou art, and cunning in thy fraud,
That, giuing me occasion of offence,
Thou pickst a quarrell to excuse thy shame.
Why, Valingford, was 't not enough for thee,
To be a ryvall twixt me and my loue,
25 But counsell her, to my no small disgrace,
That, when I came to talke with her of loue,
She should seeme deafe, as fayning not to heare?
    Val. But hath shee, Mountney, vsed thee as thou sayest?
    Mount. Thou knowest too well shee hath: wherein
30 Thou couldest not do me greater iniurie.
    Val. Then I perceiue we are deluded both,
For when I offered many gifts of Gold,

<hr>

3. *Thou hast* Qq. — 4. *as were not* A, *as wer't not* B (adopted by
Simp.), *as were it not* Del. — *that* om. by Simp. — 6. *thy ransom* Qq;
corr. by Del. — 10, 11. Form one line in Qq; divided by Del. — 11. Omitted
by Chet. — 13, 14 Divided at *confirme* | in Qq; set right by Del. — 14. *in
presence of the Gods* om. by Chet. — *Conqueror* as a dissyllable here. —
17. *villanie* may be pronounced as a dissyllable; see Abbott, ». 468. — 18. *to
concel* Del. (a misprint). — 23. *was it* Qq, *was't* Del. and Simp. — 29. End-
ing at *hath* | in Qq; corr. by Del. — 32—34. Printed as two lines in Qq,

And iewels to entreate for loue,
Shee hath refused them with a coy disdaine,
Alledging that shee could not see the sunne!   35
The same conjectured I to be thy drift,
That fayning so shee might be ridd of mee.
   Mount. The like did I by thee. But are not these
Naturall impediments?
   Val. In my coniecture merely counterfeit: 40
Therefore let us ioyne hands in frindship once againe,
Since that the iarre grew onely by coniecture.
   Mount. With all my heart: Yet lets trye th' truth thereof.
   Val. With right good will. We 'll straight vnto her father,
And there to learne whither it be so or no.   *[Exeunt.* 45

SCENE III.

Enter WILLIAM *and* BLAUNCH *disguised, with
a maske ouer her face.*

   Wm. Come on, my loue, the comfort of my life.
Disguised thus, we may remaine vnknowne,
And get we once to Seas, I force not then
We quickly shall attaine the English shore.

the first ending at *iewels* |. Arranged by Del. — 33, 34. Contracted into one
line by Chet.: *T'entreat for love, she scorn'd them with disdain.* — 34. Simp.
expunges *a.* — 38, 39. Printed as one line in Qq; divided by Del. — In Chet. l. 38
ends at *thee* (and so El. conj., Jahrb., XV, 346). — 41. *lets* A, *let's* B, *let
us* Del. — El. proposes to read: *Therefore in friendship let's join hands
again* (Jahrb., XV, 346); but, with stricter adherence to the originals, we
might restore a regular blank verse thus: *Therefore let's once again join
hands in friendship.* — 42. *yars* Del. (a misprint). — 43. *lets* Qq, *let us*
Del. and Simp. — *the truth* Qq, *th' truth* El. conj. (Jahrb., l. c.). — 44. *We
will* Qq, *We'll* Del., *we will unto her* Chet. (*straight* om.). — 45. *whither*
is to be pronounced as a monosyllable. — Although the construction is rather
a loose one, it seems unnecessary to alter it and to read with Elze either
To learn there or *And there we'll learn* (see Jahrb., XV, 347). — *And thereto
learn* Chet.

   SCENE III. 3. *I force not then*; cp. Mucedorus, Induction, l. 68: *I force
it not, I scorn what thou canst do*; New Custom (apud Dodsley, Old Plays,
ed. Hazlitt, vol. III, p. 39): *I force not, I, so the villain were dead.* — *to
sea, I doubt not then.* Chet.

5 *Blaunch.* But this I vrge you with your former oath:
You shall not seeke to violate mine honour
Vntill our marriage rights be all performed.
  Wm. Mariana, here I sweare to thee by heauen,
And by the honour that I beare to Armes,
10 Neuer to seeke or craue at hands of thee
The spoyle of honourable chastitie,
Vntill we do attaine the English coast,
Where thou shalt be my right espoused Queen.
  Blaunch. In hope your oath proceedeth from your heart,
15 Let's leaue the Court, and betake vs to his power
That gouernes all things to his mightie will,
And will reward the iust with endlesse ioye,
And plague the bad with most extreme annoy.
  Wm. Lady, as little tarriance as we may,
20 Lest some misfortune happen by the way.
        [Exit BLAUNCH *and* WILLIAM.

SCENE IV.

Enter the MILLER, *his man* TROTTER, *and* MANUILE.

  Mil. I tell you, sir, it is no little greefe to mee, you
should so hardly conseit of my daughter, whose honest report,
though I saie it, was neuer blotted with any title of de-
famation.

5 *Man.* Father Miller, the repaire of those gentlemen to
your house hath giuen me great occasion to mislike.

   7. *rights* is, of course, the old spelling for *rites* (as Del. prints); cp.
Al. Schmidt, Shak.-Lex., s. v. *rite*, p. 982$^\text{b}$. — 13. *right-espoused* Del. —
15. *betake* is to be pronounced as a monosyllable (*b'take*). — 16. *by his
mighty will* Chet. — 20. *Least* B. — *mis-fortune* Qq.
  SCENE IV. The same remarks that we have made on Act III, Scene I,
ll. 73 seqq., apply to this scene. In all probability it was originally written
in blank verse, which, in some passages, may be restored without great difficulty; but, in general, the text of the scene is so utterly corrupt that no
critic seems able to amend it except by violent and arbitrary alterations.
Here, therefore, as in all similar cases, we have thought it best to follow
Del. and Simp., who have printed the whole scene as prose. — 1—4. Printed
as four lines in Qq, ending *mee | daughter | it | defamation |*. — 5, 6. As
two lines, divided at *house |* in Qq. — 5. *these gentlemen* Chet.

Mil. As for those gentlemen, I neuer saw in them any euill intreatie. But should they haue profered it, her chaste minde hath proofe enough to preuent it.

Trot. Those gentlemen are as honest as euer I saw: 10
For yfaith one of them gaue me six pence to fetch a quart of Seck. — See, maister, here they come.

Enter VALINGFORD *and* MOUNTNEY.

Mil. Trotter, call Em. Now they are here together, Ile haue this matter throughly debated. 　　*[Exit* TROTTER.

Mount. Father, well met. We are come to confer 15 with you.

Man. Nay, with his daughter rather.

Val. Thus it is, father, we are come to craue your frindship in a matter.

Mil. Gentlemen, as you are straungers to me, yet by the 20 way of courtesie you shall demaund any reasonable thing at my hands.

Man. What, is the matter so forward they come to craue his good will?

Val. It is giuen us to vnderstand that your daughter is 25 sodenly become both blinde and deafe.

Mil. Mary, God forbid! I have sent for her. Indeed, she hath kept her chamber this three daies. It were no litle griefe to me if it should be so.

Man. This is Gods iudgement for her trecherie! 30

Enter TROTTER, *leading* EM.

Mil. Gentlemen, I feare your words are too true. See where Trotter comes leading of her. — What ayles my Em? Not blinde, I hope?

7—9. Three lines in Qq, ending *them* | *it* | *it* |. — 14. *thoroughly* Del. and Simp. — 18. *we come* Simp. — 20—22. Three lines in Qq, ending at *me* | *demaund* | *hands* |. — 21. 'Qy, read, *shall command?*' Simp. — 23, 24. Two lines in Qq, divided at *forward.* — 23. *forward? They* Del. — *came* A. — 25, 26. Two lines in Qq, the first ending at *daughter.* — 27—29. In Qq the lines end at *indeed* | *daies* | *so* |. — 28. *these three days* Chet. — 30. *is heaven's judgement* Chet. — 31—33. As three lines in Qq, ending *true* | *her* | *hope* |. — 31. *two true* Qq (followed by Simp.).

Em. [*Aside*] Mountney and Valingford both together!
35 And Manuile, to whom I haue faithfully vowed my loue! Now,
Em, suddenly helpe thy selfe.

Mount. This is no desembling, Valingford.

Val. If it be, it is cunningly contriued of all sides.

Em. [*Aside to* TROTTER] Trotter, lend me thy hand; and
40 as thou louest me, keep my counsell, and iustifie what so euer
I saie and Ile largely requite thee.

Trot. Ah, that's as much as to saie you would tell a
monstrous, terrible, horrible, outragious lie, and I shall sooth
it — no, berlady!

45   *Em.* My present extremitie wills me, if thou loue me,
Trotter.

Trot. That same word 'loue' makes me to doe any thing.

Em. Trotter, wheres my father?

Trot. Why, what a blynd dunce are you, can you not
50 see? He standeth right before you.

[*He thrusts* EM *vpon her father.*

Em. Is this my father? — Good father, giue me leaue
to sit where I may not be disturbed, sith God hath visited
me both of my sight and hearing.

Mil. Tell me, sweet Em, how came this blindnes? Thy
55 eyes are louely to looke on, and yet haue they lost the
benefit of their sight? What a griefe is this to thy poore
father!

34—36. Three lines in Qq, ending *together* | *loue* | *selfe* |. — 34. [*Aside*]
added by Del. — 38. *if ir be* A. — *on all sides* Chet. — 39—41. Three
lines in Qq, ending *hand* | *counsell* | *thee* |. El. (Notes, p. 16) arranges the
passage in this way: *Trotter,* | *Lend me thy hand, and as thou lovest me* |
Pray keep my counsel, and justify whatever | *I say, and largely I'll requite*
thee. |. The same critic (Jahrb., XV, 347) proposes another arrangement:
Trotter, | *Lend me thy hand, and as thou lovest me, keep* | *My counsel and*
justify whate'er I say, | *And largely I'll requite thee.* |. — 39. [*Aside to*
TROTTER] added by the pres. Edd. — 42. *that is* B. — 43. *monstrous* om.
by Del. — 46. *Trotrer* A. — 50. The stage-direction in Qq after l. 48. —
51—53. As four lines in Qq, ending *father?* | *sit* | *disturbed* | *hearing* |. —
52. *since* Del. — *Since fate has robb'd me of my sight and hearing.* Chet. —
55. *lovely yet to look upon,* Chet. — *they 've lost* El. conj. (Jahrb., XV, 347). —
54—57. El., who divides the lines at *blindnes* | *on* | *sight* |, proposes to add
Oh, before *what.*

Em. Good father, let me not stand as an open gazing stock to euerie one, but in a place alone, as fits a creature so miserable.   60

Mil. Trotter, lead her in, the vtter ouerthrow of poore Goddardes ioy and onely solace.

[*Exit the* MILLER, TROTTER *and* EM.

Man. Both blinde and deafe! Then is she no wife for me; and glad am I so good occasion is hapned: Now will I away to Chester, and leaue these gentlemen to their blinde   65 fortune.   [*Exit* MANUILE.

Mount. Since fortune hath thus spitefully crost our hope, let vs leaue this quest and hearken after our King, who is at this day landed at Lirpoole.

Val. Goe, my Lord, Ile follow you.   70

[*Exit* MOUNTNEY.

Well, now Mountney is gone, Ile staie behind to solicit my loue; for I imagine that I shall find this but a fained inuention, thereby to haue vs leaue off our suits.

[*Exit* VALINGFORD.

58—60. Printed as two lines in Qq, divided at *euerie one* !. El. (Notes, p. 17) arranges the passage thus: *father* | *gazing-stock* (*as om.*) | *alone* | *miserable* (inserting *that's* between *creature* and *so*) |. — 58. *let we not* Del. (a misprint). — 59. *a lone* A. — 61, 62. El. (Jahrb., XV, 347) would arrange the passage as follows: *Trotter, lead her in!* | *This is the utter overthrow of poor* | *Old Goddard's joy and only solace.* |. — 63—66. The lines end at *me* | *hapned* | *Manchester* | *fortune.* | in Qq. — *Both blind and deaf — she is no wife for me;* | *And glad am I so good occasion happen'd:* | *Now will I bend my course to Manchester,* | *And leave these gentlemen to their blind fortune.* | Chet. — For El.'s metrical reconstruction see Jahrb., XV, 348. — 63. *Then she is* Del. — 64. *glad I am* Del. — Simp. is mistaken in giving *so good an occasion* as the reading of B. — 65. *Manchester* Qq, *Chester* Del.; compare, below, IV. 3. 5, 62. — 67. *spiteful* Chet. — 68. *Let's* Chet. and El. conj. — *guest* Qq, *quest* or *gear* Simp. conj. — 69. *Liverpool* Del. — *Who is at Liv'rpool landed at this day.* El. conj. (Jahrb., XV, 348). — 70. [*Exit M.*] in Qq after l. 69. — In Chet. the end of the scene runs thus: *My lord, I'll follow you —* | *Now, that Mountney's gone,* | *I'll stay behind to solicit my fair love.* | *I love her for her virtues, lasting charms;* | *A never-fading flow'r will fill my arms.* |. — 71—73. Printed as three lines in Qq, ending *gone* | *loue* | *inuention* |. — 73. [*Exit* VAL.] added by Del.

SCENE V.

Enter MARQUES LUBECK *and the* KING OF DENMARK,
angerly with some attendants.

 Zweno. Well, Lubeck, well, it is not possible
But you must be concenting to this act.
Is this the man so highly you extold?
And play a part so hatefull with his friend?
5 Since first he came with thee into the court,
What entertainement and what countenance
He hath receiued, none better knowes than thou.
In recompence whereof, he quites me well
To steale away faire Mariana my prisoner,
10 Whose raunsome being lately greed vpon,
I am deluded of by this escape.
Besides, I know not how to answer it,
When shee shall be demaunded home to Swethia.
 Lub. My gracious Lord, coniecture not, I pray,
15 Worser of Lubeck than he doth deserue:
Your highnes knowes Mariana was my loue,
Sole paragon and mistres of my thoughts.
Is't likely I should know of her departure,
Wherein there's no man iniured more than I?
20 *Zweno.* That carries reason, Marques, I confesse.
Call foorth my daughter. Yet I am perswaded
 · That shee, poore soule, suspected not her going;
For as I heare, shee likewise loued the man,
Which he, to blame, did not at all regard.

Enter ROSILIO *and* MARIANA.

25 *Ros.* My Lord, here is the Princesse Mariana;
It is your daughter is conueyed away.

<hr>

SCENE V. 2. *in this* Del. — 5. *in to the* Simp. — 8. *quits* Simp. —
9. *fair Marian, my captive.* Chet. — 10. *lately fixed on* Chet. — 15. *More
ill of* Chet. — 18. *Is it* Qq, *Is't* Del. — 19. *there is* Qq, *there's* Del. and
Simp. — *Wherein no man is injured* Chet. — 24. The stage-direction added
by Del. — 25. *Rocilia* B, *Rozilio* Chet. — 26. For the omission of the relative
see Abbott, s. 244.

Zweno.   What, my daughter gone!
Now, Marques, your villainie breakes foorth.
This match is of your making, gentle sir,
And you shall dearly know the price thereof.   30
  Lub.   Knew I thereof, or that there was intent
In Robert thus to steale your highnes daughter,
Let heauens in iustice presently confound me!
  Zweno.   Not all the protestations thou canst vse
Shall saue thy life.   Away with him to prison!   35
And, minion, otherwise it cannot be
But you 're an agent in this trecherie.
I will reuenge it throughly on you both.
Away with her to prison!
Heres stuffe indeed!   My daughter stolen away!   40
It booteth not thus to disturbe my selfe,
But presently to send to English William,
To send me that proud knight of Windsor hither,
Here in my Court to suffer for his shame,
Or at my pleasure to be punished there,   45
Withall that Blaunch be sent me home againe,
Or I shall fetch her vnto Windsors cost,
Yea, and Williams too, if he denie her mee.
                                              [Exeunt all.

SCENE VI.

Enter WILLIAM, *taken with souldiers.*

  Wm.   Could any crosse, could any plague be worse?
Could heauen or hell, did both conspire in one
T' afflict my soule, inuent a greater scourge
Than presently I am tormented with?
Ah, Mariana, cause of my lament!   5
Ioy of my hart, and comfort of my life,
For thee I breath my sorrowes in the ayre
And tyre myself, for silently I sigh,

28. *your* may be pronounced as a dissyllable; *Now, Marques, [now]*
your Simp. — 33. *Let heaven* Chet. — 37. *you are* Qq, *you're* Del. — 38. *tho-*
roughly Chet. — 39, 40. Divided at *indeed!* | in Qq; set right by Del. —
48. [*Exit* ZWENO.] Qq; corr. by Del.
      SCENE VI.   3. *To afflict* Qq, *T'afflict* Chet. — 7, 8. *For whether I*
breathe . . . . . . or silently I sigh Simp. conj.

My sorrowes afflicts my soule with equall passion.
10   *Soul.*   Go to, sirrah, put vp, 'tis to small purpose.
      Wm.   Hence, villaines, hence!
Dare you to lay your hands vpon your Soueraigne?
      Soul.   Well, sir, we'll deale for that.
But here comes one will remedie all this.

Enter DEMARCH.

15 My Lord, watching this night in the campe
We tooke this man, and know not what he is;
And in his companie was a gallant dame,
A woman faire in outward shewe she seemd,
But that her face was masked, we could not see
20 The grace and fauour of her countenance.
      Dem.   Tell me, good fellow, of whence and what thou art.
      Soul.   Why do you not answer my Lord?
He takes scorne to answer!
      Dem.   And takest thou scorn to answer my demaund?
25 Thy proud behauiour very well deserues
This misdemeanour at the worst be construed.
Why doest thou neither know, nor hast thou heard,
That in the absence of the Saxon Duke
Demarch is his especiall Substitute,
30 To punish those that shall offend the lawes?
      Wm.   In knowing this, I know thou art a traytor;
A rebell, and mutenous conspirator.
Why, Demarch, knowest thou who I am?

9. *My griefs afflict* Chet. — *afflict* Del. — *me soule* A. — 10. *sirha* A;
cp. Marlowe's Faustus etc., ed. Ward, Note to II. 5 (p. 142). — *it is* Qq and
Edd. — 11, 12. Divided at *hands* in Qq. In the division of the lines we
have followed El.'s proposal (Notes, p. 133). — 12. *Dare you lay* Qq, *How
dare you lay* Del., *Dare you [to] lay* Simp. — 13. *we will* Qq; *we* om. by
Del. — 15. In Qq *Souldier* is prefixed also to this line. — For the dis-
syllabic pronunciation of *Lord* see Marlowe's Edward II., ed. Fleay, II. 5. 107
(and Notes, p. 117). — El., comparing l. 31, proposes to read *My Lord, in
watching* etc. (Notes, p. 17 seq.). — 17. Pronounce *comp'ny*. — 21. *what art
thou?* Simp. — 28. *The Saxon Duke.* 'He was a Norman. William is
variously termed etc.' Simp., Note ad loc. — 32. *rebel* is to be pronounced
as a monosyllable. It is, therefore, unnecessary to read with Simp. *and a
mutinous.*

Dem.   Pardon, my dread Lord, th' error of my sence,
And misdemeanour to your princely excellencie!   35
   Wm.   Why, Demarch,
What is the cause my subiects are in armes?
   Dem.   Free are my thoughts, my dread and gracious Lord,
From treason to your state and common weale;
Only reuengement of a priuate grudge,   40
By Lord Dirot lately profered me,
That stands not with the honor of my name,
Is cause I haue assembled for my guard
Some men in armes, that may withstand his force
Whose setled malice aymeth at my life.   45
   Wm.   Where's Lord Dirot?
   Dem.   In armes, my gratious Lord,
Not past two miles from hence, as credibly
I'm assertained.
   Wm.   Well, come, let us go.
I feare I shall find traytors of you both.
                     [Exeunt all.

A C T IV.

SCENE I.

Enter the CITIZEN OF CHESTER, *and his daughter*
ELNER, *and* MANUILE.

Cit.   Indeed, sir, it would do verie well if you could
intreat your father to come hither; but, if you thinke it be

---

34. *the error* Qq. — 35. El. (Notes, p. 135) substitutes *excellence* for
excellencie. — 36, 37. Printed as one line in Qq; divided by El. — 39. *and
th' common weal* El. conj. — 46—49. Six lines in Qq, ending *Dirot | Lord |
hence | assertained | go | both |.* El. (Notes, p. 18) arranges the passage thus:
WM. CONQ. *Where's Lord Dirot? |* DEM. *In arms, my gracious lord, not
past two miles | From hence, as credibly I'm ascertain'd. |.* The arrangement
as given above is that of the present editors. — 46. *Where is* Qq. — 48. *I
am* Qq. — *let's* Del. — 49. *[Exit]* Qq. — Chet. adds the following rhyme-
couplet: *Traitors to kings fly in the face of heav'n, | Since by almighty
Jove the sceptre's given.*
   SCENE I. Also this scene is printed as verse in the old copies. —
Stage-direction: *Manchester* Qq, *Chester* Del., *a Citizen of Chester* Chet. —
Eliner Chet. (throughout), *Elinor* Del. — 1. *would be very* Del. — 2. *it to
be* Del.

too farr, I care not much to take horse and ride to Manchester.   I am sure my daughter is content with either.   How
5   sayest thou, Elner, art thou not?

    El.   As you shall thinke best I must be contented.

    Man.   Well, Elner, farewell.   Only thus much, I pray:
make all things in a readines, either to serue here, or to
carry thither with vs.

10   *Cit.*   As for that, sir, take you no care; and so I betake
you to your iournie.   *[Exit* MANUILE.

Enter VALINGFORD.

But soft, what gentleman is this?

    Val.   God speed, sir.   Might a man craue a word or
two with you?

15   *Cit.*   God forbid els, sir; I pray you speake your pleasure.

    Val.   The gentleman that parted from you, was he not
of Manchester, his father lyuing there of good account?

    Cit.   Yes, mary is he, sir.   Why doe you aske?   Belike
you haue had some acquaintance with him?

20   *Val.*   I haue been acquainted, in times past, but, through
his double dealing, I am growen werie of his companie.   For,
be it spoken to you, he hath been acquainted with a poore
millers daughter, and diuers tymes hath promist her marriage.
But what with his delayes and flouts he hath brought her into
25   such a taking that I feare me it will cost her her life.

    Cit.   To be playne with you, sir, his father and I haue
been of old acquaintance, and a motion was made betweene
my daughter and his sonne, which is now throughly agreed
vpon, saue onely the place appoynted for the mariage, whether
30   it shall be kept here or at Manchester; and for no other
occasion he is now ridden.

    El.   What hath he done to you, that you should speake
so ill of the man?

    Val.   Oh, gentlewoman, I crie you mercie: he is your
35   husband that shalbe.

    4. *I'm sure* Chet. — 10. *and so betake* Chet. — 11. *[Exit M.]* added
by Del. — 27. *beteewene* A. — 28. *now is* Simp. — *thoroughly* Chet.

El. If I knew this to be true, he should not be my
husband were he neuer so good. And therefore, good father,
I would desire you to take the paines to beare this gentleman
companie to Manchester, to know whether this be true or no.

Cit. Now trust mee, gentleman, hee deales with mee very   40
hardly, knowing how well I ment to him; but I care not much
to ride to Manchester, to know whether his fathers will be he
should deale with me so badly. Will it please you, sir, to
go in? We will presently take horse and away.

Val. If it please you to go in, Ile follow you presently.   45
         [Exit ELNER *and her father.*
Now shall I be reuenged on Manuile, and by this meanes
get Em to .my wife; and therefore I will strayght to her
fathers, and informe them both of all that is hapned.

               [Exit.

SCENE II.

Enter WILLIAM, *the* AMBASSADOR OF DENAMARKE,
DEMARCH, *and other attendants.*

Wm. What newes with the Denmarke Embassador?
Emb. Mary, thus:
The King of Denmarke and my Soueraigne
Doth send to know of thee what is the cause,
That iniuriously, against the law of armes,   5
Thou 'st stolen away his onely daughter Blaunch,

----

44. *we'll presently* Chet. — 45. *Exeunt* ELINER ... Chet. — 46—48. *Now
shall l be revenged on faithless Manvile,* | *And, by this means, fair Em will
be revenged.* | Chet. — 47. *to be my* Simp. — *to her father* Del. — ,48. *has
happened.* Simp. This alteration is quite uncalled for, as in the English of
Shakespeare's time the intransitive verbs were more commonly used with *is*
than with *has.* Cp. Abbott, s. 295.
 SCENE II. 2, 3. Forming one line in Qq and Edd.; separated by El. —
4. *of the* Qq. — 5, 6. Elze, who, very likely, is right in thinking the reiteration
of *onely* in ll. 6 and 7 to be what the German critics call a 'dittography',
alters (Notes, p. 19): *That thou hast stol'n, against the law of arms* | *In-
juriously away his daughter Blanch,* |. But, in our opinion, it would be
better, not to separate *away* from its participle *stol'n,* and to read: *That
thou hast stol'n away, injuriously,* | *Against the law of armes, his daughter
Blanch* |. More conservative critics may perhaps prefer another proposal made
by El. (p. 20): *That, 'gainst the law of arms, injuriously* | *Thou'st stol'n
away his only daughter Blanch.* — 6. *Thou hast* Qq.

The onely stay and comfort of his life?
Therefore by me
He willeth thee to send his daughter Blaunch,
10   Or else foorthwith he 'll leuy such an host,
As soone shall fetch her in despite of thee.
     Wm.   Embassador, this answer I retorne thy king.
He willeth me to send his daughter Blaunch,
Saying, I conuaid her from the Danish court,
15   That neuer yet did once as thinke thereof.
As for his menacing and daunting threats,
I nill regard him nor his Danish power;
For if he come to fetch her foorth my Realme
I will prouide him such a banquet here,
20   That he shall haue small cause to giue me thanks.
     Emb.   Is this your answer, then?
     Wm.   It is; and so begone.
     Emb.   I goe; but to your cost.   *[Exit* AMBASSADOR.
     Wm.   Demarch,
25   Our subiects, earst leuied in ciuill broyles,
Muster foorthwith, for to defend the Realme.
In hope whereof, that we shall finde you true,
We freely pardon this thy late offence.
     Dem.   Most humble thanks I render to your grace.
                                              [Exeunt.

SCENE III.

Enter the MILLER *and* VALINGFORD.

     Mil.   Alas, gentleman, why should you trouble your selfe
so much, considering the imperfections of my daughter, which

8, 9. One line in Qq. — 9. El. thinks the same compositor's error as
in ll. 6, 7 to have occurred here, *his daughter Blanch* having come down
from l. 6, or up from l. 13; he, therefore, proposes to read: *Thérefore* ....
to send her.   Chet. alters: *Therefore, by me, he wills thee send her back.*
In placing *Therefore by me* in a separate line we have followed Del. and
Simp. — 10. *he will* Qq and Simp., *he'll* Del. — 14. *Saying,* a monosyllable
here. — 15. *yet once did* Simp. — 17. Simp. reads, by mistake, *I will regard.*
For the archaic form *nill = ne will,* cp. Tam., II. 1. 273, and Haml., V. 1. 19. —
18. *comes* Del. — 24, 25. As one line in Qq; divided by Del. — 26. *Mustred*
Qq; corr. by Del. and Simp.

     SCENE III.   This scene is again printed as verse in the old copies. —
Enter the Millier. A.

is able to with-draw the loue of any man from her, as
alreadie it hath done in her first choyce. Maister Manuile
hath forsaken her, and at Chester shall be maried to a mans   5
daughter of no little wealth. But if my daughter knew so
much, it would goe verie neere her heart, I feare me.

    Val. Father Miller, such is the entyre affection to your
daughter, as no misfortune whatsoeuer can alter. My fellow
Mountney, thou seest, gaue quickly ouer; but I, by reason of   10
my good meaning, am not so soone to be changed, although
I am borne off with scornes and deniall.

Enter Em *to them.*

    Mil. Trust me, sir, I know not what to saie. My daughter
is not to be compelled by me; but here she comes her selfe:
speake to her and spare not, for I neuer was troubled with   15
loue matters so much before.

    Em. [*Aside*] Good Lord! shall I neuer be rid of this
importunate man? Now must I dissemble blyndnes againe.
Once more for thy sake, Manuile, thus am I inforced, because
I shall complete my full resolued mynde to thee. Father,   20
where are you?

    Mil. Here, sweet Em. Answer this gentleman, that would
so fayne enioy thy loue.

    Em. Where are you, sir? will you neuer leaue this idle
and vaine pursuit of loue? Is not England stor'd enough   25
to content you, but you must still trouble the poore contemptible mayd of Manchester?

    Val. None can content me but the fayre maide of Man-
chester.

    Em. I perceiue loue is vainly described, that, being   30
blynd himselfe, would haue you likewise troubled with a blinde
wife, hauing the benefit of your eyes. But neither follow him
so much in follie, but loue one in whom you may better
delight.

<hr>

8. 'Qy, *my entire*' Simp. — *Father, such is th' entire* Chet. — 9—12.
My fellow . . . . deniall. Omitted by Chet. — 10. *quicly* A. — 12. *denials*
Del. — 13. *daughter's* Chet. — 17. [*Aside*] added by Del. — 19. *I am*
Del. — *insorced* A. — 25. *enought* A. — 26. *still* om. by Del.

35   *Val.* Father Miller, thy daughter shall haue honor by
graunting mee her loue. I am a Gentleman of King Williams
Court, and no meane man in King Williams fauour.

      Em. If you be a Lord, syr, as you say, you offer both
your selfe and mee great wrong; yours, as apparant, in limit-
40 ing your loue so vnorderly, for which you rashly endure re-
prochement; mine, as open and euident, when, being shut
from the vanities of this world, you would haue me as an
open gazing stock to all the world; for lust, not loue, leades
you into this error. But from the one I will keepe me as well
45 as I can; and yeeld the other to none but to my father, as
I am bound by dutie.

      Val. Why, faire Em, Manuile hath forsaken thee, and
must at Chester be married: which if I speake otherwise than
true, let thy father speake what credibly he hath heard.

50   *Em.* But can it be Manuile will deale so vnkindly to
reward my iustice with such monstrous vngentlenes? Haue I
dissembled for thy sake, and doest thou now thus requite it?
In deed these many daies I haue not seen him, which hath
made me marueile at his long absence. But, father, are you
55 assured of the words he spake were concerning Manuile?

      Mil. In sooth, daughter, now it is foorth I must needs
confirme it: Maister Manuile hath forsaken thee, and at Chester
must be married to a man's daughter of no little wealth. His
owne father procures it, and therefore I dare credit it; and
60 doe thou beleeue it, for trust me, daughter, it is so.

      Em. Then, good father, pardon the iniurie that I haue
don to you, onely causing your griefe, by ouer-fond affecting
a man so trothlesse. And you likewise, sir, I pray hold me
excused, as I hope this cause will allow sufficiently for mee:
65 My loue to Manuile, thinking he would requite it, hath made

38. *man in favour with my prince.* Chet. — 39. *your's* Chet. —
41. *which, being* Del. — 41, 42. *shut out from* Simp. — 42. *of the world*
Del. — 42, 43. *have me u gazing-stock* Chet. — 44, 45. *I'll keep me as I
can* Chet. — 49. *credibly I have heard* Del. — 54, 55. *are you assured
of the words he speak were true concerning Manvile?* Chet.; *are you assured
if the words he spake were true, concerning Manvile?* Del. — 56. *Indeed,
daughter, now it is such, I must* Del. — 63. *I pray you* Del.

me double with my father and you, and many more besides,
which I will no longer hyde from you: That inticing speeches
should not beguile mee, I haue made my selfe deafe to any
but to him; and lest any mans person should please mee
more than his, I haue dissembled the want of my sight: Both   70
which shaddowes of my irreuocable affections I haue not
spar'd to confirme before him, my father, and all other
amorous soliciters — wherewith not made acquainted, I perceiue my true intent hath wrought mine owne sorrow, and
seeking by loue to be regarded, am cut of with contempt,   75
and dispised.

Mil. Tell me, sweet Em, hast thou but fained all this
while for his loue, that hath so descourteously forsaken thee?

Em. Credit me, father, I haue told you the troth; wherewith I desire you and Lord Valingford not to be displeased.   80
For ought else I shall saie, let my present griefe hold me
excused. But, may I liue to see that vngratfull man iustly
rewarded for his trecherie, poore Em would think her selfe
not a little happie. Favour my departing at this instant; for
my troubled thought desires to meditate alone in silence.   85
[Exit Em.

Val. Will not Em shew one cheerefull looke on Valingford?

Mil. Alas, sir, blame her not; you see shee hath good
cause, being so handled by this gentleman! And so Ile leaue
you, and go comfort my poore wench as well as I may.
[Exit the Miller.

Val. Farewell, good father.   90
[Exit Valingford.

<hr>

77. *but* om. by Del. — 77, 78. *all this only for his* Chet. — 79. *told
you truth* Chet. — 80. *desire yon* A. — 85. *in silence* om. by Chet. —
88. *being so handled by this gentleman* om. by Chet. — 89. *as well as I
may* om. by Chet. — 90 Chet. adds the following rhyme couplet: *O loue!
deceiving mirror, bane to joy,* | *Who lights a flame, whose lustre will destroy* |.

A C T V.

SCENE I.

Enter ZWENO, *King of Denmarke, with* ROSILIO
and other attendants.

Zweno.   Rosilio, is this the place whereas
The Duke William should meet mee?
   Ros.   It is, and like your grace.
   Zweno.   Goe, captaine!   Away, regard the charge I gaue:
5 See all our men be martialed for the fight;
Dispose the wards, as lately was deuised;
And let the prisoners, vnder seuerall gards,
Be kept apart, vntill you heare from us.
Let this suffice, you know my resolution.
10 If William, Duke of Saxonie, be the man,
That by his answer sent us, he would send
Not words, but wounds; not parleis, but alarms,
Must be descider of this controuersie.
Rosilio, stay with mee; the rest begone.   *[Exeunt.*

Enter WILLIAM, *and* DEMARCH *with other attendants.*

15   *Wm.*   All but Demarch go shroud you out of sight;
For Ile goe parley with the Prince my selfe.
   Dem.   Should Zweno, by this parley, call you foorth,
Vpon intent iniuriously to deale,
This offereth too much oportunitie.
20   *Wm.*   No, no, Demarch,
That were a breach against the law of Armes.
Therefore be gone, and leaue vs here alone.   *[Exeunt.*

SCENE I. 1, 2. Divided in Qq at *William* |; corr. by Del. — 3. *an't*
Del. — 10. *Duke of Saxon* Qq, *Duke of Normandy* Chet. *Saxony,* as we
have given in our text, is written in the margin of the copy, which was used
by Malone (the undated Q, Bodl. Libr.). — 11. *he would seem* Simp. conj. —
13. *deciders* Del.; cp., however, As You Like It, III. 4. 33 seqq.: *the oath of
a lover is no stronger than the word of a tapster; they are both the confirmer
of false reckonings.* — 15. Here begins another scene in Del.'s edition. But
Zweno and *Ros.* remain on the stage, and *Wm.* and *Dem.* enter to them. —
shroud yon Del. (a misprint). — 16. *For I will go parley* Qq, *For I will
parley* Del., *For I'll go parley* Simp. — 20—22. As three lines in Qq, ending
breach | *begone* | *alone* !; corr. by Del.

I see that Zweno's maister of his word,
Zweno, William of Saxonie greeteth thee,
Either well or yll, according to thy intent.   25
If well thou wish to him and Saxonie,
He bids thee frindly welcome as he can;
If yll thou wish to him and Saxonie,
He must withstand thy mallice as he may.
    Zweno. William,   30
For other name and title giue I none
To him, who, were he worthie of those honours
That Fortune and his predecessors left,
I ought, by right and humaine courtesie,
To grace his style the duke of Saxonie;   35
But, for I finde a base, degenerate mynde,
I frame my speech according to the man,
And not the state that he vnworthie holds.
    Wm. Herein, Zweno, doest thou abase thy state,
To breake the peace which by our auncesters   40
Hath heretofore been honourably kept.
    Zweno. And should that peace for euer haue been kept,
Had not thy selfe been author of the breach:
Nor stands it with the honor of my state,
Or nature of a father to his childe,   45
That I should so be robbed of my daughter,
And not, vnto the vtmost of my power,
Reuenge so intollerable an iniurie.
    Wm. Is this the colour of your quarrell, Zweno?
I well perceiue the wisest men may erre.   50
And thinke you I conueied away your daughter Blaunch?

23. In Del.'s edition *Zweno* and *Ros.* reenter here. — *Zweno is* Qq. — 24. *William of England* Chet. — 26. *to him, and England's crown.* Chet. — 28. *to him, and this my realm.* Chet. — *Saxanie* A. — 30, 31. One line in Qq and Edd. — 34. *common courtesy* El. conj. — 35. *To grace his style with King of England.* Chet. — *To style his grace* Simp. — 39. *abuse thy* Del. — 42. El. proposes to read: *And that peace should for ever have been kept.* — 44. *of thy state* Del. — 50. *man* Del. — 51. El. supposes *Blaunch* to have been inserted here by faulty anticipation from l. 56. In the same critic's opinion the metre of this line might also be regulated by omitting either *And* or *away* (see Notes, p. 135 seq.).

Zweno.   Art thou so impudent to deny thou didst,
When that the proofe thereof is manifest?
    Wm.   What proofe is there?
55   *Zweno.*   Thine owne confession is sufficient proofe.
    Wm.   Did I confesse I stole your daughter Blaunch?
    Zweno.   Thou didst confesse thou hadst a Ladie hence.
    Wm.   I haue, and do.
    Zweno.   Why, that was Blaunch, my daughter.
    Wm.   Nay, that was Mariana,
60   Who wrongfully thou detainest prisoner.
    Zweno.   Shamelesse persisting in thy ill!
Thou doest mayntaine a manifest vntroth,
As shee shall iustifie vnto thy teeth.
Rosilio, fetch her and the Marques hether.
                      [Exit Rosilio *for* Mariana.
65   *Wm.*   It cannot be I should be so deceiued.
    Dem.   I heard this night among the souldiers
That in their watch they tooke a pensiue. ladie,
Who, at th' appoyntment of the Lord Dirot,
Is yet in keeping.   What shee is I know not:
70   Onely thus much I ouer-heard by chance.
    Wm.   And what of this?
    Dem.   It may be Blaunch, the King of Denmarkes daughter.
    Wm.   It may be so; but on my lyfe it is not;
Yet, Demarch, goe, and fetch her strayght.   *[Exit* Demarch.

Enter Rosilio *with the* Marques.

75   *Ros.*   Pleaseth your highnes, here is the Marques and Mariana.
    Zweno.   Seé here, Duke William, your competitors,
That were consenting to my daughters scape:
Let them resolue you of the truth herein.
And here I vow and solemly protest,

That in thy presence they shall lose their heds,   80
Vnlesse I here whereas my daughter is!
    Wm. Oh, Marques Lubeck, how it grieueth me,
That for my sake thou shouldest indure these bondes!
Be iudge, my soule, that feeles the martirdome!
    Lub. Duke William, you know it's for your cause   85
It pleaseth thus the King to misconceiue of me,
And for his pleasure doth me iniurie.

Enter DEMARCH with the Ladie BLAUNCH.

    Dem. May it please your highnesse,
Here is the Ladie whom you sent me for.
    Wm. Away, Demarch! what tellest thou me of Ladies? 90
I so detest the dealing of their sex,
As that I count a louers state to be
The base and vildest slaueric in the world!
    Dem. What humors are these? Heres a straunge alteration!
    Zweno. See, Duke William, is this Blaunch or no?   95
You know her if you see her, I am sure.
    Wm. Zweno,
I was deceiued, yea vtterly deceiued;
Yet this is shee: this same is Ladie Blaunch.
And for mine error, here I am content   100
To do whatsoeuer Zweno shall set downe.
Ah, cruell Mariana, thus to vse
The man which loued and honoured thee with's heart!

---

85. *it is* Qq and Del., *it's* Simp. — 86. *It pleaseth th' King to mis-
conceive of me* El. conj. — 89. *whom* not in Qq; inserted on El.'s authority
(Notes, p. 136). — 92, 93. Divided at *the base* in Qq. — 93. *vilest* Chet. —
i' th' world Simp. — 94. As two lines in Chet., the first ending at *these?* |.
— 95. *See* is to be considered as a 'monosyllabic foot. — 96. The words of
ZWENO: *You know her, if you see her* bring to mind the title of Sam.
Rowley's chronicle-history 'When you see me, you know me' Compare Mucedorus, I. 4. 62 (in Warnke and Proescholdt's ed. I. 4. 30; p. 31) where the words
of *Mouse: Why, then you know nobody, an you know not me* seem to refer to
the title of Tho. Heywood's play 'If you know not me, you know nobody'. —
97, 98. Forming one line in Qq and Edd. — 99. El. proposes *Yes* for *Yet.* —
101. *whatever* Simp.; *whatsoeuer* to be pronounced as a trisyllable. — 103. *with*
his Qq and Del., *with's* Simp. — *thee so much* Chet.

Mar. When first I came into your highnes court,

105 And William oft importuning me of loue,

I did deuise, to ease the griefe your daughter did sustain,

Shee'ld meete Sir William masked, as I it were.

This put in proofe did take so good effect,

As yet it seemes his grace is not resolued,

110 But it was I which he conueied away.

Wm. May this be true? It cannot be but true.

Was 't Ladie Blaunch which I conueied away?

Vnconstant Mariana, thus to deale

With him which meant to thee nought but faith!

115 *Blaunch.* Pardon, deere father, my follyes that are past,

Wherein I haue neglected thus my dutie,

Which I in reuerence ought to shew your grace;

For, led by loue, I thus haue gone astray,

And now repent the errors I was in.

120 *Zweno.* Stand vp, deare daughter. Though thy fault deserues

For to be punisht in th' extremest sort,

Yet loue, that couers multitude of sinns,

Makes loue in parents winke at childrens faults.

Sufficeth, Blaunch, thy father loues thee so,

125 Thy follies past he knowes, but will not know.

---

104. El. proposes *unto your;* cp. I. 1. 78. — 105. *often importing* Qq, *oft' importing* Simp., *oft importuning* El. conj.; cp. III. 1. 81. — 107. *Shee should* Qq, *She 'ld* El. conj. — *meet, Sir, William* Chet. — 111. Simp. proposes to read *It cannot but be true.* — 112. *Was it* Qq, *Was't* Del. and Simp. — 113, 114. Divided at *Mariana | in* Qq; corr. by Del. — 114. *nought* is to be pronounced as a dissyllable; cp. *Which else | would frée | have wró | ught. All | is wéll |,* Macb. II. 1. 19, quoted by Abbott, s. 484, p. 381 (El., Jahrb., XV, 349). — 115. Almost the same line (*Pardon, dear father, the follies that are past*) occurs in The London Prodigal (Doubtful Plays of Wm. Shakespeare, ed. Moltke; Leipzig, Tauchnitz) V. 1. (p. 276). — *are pas* Del. (a misprint). — 116. *thus* not in Qq, added by Del. — *this my duty* Chet. — *me dutie* A. — 118. *For led by loue* Qq and Simp.; the punctuation added by the pres. Edd. — *Forled by love* Del.; the verb *forlead,* however, occurs so seldom in the Elizabethan literature, that we have not ventured to admit the reading of Del. into the text. See Nares, Gloss., and Halliwell, Dict. of Arch. and Prov. Words, s. v. — 121. *the* Qq. — 122. *multitudes* Chet. — 123. *Makes loving parents* Chet. and Del. — 124. *Suffice it* Simp. conj.; but *sufficeth* without *it* often occurs in Shak.

And here, Duke William, take my daughter to thy wife,
For well I am assured shee loues thee well.
   Wm.   A proper coniunction!
As who should say, lately come out o' th' fyer,
I would go thrust my selfe into the flame.   130
Let Maistres nice go saint it where shee list,
And coyly quaint it with dissembling face;
I hold in scorne the fooleries that they vse:
I being free, will ne'er subiect my selfe
To any such as shee is underneath the sunne.   135
   Zweno.   Refusest thou to take my daughter to thy wife?
I tell thee, Duke, this rash deniall may bring
More mischiefe on thee then thou canst auoyd.
   Wm.   Conseit hath wrought such generall dislike,
Through the false dealing of Mariana,   140
That vtterly I doe abhor their sex.
They're all disloyall, vnconstant, all vniust:
Who tryes as I haue tryed, and findes as I haue found,
Will say there's no such creatures on the ground.
   Blaunch. Vnconstant Knight, though some deserue no trust, 145
Thers others faithfull, louing, loyall, and iust!

Enter to them VALINGFORD *with* EM *and the* MILLER, *and*
      MOUNTNEY, *and* MANUILE, *and* ELNER.

   Wm. How now Lord Valingford, what makes these women here?
   Val.   Here be two women, may it please your grace,
That are contracted to one man, and are   :
In strife whether shall haue him to their husband.   150
   Wm.   Stand foorth, women, and saie
To whether of you did he first giue his faith.
   Em.   To me, forsooth.

128, 129. Divided at *say* | in Qq; corr. by Del. — 128. *coniuntion* A.
— 129. *of the* Qq, *o' th'* pres. Edd. — 132. *cryly* Del. (a misprint). — 134.
neuer Qq, *ne'er* Del. — 135. *such as* om. Simp. conj. — 137, 138. Divided
at *deniall* in Qq; corr. by Del. — 141. *abhor the sex* Chet. — 142. *they are*
Qq, *they're* Del. — 143. Two lines in Qq, the first ending at *tryed* |; corr.
by Del. — 145. *though same* Del. (a misprint). — 146. *and* om. by Chet. —
148. *Here is two* Del. — 149, 150. Divided at *man* | in Qq. — 150. *to her*
husband Simp. — 152. *first giue faith* Chet. — 153. *To me, my liege.* Chet.

El. To me, my gracious Lord.

155   *Wm.* Speake, Manuile: to whether didst thou giue thy faith?

Man. To, saie the troth, this maid had first my loue.

El. Yea, Manuile, but there was no witnesse by.

Em. Thy conscience, Manuile, is a hundred witnesses.

El. Shee hath stolne a conscience to serue her owne
160 turne; but you are deceiued, yfaith, he will none of you.

Man. Indeed, dred Lord, so deere I held her loue

As in the same I put my whole delight;

But some impediments, which at that instant

Hapned, made me forsake her quite;

165 For which I had her fathers franke consent.

Wm. What were th' impediments?

Man. Why, shee could neither heare nor see.

Wm. Now shee doth both. Mayden, how were you cured?

Em. Pardon, my Lord, Ile tell your grace the troth,

170 Be't not imputed to me as discredit.

I loued this Manuile so much, that still my thought,

When he was absent, did present to mee

The forme and feature of that countenance

Which I did shrine an ydoll in mine heart.

175 And neuer could I see a man, methought,

That equald Manuile in my partiall eye.

Nor was there any loue betweene us lost,

But that I held the same in high regard,

Vutill repaire of some vnto our house,

180 Of whom my Manuile grew thus iealous·

As if he tooke exception, I vouchsafed

To heare them speake, or saw them when they came:

155. *faitth* A. — 158. QA omits *is.* — By a mistake Simp. gives *is a
thousand witnesses* as the reading of QB. — 159, 160. Printed as two lines
in Qq, the first ending at *turne.* — 163. Ending at *hapned* in Qq. — 166.
the impediments Qq, *th' impediments* Simp. — 168. Two lines in Chet., ending
both | cured |. — 170. *Be it* Qq, *Be't* Del. — 171. *me thought* Qq, *mythought*
Del., *methought* Simp. The emendation *my thought* is to be found in the
margin of QA, written by the same hand as above, l. 10. As to the use of
me for *my* in A, cp. III. 6. 9, and V. 1. 116. — 173. *The frame and* Del. —
174. *in my heart* B. — 180. *iealous* is to be pronounced as a trisyllable
(*ieal-i-ous*); cp. S. Walker, Versif., p. 154 seqq., El. Jahrb., XV, 350.

On which I straight tooke order with my selfe,
To voyde the scrupule of his conscience,
By counterfaiting that I neither saw   185
Nor heard, any wayes to rid my hands of them.
All this I did to keepe my Manuiles loue,
Which he vnkindly seekes for to reward.

   Man.   And did my Em, to keepe her faith with mee,
Dissemble that shee neither heard nor sawe?   190
Pardon me, sweet Em, for I am onely thine!

   Em.   Lay off thy hands, disloyall as thou art!
Nor shalt thou haue possession of my loue,
That canst so finely shift thy matters off!
Put case I had been blind, and could not see —   195
As often times such visitations falles
That pleaseth God, which all things doth dispose —
Shouldest thou forsake me in regard of that?
I tell thee Manuile, hadst thou been blinde,
Or deafe, or dumbe,   200
Or else what impediments might befall to man,
Em would haue loued, and kept, and honoured thee;
Yea, begg'd, if wealth had faylde, for thy releefe.

   Man.   Forgiue me, sweet Em!

   Em.   I do forgiue thee, with my heart,   205
And will forget thee too, if case I can:
But neuer speake to mee, nor seeme to know mee!

   Man.   Then farewell, frost! farewell a wench that will!
Now, Elner, I am thine owne, my gyrl.

   El.   Myne, Manuile? thou neuer shalt be myne.   210

185, 186. Divided at *heard* | in Qq; our division has been proposed by
El. — 196. *visitation* Del. — 199. El. proposes *haddest* for *hadst.* — 200—
203. In Qq the lines end *impediments* | *kept* | *faylde* | *releefe* |. — 201. The
line is to be scanned: *Or élse* | *what 'mpéd* | *'ments míght* | &c. See Jahrb.,
XV, 350. It is therefore unnecessary to read with Simp.: *Or what impediments
else might befal man.* — 205. *I do forgive with all my heart.* Del. — 207.
now seem Del. (a misprint). — 208. Printed as two lines in Qq, ending *frost* |
will |. — Del.'s and Simp.'s transposition *Well-fare a wench* is an unneces-
sary alteration of the text, *farewell* having a shifting accent; cp. K. John,
III. 3. 17; Mucedorus, III. 4. 34; see also above, II. 1. 157, and Abbott, ∍.
475, p. 361. — 209. We must either pronounce *Elner* as a trisyllable (*Eliner*),
or consider the line with Simp. as a verse of four accents, and read *I'm.*

I so detest thy villanie,
That whilest I liue I will abhor thy companie!
   Man. Is't come to this? Of late I'd choyce of twaine,
On either side, to haue mè to her husband,
215 And now am vtterly reiected of them both.
   Val. My Lord,
This gentleman stood something in our light,
When time was; now I thinke it not amisse
To laugh at him that sometime scorned at vs.
220   *Mount.* Content my Lord, inuent the forme.
   Val. Then thus.
   Wm. I see that women are not generall euils,
Blaunch is faire: methinkes I see in her
A modest countenance, a heauenly blush.
225 Zweno, receiue a reconciled foe,   .
Not as thy friend, but as thy sonne-in-law,
If so that thou be thus content.
   Zweno. I ioy to see your grace so tractable.
Here, take my daughter Blaunch;
230 And after my desease the Denmarke Crowne.
   Wm. Now, sir, how stands the case with you?
   Man. I partly am perswaded as your grace is;
My Lord, he's best at ease that medleth least.
   Val. Sir, may a man
235 Be so bold as to craue a word with you?
   Man. Yea, two or three. What are they?
   Val. I say, *this* maid will haue thee to her husband.
   Mount. And I say *this:* and thereof will I lay
An hundred pound.

<hr>

213. *Is it* Qq, *Is't* Del. — *I had* Qq. — 216—218. *My Lord, this
gentleman, when time was,* | *Stood something in our light,* | *And now I thinke
it not amisse* | Qq; we have adopted El.'s arrangement. — 221. El. thinks
the conclusion of the play to be corrupt, or, at least, in great disorder. He
proposes to arrange the lines that follow in this way: 221, 234—254, 231—
233, 222—230, 255—278. For further particulars see Jahrb., XV, 351 seq. —
233. *he is* Qq, *he's* Chet. and Simp. — 234, 235. Divided at *bold* | in Qq. —
238, 239. Forming one line in Qq. — 238—240. *thereof . . . whereon,* a striking
example for the free interchange between *on* and *of.* See Doctor Faustus, ed.
Ward, note to II. 15, p. 142 seq., and Abbott, s. 181.

Val. And I say *this:* whereon Ile lay as much.   240
Man. And I say neither: what say you to that?
Mount. If that be true, then are we both deceiued.
Man. Why, it is true, and you are both deceiued.
Lub. In mine eyes this' the properest wench;
Might I aduise thee, take her to thy wife!   245
Zweno. It seemes to me, shee hath refused him.
Lub. Why, theres the spite.
Zweno. If one refuse him, yet may he haue the other.
Lub. He'll aske but her good will, and all her friends.
Zweno. Might I aduise thee? Let them both alone. 250
Man. Yea, thats the course, and thereon will I stand;
Such idle love hencefoorth I will detest.
Val. The foxe will eat no grapes, and why?
Mount. I know full well, because they hang too hye.
Wm. And may it be a Millers daughter by her birth? 255
I cannot thinke but shee is better borne.
Val. Sir Thomas Goddard hight this reuerent man
Famed for his virtues, and his good successe,
Whose fame hath been renowmed through the world.
Wm. Sir Thomas Goddard, welcome to thy Prince; 260
And, faire Em, frolike with thy good father;
As glad am I to find Sir Thomas Goddard,
As good Sir Thomas Treford, on the plaines,
He like a sheepheard, and thou our countrie Miller.
Mil. And longer let not Goddard liue a day 265
Than he in honour loves his soueraigne.
Wm. But say, Sir Thomas, shall I giue thy daughter?

240. *I will* Qq, *I'll* Del. and Simp. — 242. *we are* Del. — 244, 245. Printed as three lines in Del. and Simp., ending *eyes* | *thee* | *wife* |. We have retained the arrangement of the original and printed the lines according to El.'s corrections. The old copies read *this is* for *this'* and *unto* for *to.* As to the contraction *this'*, see S. Walker, Versif., p. 80 seqq., and Abbott, s. 461. — 244. *In my eyes* Del. -- 248. *he may* Del. — 249. *He will* Qq, *He'll* Del. — 255. *may't* Simp. — 259. *renown'd throughout the world.* Chet. — 261. Simp., in order to improve the metre, inserts *thou* after *frolic.* This insertion, however, seems needless, as the line may perhaps be scanned thus: *Ánd* | *fair Ém* | *frólic* | *with thý* | *good fá* | *ther.* See El., Jahrb., XV, 352. — 262. *I am* Del. — 263. *Edmund Troferd* Del., *Edmond Treford* Simp. — 264. *and* om. by Del.

Mil. Sir Thomas Goddard, and all that he hath,
Doth rest at th' pleasure of your Maiestie.

270   *Wm.* And what sayes Em to louely Valingford?
It seemed he loued you well, that for your sake
Durst leaue his King.

Em. Em restes at the pleasure of your highnes;
And would I were a wife for his desert.

275   *Wm.* Then here, Lord Valingford, recciue faire Em.
Here take her, make her thy espoused wife.
Then goe we in, that preparation may be made,
To see these nuptials solemly performed.

> *[Exeunt all. Sound Drummes and Trumpets.*

268. *Sir Thomas* not in Qq; added by Simp. — 269. *the* Qq. — 270.
says lovely Em to Valingford? Del. — 271, 272. Divided at *well* | in Qq. —
271. *It seem's* Del. — 272. *Darst* Del. — 273. *rests* B. — 274. Chet. adds
a line: *I know his merit, and I know his truth.* — 275. Printed as two lines
in Qq, ending *Valingford* | *Em* |. — 276. Chet. inserts two lines: VAL. *I
take her as the treasure of my life.* | EM. *And with this hand I give thee
all my heart.* — 278. Chet. ends the play with the following rhyme couplet:
Thus war tumultuous flies to banishment, | *And England's breast is fraught
with rich content.*

THE END.

APPENDIX.

A. II. Sc. 2. In all probability, the whole scene was originally written in verse. Prof. Elze (Notes, p. 128 seqq.) has tried to restore the shape in which, in his opinion, it came from the author's pen. His arrangement is, as follows:

Mar. Trust me, my Lord, I'm sorry for your hurt.

Lub. Gramercy, madam; but it is not great,

Only a thrust, prick'd with a rapier's point.

Mar. How grew the quarrel, my Lord?

Lub.   Sweet, for thy sake.

There was last night two maskers in our company,

Myself the foremost; the others strangers were

'Mongst which, when th'music 'gan to sound the measures,

Each masker made choice of his lady; and one,

More forward than the rest, stept towards thee;

Which I perceiving

Thrust him aside and took thee out myself.

But this was taken in so ill a part

That at my coming out of the court-gate,

With justling together, it was my chance to be

Thrust into th'arm. The doer thereof, because

He was th'original cause of the disorder,

At th' inconvenient time, was presently

Committ'd, and is this morning sent for hither

To answer th'matter; and here, I think, he comes.

Enter WILLIAM THE CONQUEROR *with a* JAILOR.

What, Sir Robert of Windsor? How now!

Wm. Conq. I' faith, a prisoner; but what ails your arm?

Lub. Hurt by mischance last night.

Wm. Conq. What? Not in the mask at the court-gate?
Lub. Yes, trust me, there.
Wm. Conq. Why then, my Lord, I thank you for my lodging.
Lub. And I you for my hurt, if it were so.
Keeper, away!
I here discharge you of your prisoner.   *[Exit Keeper.*
  Wm. Conq. Lord Marquess!
You offer'd me disgrace to shoulder me.
  Lub. Sir!
I knew you not, and therefore pardon me,
And th'rather as it might be alleged to me
Of mere simplicity, to see another
Dance with my mistress, disguis'd, myself in presence.
But seeing it was our haps to damnify
Each other unwillingly, let's be content
With both our harms and lay the fault where 't was,
And so be friends.
  Wm. Conq. I' faith, I am content with my night's lodging,
If you be with your hurt.
  Lub.   Not that I have't,
But I'm content to forget how I came by't.
  Wm. Conq. My Lord,
Here comes the lady Blanch, let us away.

Enter BLANCH.

  Lub. With right good will. *[To Mariana]* Lady, will you stay?
  Mar. Madam — *[Exeunt William the Conqueror and Lubeck.*
  Blanch. Mariana, as I'm griev̀ed with thy presence,
So am I not offended for ·thy absence,
And, were it not a breach to modesty,
Thou shouldest know before I left thee.
  Mar. [Aside] How near this humour is akin to madness!
If you hold on to talk as you begin,
You're in a pretty way to scolding.
  Blanch. To scolding, huswife?
  Mar.   Madam, here comes one.

Enter a MESSENGER *with a Letter.*

  Blanch. There does indeed. Fellow, wouldst thou
Have anything with anybody here?

Mess. I have a letter to deliver to the Lady Mariana.

Blanch. Give it me.

Mess. There must none but she have it.

                   [Blanch snatcheth the letter from him.

Blanch. Go to, foolish fellow.   *[Exit Messenger.*

And, therefore, to ease the anger I sustain,

I'll be so bold to open it. What's here?

'Sir Robert greets you well!'

You, mistress, his love, his life? Oh, amorous man,

How he his new mistress entertains,

And on his old friend Lubeck doth bestow

A horned nightcap to keep in his wit.

    Mar. Madam,

Though you discourteously have read my letter,

Yet, pray you, give it me.

    Blanch. Then take it, there, and there, and there.

                [She tears it. Exit Blanch.

    Mar. How far doth this differ from modesty!

Yet I will gather up the pieces, which,

Haply, may show to me th' intent thereof,

Though not the meaning.

           [She gathers up the pieces and joins them.

    [Reads] 'Your servant and love, Sir Robert of Windsor, alias

William the Conqueror, wisheth long health and happiness.'

Is this then William the Conqueror

Shrouded under th' name of Sir Robert of Windsor?

Were he the monarch of the world, he should

Not dispossess my Lubeck of his love.

Therefore I'll to the court, there, if I can,

Close to be friends with Lady Blanch, thereby

To keep my love, my Lubeck, for myself,

And further the Lady Blanch in her own suit,

As much as e'er I may.

E. Karras, Printer, Halle.

PSEUDO-SHAKESPEARIAN PLAYS.

EDITED

BY

KARL WARNKE, PH. D.

AND

LUDWIG PROESCHOLDT, PH. D.

II. THE MERRY DEVIL OF EDMONTON.

HALLE:
MAX NIEMEYER.
1884.

THE
MERRY DEVIL OF EDMONTON.

REVISED AND EDITED

WITH INTRODUCTION AND NOTES

BY

KARL WARNKE, PH. D.

AND

LUDWIG PROESCHOLDT, PH. D.

HALLE:

MAX NIEMEYER.

1884.

A.257859

INTRODUCTION.

THE earliest known edition of The Merry Devil of Edmonton was published in 1608, with the title: '*The Merry Devill of Edmonton. As it hath beene sundry times Acted, by his Maiesties Seruants, at the Globe on the bank-side. London, Printed by Henry Ballard for Arthur Johnson, dwelling at the signe of the white-horse in Paules Churchyard, ouer against the great North doore of Paules. 1608.*' (A). In the course of the next fifty years five more editions of the play were issued, the first two of which were likewise printed for Arthur Johnson in 1612 and 1617 (BC), the third and fourth for Francis Falkner in 1626 and 1631 (DE), and the fifth for W. Gilbertson in 1655 (F).

The *Editio princeps* of the play has been accessible to us in a copy, preserved in Trinity College, Cambridge, and bearing the press-mark *Capell R. 23*. The edition of 1612 is, as far as we know, not to be found in any public library; we owe the knowledge of it to the liberality of Mr. A. H. Huth, who kindly allowed us to make a transcript from his own copy of it. The remaining four editions of the play have been collated by us after copies preserved in the British Museum and bearing the press-marks C. 24. l. 12 (C), C. 34. b. 19 (D), 161. a. 23 and 643. c. 12 (E, two copies), 643. c. 13 (F).

Even *a priori* it may be supposed that the first three editions of the play, being printed for the same publisher, are nearly related to each other. And indeed, in a number of cases B and C show the same mistakes as the edition of 1608. So *panting* is printed for *parting* II. 3. 16, *steale* for *stealth* II. 3. 27, *parsonages* for *parsonage* IV. 2. 34; wrong prefixes are put before the lines I. 3. 31; II. 2. 20; IV. 1. 12; IV. 2. 63; V. 1. 72, 113; stage-directions are omitted IV. 1. 172; V. 1. 111; V. 2. 104. On the other hand, not unfrequently two of the editions exhibit a mistake, avoided or corrected by the third. So AB Ind. 72; III. 1. 11; V. 2. 44; AC I.

I. 33, 40; I. 2. 23; BC II. 3. 56; III. 2. 11; IV. 2. 67. It is evident that C, having some mistakes or misprints in common only with A, others only with B, cannot have been directly derived either from A or from B. On the contrary we must suppose that B and C are independent of each other, and that both of them are based on a lost or at least unknown edition of our play (A'). This hypothetical edition preserved part of the mistakes of A, and added a few more of its own. To the former class belong all those which are to be met with either in AB or in AC, to the latter those which we find in BC. At any rate, A' seems to have been of little intrinsic value and was probably a mere reprint of A. For C, though deriving from A', differs from A only in subordinate and unimportant points. So C prints *shall* for *can* I. 2. 50, *toward* for *towards* I. 3. 66, *this night* for *to night* II. 2. 79, *yonder* for *yond* II. 3. 17, *betweene* for *betwixt* ib. 50, *some* for *such* III. 2. 64, *your* for *our* ib. 157, *at* for *in* IV. 1. 20, *blacke* for *dark* IV. 2. 1.[1]) Whilst C in all essential points agrees with the *Editio princeps* of the play, B offers a great many different readings from A. As all subsequent editions are, directly or indirectly, based on B, it matters much to know whether the readings of B are to be considered as corrections of the poet himself, or as the arbitrary alterations of some unknown editor. Setting aside all those readings which may be quite as genuine and quite as correct in B as in A, we shall turn our eye only to those passages in which either of the editions presents a reading decidedly superior to the other. There can be little doubt that the reading of A must be preferred by us Ind. 39; I. 1. 3; I. 2. 25; I. 3. 68; I. 3. 85, 86; III. 2. 90; IV. 2. 6. To these passages we add II. 1. 23 and V. 1. 72 where, in all probability at least, A presents the original reading. B, on the other hand, exhibits a better reading than A I. 1. 40; I. 3. 91; II. 1. 44. The misprint in A I. 3. 98 was already corrected in A', as the reading of C agrees with that of B. Thus we see that only in a few instances the editor of B succeeded in removing a wrong reading, but that, on the contrary, he introduced into the text a number af alterations which must be rejected by us. As to the indifferent passages, it will therefore certainly be best not to depart from the reading of A, particularly when supported by C.

---

[1]) A' added I. 3. 111 which had dropped out in A (only in some copies?).

It is easily to be seen that D and E, which form the second group of the old editions, directly emanate from B. We meet in them not only with the same mistakes which we have pointed out in B, but with some misprints not contained either in A or in C; cp. I. 2. 19 *discontinnance* BD for *discontinuance,* II. 2. 25 *no* om. BDE, V. 2. 26 *Venere* BDEF for *Cerere.* Far however from merely re-printing B, the editor of D tried to adapt the text of the play as much as possible to his own age. So he wrote *miles* for *mile* Pr. 13, *cough o'th lungs* for *cough a'th lungs* I. 3. 50, *horse is* for *horses* I. 3. 126, *frowardnesse* for *soares* II. 2. 57, *you* for *yee* V. 1. 39, *at the next assizes* for *at next a.* V. 2. 11, *doe you see* for *dee see* A, *doe see* B V. 2. 44; cp., besides, *to acquaint* for *t'acquaint* III. 2. 165, *Metropolitane* for *Metrapolitan* IV. 1. 64 &c. In conformity with the statute of King James I., the editor of D either omitted or altered the name of God; so he omitted *to God* IV. 2. 44, *Lord* ib. 57, and wrote *by the mass* for *by the Lord* ib. 43, *before Iove* for *before God* V. 1. 125, *by my sword* for *by the Lord* II. 1. 59. For the same reason he always printed *blood* for *zblood, hart* for *zhart, foot* for *zfoot, life* for *slife, nounes* for *zounds* &c. Of greater interest to us are those alterations by which the editor of D tried to restore the defective sense of some passages. In our opinion he succeeded in giving a right or at least an acceptable reading I. 1. 16; II. 1. 6; II. 2. 5; ib. 54; II. 3. 2; ib. 27; III. 2. 127; IV. 2. 34; V. 2. 142. Besides D is right in assigning I. 3. 31 to *Ierningham,* II. 2. 20 to *Sir Arthur,* IV. 2. 63 to *Sexton,* and in adding stage-directions where they are wanted. In all other cases, however, where D differs from A (AC), we have not deviated from the reading which must be considered by us as the original one.

The same remark applies to E. Published five years afterwards by the same book-seller, it agrees in all essential points with D; the few slight alterations which it offers are of little or no interest for the modern reader of the play.

A similar place to that of D is held by F, published twenty-four years after E (1655). The editor of F chose the last edition published (E) as the model to work on, and followed it so closely as to adopt even some glaring mistakes; cp. the notes to Pr. 36; Ind. 70; I. 1. 99; I. 3. 30; ib. 42; II. 2. 7; III. 2. 19; IV. 1. 77; IV. 2. 30; V. 1. 66; V. 2. 66; besides V. 2. 10; ib. 31; ib. 116. Notwithstanding we owe to F the correction of a number of passages which had been quite disregarded by all preceding editors. Not unfrequently it happens that the names of Raph, Harry, Arthur, Clare and Ierningham are confounded with one another in ABCDE; cp. II. 2. 44; III. 1. 68; III. 2. 150; IV. 1. 99; V. 1 Stage-dir.; ib. 106, 107. As in some of these passages the verse suffers from the alteration required by the sense, we have perhaps to suppose that the poet himself, carelessly preparing his manuscript for the press, committed the blunders which were faithfully preserved in the following editions. Be that as it may, there can be no doubt that the alterations of F must be considered as corrections and are to be put into the critical text of the play. Besides, the editor took care to regulate the versification of the play, in printing as verse a number of prose-passages which doubtless must be read as verse; s. II. 3. 22—24; III. 2. 128, 129; V. 1. 43—45; ib. 97—105; V. 2. 82, 83. In a few isolated cases some trivial mistakes of a different kind were removed by F; cp. the notes to I. 1. 70, 72; II. 3. 27; III. 2. 28; IV. 1. 134.

Eighty-nine years after F the first modern edition of the play was published in 'A Select Collection of Old Plays. London, Printed for R. Dodsley in Pall-Mall, 1744, Vol. XI, pp. 123—169' (G). In the Introductory Notice it is distinctly stated that this edition was printed from the one published in 1655; and even without that notice it might easily be seen that the editor of G did not resort to any of the earlier editions; cp. ad I. 3. 23; II. 2. 69; II. 3. 72; III. 1. 117; V. 1. 70; V. 2. 31. The meaning of many an expression having become obsolete and obscure in the course of a century, a number of passages were altered in G; cp. the notes to I. 2. 4; I. 3. 73; II. 1. 56; ib. 60; III. 1. 77; III. 2. 89; ib. 158; IV. 1. 79 &c. Only in two cases (I. 1. 70 and II. 1. 68) we have thought fit to avail ourselves of the alterations of G.

The second edition of Dodsley's Select Collection of Old Plays was published by Isaac Reed, London 1780 (H). The title asserts that this edition has been 'corrected and collated with the old copies', and at the end of the Merry Devil of Edmonton (Vol. V, 245—306) Isaac Reed says: 'That (the edition) of 1655, from which the former edition of this play was printed, is unworthy of any notice from the number of errors it contains.' Notwithstanding this, Reed did not hesitate substantially to reprint G; cp. I. 1. 101; I. 3. 42; ib. 48; ib. 110; II. 3. 40; III. 1. 77; IV. 1. 79; ib. 118 &c. Now and then,

it is true, he must have had recourse to one of the older editions;
for in some few cases he disdains the reading of DEFG and agrees
with ABC, s. I. 3. 133; II. 2. 38; IV. 2. 57. That old edition was
in all probability C, cp. I. 2. 25; I. 3. 98 and V. 2. 56. On the
whole, however, the editor of H stuck to G, i. e. to BDEFG,
and only in the few instances just mentioned he preferred the
reading of A (C). As the editor did not choose to add any corrections, the addition of *the* II. 2. 71 may be considered merely as
a mistake.

A new edition of the comedy was published in 'The Ancient
British Drama. London, Printed for William Miller, Albemarle
Street, By James Ballantyne and Co. Edinburgh 1810', 3 voll.,
vol. II, 238—257 (I). This edition, though superintended by Walter
Scott, is of little interest to the critic; it is evidently based on H,
and it is certainly only a matter of chance if it agrees with other
editions, as Ind. 1; IV. 1. 86; V. 1. 118.

H was likewise the basis of the reprint of our play in the
third edition of Dodsley's Collection, ed. J. P. Collier, London 1825,
vol. V, p. 221—274 (K). Now and then, however, G also must
have been compared by the editor; cp. I. 2. 25; I. 3. 98, and particularly II. 1. 68. Only in few instances Collier corrected the verse
or tried to throw light on an obscure passage by adding a conjecture of his own.

Lastly the comedy of the Merry Devil was published in the
fourth edition of Dodsley's Collection, ed. W. Carew Hazlitt, London 1875, vol. X, p. 201—264 (L). This edition is doubtless
superior to all preceding it; Mr. Hazlitt collated some of the old
editions and in many cases tried to re-establish the sense and the
metre of an apparently corrupt passage. But as Mr. Hazlitt did
not examine the *Editio princeps* and was not aware of the second
edition of the play, his edition too, careful as it is, cannot stand
the test to which we now-a-days submit a critical edition.

Three different Elizabethan dramatists, Shakespeare, Drayton,
and Heywood, have been proposed as presumptive authors of the
play; but as cogent arguments are absolutely wanting, it will hardly
ever be possible to settle the question definitively.

In the Library of King Charles II., we are told, there existed
a volume, containing Mucedorus, The Merry Devill of Edmonton

and Faire Em, and labelled *Shakespeare, vol. I.*[1]) On the authority of that inscription, Kirkman, the bookseller, registered the play in his catalogue as a comedy of Shakespeare's. In England that tradition seems not to have met with any advocate; in Germany, however, two well-known Shakespearian critics, L. Tieck and H. von Friesen, felt inclined to attribute the play to Shakespeare.

In Tieck's opinion[2]), the whole play is of a piece with the Merry Wives of Windsor, particularly in the form which the latter comedy had in its first edition; some of the personages closely resemble Shakespearian characters; the Induction as well as the scene in the forest bear the stamp of Shakespeare's genius. Tieck's opinion as to the author of the play has been adopted and supported by H. von Friesen.[3]) Friesen, it is true, owns that one of the most striking characteristics of Shakespeare's art, the symmetry and skilful arrangement of the whole, is wanting; yet he is of opinion that the play, both in language and contents, is not unworthy of Shakespeare. The Host in the Merry Devil of Edmonton is cast in the same mould as the Host in the Merry Wives, and the conversation between Sir Arthur, Sir Raph and Friar Hildersham reminds the reader of the Comedy of Errors; some parallel thoughts and expressions may be traced in Romeo and Juliet, Richard II., the Merchant of Venice, and even the Sonnets; the trochaic shortlines III. 1 and 2 are something like to the invocations and magical charms of the elves in the Midsummernight's-Dream. All such analogies and parallel passages, however, amount to little in the way of evidence. Besides, in nothing do scholars disagree more than in literary questions of the kind. The very resemblance of the two hosts makes Ch. Knight[4]) think it impossible that Shakespeare wrote the play, since he, in the abundance of his riches, would certainly not have repeated himself. The same forest scene, which to Tieck seems to have a Shakespearian touch, lacks in Ulrici's opinion[5]) all that fine irony which is characteristic of the comical

---

[1]) Afterwards in Garrick's Collection; now, broken up, in the British Museum. According to Simpson, Transactions of the New-Shakspere-Society, the label was *Shakespeare, vol. II.*

[2]) Tieck, Alt-Englisches Theater, vol. II, pp. 7—9.

[3]) H. von Friesen, Flüchtige Bemerkungen über einige Stücke, welche Shakespeare zugeschrieben werden. Shakespeare-Jahrbuch, vol. I, pp. 160—165.

[4]) Charles Knight, Studies on Shakespeare, p. 288 seqq.

[5]) Ulrici, Shakespeare's Dramatische Kunst, ed. 2, vol. III, p. 71 seqq.

episodes in Shakespeare's plays. The action of the play, the same critic continues, is likewise destitute of that unity which we admire in all the plays of the great dramatist; the story of Fabell's treaty with the devil has nothing to do with the subject of the play; the love-affair between Milliscent and Young Mountchensey is but loosely and quite externally connected with the pranks of Sir John and his merry companions. The conclusion, arrived at by Ulrici, is that the author of the Merry Devil of Edmonton must have been a not unskilful poet, endowed particularly with a certain talent for popular poetry, and grown up under Shakespeare's influence, but that we can by no means set down Shakespeare himself as the author of the play. Every reader, we feel sure, will subscribe to Ulrici's opinion, and hardly any critic will now-a-days venture to claim the play for England's greatest poet.

In his Dramatic Literature of the Age of Elizabeth 1820, p. 221, Hazlitt proposes Thomas Heywood as the author of the play. 'The Merry Devil of Edmonton', he says, 'which has been sometimes attributed to Shakespeare, is assuredly not unworthy of him. It is more likely, however, both from the style and subject-matter, to have been Heywood's than any other person's. Romantic, sweet, tender, it expresses the feelings of honour, of love, and friendship in their utmost delicacy, enthusiasm and purity.' Also Ulrici is of opinion that the management of the fable as well as the style of the comedy remind the reader of Heywood's plays. The exterior evidence, however, which the same learned gentleman has adduced in favour of his theory, is based on a mistake and cannot be turned to any account. On March 5th 1608 the two booksellers Joseph Hunt and Thomas Archer had a book registered with the title: 'A Book called the Lyfe and Deathe of the Merry Devil of Edmonton, with the pleasant Pranks of Smugge the Smyth, Sir John and mine Hoste of the George, about their stealing of Venison. By T. B.' This 'book' is certainly identical with the prose-tract which was published (for the second time?) in 1631 and the author of which was Tony Brewer.[1]) Ulrici, however, identifies this tract

---

[1]) The prose-tract has been described by Dr. L. Proescholdt in 'Eine prosaische Nachbildung der Erzählung des Müllers aus Chaucer's Canterbury Tales', Anglia VII, p. 116 seqq. According to the entry in the catalogue of the British Museum Dr. P. stated the author of the book to have been *Thomas Brewer*. Mr. Bullen kindly hinted to us that the author's name was *Tony*

with our comedy and supposes T. B. to have been the initials of
the author of our play. As there is no dramatic poet known to
him, whose name shows the initials T. B., Ulrici thinks T. B. to be
a misprint for T. H. i. e. Thomas Heywood.[1])

For completeness' sake we add that Thomas Coxeter (d. 1747)
and Oldys have ascribed our play to Michael Drayton, perhaps only
because he has in his Polyolbion described the localities mentioned
in our play.

The comedy of the Merry Devil of Edmonton is, as far as we
know, mentioned for the first time in the Blacke Booke by T. M.,
1604: 'Giue him leaue to see the Merry Devil of Edmunton, or A
Woman kill'd with kindness.' The play was not entered into the
Stationers' Registers till on the 22d October 1607; the earliest edition
extant (1608) seems in fact to be the *Editio princeps* of the play.
The resemblance to the Merry Wives induced Tieck to assign it
to the year 1600; but A. W. Ward, l. c. I. 463, is probably right
in believing this year in any case too late a date. The battle of
S. Quentins (1558) would indeed hardly have been mentioned in
a comedy like ours, if the remembrance of it had no more been
within the memory of men.

The Merry Devil of Edmonton must have been a highly
popular performance. This not only appears from the number of
early editions, but is attested in plain words by Ben Jonson, who
in the prologue of 'The Devil is an Ass' says[2]):

'And show this but the same face you have done
Your dear delight, the Devil of Edmonton.'

Of modern critics Ch. Lamb in his 'Specimens of English Dramatic
Poets' I. 55—60 speaks with great warmth and admiration of the
play, and Ch. Knight and Ulrici pronounce a by no means un-
favourable judgment on it. Mr. Swinburne in his 'Sonnets on the
English Dramatic Poets', No. XVIII, calls our comedy

Brewer, whose initials 'T. B.' also stand on the titlepage of the 'Country
Girl', the scene of which is laid in Edmonton.

[1]) The same mistake occurs again in A. W. Ward, History of English
Dramatic Literature I, p. 463: 'The first edition of the play did not bear the
initials of Shakspere, but those of T. B.'

[2]) Ben Jonson, ed. Cunningham, vol. II, p. 212.

'that sweet pageant of the kindly fiend
Who, seeing three friends in spirit and heart made one,
Crowned with good hap the true love-wiles he screened
In the pleached lanes of pleasant Edmonton.'

The principal charm of the play lay for contemporaries doubtless
in the comical scenes; and also Peter Fabell, the merry Fiend of
Edmonton, may be supposed to have been a favourite personage
with them. It is much to be regretted that all we know about
Peter Fabell amounts to little more than what we learn from our
comedy. In T. Brewer's prose-tract only the first four chapters treat
of Maister Peter, all the rest is devoted to Smug and his 'pleasant
Prancks.' 'In Edmonton', Brewer says, 'he was borne, liued and
died, in the reign of King H. VII [1485—1509]. He was a man
of good discent: and a man, either for his gifts externall or internall,
inferior to few. For his person he was absolute. Nature had never
showne the fulnesse of her skill more in any then in him. For the
other, I meane his great learning (including many misteries), hee
was as amply blest as any.'[1] As early as 1533 Peter Fabell was
made the hero of a ballad, entitled Fabyls Ghoste. Th. Warton,
in his History of English Poetry, ed. W. C. Hazlitt (London, 1871),
vol. IV, p. 76, says: 'In the dispersed library of the late Mr. William
Collins I saw a thin folio of two sheets in black letter, containing
a poem in the octave stanza, entitled Fabyls Ghoste, printed by
John Rastell in the year 1533. The piece is of no merit ... [The
old play] has nothing, except the machine of the chime, in common
with Fabyll's Ghoste.'

As in most comedies of the age, the blank-verse in the Merry
Devil of Edmonton is interspersed with numerous prose-passages.
All persons of an essentially comical character do not 'speake in
Numbers', as the Host calls it. Thus Master Blague the Host, and
his boon-companions Banks and Smug, Sir John the priest[2], and
his Sexton, Bilbo and the Chamberlain speak in prose, and so do
the other persons when conversing with them; s. I. 1; I. 2; II. 3.
44 seqq.; V. 1. 111; V. 2. When any of the other persons are joking,
they also use prose instead of verse; cp. the scene in the Abbey

---

[1] Quoted by Nares, s. v. Fabell.
[2] But cp. II. 1. 22 seqq.

III. 1. 12 seqq.; ib. 27; ib. 36; ib. 45 seqq.; III. 2. 132.   Prose is
also used to express passion or anger; cp. especially V. 1. 19 seqq.
where the comical effect is heightened by the sudden change of
verse and prose; V. 1. 49 seqq.; ib. 54 seqq.; V. 2. 65 seqq.   Therefore we have thought it best to print A. Jerningham's speech and
H. Clare's answer to it as prose I. 3. 61 seqq. and 67 seqq.   In
some other instances prose is intended to lower the dramatic pitch.
Harry Clare and Arthur Jerningham, when in the forest with Milliscent, use prose when talking about the way and the time (IV. 1.
33—45), but they pass to verse as soon as they address Milliscent
(ib. 46).   Raph, Brian's man, speaks in prose IV. 1. 72; Brian's
words are printed in the editions partly as prose, partly as verse.   It
seems possible to re-establish verse in most passages; the two prose-
passages which we admit may be explained as spoken in anger.

Frequently passages which must doubtless be regarded as verse
are printed as prose in the old editions.   In most cases the metre
is restored by the subsequent editions; so by D II. 2. 90; by F II.
3. 22; III. 2. 128; V. 1. 43; ib. 97; by K III. 2. 123; ib. 162; by L
III. 1. 112; by the present Edd. III. 2. 139; IV. 1. 161 &c.   On the
other hand a prose-passage is printed as verse by part of the Edd.
I. 3. 61 seqq.

Proper Alexandrines with six accents are seldom to be met
with in our play.   As apparent Alexandrines may be considered
I. 3. 40; III. 1. 1; III. 2. 4 where the redundant two or three syllables are best put in separate lines; besides III. 1. 94; V. 1. 38;
ib. 92; ib. 107.   Real Alexandrines seem to be II. 2. 66; III. 1. 68;
IV. 1. 129; ib. 145.

The Prioress and Raymond, in the disguise of Benedick, speak
in rhymed lines with four accents; the metre is generally trochaic,
but is frequently interchanged with iambic lines.   Bilbo, finally, uses
some short-lines (II. 3. 58 — 63), the rhythm of which agrees very
well with their contents.

The text of the present edition of the Merry Devil of Edmonton has been based on the edition of 1608.   Wherever the text of
A offers a mistake, we have tried to correct it according to the
subsequent editions; wherever, on the other hand, the original
reading may be justified, we have taken care not to depart from
it in an arbitrary manner.   Only in a few isolated instances where

the tradition was in all appearance corrupt, we have ventured to emend the passage to the best of our power. The readings of all subsequent editions have been embodied by us in the foot-notes, which, we hope, will prove to be faithful and complete. It seemed, however, unnecessary to swell the foot-notes by pointing out the merely orthographical changes of the different editions. The text of the play has been printed in the orthography exhibited by A. The two or three words where for distinctness' sake we have altered the original spelling, have been indicated in the notes. We have not thought it necessary to smooth the metre by contracting forms like *ouer*, *we haue*, *we will* &c., where the verse requires a mono-syllable, or by dissolving forms like *o're*, *nunry*, *absolude*, where the metre requires a word of two or three syllables.

The Explanatory Notes, added to our text, are intended to expound the sense of an obscure passage, or to give the meaning of a word now out of use.[1]) The parallel passages from Shakespeare and other contemporary poets, by which some passages and con-structions have been illustrated, will, we hope, not be disdained by the reader of the play.

In the old editions our play is not divided into acts and scenes. Tieck first divided the play into eleven scenes; we have styled the first scene Induction and have divided the remainder of the play into five acts and twelve scenes.

---

[1]) We beg the reader's indulgence for a mistake occurring in the Notes, ad I. 2. 26. Cooper's Dictionary bears the title 'Thesaurus Linguae Romanae et Britannicae', and was first published in 1565.

DRAMATIS PERSONÆ.

SIR ARTHUR CLARE.	SIR IOHN, *a Priest.*
SIR RICHARD MOUNCHENSEY.	BANKS, *the Miller of Waltham.*
SIR RAPH IERNINGHAM.	SMUG, *the Smith of Edmonton.*
HARRY CLARE, *son to Sir Arthur.*	SEXTON.
RAYMOND MOUNCHENSEY, *son to Sir Richard.*	BILBO.
	BRIAN.
FRANCKE IERNINGHAM, *son to Sir Raph.*	RAPH, *Brian's man.*
	FRIAR HILDERSHAM.
PETER FABELL, *the Merry Devil.*	BENEDICK.
COREB, *a Spirit.*	CHAMBERLAINE.
BLAGUE, *the Host.*	

LADY DORCAS CLARE.
MILLISCENT CLARE, *her Daughter.*
THE PRIORESSE *of Cheston Nunnery.*
NUNS *and* ATTENDANTS.

———

THE PROLOGUE.

Your silence and attention, worthy friends,
That your free spirits may with more pleasing sense
Relish the life of this our actiue sceane!
To which intent, to calme this murmuring breath,
We ring this round with our inuoking spelles;   5
If that your listning eares be yet prepard
To entertayne the subiect of our play,
Lend vs your patience!
Tis Peter Fabell, a renowned Scholler,
Whose fame hath still beene hitherto forgot   10
By all the writers of this latter age.
In Middle-sex his birth and his abode,
Not full seauen mile from this great famous Citty,
That, for his fame in sleights and magicke won,
Was calde the merry Fiend of Edmonton.   15
If any heere make doubt of such a name,
In Edmonton yet fresh vnto this day,
Fixt in the wall of that old antient Church,
His monument remayneth to be seene;
His memory yet in the mouths of men,   20
That whilst he liude he could deceiue the Deuill.
Imagine now that whilst he is retirde
From Cambridge backe vnto his natiue home,
Suppose the silent, sable-visagde night
Casts her blacke curtaine ouer all the World;   25
And whilst he sleepes within his silent bed,
Toylde with the studies of the passed day,

PROLOGUE. 13. *miles* D and the rest. — 14. *in sseights* A, *in flights* I. —
20. *yet lives in* or *yet is in* Collier conj. —√24. *visage* C.

1*

The very time and houre wherein that spirite
That many yeeres attended his commaund,

30   And oftentimes twixt Cambridge and that towne
Had in a minute borne him through the ayre,
By composition twixt the fiend and him,
Comes now to claime the Scholler for his due.

                                  [*Draw the Curtaines.*

Behold him heere, laide on his restlesse couch,

35   His fatall chime prepared at his head,
His chamber guarded with these sable slights,
And by him stands that Necromanticke chaire,
In which he makes his direfull inuocations,
And binds the fiends that shall obey his will.

40   Sit with a pleased eye, vntill you know
The Commicke end of our sad Tragique show.   [*Exit.*

33. The stage-dir. after l. 32 in the old copies. — 36. *with his sable* EFG.

INDUCTION.

*The Chime goes, in which time Fabell is oft seene to stare about him, and
hold vp his hands.*

 Fab. What meanes the tolling of this fatall chime?
O, what a trembling horror strikes my hart!
My stiffned haire stands vpright on my head,
As doe the bristles of a porcupine.

Enter Coreb, a Spirit.

 Cor. Fabell, awake! or I will beare thee hence   5
Hedlong to hell.
 Fab. Ha, ha,
Why dost thou wake me? Coreb, is it thou?
 Cor. Tis I.
 Fab. I know thee well: I heare the watchfull dogs 10
With hollow howling tell of thy approch;
The lights burne dim, affrighted with thy presence;
And this distemperd and tempestuous night
Tells me the ayre is troubled with some Deuill.
 Cor. Come, art thou ready?   15
 Fab.   Whither? or to what?
 Cor. Why, Scholler, this the houre my date expires;
I must depart, and come to claime my due.
 Fab. Hah, what is thy due?
 Cor.   Fabell, thy selfe!
 Fab. O, let not darkenes heare thee speake that word,
Lest that with force it hurry hence amaine,   20

INDUCTION. *Induction* pres. Edd., not marked in the old copies; *Scene I.*
Tieck. 1. *rouling* FGI, *trolling* H. — 5. *for I* L. — 7, 8. Divided at *me* |
in all former Edd. — 16. *this is the hour* GHI.

And leaue the world to looke vpon my woe:
Yet ouerwhelme me with this globe of earth,
And let a little sparrow with her bill
Take but so much as shee can beare away,
25 That, euery day thus losing of my load,
I may againe in time yet hope to rise.
    Cor. Didst thou not write thy name in thine owne blood,
And drewst the formall deed twixt thee and mee,
And is it not recorded now in hell?
30 *Fab.* Why comst thou in this sterne and horred shape,
Not in familiar sort, as thou wast wont?
    Cor. Because the date of thy command is out,
And I am master of thy skill and thee.
    Fab. Coreb, thou angry and impatient spirit,
35 I haue earnest busines for a priuate friend;
Reserue me, spirit, vntill some further time.
    Cor. I will not for the mines of all the earth.
    Fab. Then let me rise, and ere I leaue the world,
Dispatch some busines that I haue to doe;
40 And in meane time repose thee in that chayre.
    Cor. Fabell, I will.   [*Sit downe.*
    Fab. O, that this soule, that cost so great a price
As the deere pretious blood of her redeemer,
Inspirde with knowledge, should by that alone
45 Which makes a man so <u>meane</u> vnto the powers,
Euen lead him downe into the depth of hell,
When men in their owne pride striue to know more
Then man should know!
For this alone God cast the Angelles downe.
50 The infinity of Arts is like a sea,
Into which, when man will take in hand to saile
Further then reason, which should be his Pilot,
Hath skill to guide him, losing once his compasse,
He falleth to such deepe and dangerous whirlepooles,
55 As he doth lose the very sight of heauen:

27. *name with thine* G and the rest. — 36. *farther* G and the rest. —
39. *Ile dispatch* BDEFG. — 41. [Stage-dir.] *Sits down in the necromantic
chair.* L. — 42. *great*] *dear* G and the rest. — 45. *meane*] *near* FG. —
52, 57. *farther* G and the rest. — 55. *haven* I.

The more he striues to come to quiet harbor,
The further still he finds himselfe from land.
Man, striuing still to finde the depth of euill,
Seeking to be a God, becomes a Diuell.

   Cor. Come, Fabell, hast thou done?   60
   Fab.   Yes, yes. Come hither!
   Cor. Fabell, I cannot.
   Fab. Cannot? — What ailes your holownes?
   Cor. Good Fabell, helpe me!
   Fab. Alas! where lies your griefe? some *Aqua-vitae*!
The Deuil's very sicke, I feare hee'le die;   65
For he lookes very ill.
   Cor. Darst thou deride the minister of darkenes?
In Lucifers dread name Coreb coniures thee
To set him free.
   Fab. I will not for the mines of all the earth,   70
Vnles thou giue me libertie to see
Seauen yeares more, before thou seaze on mee.
   Cor. Fabell, I giue it thee.
   Fab.   Sweare, damned fiend!
   Cor. Vnbind me, and by hell I will not touch thee,
Till seauen yeares from this houre be full expirde.   75
   Fab. Enough, come out.
   Cor.   A vengeance take thy art!
Liue and conuert all piety to euill:
Neuer did man thus ouer-reach the Deuill.
No time on earth like Phaetontique flames
Can haue perpetuall being. Ile returne   80
To my infernall mansion; but be sure,
Thy seauen yeeres done, noe tricke shall make me tarry,
But, Coreb, thou to hell shalt Fabell carry.   *[Exit.*
   Fab. Then thus betwixt vs two this variance ends,
Thou to thy fellow Fiends, I to my friends!   *[Exit.* 85

   58. *finde*] *know* C. — 68. *dread*] *great* D and the rest. — 70. *for all the mines* EF. — 72. *yeares*] *fiends* AB. — 79. *Phaetentique* ABC, *Phaetontic* L. — 83. *Exit* om. BDEFG. — 84. *between* F and the rest.

A C T I.

SCENE I.

Enter SIR ARTHUR CLARE, DORCAS, *his Lady*, MILLISCENT, *his daughter,
yong* HARRY CLARE, *the men booted, the Gentlewomen in Cloakes and safe-
- guardes*, BLAGUE, *the merry host of the George, comes in with them.*

Host. Welcome, good knight, to the George at Waltham,
my free-hold, my tenements, goods and chattels! Madam,
heer's a roome is the very *Homer* and *Iliads* of a lodging,
it hath none of the foure elements in it; I built it out of the
5   Center, and I drinke neere the lesse sacke. Welcome, my
little wast of maiden-heads! What? I serue the good Duke
of Norfolke.

Sir Ar. God a mercie, my good host Blague! Thou hast
a good seate here.

10   *Host.* Tis correspondent or so: there's not a Tartarian nor
a Carrier, shall breath vpon your geldings; they haue villanous
rancke feete, the rogues, and they shall not sweat in my linnen.
Knights and Lords too haue bene drunke in my house, I thanke
the destinies.

15   *Y. Cla.* Pre' the, good sinful Inkeeper, wil that corruption,
thine Ostler, looke well to my gelding. Hay, a poxe of these
rushes!

Host. You, Saint Dennis, your gelding shall walke without
doores, and coole his feete for his masters sake. By the body
20   óf S. George, I haue an excellent intillect to goe steale som
venison. Now, when wast thou in the forrest?

SCENE I. *Scene II.* Tieck. 3. *is] in* BDEF. — 16. *Ostler to looke* F
and the rest. — 16, 18. *geldings* ABC. -- 19. *feete] heels* FG. — 20. *goe*
om. F; *go to steale* C. — 21. *venison now, when* AC, *venison, Now when* B,
venison: Now when the rest.

Y. Cla. Away, you stale messe of white-broth! Come hither,
sister, let me helpe you.

Sir Ar. Mine Host, is not Sir Richard Mounchensey come
yet, according to our appointment, when we last dinde here?   25

Host. The knight's not yet apparent. — Marry, heere's a
forerunner that summons a parle, and saith, heele be here top
and top-gallant presently.

Sir Ar. Tis well. Good mine host, goe downe, and see
breakfast be prouided.   30

Host. Knight, thy breath hath the force of a woman, it takes
me downe; I am for the baser element of the kitchin: I retire
like a valiant souldier, face point-blanke to the foe-man, or,
like a Courtier, that must not shew the Prince his posteriors;
I vanish to know my canuasadoes, and my interrogatories, for   35
I serue the good Duke of Norfolke.   [*Exit.*

Sir Ar. How doth my Lady? are you not weary, Madam?
Come hither, I must talke in priuate with you;
My daughter Milliscent must not ouer-heare.

Mil. I, whispring, pray God it tend to my good!   40
Strange feare assailes my heart, vsurps my blood.

Sir Ar. You know our meeting with the knight Mounchensey
Is to assure our daughter to his heire.

L. Dor. Tis, without question.

Sir Ar. Two tedious winters haue past ore, since first   45
This couple lou'd each other, and in passion
Glewd first their naked hands with youthfull moysture —
Iust so long, on my knowledge.

L. Dor.   And what of this?

Sir Ar. This morning should my daughter lose her name,
And to Mounchenseys house conuey our armes,   50
Quartered within his scutchion; th' affiance, made
Twixt him and her, this morning should be sealde.

L. Dor. I know it should.

<hr>

27. *a parley and saith* B, *a parle and faith* C, *a parley and faith* the
rest. — 33. *souldiers face, point blanke* AC. — 34. *the*] *his* F and the rest. —
35. *I* added by the present Edd. — 36. *Exit* om. EFG. — 39. [Stage-dir.]
Speaking low added by L. — 40. *tend my good* AC. — 41. *feares assailes* E,
fears assail F, *fears assail* G. — 46. *These couple* all Edd., except FG. —
51. *the affiance* F and the rest.

Sir Ar. But there are crosses, wife; heere's one in Waltham,
55 Another at the Abby, and the third
At Cheston; and tis ominous to passe
Any of these without a pater-noster.
Crosses of loue still thwart this marriage,
Whilst that we two, like spirits, walke in night
60 About those stony and hard hearted plots.
 Mil. O God, what meanes my father?
 Sir Ar. For looke you, wife, the riotous old knight
Hath ouer-run his annual reuenue
In keeping iolly Christmas all the yeere:
65 The nostrilles of his chimny are still stuft
With smoake, more chargeable then Cane-tobacco;
His hawkes deuoure his fattest dogs, whilst simple,
His leanest curres eate his hounds carrion.
Besides, I heard of late, his yonger brother,
70 A Turky merchant, hath sore suck'de the knight
By meanes of some great losses on the sea;
That, you conceiue mee, before God all's naught,
His seate is weake. Thus, each thing rightly scand,
You'le see a flight, wife, shortly of his land.
75 *Mil.* Treason to my hearts truest soueraigne!
How soone is loue smothered in foggy gaine!
 L. Dor. But how shall we preuent this dangerous match?
 Sir Ar. I haue a plot, a tricke; and this it is —
Vnder this colour Ile breake off the match:
80 Ile tell the knight that now my minde is changd
For marrying of my daughter: for I intend
To send her vnto Cheston Nunry.
 Mil. O me accurst!

<hr>

54. *in*] *at* FG. — 55. *and a third* G and the rest. — 56. *it is* E and the rest. — 58. *marriage* has the quality of a trisyllable here. — 59. *sprites* C. — 65. *chimneys* D and the rest. — 67, 68. *His hawks devour his fattest hogs, whilst Simple, His leanest cur, eats his hounds' carrion* L. — 68. *eate him hounds* AC. — 70. *Or Turkey* all Edd., except GL; *sure* most Edd., *sore* only FGL. — 72. *all naught* ABCDE, *all is naught* FGHI, *all's naught* KL. — 80. *knights* DE. — 81. For the monosyllabic pronunciation of *daughter* cp. Faire Em, I. 4. 55. — 82. *Nunry* to be pronounced as a trisyllable.

Sir Ar. There to become a most religious Nunne.
Mil. Ile first be buried quicke.   85
Sir Ar. To spend her beauty in most priuate prayers.
Mil. Ile sooner be a sinner in forsaking
Mother and father.
Sir Ar.   How dost like my plot?
L. Dor. Exceeding well; but is it your intent
Shee shall continue there?   90
Sir Ar. Continue there? Ha, ha, that were a iest!
You know a virgin may continue there
A twelue moneth and a day onely on triall.
There shall my daughter soiourne some three moneths,
And in meane time Ile compasse a faire match   95
Twixt youthfull Ierningham, the lusty heire
Of Sir Raph Ierningham, dwelling in the forrest.
I thinke they'le both come hither with Mounchensey.
L. Dor. Your care argues the loue you beare our childe;
I will subscribe to any thing youle haue me.   [*Exeunt.* 100
Mil. You will subscribe to it! Good, good, tis well;
Loue hath two chaires of state, heauen and hell.
My dear Mounchensey, thou my death shalt rue,
Ere to thy heart Milliscent proue vntrue.   •   [*Exit.*

SCENE II.

Enter BLAGUE.

Host. Ostlers, you knaues and commanders, take the horses
of the knights and competitors: your honourable hulkes haue
put into harborough, theile take in fresh water here, and I
haue prouided cleane chamber-pots. Via, they come!

Enter SIR RICHARD MOUNCHENSEY, SIR RAPH IERNINGHAM, *young*
FRANKE IERNINGHAM, RAYMOND MOUNCHENSEY, PETER FABELL,
and BILBO.

---

84. Prefix om. B. — 93. *onely* om. L. — 99. *beare your childe* EFG. —
100. *Exeunt.* The stage-direction is put after l. 98 in ABC; *Exeunt Sir Arthur and Dorcas* IKL; om. in DEFGH. — 101. *good* only once in GHI. —
104. *Exeunt* G.
    SCENE II. *Scene III.* Tieck. — 4. *Via they come* printed as stage-direction
in Edd., *voyez — they come* G.

5   *Host.* The destinies be most neate Chamberlaines to these
swaggering puritanes, knights of the subsidy.

Sir Rich. God a mercy, good mine host.

Sir Raph. Thankes, good host Blague.

Host. Roome for my case of pistolles, that haue Greeke
10 and Latine bullets in them; let me cling to your flanks, my
nimble Giberalters, and blow wind in your calues to make
them swell bigger. Ha, lle caper in mine owne fee-simple.
Away with puntillioes and Orthography! I serue the good
Duke of Norfolke. Bilbo, *Titere tu. patulae recubans sub teg-*
15 *mine fagi.*

Bil. Truely, mine host, Bilbo, though he be somewhat out
of fashion, will be your onely blade still. I haue a villanous
sharp stomacke to slice a breakfast.

Host. Thou shalt haue it without any more discontinuance, ·
20 releases, or atturnement. What! we know our termes of hunting and the sea-card.

Bil. And doe you serue the good Duke of Norfolke still?

Host. Still, and still, and still, my souldier of S. Quintins!
Come, follow me; I haue Charles waine below in a but of
25 sacke, 't will glister like your Crab-fish.

Bil. You haue fine Scholler-like tearmes; your Coopers
Dixionary is your onely booke to study in a celler, a man
shall finde very strange words in it. Come, my host, lets
serue the good Duke of Norfolke.

30 *Host.* And still, and still, and still, my boy, lle serue the
good Duke of Norfolke.   [*Exeunt* HOST *and* BILBO.

Enter SIR ARTHUR CLARE, HARRY CLARE *and* MILLISCENT.

Sir Raph. Good Sir Arthur Clare!

Sir Ar. What Gentleman is that? I know him not.

Sir Rich. Tis M. Fabell, Sir, a Cambridge scholler,
35 My sonnes deere friend.

Sir Ar.   Sir, I intreat you know me.

11. *Giberlaters* EFG. — 14. The words *Titere tu* &c. are given to Bilbo
in D and the rest, the word *Bilbo* being erroneously taken for a prefix. —
19. *discontinnance* BD. — 20. *release* L. — 23. *S. Quintus* AC. — 25. *sacke,
I will* BDEFGK. — 31. No stage-direction in most Edd. In KL *Enter Sir
Arthur Clare, Harry Clare, and Milliscent.*

Fab. Command me, sir; I am affected to you
For your Mounchenseys sake.
    Sir Ar.   Alas, for him,
I not respect whether he sinke or swim!
A word in priuate, Sir Ralph Ierningham.
    Ray. Methinks your father looketh strangely on me: 40
Say, loue, why are you sad?
    Mil.   I am not, sweete;
Passion is strong, when woe with woe doth meete.
    Sir Ar. Shall's in to breakfast?   After wee'l conclude
The cause of this our comming: in and feed,
And let that vsher a more serious deed.   45
    Mil. Whilst you desire his griefe, my heart shall bleed.
    Y. Ier. Raymond Mounchensey, come, be frolick, friend,
This is the day thou hast expected long.
    Ray. Pray God, deere Ierningham, it proue so happy.
    Y. Ier. There's nought can alter it!   Be merry, lad!   50
    Fab. There's nought shall alter it!   Be liuely, Raymond!
Stand any opposition gainst thy hope,
Art shall confront it with her largest scope.   *[Exeunt.*

SCENE III.

PETER FABELL, *solus.*

Fab. Good old Mounchensey, is thy hap so ill,
That for thy bounty and thy royall parts
Thy kind alliance should be held in scorne,
And after all these promises my Clare
Refuse to giue his daughter to thy sonne,   5
Onely because thy Reuenues cannot reach
To make her dowage of so rich a ioynture
As can the heire of wealthy Ierningham?
And therefore is the false foxe now in hand
To strike a match betwixt her and th' other;   10

<hr>

41. *are you so sad* C. — 42. *woe doe mete* E. — 47, 50. Given to *Y.
Clare* in L. — 49. *deere Harry Clare* Edd. — 50. *nought shall alter* C. —
53. *Exeunt, save Fabel* L.
    SCENE III. 4. *promises by Clare* Edd., corr. by L. — 10. *the other*
F and the rest.

And the old gray-beards now are close together,
Plotting it in the Garden. Is't euen so?
Raymond Mounchensey, boy, haue thou and I
Thus long at Cambridge read the liberall Arts,
15 The Metaphisickes, Magicke, and those parts
Of the most secret deepe Philosophy?
Haue I so many melancholy nights
Watch'd on the top of Peter-house highest tower,
And come we backe vnto our natiue home,
20 For want of skill to lose the wench thou lou'st?
Weele first hang Enfield in such rings of miste
As neuer rose from any dampish fenne:
Ile make the brinde sea to rise at Ware,
And drowne the marshes vnto Stratford bridge;
25 Ile driue the Deere from Waltham in their walkes,
And scatter them like sheepe in euery field.
We may perhaps be crost; but, if we be,
He shall crosse the Deuill, that but crosses me.

Enter RAYMOND, *yong* IERNINGHAM *and yong* CLARE.

But here comes Raymond, disconsolate and sad,
30 And heeres the gallant that must haue the wench.
     Y. Ier. I pri'thee, Raymond, leaue these solemne dumps:
.Reuiue thy spirits, thou that before hast beene
More watchfull then the day-proclayming Cocke,
As sportiue as a Kid, as francke and merry
35 As mirth herselfe!
If ought in me may thy content procure,
It is thine owne, thou mayst thy selfe assure.
     Ray. Ha, Ierningham, if any but thy selfe
Had spoke that word, it would haue come as cold
40 As the bleake Northerne winds upon the face
Of winter.

From thee they haue some power vpon my blood;
Yet being from thee, had but that hollow sound
Come from the lips of any liuing man,
It might haue won the credite of mine eare;   45
From thee it cannot.

   Y. Ier. If I vnderstand thee, I am a villain:
What, dost thou speake in Parables to thy friends?

   Y. Cla. Come, boy, and make me this same groning loue,
Troubled with stitches and the cough a'th lungs,   50
That wept his eyes out when he was a Childe,
And euer since hath shot at hudman-blind,
Make her leape, caper, ierke, and laugh, and sing,
And play me horse-trickes;
Make Cupid wanton as his mothers doue: 55
But in this sort, boy, I would haue thee loue.

   Fab. Why, how now, Mad cap? What, my lusty Franke,
So neere a wife, and will not tell your friend?
But you will to this geere in hugger-mugger;
Art thou turnde miser, Rascall, in thy loues?   60

   Y. Ier. Who, I? z'sblood, what should all you see in me,
that I should looke like a married man, ha? am I balde? are
my legs too little for my hose? If I feele any thing in my
forehead, I am a villain. Doe I weare a night-cap? doe I
bend in the hams? What dost thou see in mee, that I should 65
be towards marriage, ha?

   Y. Cla. What, thou married? let me looke vpon thee, Rogue;

---

42. *power* a monosyllable here. — *vpon*] *of* EF, *on* GHI. — 48. *friend*
G and the rest. — 50. *o'th* D and the rest. — 56. *But, in* Edd. — 61—66.
Printed partly as verse in ABC, the lines ending at *in me | ha | hose | I
am | .* The rest is printed as prose. In DEFGHI the passage is printed
in six lines, divided at *me | ha | hose | villaine | hams | ha.* If, indeed, the
passage is to be considered as verse corrupted into prose, we should per-
haps scan it: *Who I? | Z'sblood, what should all you see in mee, that
I should | Looke like a married man? ha, am I balde? | Are my legs too little
for my hose? If I | Feele anything in my forehead, I am | A villain; doe
I weare a night-cap? doe | I bend i'th hams? What doest thou see in
mee | That I should be towards marriage, ha?* We have thought it best
to follow KL and print the whole passage as prose. — 66. *toward* C. —
67—69. Apparently a prose-passage (KL). In ABC divided at *thee | how |
company | in | .*

who has giuen out this of thee? how camst thou into this ill
name?   What company hast thou bin in, Rascall?

70   *Fab.* You are the man, sir, must haue Millescent,
The match is making in the Garden now;
Her ioynture is agreed on, and th' old men,
Your fathers, meane to lanch their busie bags,
But in meane time to thrust Mountchensey off.

75   For colour of this new intended match,
Faire Millescent to Cheston must be sent,
To take the approbation for a Nun.   ,
Nere looke vpon me, Lad, the match is done.

     Y. Ier. Raymond Mountchensey, now I touch thy griefe
80   With the true feeling of a zealous friend.
And as for faire and beauteous Millescent,
With my vaine breath I will not seeke to slubber
Her angell-like perfections; but thou know'st
That Essex hath the Saint that I adore.

85   Where ere did we meete thee and wanton springs,
That like a wag thou hast not laught at me,   /
And with regardles iesting mockt my loue?
How many a sad and weary summer night
My sighs haue drunke the dew from off the earth,

90   And I haue taught the Nighting-gale to wake,
And from the meadowes sprung the earely Larke
An houre before she should haue list to sing:
I haue loaded the poore minutes with my moanes,
That I haue made the heauy slow-pasde houres

95   To hang like heauie clogs vpon the day.
But, deere Mounchensey, had not my affection
Seazde on the beauty of another dame,
Before I'de wrong the chase, and o'regiue th' loue

68. *giuen this out of* BD and the rest. — 69. *ill-name* L. — 73. *pursy
bags* G. — 81. *And as for thy fair beauteous* G. — 85—86. *Where ere did'st
meete me, but we two were Iouiall,* | *But like a wag* &c. BDE; *Where ere
didst meet me, that we two were jovial,* | *But like a wag* &c. F and the rest. —
88. *How*] *Now* ABCDEF; *summer's night* GHIK. — 89. *sights* C. — 90. *And*
om. AC. — 91. *spring* AC. — 92. *list*] *rest* AC. — 98. *Before I would vnage
the chase, and ouergiue loue* A, *Before I'de wrong the chase, and o'regiue
loue* C, *Before I would wrong the chase and leaue the loue* BDEFG, *Before
I'ld wrong the chase and leaue the loue* KL.

Of one so worthy and so true a friend,
I will abiure both beauty and her sight,   100
And will in loue become a <u>counterfeit.</u>

  Ray. Deere Ierningham, thou hast begot my life,
And from the mouth of hell, where now I sate,
I feele my spirit rebound against the stars:
Thou hast conquerd me, deere friend; in my free soule   105
Neither time nor death can by their power controule.

  Fab. Franke Ierningham, thou art a gallant boy;
And were he not my pupill, I would say
He were as fine a metled Gentleman,
Of as free spirit, and of as fine a temper   110
As is in England; and he is a man
That very richly may deserue thy loue.
But, noble Clare, this while of our discourse,
What may Mounchenseys honour to thy selfe
Exact vpon the measure of thy grace?   115

  Y. Cla. Raymond Mounchensey? I would haue thee know,
He does not breath this ayre,
Whose loue I cherish, and whose soule I loue
More then Mounchenseyes:
Nor euer in my life did see the man   120
Whom, for his wit and many vertuous parts,
I thinke more worthy of my sisters loue.
But since the matter growes vnto this <u>passe,</u>
I must not seeme to crosse my Fathers will;
But when thou list to visit her by night,   125
My horses sadled, and the stable doore
Stands ready for thee; vse them at thy pleasure.
In honest marriage wed her frankly, boy,
And if thou getst her, lad, God giue thee joy!

  Ray. Then, care, away! Let fates my fall pretend,   130
Backt with the fauours of so true a friend!

<hr>

105. *friend, and my free soul* G. — 106. *Their time or death* AB, *Their
time nor death* C, *There time or death* DEF, *Nor time nor death* G, *There
time, nor death* HIKL. — 110. *and as* GHI. — 111. Dropped out in A;
As is] *As any* G. — 117—119. As two lines in L, divided at *cherish.* —
122. *more worthy*] *no more* B. — 126. *horse is sadled* D and the rest. —
130. The prefix *Ray.* wanting in B; *Fate* D and the rest.

Fab. Let vs alone, to bussell for the set;

For age and craft with wit and Art haue met.

Ile make my spirits to dance such nightly Iigs

135 Along the way twixt this and Totnam crosse,

The Carriers Iades shall cast their heauie packs,

And the strong hedges scarse shall keepe them in:

The Milke-maides Cuts shall turne the wenches off,

And lay the Dossers tumbling in the dust:

140 The franke and merry London Prentises,

That come for creame and lusty country cheere,

Shall lose their way; and, scrambling in the ditches,

All night shall whoop and hollow, cry and call,

Yet none to other finde the way at all.

145   *Ray.* Pursue the proiect, scholler: what we can do

To helpe indeauour, ioyne our liues thereto!   [*Exeunt.*

A C T   II.

SCENE I.

Enter BANKS, SIR IOHN *and* SMUG.

Banks. Take me with you, good Sir Iohn! A plague on thee, Smug, and thou touchest liquor, thou art founderd straight. What! are your braines alwayes water-milles? must they euer runne round?

5   *Smug.* Banks, your ale is a Philistine fox; z' hart, theres fire i'th taile on't; you are a rogue to charge vs with Mugs i'th rereward. A plague of this winde; O, it tickles our Cata-strophe.

Sir Io. Neighbour Banks of Waltham, and Goodman Smug, 10 the honest Smith of Edmonton, as I dwell betwixt you both at Enfield, I know the taste of both your ale houses, they are good both, smart both. Hem, Grasse and hay! we are

---

133. *haue*] *hath* DEFG. — 134. *sprites* B; *to* om. G; *Iigs* om. C. — 135. *Totnan* C. — 139. *their Dossers* D and the rest. — 143. *hallow* D, *hallo* L. — 144. *Yet*] *And* BDEFG. — 146. *Exeunt* first added in D.

SCENE I. *Scene IV.* Tieck. — 5. *is a*] *is as a* E and the rest; *there* C; *nounes theres* D and the rest. — 6. *taile : out* ABC.

all mortall; lets liue till we die, and be merry; and theres
an end.

Banks. Well said, Sir Iohn, you are of the same humor   15
still; and doth the water runne the same way still, boy?

Smug. Vulcan was a rogue to him; Sir Iohn, locke, lock,
lock fast, sir Iohn; so, sir Iohn.   Ile one of these yeares, when
it shall please the Goddesses and the destinies, be drunke in
your company; thats all now, and God send vs health.   Shall   20
I sweare I loue you?

Sir Io. No oathes, no oaths, good neighbour Smug;
Weel wet our lips together in hugge;
Carrouse in priuate, and eleuate the hart,
And the liuer and the lights, and the lights, marke you me,   25
within vs; for hem, Grasse and hay! we are all mortall, lets
liue till we die, and bee Merry, and thers an end.

Banks. But to our former motion about stealing some venison;
whither goe we?

Sir Io. Into the forrest, neighbour Banks, into Brians walke,   30
the madde keeper.

Smug. Z' blood!   Ile tickle your keeper.

Banks. Yfaith, thou art alwayes drunke when we haue neede
of thee.

Smug. Neede of mee? z' hart! you shall haue neede of mee   35
alwayes while theres yron in an Anuill.

Banks. M. Parson, may the Smith goe, thinke you, being
in this taking?

Smug. Go? Ile goe in spight of all the belles in Waltham.

Sir Io. The question is, good neighboure Banks — let   40
mee see: the Moone shines to night, — ther's not a narrow
bridge betwixt this and the forrest, — his braine will be setled
ere night; he may go, he may go, neighbour Banks.   Now
we want none but the company of mine host Blague of the
George at Waltham; if he were here, our Consort were full.   45

13, 26. *we are not yet all* G. — 13. *till he die* B. — 23. *together and hugge*
BD and the rest. — 25. *and the lights* only once in EFG. — 31. *madkeeper*
H, *mad-keeper* KL. — 32. *Blood* D and the rest. — 35. *hart* D and the
rest. — 36. *there is* F and the rest. — 40. *The question is good, neigh-
bour* L. — 42. *will*] *may* BD and the rest. — 44. *Blague at the George*
AC. — 45. *our comfort were full.* I.

Looke where comes my good host, the Duke of Norfolks man!
and how? and how? a hem, grasse and hay! wee are not
yet mortall; lets liue till we die, and be merry; and ther's
an end.

Enter HOST.

50   *Host.* Ha, my Castilian dialogues! and art thou in breath
stil, boy? Miller, doth the match hold? Smith, I see by thy
eyes thou hast bin reading little Geneua print: but wend we
merrily to the forrest, to steale some of the kings Deere! Ile
meet you at the time apointed. Away, I haue Knights and
55   Colonells at my house, and must tend the Hungarions. If we
be scard in the forrest, weele meete in the Church-porch at
Enfield; ist Correspondent?

     Banks. Tis well; but how, if any of vs should be taken?
     Smug. He shall haue ransome, by the Lord.
60   *Host.* Tush, the knaue keepers are my bosonians and my
pensioners. Nine a clock! be valiant, my little Gogmagogs;
Ile fence with all the lustices in Hartfordshire. Ile haue a
Bucke till I die; Ile slay a Doe while I liue. Hold your bow
straight and steady! I serue the good Duke of Norfolke.
65   *Smug.* O rare! who, ho, ho, boy!
     Sir Io. Peace, neighbor Smug! You see this is a Boore, a
Boore of the country, an illiterate Boore, and yet the Cittizen
of good fellowes. Come, lets prouide; a hem, Grasse and
hay! wee are not yet all mortall; weel liue till we die, and
70   be merry; and theres an end. Come, Smug!
     Smug. Good night, Waltham — who, ho, ho, boy! [*Exeunt.*

SCENE II.

Enter the Knights and Gentlemen from breakfast againe.

     Sir Rich. Nor I for thee, Clare, not of this.
What? hast thou fed me all this while with shalles?
And com'st to tell me now, thou lik'st it not?

---

48. *let vs liue* F and the rest. — 52. *reading a little* D and the rest. —
55. *Hungarians* F and the rest. — 56. *scatter'd* G. — 59. *ransome by my
Sword* D and the rest. — 60. *knaues* D and the rest, except L; *my bonasosis*
DEF; *my bona socias* G and the rest. — 66. *is a* om. BD and the rest. —
68. *good-fellows* KL; *lets prouide a hen, grass* most Edd. The mistake is
corrected in GKL.

Sir Ar. I doe not hold thy offer competent;
Nor doe I like th' assurance of thy land,   5
The title is so <u>brangled</u> with thy debts.
  Sir Rich. Too good for thee; and, knight, thou knowest it well,
I fawnd not on thee for thy goods, not I;
Twas thine owne motion; that thy wife doth know.
  L. Dor. Husband, it was so; he lies not in that.   10
  Sir Ar. Hold thy chat, queane.
  Sir Rich. To which I hearkned willingly, and the rather,
Because I was perswaded it proceeded
From loue thou bor'st to me and to my boy;
And gau'st him free accesse vnto thy house,   15
Where he hath not behaude him to thy childe,
But as befits a Gentleman to doe:
Nor is my poore distressed state so low,
That Ile shut vp my doores, I warrant thee.
  Sir Ar. Let it suffice, Mounchensey, I mislike it;   20
Nor thinke thy sonne a match fit for my childe.
  Sir Rich. I tell thee, Clare, his blood is good and cleere,
As the best drop that panteth in thy veines:
But for this maide, thy faire and vertuous childe,
She is no more disparagd by thy basenes   25
Then the most <u>orient</u> and the pretious iewell,
Which still retaines his lustre and his beauty,
Although a slaue were owner of the same.
  Sir Ar. She is the last is left me to bestow,
And her I meane to dedicate to God.   30
  Sir Rich. You doe, sir?
  Sir Ar.   Sir, sir, I doe, she is mine owne.
  Sir Rich. And pity she is so!   [*Aside.*
Damnation dog thee and thy wretched pelfe!
  Sir Ar. Not thou, Mounchensey, shalt bestow my childe.
  Sir Rich. Neither shouldst thou bestow her where thou mean'st. 35

<hr>

SCENE II. *Scene V.* Tieck. — 5. *the assurance* F and the rest; *of
thy loue* ABC. — 7, 8. Divided at *knowst it* EFG. — 20, 21. Added to
Moun.'s speech in ABC. — 22. *To tell thee* ABC. — 25. *no* om. BDE. —
26. *and most precious* L. — 28. *were the owner* C. — 33. *damnation,
dog* Edd.; *pelfe aside* ABC, *aside* a stage‑direction in D and the rest. —
35. *shall'st* L.

Sir Ar. What wilt thou doe?

Sir Rich.   No matter, let that bee;
I wil doe that, perhaps, shall anger thee:
Thou hast wrongd my loue, and, by Gods blessed Angell,
Thou shalt well know it.

Sir Ar.   Tut, braue not me!

40   *Sir Rich.* Braue thee, base Churle! Were't not for man-hood
I say no more, but that there be some by   [sake —
Whose blood is hotter then ours is,
Which, being stird, might make vs both repent
This foolish meeting. But, Harry Clare,

45   Although thy father haue abused my friendship,
Yet I loue thee, I doe, my noble boy,
I doe, yfaith.

   L. Dor. I, doe, do,
Fill all the world with talke of vs, man, man;
50   I neuer lookt for better at your hands.

   Fab. I hoped your great experience and your yeeres
Would haue prou'de patience rather to your soule,
Then with this frantique and vntamed passion
To whet their skeens. And, but for that

55   I hope their friendships are too well confirmd,
And their minds temperd with more kindly heat,
Then for their froward parents soares,
That they should breake forth into publique brawles.
Howere the rough hand of th' vntoward world

60   Hath moulded your proceedings in this matter,
Yet I am sure the first intent was loue:
Then since the first spring was so sweet and warme,
Let it die gently; ne're kill it with a scorne.

   Ray. O thou base world, how leprous it that soule
65   That is once lim'd in that polluted mudde!

38. *Gods*] *u* DEFG. — 42. *Whose youthful blood* pres. Edd. conj.; cp.
Sh., Rich. II., I. 3. 83: *Rouse up thy youthful blood*, and Rom., II. 5. 12:
Had she affections and warm youthful blood. — 44. *Raph Clare* ABCDE. —
45. *hath* E and the rest. — 51. *hope* ABC. — 54. *and but that* ABC. —
57. *forward* B; *their forward Parents frowardnesse* DEFGKL, *their froward
parent's frowardness* HI. — 59. *the untoward* F and the rest. — 63. *with
scorn* L. — 65. *in thy polluted* G.

Oh, sir Arthur, you haue startled his free actiue spirits
With a too sharpe spur for his minde to beare.
Haue patience, sir; the remedy to woe
Is to leaue what of force we must forgoe.
   Mil. And I must take a twelue moneths approbation,   70
That in meane time this sole and priuate life
At the yeares end may fashion me a wife.
But, sweet Mounchensey, ere this yeare be done,
Thou'st be a frier, if that I be a Nun.
And, father, ere young Ierninghams Ile bee,   75
I will turne mad to spight both him and thee.
   Sir Ar. Wife, come to horse, and, huswife, make you ready;
For, if I liue, I sweare by this good light,
Ile see you lodgde in Chesson house to night.   [*Exeunt.*
   Sir Rich. Raymond, away! Thou seest how matters fall.   80
Churle, hell consume thee, and thy pelfe, and all!
   Fab. Now, M. Clare, you see how matters fadge;
Your Milliscent must needes be made a Nun.
Well, sir, we are the men must plie this match:
Hold you your peace, and be a looker on,   85
And send her vnto Chesson where he will;
Ile send mee fellowes of a handfull hie
Into the Cloysters where the Nuns frequent,
Shall make them skip like Does about the Dale,
And make the Lady prioresse of the house   90
To play at leape-frogge, naked in their smockes,
Untill the merry wenches at their masse
Cry teehee weehee;
And tickling these mad Lasses in their flanckes,
Shall sprawle, and squeake, and pinch their fellow Nunnes.   95
Be liuely, boyes, before the Wench we lose,
Ile make the Abbas weare the Cannons hose.   [*Exeunt.*

<hr>

66. *spirit* L. — 67. *With too sharp a spur* G. — 69. *what*] *that* D
and the rest; *we must of force* FG. — 71. *in the mean* HIKL. — 79. *this
night* C; *Exeunt* first in D. — 84. *the match* E and the rest. — 86. *when
he will* L. — 90, 91. Divided at *play* in ABC. — 91. *in her smock* GL. —
96. *we'll lose* G.

SCENE III

Enter HARRY CLARE, FRANKE IERNINGHAM, PETER FABELL,
and MILLESCENT.

   Y. Cla. Spight now hath done her worst; sister, be patient!
   Y. Ier. Forewarnd, poore Raymonds company! O heauen!
When the composure of weake frailtie meete
Vpon this mart of durt, o, then weake loue
5 Must in hir owne vnhappines be silent,
And winck on all deformities.
   Mil.   Tis well:
Whers Raymond, Brother? Whers my deere Mounchensey?
Would wee might weepe together and then part;
Our sighing parle would much ease my heart.
10 *Fab.* Sweete beautie, fould your sorrowes in the thought
Of future reconcilement. Let your teares
Shew you a woman; but be no farther spent
Then from the eyes; for, sweet, experience sayes
That loue is firme thats flatterd with delayes.
15 *Mil.* Alas, sir, thinke you I shall ere be his?
   Fab. As sure as parting smiles on future blisse.
Yond comes my friend! See, he hath doted
So long vpon your beautie, that your want
Will with a pale retirement wast his blood;
20 For in true loue Musicke doth sweetly dwell:
Seuerd, these lesse worlds beare within them hell.

Enter RAYMOND MOUNCHENSEY.

   Ray. Harry and Francke, you are enioynd to <u>waine</u>
Your friendship from mee; we must part the breath.
Of all aduised corruption pardon mee!
25 Faith, I must say so; you may thinke I loue you;
I breath not, rougher spight do seuer vs;

<hr>

SCENE III. *Scene VI.* Tieck. — 2. *company to heauen* ABC. —
3. *meet*[*s*] L. — 9. *parley* BDEFGK; *One sighing parley* L. Pronounce
par'le. — 12. *be* om. L.; *further* CDEF. — 14. *for, sweet experience* H, *for
sweet experience* KL. — 16. *panting* ABC. — 17. *Yonder* C. — 22—24.
Printed as prose in ABCDE. — 23, 24. *part the breath Of all a. c., pardon
mee.* all Edd. — 24. *of ill advis'd* L. — 26. *Tho' I breathe not, and tho' rough
spite do sever us* G; *to sever* L.

Weele meete by stealth, sweet friends, by stealth you twaine;
Kisses are sweetest got with strugling paine.   •
   Y. Ier. Our friendship dies not Raymond.
   Ray.   Pardon mee:
I am busied; I haue lost my faculties,   30
And buried them in Milliscents cleere eyes.
   Mil. Alas, sweete Loue, what shall become of me?
I must to Chesson to the Nunery,
I shall nere see thee more.
   Ray.   How, sweete?
Ile be thy votary, weele often meete: 35
This kisse diuides vs, and breathes soft adiew, —
This be a double charme to keepe both true.   •
   Fab. Haue done: your fathers may chance spie your parting.
Refuse not you by any meanes, good sweetnes,
To goe vnto the Nunnery; farre from hence   40
Must wee beget your loues sweete happines.
You shall not stay there long; your harder bed
Shall be more soft when Nun and Maide are dead.

Enter BILBO.

   Ray. Now, sirra, whats the matter?
   Bil. Marry, you must to horse presently; that villanous   45
old gowty churle, Sir Arthur Clare, longs till he bee at the
Nunry.
   Y. Cla. How, sir?
   Bil. O, I cry you mercy, he is your father, sir, indeed; but
I am sure that theres lesse affinitie betwixt your two natures   50
then there is betweene a broker and a Cutpurse.
   Ray. Bring my gelding, sirra.
   Bil. Well, nothing greeues me, but for the poore wench;
she must now cry *vale* to Lobster pies, hartichokes, and all
such meates of mortalitie; poore gentlewoman, the signe must   55

not be in *Virgo* any longer with her, and that me grieues
ful wel.

                Poor Milliscent
                Must pray and repent:
60   O fatalle wonder!
                Sheele now be no fatter,
                Loue must not come at her,
                Yet she shall be kept vnder.   *[Exit.*
   Y. Ier. Farewell, deere Raymond.
   Y. Cla.   Friend, adew.
   Mil.   Deere sweete,
65 No ioy enioyes my hearte till wee next meete.   *[Exeunt.*
   Fab. Well, Raymond, now the tide of discontent
Beats in thy face; but, er't be long, the wind
Shall turne the flood. Wee must to Waltham Abby,
And as faire Milliscent in Cheston liues,
70 A most vnwilling Nun, so thou shalt there
Become a beardles Nouice; to what end,
Let time and future accidents declare:
Tast thou my sleights, thy loue Ile onely share.
   Ray. Turne frier? Come, my good Counsellor, lets goe,
75 Yet that disguise will hardly shrowd my woe.   *[Exeunt.*

ACT III.

SCENE I.

Enter the Prioresse of Cheston, with a Nun or two, Sir Arthur
Clare, Sir Ralph Ierningham, Henry *and* Francke, *the Lady,
and* Bilbo, *with* Milliscent.

   L. Dor. Madam,
The loue vnto this holy Sister-hood,
And our confirmd opinion of your zeale
Hath truely wonne vs to bestow our Childe
5 Rather on this then any neighbouring Cell.
   Pri. Iesus, Daughter Maries childe,

Holy Matron, woman milde,
For thee a masse shall still be sayd,
Euery Sister drop a bead;
And those again succeeding them   10
For you shall sing a Requiem.

Y. Ier. The wench is gone, Harry; she is no more a woman of this world. Marke her well, shee lookes like a Nun already. What thinkst on her?

Y. Cla. By my faith, her face comes handsomly to 't. But   15 peace, lets heare the rest.

Sir Ar. Madam, for a twelue-months approbation,
Wee meane to make this triall of our childe.
Your care and our deere blessing, in meane time,
Wee pray, may prosper this intended worke.   20

Pri. May your happie soule be blithe,
That so truely pay your Tithe:
He who many children gaue,
Tis fit that he one child should haue.
Then, faire Virgin, heare my spell,   25
For I must your duty tell.

Mil. Good men and true, stand together, and heare your charge!

Pri. First, a mornings take your booke,
The glasse wherein your selfe must looke;
Your young thoughts, so proud and iolly,   30
Must be turnd to motions holy;
For your buske, attires, and toyes
Haue your thoughts on heauenly ioyes;
And for all your follies past
You must doe penance, pray, and fast.   35

Bil. Let her take heed of fasting; and if euer she hurt her selfe with praying, Ile nere trust beast.

Mil. This goes hard, berladye!

Pri. You shal ring the sacring Bell,
Keepe your howers, and toll your knell,   40
Rise ad midnight to your Mattins,

Read your Psalter, sing your <u>Lattins</u>,
And when your blood shall kindle pleasure,
Scourge your selfe in plenteous measure.

45   *Mil.* Worse and worse, by Saint Mary!

Y. Ier. Sirra Hal, how does she hold her countenance?
Wel, goe thy wayes, if euer thou proue a Nunne, Ile build
an Abby.

Y. Cla. She may be a Nun; but if euer shee prooue an
50   Anchoresse, Ile dig her graue with my nailes.

Y. Ier. To her againe, mother!

Y. Cla. Hold thine owne, wench!

Pri. You must read the mornings Masse,
You must creepe vnto the Crosse,
55   Put cold Ashes on your head,
Haue a Haire-cloth for your bed.

Bil. She had rather haue a man in her bed.

Pri. Bid your beads, and tell your needs,
Your holy *Avies,* and your Creedes;
60   Holy maide, this must be done,
If you meane to liue a Nun.

Mil. The holy maide will be no Nun.

Sir Ar. Madam, we haue some busines of import,
And must be gone.

65   Wilt please you take my wife into your closet,
Who further will acquaint you with my mind;
And so, good madam, for this time Adiew. [*Exeunt women.*

Sir Raph. Well now, Francke Ierningham, how sayest thou?
                              To be briefe, —
What wilt thou say for all this, if we two,
70   Her father and my selfe, can bring about,
That we conuert this Nun to be a wife,
And thou the husband to this pretty Nun?
How then, my Lad? ha, Francke, it may be done.

Y. Cla. I, now it workes.

75   *Y. Ier.* O God, sir, you amaze mee at your words;

Thinke with your selfe, Sir, what a thing it were
To cause a Recluse to remoue her vow:
A maymed, contrite, and repentant soule,
Euer mortified with fasting and with prayer,
Whose thoughts, euen as hir eyes, are fixd on heauen,   80
To drawe a virgin, thus deuour'd with zeale,
Backe to the world: O impious deede!
Nor by the Canon Law can it be done
Without a dispensation from the Church;
Besides, she is so prone vnto this life,   85
As sheele euen shreeke to heare a husband namde.

   Bil. I, a poore innocent shee! Well, heres no knauery; hee
flowts the old fooles to their teeth.

   Sir Raph. Boy, I am glad to heare
Thou mak'st such scruple of that <u>conscience</u>;   90
And in a man so young as is your selfe,
I promise you tis very seldome seene.
But Franke, this is a tricke, a meere deuise,
A sleight plotted betwixt her father and my selfe,
To thrust Mounchenseyes nose besides the <u>cushion</u>;   95
That, being thus debard of all accesse,
Time yet may worke him from her thoughts,
And giue thee ample scope to thy desires.

   Bil. A plague on you both for a couple of Iewes!

   Y. Cla. How now, Franke, what say you to that?   100

   Y. Ier. Let me alone, I warrant thee.
Sir,
Assurde that this motion doth proceede
From your most kinde and fatherly affection,
I do dispose my liking to your pleasure: 105
But for it is a matter of such moment
As holy marriage, I must craue thus much,
To haue some conference with my ghostly father,
Frier Hildersham, here by, at Waltham Abby,

<hr>

77. *renounce* GHI. — 78. *maymed*] *sainted* L. — 81. *deuout* D and
the rest. — 87. *innocent, she* L. — 90. *of thy conscience* L. — 93. *is* om.
B. — 94. Scan: *A sleight | plott(ed) 'twixt | her fáth | er* etc. — 95. *beside*
BCDEKL. — 102. *Sir* placed in a separate line by the pres. Edd. — 103.
Assurde to be pronounced as a trisyllable.

110 To be absolute of things, that it is fit
    None only but my confessor should know.
        Sir Raph. With all my heart. He is a reuerend man;
    And to morrow-morning wee will meet all at the Abby,
    Where by th' opinion of that reuerend man
115 Wee will proceede; I like it passing well.
    Till then we part, boy; I thinke of it; farewell!
    A parents care no mortall tongue can tell.   [*Exeunt.*

SCENE II.

Enter SIR ARTHUR CLARE, *and* RAYMOND MOUNCHENSEY, *like a Frier.*

        Sir Ar. Holy yong Nouice, I haue told you now
    My full intent, and doe refer the rest
    To your professed secrecy and care:
    And see,
  5 Our serious speech hath stolne vpon the way,
    That we are come vnto the Abby gate.
    Because I know Mountchensey is a foxe,
    That craftily doth ouerlooke my doings,
    Ile not be seene, not I; tush, I haue done,
 10 I had a Daughter, but shee's now a Nun.
    Farewell, deere sonne, farewell.   [*Exit.*
        Ray. Fare you well! — I, you haue done!
    Your daughter, sir, shall not be long a Nun.
    O my rare Tutor, neuer mortall braine
 15 Plotted out such a masse of pollicie;
    And my deere bosome is so great with laughter,
    Begot by his simplicity and error,
    My soule is fallen in labour with her ioy.
    O my true friends, Franke Ierningham and Clare,
 20 Did you now know but how this iest takes fire —

112—117 wrongly given to *Sir Arthur* in ABCDE. — 112—114. Printed
as prose in Edd., only L divides the lines at *man* | *abbey* | *man* | . — 112.
hees BCDE. — 114. *the opinion* F and the rest. — 116. *boy. Ay, think* L. —
117. *Exeunt* om. FG.

    SCENE II. *Scene VIII.* Tieck. — 10. *she is* G. — 11. *deere onne* B,
deare one C. — 15. *masse*] *plot* DEHIK, *piece* FG, *mesh* L. — 18. *in* om.
B. — 19. *true* om. E and the rest. — 20. *Did you but know, but how* D and
the rest, except G: *Did you but know, how this.*

That good sir Arthur, thinking me a Nouice,
Had euen powrd himselfe into my bosome,
O, you would vent your spleenes with tickling mirth!
But, Raymond, peace, and haue an eye about,
For feare perhaps some of the Nuns looke out.   25
> Peace and charity within,
> Neuer toucht with deadly sin;
> I cast my holy water pure
> On this wall and on this doore,
> That from euill shall defend,   30
> And keepe you from the vgly fiend:
> Euill spirit, by night nor day,
> Shall approch or come this way;
> Elfe nor Fairy, by this grace,
> Day nor night shall haunt this place.   35
Holy maidens!   [*Knocke.*
[*Answere within.*] Who's that which knocks? ha, who is there?
   Ray. Gentle Nun, here is a Frier.

Enter NUN.

   Nun. A Frier without, now Christ vs saue!
> Holy man, what wouldst thou haue?   40
   Ray. Holy Mayde, I hither come
> From Frier and Father Hildersome,
> By the fauour and the grace
> Of the Prioresse of this place
> Amongst you all to visit one   45
> That's come for approbation;
> Before she was as now you are,
> The Daughter of Sir Arthur Clare,
> But since she now became a Nun,
> Call'd Milliscent of Edmunton.   50
   Nun. Holy man, repose you there;
> This newes Ile to our Abbas beare,
> To tell her what a man is sent,
> And your message and intent.

55   *Ray.* Benedicite.
     Nun. Benedicite.   [*Exit.*
     Ray. Doe, my good plumpe wench; if all fall right,
     Ile make your sister-hood one lesse by night.
     Now happy fortune speede this merry drift,
60   I like a wench comes roundly to her shrift.

                Enter LADY *and* MILLISCENT.

     L. Dor. Haue Friers recourse then to the house of Nuns?
     Mil. Madam, it is the order of this place,
     When any Virgin comes for approbation, —
     Lest that for feare or such sinister practise
65   Shee should be forcde to vndergoe this vaile,
     Which should proceed from conscience and deuotion, —
     A visitor is sent from Waltham house,
     To take the true confession of the maide.
     L. Dor. Is that the order? I commend it well:
70   You to your shrift, Ile backe vnto the Cell.   [*Exit.*
     Ray. Life of my soule! bright Angel!
     Mil. What meanes the Frier?
     Ray.   O Milliscent, tis I.
     Mil. My heart misgiues me; I should know that voyce.
     You? who are you? the holy virgin blesse me!
75   Tell me your name: you shall, ere you confesse me.
     Ray. Mountchensey, thy true friend.
     Mil. My Raymond, my deere heart!
     Sweete life, giue leaue to my distracted soule,
     To wake a little from this swoone of joy.
80   By what meanes camst thou to assume this shape?
     Ray. By meanes of Peter Fabell, my kind Tutor,
     Who in the habite of Frier Hildersham,
     Franke Ierninghams old friend and confessor,
     Plotted by Francke, by Harry and my selfe,
85   And so deliuered to Sir Arthur Clare,
     Who brought me heere vnto the Abby gate,
     To be his Nun-made daughters visitor.

     60. [Stage-dir.] *Enter Lady, Milliscent* ABC. — 64. *feare of some
sinister* C. — 84. *by Fabell and* all Edd.

Mil. You are all sweete traytors to my poore old father.
O my deere life! I was a dream't to night
That, as I was a-praying in mine Psalter,   90
There came a spirit vnto me as I kneeld,
And by his strong perswasions tempted me
To leaue this Nunry; and methought
He came in the most glorious Angell-shape,
That mortall eye did euer looke vpon.   95
Ha, thou art sure that spirit, for theres no forme
Is in mine eye so glorious as thine owne.'

Ray. O thou Idolatresse, that dost this worship
To him whose likenes is but praise of thee!
Thou bright vnsetting star, which through this vaile,   100
For very enuy, mak'st the Sun looke pale! ·

Mil. Well, Visitor, lest that perhaps my mother
Should thinke the Frier too strict in his decrees,
I this confesse to my sweet ghostly father:
If chast pure loue be sin, I must confesse,   105
I haue offended three yeares now with thee.

 Ray. But doe you yet repent you of the same?
 Mil. Yfaith, I cannot.
 Ray.   Nor will I absolue thee
Of that sweete sin, though it be venial;
Yet haue the pennance of a thousand kisses,   110
And I enioyne you to this pilgrimage:
That in the euening you bestow your selfe
Heere in the walke neere to the willow ground,
Where Ile be ready both with men and horse
To waite your comming, and conuey you hence   115
Vnto a lodge I haue in Enfield chase.
No more replie, if that you yeeld consent —
I see more eyes vpon our stay are bent.¯

 Mil. Sweete life, farewell! Tis done: let that suffice;
What my tongue failes, I send thee by mine eyes.· [*Exit.*   120

Enter FABELL, CLARE, *and* IERNINGHAM.

Y. Ier. Now, Visitor, how does this new made Nun?

<hr>

89. *a dreaming* G. — 90. *was praying* B and the rest; *in my Psalter*
CE and the rest. — 94. *Angell-shape.* The hyphen added by L.

3

Y. Cla. Come, come, how does she, noble Capouchin?

Ray. She may be poore in spirit, but for the flesh,

Tis fatte and plumpe, boyes. Ah, rogues, there is

125 A company of girles would turn you all Friers.

Fab. But how, Mountchensey, how, lad, for the wench?

Ray. Sounds, lads, y'faith, I thanke my holy habit,

I haue confest her, and the Lady Prioresse

Hath giuen me ghostly counsell with her blessing.

130 And how say yee, boyes,

If I be chose the weekely visitor?

Y. Cla. Z'blood, sheel haue nere a Nun vnbagd to sing

masse then.

Y. Ier. The Abbot of Waltham will haue as many Children

135 to put to nurse as he has calues in the Marsh.

Ray. Well, to be breefe, the Nun will soone at night turne

tippit; if I can but deuise to quit her cleanly of the Nunry,

she is mine owne.

Fab. But, Sirra Raymond,

140 What newes of Peter Fabel at the house?

Ray. Tush, hees the onely man;

A Necromancer and a Coniurer

That workes for yong Mountchensey altogether;

And if it be not for Fryer Benedicke,

145 That he can crosse him by his learned skill,

The Wench is gone;

Fabell will fetch her out by very magicke.

Fab. Stands the winde there, boy? Keepe them in that key,

The wench is ours before to-morrow day.

150 Well, Harry and Franke, as ye are gentlemen,

Sticke to vs close this once! You know your fathers

Haue men and horse lie ready still at Chesson,

123—125. Printed as two lines, the first ending at *boyes* in most Edd., first set right in K. — 125. *you Friers all.* pres. Edd. conj. — 127. *Sound* ABC. — 128, 129. Printed as prose in ABCDE. — 132. *Blood* D and the rest. — 134. *Waltham-house will* BC. — 136, 137. *turne lippet* most Edd., *lippet* first in K. — 137. *can* om. C. — 139—147. Printed as prose in Edd. — 141. *he is* F and the rest. — 145. *him by* om. C. — 148. *keeps* C. — 150—158. Printed as prose in most Edd., printed as verse in KL. — 150. *Raph and Franke* ABCDE.

To watch the coast be cleere, to scowt about,
And haue an eye vnto Mountchenseys walks:
Therfore you two may houer thereabouts,   155
And no man will suspect you for the matter;
Be ready but to take her at our hands,
Leaue vs to scamble for hir getting out.

   Y. Ier. Z'bloud, if al Herford-shire were at our heeles,
Weele carry her away in spight of them.   160

   Y. Cla. But whither, Raymond?

   Ray. To Brians vpper lodge in Enfield Chase;
He is mine honest Friend and a tall keeper;
Ile send my man vnto him presently
T' acquaint him with your comminge and intent.   165

   Fab. Be breefe and secret!

   Ray.   Soon at night remember
You bring your horses to the willow ground.

   Y. Ier. Tis done; no more!

   Y. Cla.   We will not faile the hower.
My life and fortune now lies in your power.

   Fab. About our busines! Raymond, lets away!   170
Thinke of your hower; it drawes well of the day.   [*Exeunt.*

ACT IV.

SCENE I.

Enter BLAGUE, BANKS, SMUG, *and* SIR IOHN.

   Host. Come, yee Hungarian pilchers, we are once more
come vnder the *zona torrida* of the forrest. Lets be resolute,
lets flie to and againe; and if the deuill come, weele put him
to his Interogatories, and not budge a foote. What? s' foote,
ile put fire into you, yee shall all three serue the good Duke   5
of Norfolke.

Smug. Mine host, my bully, my pretious consull, my noble
Holefernes, I haue bin drunke i' thy house twenty times and
ten, all's one for that: I was last night in the third heauens,
10   my braine was poore, it had yest in 't; but now I am a man
of action; is 't not so, lad?

Banks. Why, now thou hast two of the liberall sciences
about thee, wit and reason, thou maist serue the Duke of
Europe.

15   *Smug.* I will serue the Duke of Christendom, and doe him
more credit in his celler then all the plate in his buttery; is 't
not so, lad?

Sir Io. Mine host and Smug, stand there; Banks, you and
your horse keepe together; but lie close, shew no trickes, for
20   feare of the keeper. If we be scard, weele meete in the Church
-porch at Enfield.

Smug. Content, sir Iohn.

Banks. Smug, dost not thou remember the tree thou fellst
out of last night?

25   *Smug.* Tush, and 't had bin as high as the Abby, I should
nere haue hurt my selfe; I haue fallen into the riuer, comming
home from Waltham, and scapt drowning.

Sir Io. Come, scuer, feare no spirits! Weele haue a Bucke
presently; we haue watched later then this for a Doe, mine
30   Host.

Host. Thou speakst as true as veluet.

Sir Io. Why then, come! Grasse and hay, &c.   [*Exeunt.*

Enter CLARE, IERNINGHAM *and* MILLESCENT.

Y. Cla. Franke Ierningham!

Y. Ier. Speake softly, rogue; how now?

35   *Y. Cla.* S' foot, we shall lose our way, its so darke; where-
abouts are we?

Y. Ier. Why, man, at Potters gate; the way lies right:
hearke! the clocke strikes at Enfield; whats the houre?

8. *i' th house* C, *in thy house* E and the rest. — 9. *heauen* D and
the rest. — 12—14. Given to *Bil.* in ABC; corr. in D. — 17. *so, lad* om.
C. — 20. *in*] *at* C. — 25. The prefix *Smug* om. C; *the*] *an* BD and the
rest. — 26. *I* om. D. — 28. *feare*] *eare* A. — 37. *Potters*] *Poiters* BDEF,
Porter's GHIKL.

Y. Cla. Ten, the bell sayes.

Y. Ier. A lies in's throate, it was but eight when we set   40
out of Cheston. Sir Iohn and his Sexton are at ale to night,
the clocke runs at random.

Y. Cla. Nay, as sure as thou liu'st, the villanous vicar is
abroad in the Chase this darke night: the stone Priest steales
more venison then halfe the country.   45

Y. Ier. Milliscent, how dost thou?

Mil.   Sir, very well.
I would to God we were at Brians Lodge.

Y. Cla. We shall anon; z'ounds, harke! what meanes this noyse?

Y. Ier. Stay, I heere horsemen.

Y. Cla.   I heare footmen too.

Y. Ier. Nay, then I haue it: we haue bin discouerd,   50
And we are followed by our fathers men.

Mil. Brother and friend, alas, what shall we doe?

Y. Cla. Sister, speake softly, or we are describe.
They are hard vpon vs, what so ere they be;
Shadow your selfe behind this brake of ferne,   55
Weele get into the wood, and let them passe.

Enter Sir Iohn, Blague, Smug, *and* Banks, *one after another.*

Sir Io. Grasse and hay! wee are all mortall; the keeper's
abroad, and there's an end.

Banks. Sir Iohn!

Sir Io. Neighbour Bankes, what newes?   60

Banks. Z'wounds, Sir Iohn, the keepers are abroad; I was
hard by 'am.

Sir Io. Grasse and hay! wher's mine host Blague?

Host. Here, Metrapolitane. The Philistines are vpon vs, be
silent; let vs serue the good Duke of Norfolke. But where   65
is Smug?

Smug. Here; a poxe on yee all, dogs; I haue kild the
greatest Bucke in Brians walke. Shift for your selues, all the
keepers are vp. Lets meete in Enfield Church porch; away,
we are all taken els.   [*Exeunt.*   70

Enter BRIAN, *with* RAPH, *his man, and his hound.*

Bri. Raph, hearst thou any stirring?

Raph. I heard one speake here hard by, in the bottome.
Peace, Maister, speake low; zownes, if I did not heare a bow
goe off, and the Bucke bray, I neuer heard deere in my life.

75   *Bri.* When went your fellowes out into their walks?

Raph. An hower agoe.

Bri. S' life, is there stealers abroad, and they cannot heare
Of them: where the deuill are my men to night?
Sirra, goe vp the wind towards Buckleys lodge!

80 Ile cast about the bottome with my hound,
And I will meete thee vnder Cony oke.

Raph. I will, Sir.

Bri. How now? by the masse, my hound stayes vpon some-
Harke, harke, Bowman, harke, harke, there!   [thing;

85   *Mil.* Brother, Franke Ierningham, brother Clare!

Bri. Peace; thats a womans voyce! Stand! who's there?
Stand, or Ile shoote.

Mil. O Lord! hold your hands, I meane no harme, sir.

Bri. Speake, who are you?

90   *Mil.* I am a maid, sir; who? M. Brian?

Bri. The very same; sure, I should know her voyce;
Mistris Milliscent?

Mil. I, it is I, sir.

Bri. God for his passion! what make you here alone?
95 I lookd for you at my lodge an hower agoe.
What meanes your company to leaue you thus?
Who brought you hither?

Mil. My brother, Sir, and M. Ierningham,
Who, hearing folks about vs in the Chase,
100 Feard it had bin sir Raph and my father,

77. In C this line (*Bri. S' life .... of*) has been erroneously placed
between ll. 74 and 75. — *Life* D and the rest, *they*] *wee* E and the rest. —
79. *vp the*] *up and* G and the rest; *toward* BD and the rest. — 78. *Of
them* put in a separate line in L. — 86. *that a* GHKL. — 90. *Master Brian?*
D and the rest. — 96. *your*] *you* E. — 97. *Master Ierningham* D and the rest. —
99, 100. *Chase, and fearing it had* G; *sir Arthur and my father* ABCDE,
sir Raph and m. f. FG, *Sir Arthur, my father,* HIKL; *feard* pron. *fearèd.*
The metre would be smoothed by transposing *bin my father and sir Raph.*

Who had pursude vs, thus dispearsed our selues,
Till they were past vs.

   Bri. But where be they?

   Mil. They be not farre off, here about the groue.

Enter CLARE *and* IERNINGHAM.

   Y. Cla. Be not afraid! man, I heard Brians tongue,   105
Thats certain.

   Y. Ier. Call softly for your sister.

   Y. Cla. Milliscent!

   Mil. I, brother, heere.

   Bri. M. Clare!   110

   Y. Cla. I told you it was Brian.

   Bri. Whoes that? M. Ierningham, you are a couple of hot
-shots; does a man commit his wench to you, to put her to
grasse at this time of night?

   Y. Ier. We heard a noyse about here in the Chase,   115
And fearing that our fathers had pursude vs,
Seuerd our selues.

   Y. Cla.   Brian, how hapd'st thou on her?

   Bri. Seeking for stealers are abroad to night,
My hound staied on her, and so found her out.

   Y. Cla. They were these stealers that affrighted vs;   120
I was hard vpon them, when they horst their Deere,
And I perceiue they tooke me for a keeper.

   Bri. Which way tooke they?

   Y. Ier. Towards Enfield.

   Bri. A plague vpon 't, thats that damned Priest, and Blague 125
of the George — he that serues the good Duke of Norfolke.

A noyse within: Follow, follow, follow.

   Y. Cla. Peace, thats my fathers voyce.

   Bri. Z'ownds, you suspected them, and now they are heere indeed.

   Mil. Alas, what shall we doe?   130

---

    101. *vs, and thus* L. — 105. *I hear* L. — 110. *Master Clare* D and
the rest. — 112. *Who is that* F and the rest; *Master I.* D and the rest. —
115. *here*] *her* ABC, *vs* D and the rest. — 117. *hapnedst* BDEFG, *happedst*
L. — 118. *stealers that are* G and the rest. — 125. *that's the damnd* E and
the rest. — 129. *Nownes* D and the rest; *you haue suspected* EFG.

Bri. If you goe to the lodge, you are surely taken;

Strike downe the wood to Enfield presently,

And if Mounchensey come, Ile send him t'yee.

Let mee alone to bussle with your Fathers;

135 I warrant you that I will keepe them play

Till you haue quit the Chase; away, away! [*Exeunt all but* BRIAN.

Whoes there?

Enter the Knights.

Sir Raph. In the kings name, pursue the Rauisher!

Bri. Stand, or Ile shoote.

140   *Sir Ar.* Whoes there?

Bri. I am the keeper that doe charge you stand;

You haue stollen my Deere.

    Sir Ar. We stolne thy Deere? we doe pursue a thiefe.

Bri. You are arrant theeues, and ye haue stolne my Deere.

145   *Sir Raph.* We are Knights; Sir Arthur Clare, and Sir Raph

                          [Ierningham.

Bri. The more your shame, that Knights should bee such

Sir Ar. Who, or what art thou?   [thieues.

Bri. My name is Brian, keeper of this walke.

Sir Raph. O Brian, a villain!

150 Thou hast receiu'd my Daughter to thy Lodge.

Bri. You haue stolne the best Deere in my walke to night.

My Deere!

    Sir Ar. My daughter!

Stop not my way!

    Bri.   What make you in my walke?

155 You haue stolne the best Bucke in my walke to night.

    Sir Ar. My Daughter!

    Bri. My Deere!

    Sir Raph. Where is Mountchensey?

    Bri. Wheres my Bucke?

160   *Sir Ar.* I will complaine me of thee to the king.

<hr>

131. The prefix *Bri.* om. B. — 133. *to you* F and the rest. — 134. *Father* ABCDE. — 135. *Keepe him play* C. — 136. Stage-direction added by the present Edd. — 137. [Stage-dir.] *Enter the knight* B, *Enter the two knights* C. — 151, 152. One line in Edd. — 153, 154 (*My … way*). One line in Edd. — 154, 155. (*What .. night*) printed as prose in Edd. — 159. *Where is my* L.

Bri. Ile complaine vnto the king you spoile his game:
Tis strange that men of your account and calling
Will offer it!
I tell you true, Sir Arthur and Sir Raph,
That none but you haue onely spoild my game.   165
   Sir Ar. I charge you, stop vs not!
   Bri. I charge you both ye get out of my ground!
Is this a time for such as you,
Men of your place and of your grauity,
To be abroad a-theeuing? Tis a shame;   170
And, afore God, if I had shot at you,
I had serude you well enough.   [*Exeunt.*

SCENE II.

Enter Banks the Miller, *wet on his legges.*

Banks. S' foote, heeres a darke night indeed! 1 thinke I
haue bin in fifteene ditches betweene this and the forrest.
Soft, heers Enfield Church: 1 am so wet with climing ouer
into an orchard for to steale some filberts. Well, heere
lle sit in the Church porch, and wait for the rest of my   5
consort.

Enter the Sexton.

Sex. Heeres a skye as blacke as Lucifer, God blesse vs!
Heere was goodman Theophilus buried; hee was the best
Nutcracker that euer dwelt in Enfield. Well, tis 9. a clock,
tis time to ring curfew. Lord blesse vs, what a white thing   10
is that in the Church porch! O Lord, my legges are too
weake for my body, my haire is too stiffe for my night-cap,
my heart failes; this is the ghost of Theophilus. O Lord,
it followes me! I cannot say my prayers, and one would
giue me a thousand pound. Good spirit, I haue bowld   15
and drunke and followed the hounds with you a thousand

161—165, 167—172. Printed as prose in Edd. — 167. *ye* om. BD and
the rest. — 169. *Men of place* most Edd., *men of your place and of your
grauity* G, *men of place and grauity* C. — 172. *Exeunt* om. ABC.
   Scene II. *Scene X.* Tieck. — 1. *Foote* D and the rest; *darke*] *blacke*
C. — 6. *consorts* BD and the rest. — *Enter Sexton and Priest.* G. — 9. *in
England* L. — 10. *what white* BC. — 15. *me thousand* C.

times, though I haue not the spirit now to deale with you.
O Lord!

Enter Priest.

Sir Io. Grasse and hay! we are all mortall. Who's there?
20   *Sex.* We are grasse and hay indeede; I know you to bee
Master Parson by your phrase.

Sir Io. Sexton!

Sex. I, Sir!

Sir Io. For mortalities sake, whats the matter?

25   *Sex.* O Lord, I am a man of another element; Maister
Theophilus Ghost is in the Church porch. There was a hundred
Cats, all fire, dancing here euen now, and they are clombe
vp to the top of the steeple; ile not into the bellfree for a
world.

30   *Sir Io.* O good Salomon; I haue bin about a deede of
darknes to night: O Lord, I saw fifteen spirits in the forrest,
like white bulles; if I lye, I am an arrant theefe: mortalitie
haunts vs — grasse and hay! the deuills at our heeles, and
lets hence to the parsonage.   [*Exeunt.*
                               [*The Miller comes out very softly.*
35   *Banks.* What noise was that? Tis the watch, sure; that
villanous vnlucky rogue, Smug, is taine, vpon my life; and then
all our villeny comes out; I heard one cry, sure.

Enter HOST BLAGUE.

Host. If I go steale any more veneson, I am a Paradox!
S'foot, I can scarce beare the sinne of my flesh in the day,
40   tis so heauy; if I turne not honest, and serue the good Duke
of Norfolke, as true mareterraneum skinker should doe, let
me neuer looke higher then the element of a Constable.

Banks. By the Lord, there are some watchmen; I heare
them name Maister Constable; I would to God my Mill were
45   an Eunuch, and wanted her stones, so I were hence.

Host. Who's there?

26. *an hundred* F and the rest. — 27. *here* om. BD and the rest. —
30. *O goodman Salomon* EF, *O goodman Solomon* GHIKL. — 34. *parsonages* ABC. — 37. *villeny*] *knauerie* D and the rest. — 39. *Foot* D and the
rest. — 41. *as a true* D and the rest; *skinner* EFG. — 43. *By the masse*
D and the rest. — 44. *to God* om. D and the rest.

Banks. Tis the Constable, by this light; Ile steale hence, and if I can meete mine Host Blague, ile tell him how Smug is taine, and will him to looke to himselfe.   [*Exit.*

Host. What the deuill is that white thing? this same is a 50
Church-yard, and I haue heard that ghosts and villenous goblins haue beene seene here.

Enter Sexton and Priest.

Sir Io. Grasse and hay! O, that I could coniure! wee saw a spirite here in the Church-yard; and in the fallow field ther's the deuill with a mans body vpon his backe in a white sheet. 55

Sex. It may be a womans body, Sir Iohn.

Sir Io. If shee be a woman, the sheets damne her; Lord blesse vs, what a night of mortalitie is this!

Host. Priest!

Sir Io. Mine host!   60

Host. Did you not see a spirit all in white crosse you at the stile?

Sex. O no, mine host; but there sate one in the porch; I haue not breath ynough left to blesse me from the Deuill.

Host. Whoes that?   65

Sir Io. The Sexton, almost frighted out of his wits. Did you see Banks or Smug?

Host. No, they are gone to Waltham, sure. I would faine hence; come, lets to my house: Ile nere serue the Duke of Norfolk in this fashion againe whilst I breath. If the deuill 70 be amongst vs, tis time to hoist saile, and cry roomer. Keepe together; Sexton, thou art secret, what? Lets be comfortable one to another.

Sir Io. We are all mortall, mine host.

Host. True; and Ile serue God in the night hereafter afore 75 the Duke of Norfolke.   [*Exeunt.*

57. *Lord* om. DEFG. — 63, 64. Assigned to the *Priest* in ABC. — 66. *frightened* L. — 67. *Bank* BC. — 71. *among* L. — 76. *Exeunt* om. FG.

ACT V.

SCENE I.

Enter Sir Arthur Clare *and* Sir Raph Ierningham,
trussing their points as new vp.

Sir Raph. Good morrow, gentle knight.
A happy day after your short nights rest!
   Sir Ar. Ha, ha, sir Raph, stirring so soone indeed?
Birlady, sir, rest would haue done right well;
5 Our riding late last night has made me drowsie.
Goe to, goe to, those dayes are gone with vs.
   Sir Raph. Sir Arthur, Sir Arthur, care go with those dayes,
Let 'am euen goe together, let 'am goe!
Tis time, yfaith, that wee were in our graues,
10 When children leaue obedience to their Parents,
When there's no feare of God, no care, no dutie.
Well, well, nay, nay, it shall not doe, it shall not;
No, Mountchensey, thou'lt heare on't, thou shalt,
Thou shalt yfaith!
15 Ile hang thy son, if there be law in England.
A mans Child rauisht from a Nunry!
This is rare!
Well, well, ther's one gone for Frier Hildersham.
   Sir Ar. Nay, gentle knight, do not vexe thus,
20 It will but hurt your health.
You cannot greeue more then I doe, but to what end? But
harke you, Sir Raph, I was about to say somthing — it makes
no matter. But hearke you in your eare: the Frier's a knaue;
but God forgiue me, a man cannot tell neither; s'foot, I am
25 so out of patience, I know not what to say.
   Sir Raph. Ther's one went for the Frier an hower agoe.
Comes he not yet? s'foot, if I doe find knauery unders cowle,

Ile tickle him, Ile <u>firke</u> him. Here, here, hee's here, hee's
here. Good morrow, Frier; good morrow, gentle Frier.

Enter HILDERSHAM.

Sir Ar. Good morrow, Father Hildersham, good morrow.   30
Hil. Good morrow, reuerend Knights, vnto you both.
Sir Ar. Father, how now? you heare how matters goe;
I am vndone, my Childe ist cast away.
You did your best, at least I thinke the best;
But we are all crost; flatly, all is dasht.   35
Hil. Alas, good knights, how might the matter be?
Let mee vnderstand your greefe for Charity.
Sir Ar. Who does not vnderstand my griefes? Alas, alas!
And yet yee do not! Will the Church permit
A Nun in approbation of her habit   40
To be rauished?
Hil. A holy woman, benedicite!
Now God forfend that any should presume
To touch the sister of a holy house.
Sir Ar. Ihesus deliuer mee!   45
Sir Raph. Why, Milliscent, the daughter of this knight,
Is out of Cheston taken the last night.
Hil. Was that faire maiden late become a Nun?
Sir Raph. Was she, quotha? Knauery, knauery, knauery;
I smell it, I smell it, yfaith; is the wind in that dore? is it   50
euen so? doost thou aske me that now?
Hil. It is the first time that I ere heard of it.
Sir Ar. That's very strange.
Sir Raph. Why, tell me, Frier, tell mee; thou art counted
a holy man; doe not play the hypocrite with me, nor   55
beare with mee. I cannot dissemble. Did I ought but by
thy own consent, by thy allowance — nay, further, by thy
warrant?
Hil. Why, Reuerend knight —
Sir Raph. Vnreuerend Frier —   60

38. *my griefe?* C and the rest. — 39. *yet you doe* D and the rest. —
43—45. Printed as prose in ABCDE. — 47. *the*] *this* BD and the rest. —
49. *knauery* four times in BD and the rest. — 52. *that ere I heard* B. —
55. *nor*] *now* Collier conj. — 57. *farther* GHIK.

Hil. Nay, then giue me leaue, sir, to depart in quiet; I
had hopd you had sent for mee to some other end.

Sir Ar. Nay, stay, good Frier; if any thing hath hapd
About this matter in thy loue to vs,
65 That thy strickt order cannot iustifie,
Admit it be so, we wlll couer it.
Take no care, man:
Disclayme not yet thy counsell and aduise,
The wisest man that is may be orereacht.
70 *Hil.* Sir Arthur, by my order and my faith,
I know not what you meane.

Sir Raph. By your order and your faith?
This is most strange of all: Why, tell me, Frier,
Are not you Confessor to my Son Francke?
75 *Hil.* Yes, that I am.

Sir Raph. And did not this good knight here and my selfe
Confesse with you, being his ghostly Father,
To deale with him about th'intended marriage
Betwixt him and that faire young Milliscent?
80 *Hil.* I neuer heard of any match intended.

Sir Ar. Did not we breake our minds that very time,
That our deuice of making her a Nun
Was but a colour and a very plotte
To put by young Mountchensey? Ist not true?
85 *Hil.* The more I striue to know what you should meane,
The lesse I vnderstand you.

Sir Raph. Did not you tell vs still how Peter Fabell
At length would crosse vs, if we tooke not heed?

Hil. I haue heard of one that is a great magician,
90 But hees about the Vniversity.

Sir Raph. Did not you send your nouice Benedic
To perswade the girle to leaue Mountchenseys loue,
To crosse that Peter Fabell in his art,
And to that purpose made him visitor?

66. *it to be so* E and the rest. — 68. *yet my counsell* D and the rest. —
70. *and by my* FG. — 72—74. Two lines in Edd., ending at *all | Frier.* —
72. Prefixed *Sir Arthur* in ABC; *and by your* BD and the rest. — 73. *of all*
om. EFG. — 78. *vnbanded* Edd.; for *intended* the pres. Edd. are answerable. —
82. *of*] *in* B and the rest. — 87, 88. Printed as prose in Edd. — 91. *Did
you not* BEF.

Hil. I neuer sent my nouice from the house,   95
Nor haue we made our visitation yet.

Sir Ar. Neuer sent him? Nay, did he not goe?
And did not I direct him to the house,
And conferre with him by the way? and did he not
Tell me what charge he had receiued from you,   100
Word by word, as I requested at your hands?

Hil. That you shall know; hee came along with me,
And stayes without. Come hither, Benedic!

Enter BENEDIC.

Yong Benedic, were you ere sent by me
To Cheston Nunnery for a visitor?   105

Ben. Neuer, sir, truely.

Sir Raph.   Stranger then all the rest!

Sir Ar. Did not I direct you to the house? Confer with you
From Waltham Abby vnto Cheston wall?

Ben. I neuer saw you, sir, before this hower!

Sir Raph. The deuill thou didst not! Hoe, Chamberlen!   110

Enter CHAMBERLAINE.

Cham. Anon, anon.

Sir Raph. Call mine host Blague hither!

Cham. I will send one ouer to see if he be vp; I thinke
he bee scarce stirring yet.

Sir Raph. Why, knaue, didst thou not tell me an hower 115
ago, mine host was vp?

Cham. I, sir, my Master's vp.

Sir Raph. You knaue, is a vp, and is a not vp? Doest
thou mocke me?

Cham. I, sir, my M. is vp; but I thinke M. Blague indeed 120
be not stirring.

Sir Raph. Why, who's thy Master? is not the Master of
the house thy Master?

Cham. Yes, sir; but M. Blague dwells ouer the way.

125   *Sir Ar.* Is not this the George? Before God, theres some
[villany in this.

Cham. S'foote, our signe's remoou'd; this is strange!

[*Exeunt.*

SCENE II.

Enter BLAGUE, *trussing his points.*

Host. Chamberlen, speake vp to the new lodgings, bid Nell
looke well to the bakt meats!

Enter SIR ARTHUR *and* SIR RAPH.

How now, my old Ienerts bauke my house, my castle, lie in
Waltham all night, and not vnder the Canopie of your host
5   Blagues house?

Sir Ar. Mine host, mine host, we lay all night at the George
•in Waltham; but whether the George be your fee-simple or no,
tis a doubtfull question. Looke vpon your signe!

Host. Body of Saint George, this is mine ouerthwart neigh-
10   bour hath done this to seduce my blind customers. Ile tickle
his catastrophe for this; if I do not indite him at next assises
for Burglary, let me die of the yellowes; for I see tis no
boote in these dayes to serue the good Duke of Norfolke. The
villanous world is turnd manger; one Iade deceiues another,
15   and your Ostler playes his part commonly for the fourth share.
Haue wee Commedies in hand, you whorson, villanous male
London letcher?

Sir Ar. Mine host, we haue had the moylingst night of it
that euer we had in our liues.

20   *Host.* Ist certaine?

124. *dwells* om. B. — 125. *before Ioue theres* D and the rest. — 126.
Foote D and the rest. — *Exeunt* om. Edd.

SCENE II. The scene is continued in Tieck. — 1—5. Divided at *lodg-
ings | meats | horse | not | house* in Edd. — 1. *speake*] *speed* L. — 2. *meat*
F and the rest; the stage-dir. *Enter . . .* added by the pres. Edd. — 3. *my
old Iennerts banke, my horse, my castle* most Edd., *old jennet's back, my
house [Is] my castle* L. *house* for *horse* first conj. by Steevens. — 8. *doubtfull* om. BD and the rest. — 10, 11. *to seduce . . . for this* om. EFG. —
11. *at the next* D and the rest. — 12. *see it is* L. — 14. *mangy* L. —
17. *London-lecther* D, *London leether* E, *London-leather* FG. — 20. *Is it* F
and the rest.

Sir Raph. We haue bin in the Forrest all night almost.

Host. S'foot, how did I misse you? Hart, I was a-stealing a Bucke there.

Sir Ar. A plague on you; we were stayed for you.

Host. Were you, my noble Romanes? Why, you shall share; 25 the venison is a footing. *Sine Cerere & Baccho friget Venus*; that is, theres a good breakfast prouided for a marriage thats in my house this morning.

Sir Ar. A marriage, mine host?

Host. A coniunction copulatiue; a gallant match betweene 30 your daughter and M. Raymond Mountchensey, yong Iuuentus.

Sir Ar. How?

Host. Tis firme, tis done. Weele shew you a president i'th

Sir Raph. How? married?   [ciuill law for't.

Host. Leaue trickes and admiration. Theres a cleanely paire 35 of sheetes in the bed in the Orchard chamber, and they shall lie there. What? Ile doe it; Ile serue the good Duke of Norfolke.

Sir Ar. Thou shalt repent this, Blague.

Sir Raph. If any law in England will make thee smart for this, expect it with all seucrity.   40

Host. I renounce your defiance, if you parle so roughly. Ile barracado my gates against you. Stand, faire bully; Priest, come off from the rereward! What can you say now? Twas done in my house; I haue shelter i'th Court for't. D'yee see yon bay window? I serue the good Duke of Norfolk, and tis his lodg- 45 ing. Storm, I care not, seruing the good Duke of Norfolk. Thou art an Actor in this, and thou shalt carry fire in thy face eternally.

Enter SMUG, MOUNTCHENSEY, HARRY CLARE, *and* MILLISCENT.

Smug. Fire, s'blood, theres no fire in England like your Trinidado sack. Is any man heere humorous? We stole the venison, and weele iustifie it: say you now!   50

---

21. Assigned to *Sir Ar.* in L. — 22. *Foote* D and the rest; *was stealing of a* D and the rest. — 26. *Venere* BDEF. — 27. *there is* CFG and the rest; *that is* CFG and the rest. — 31. *M.* (i. e. *Master*) om. L; *juvents* FG. — 33. *in the* F and the rest. — 36. *sheets on the bed* D and the rest; *bed on the Orchard* B, *in Orchard Chamber* A. — 37. *I serue* D and the rest. — 43. *reward* EF. — 44. *in the* F and the rest. — 44, 45. *Dee see your bay* A, *Doe see your bay* B, *Doe you see yon bay* D and the rest. — 48. *Fire, nouns, ther's* D and the rest.

Host. In good sooth, Smug, theres more sacke on the fire, Smug.

Smug. I do not take any exceptions against your sacke; but if youle lend mee a picke staffe, ile cudgle them all hence, by this hand.

55   *Host.* I say thou shalt into the Celler.

Smug. S'foot, mine Host, shalls not grapple? Pray, pray you; I could fight now for all the world like a Cockatrices ege. Shalls not serue the Duke of Norfolk?   [*Exit.*

Host. In, skipper, in!

60   *Sir Ar.* Sirra, hath young Mountchensey married your sister?

Y. Cla. Tis certaine, Sir; here's the Priest that coupled them, the parties ioyned, and the honest witnesse that cride Amen.

Ray. Sir Arthur Clare, my new created Father,
I beseech you, heare mee.

65   *Sir Ar.* Sir, sir, you are a foolish boy; you haue done that you cannot answere; I dare be bould to ceaze her from you; for shee's a profest Nun.

Mil. With pardon, sir, that name is quite vndone;
This true-loue knot cancelles both maid and Nun.
70   When first you told me I should act that part,
How cold and bloody it crept ore my hart!
To Chesson with a smiling brow I went;
But yet, deere sir, it was to this intent,
That my sweete Raymond might find better meanes
75   To steale me thence. In breefe, disguised he came,
Like Nouice to old father Hildersham;
His tutor here did act that cunning part,
And in our loue hath ioynd much wit to art.

Sir Ar. Is't euen so?

80   *Mil.* With pardon therefore wee intreat your smiles;
Loue, thwarted, turnes itselfe to thousand wiles.

Sir Ar. Young Maister Ierningham, were you an actor
In your owne loues abuse?

Y. Ier.   My thoughts, good sir,
Did labour seriously vnto this end,
85   To wrong my selfe, ere ide abuse my friend.

---

53. *you lend* L. — 56, 57. *pray you, pray you* CHIKL. — 66. *to ceaze on her* EFG. — 79. *Is it* F and the rest. — 82, 83 (. . *abuse*). Printed as prose in ABCDE.

Host. He speakes like a Batchelor of Musicke, all in Numbers. Knights, if I had knowne you would haue let this couy of Partridges sit thus long vpon their knees vnder my signe post, I would haue spred my dore with old Couerlids.

Sir Ar. Well, sir, for this your signe was remoued, was it?　90

Host. Faith, wee followed the directions of the deuill, Master Peter Fabell; and Smug, Lord blesse vs! could neuer stand vpright since.

Sir Ar. You, sir, twas you was his minister that married them?

Sir Io. Sir, to proue my selfe an honest man, being that I　95 was last night in the forrest stealing Venison — now, sir, to haue you stand my friend, if that matter should bee calld in question, I married your daughter to this worthy gentleman.

Sir Ar. I may chaunce to requite you, and make your necke crack for't.　100

Sir Io. If you doe, I am as resolute as my Neighbour vicar of Waltham Abby; a hem, grasse and hay! wee are all mortall; lets liue till we be hangd, mine host, and be merry, and theres an end.

Enter FABELL.

 Fab. Now, knights, I enter; now my part begins.　105
 To end this difference, know, at first I knew
 What you intended, ere your loue tooke flight
 From old Mountchensey; you, sir Arthur Clare,
 Were minded to haue married this sweete beauty
 To yong Franke Ierningham; to crosse which match,　110
 I vsde some pretty sleights; but I protest
 Such as but sate vpon the skirts of Art;
 No coniurations, nor such weighty spells
 As tie the soule to their performancy.
 These for his loue, who once was my deere puple,　115
 Haue I effected. Now, mee thinks, tis strange
 That you, being old in wisedome, should thus knit
 Your forehead on this match, since reason failes;
 No law can curbe the louers rash attempt;

89. *old* om. D and the rest. — 97. *that*] *the* D and the rest. — 98. *your*] *you* A. — 104. *Enter Fabell* om. ABC, *Enter Fabian* DE. — 108. *you*] *your* B. — 110. *which*] *this* E. and the rest. — 116. *affected* EF. -- 119. *lover's* L.

4*

120 Yeares, in resisting this, are sadly spent.
　　Smile, then, vpon your daughter and kind sonne,
　　And let our toyle to future ages proue,
　　The Deuill of Edmonton did good in Loue.
　　　Sir Ar. Well, tis in vaine to crosse the prouidence:
125 Deere Sonne, I take thee vp into my hart;
　　Rise, daughter; this is a kind fathers part.
　　　Host. Why, Sir Iohn, send for Spindles noise, presently: Ha,
　　er't be night, Ile serue the good Duke of Norfolke.
　　　Sir Io. Grasse and hay! mine Host, lets live till we die, and
130 be merry, and theres an end.
　　　Sir Ar. What, is breakfast ready, mine Host?
　　　Host. Tis, my little Hebrew.
　　　Sir Ar. Sirra, ride straight to Chesson Nunry,
　　Fetch thence my Lady; the house, I know,
135 By this time misses their yong votary.
　　Come, knights, lets in!
　　　Bil. I will to horse presently, sir. — A plague a my Lady,
　　I shall misse a good breakfast. Smug, how chaunce you cut
　　so plaguely behind, Smug?
140　　*Smug.* Stand away, Ile founder you else.
　　　Bil. Farewell, Smug, thou art in another element.
　　　Smug. I will be by and by; I will be Saint George againe.
　　　Sir Ar. Take heed the fellow doe not hurt himselfe.
　　　Sir Raph. Did we not last night find two S. Georges here?
145　　*Fab.* Yes, knights, this martialist was one of them.
　　　Y. Cla. Then thus conclude your night of merriment!

　　　　　　　　　　　　　　　　　　[Exeunt omnes.

126. *This is a kind father's part* given to *Mil.* in L. — 127. *Why, Sir George* the old copies; corr. in L. — 132. Prefix *Host* om. C. — 137. *a my*] *o my* D, *on my* E and the rest. — 142. *Sir George* ABC; corr. in D. —

The End.

NOTES.

THE PROLOGUE.

5. *round*, the interior of the play-house, on account of its circular form. For the same reason the circle of the theatre is called a *wooden O* H. V. Prol. 13.

7. *to enterlayne*, to enter into, to admit. Cp. Shak. Lucr. 1629

> *Awake, thou Roman dame*
> *And entertain my love.*

14. *that* refers to *his*, l. 12: the birth and the abode of him who was called the merry Fiend of Edmonton.

19. *His monument remayneth to be seene.* 'A monument, reputed to be his, was shown in Edmonton Church, in the time of Weaver and of Norden: but it was without inscription, and therefore could throw no light on his history'. Nares, s. v. Fabell.

20. *His memory*, scil. *remaineth*, l. 19.

22 seqq. The construction of the whole sentence, in which ll. 24, 25 form a sort of parenthesis, is somewhat inexact, as the verb which ought to join *that* (l. 22) and *The very time and houre* (l. 28) is wanting.

36. *guarded with these sable slights*, ornamented with sable decorations or devices. *slight*, originally, artifice, contrivance; thence, anything artfully conceived or contrived, ornaments. Similarly, *device* originally means contrivance, stratagem; thence, anything fancifully conceived; cp. K. John I. 210

> *Not alone in habit and device,*
> *Exterior form, outward accoutrement.*

INDUCTION.

3, 4. Cp. Haml. I. 5. 19, 20

> *And each particular hair to stand an-end,*
> *Like quills upon the fretful porpentine.*

16. *this*, i. e. *this is*; see Abbot, A Shakespearian Grammar, s. 461.

22 seqq. Rather than so abruptly be carried to hell, Fabell will bear on his shoulders the whole globe of earth like Hercules,

and at the same time endure the sufferings by which Prometheus was tormented.

45. *meane*, despicable. The sense of the lines is: Immoderate desire of knowledge renders man contemptible to the powers and may even lead him down to hell.

62. *holowness*, properly, deceitfulness, treachery; as a title given to Coreb it was probably suggested by the expression *his holiness*, the appellation of the Pope of Rome.

79. *like Phaetontique flames*, such Phaetonic endeavours. As Phaeton perished in trying to take Phœbus' place, so Fabell will finally fail in attempting to out-wit the Devil.

ACT I.

1. [Stage-dir.] *Blague*, from the French *blague*, swaggering, bragging.

Ib. *Safe-guardes*, large petticoats, worn over the other clothes, to protect them from dirt; see Nares, Gloss., s. v.

1, 5. *my little wast of maiden-heads*, addressed to Harry Clare. The abstract substantive *waste* is used here for the concrete noun *waster, destroyer*. Cp. the similar use of *corruption*, l. 15.

1, 10. *a Tartarian*. Nares and Webster give *thief* as the meaning of the word. More properly, *a Tartarian* seems to be any person of low order who strolls about the country like a gypsy. Cp. *a Bohemian Tartar* M. Wives IV. 5. 21; *tawny Tartar* Mids. III. 2. 101.

1, 15. *wil that corruption looke well*. As to the construction of *wil*, cp. H. V. II. 4. 90 *willing you overlook this pedigree*, Tit. V. 1. 160 *willing you to demand your hostages*.

1, 27. The Host, having a great predilection for nautical terms (cp. I. 2. 1 seqq.), means to enhance the idea of *presently* by adding *top and top-gallant*.

1, 35. *my canuasadoes and my interrogatories. canvasado,* a burlesque form for *canvass*, inspection, examination; *interrogatory* occurs again IV. 1. 4.

1, 43. *assure*, to engage, to affiance.

1, 54. Near Waltham King Edward I. had a cross erected in remembrance of Queen Elinor. — Clare first uses *crosses* in the sense of disappointment, vexation; in order to avert Milliscent's attention, he then speaks of crosses in the proper sense of the word, and gives his whole speech such an obscure and unintelligible turn that Milliscent is right in exclaiming:

> *O God, what meanes my father?*

1, 57, 58. Cp. Merch. of Ven. V. 1. 30—32

> *she doth stray about*
> *By holy crosses, where she kneels and prays*
> *For happy wedlock hours.*   (Quoted by Hazlitt.)

1, 66. *Cane-tobacco.* 'Tobacco made up in a particular form, highly esteemed and dear.' Nares, Gloss., s. v.

1, 67, 68. Convinced that Mr. Hazlitt's alteration of the text does not hit the mark, and unable to proffer an emendation that would remove the difficulties of this puzzling passage once for all, we have left the reading of the originals unchanged. Tieck's translation of the two lines is to the following effect:

> *Was Hunde haben sollten frisst der Falk,*
> *Ihn kost't der Spitz mehr als der Solofänger.*

1, 74. *You'le see a flight, wife, shortly of his land,* i. e. you will soon see how his land passes away; cp. V. 2. 107 *ere your loue took flight.*

2, 1. *Ostlers, you knaues and commanders.* The Host considers his ostlers as his officers, *commander* being the officer who ranks next above a lieutenant in the Navy.

2, 2. *your honourable hulkes.* As to the use of *your*, Lat. *iste,* cp. Abbott, s. 221.

2, 4. *Via* is, according to Florio, 'an adverb of encouraging, much used by commanders, as also by riders to their horses'. (Quoted by Al. Schmidt, Shakespeare-Lexicon, s. v.).

2, 5, 6 and 9—14. Tieck translates these quaint speeches of *mine Host Blague* thus: *Mögen die Verhängnisse saub're Kammerdiener diesen landstreichenden Puritanern werden, ihr Ritter der Subsidien! ... Ha! Platz da für mein Paar Pistolen, die mit griechischen und lateinischen Kugeln geladen sind; lasst mich euch in die Flanken fallen, ihr meine behenden Gibraltars, und Wind in eure Lendenstücke blasen, dass sie dicker auflaufen! Ha! springen will ich in meinem Besitzthum! Weg mit allen Punctilio's und aller Orthographie! ich diene dem guten Herzog von Norfolk!*

2, 14. *Titere tu* &c. Verg. Ecl. I. 1 *Tityre tu* &c.

2, 16. *Bilbo,* prop., a rapier, a sword, from the town of Bilboa, in Spain, famous for the manufacture of good blades.

2, 19, 20. *without any more discontinuance, releases, or atturnement.* Besides its proper meaning, the word *discontinuance* is an English law-term and refers to the alienation of an estate. The use of this word induces the loquacious Host to add two other law-terms of a similar sense, but which have nothing to do with the idea he will express.

2, 21. *sea-card,* mariner's card, compass.

2, 23. *my souldier of S. Quintins.* Eight thousand English soldiers, under the command of the Earl of Pembroke, were present at the battle of S. Quentins, 1557.

2, 24 seq. The Host compares his sack to the stars commonly called Charles' wain or the Great Bear, and to a crabfish glistening in the dark.

2, 26. *your Coopers Dixionary.* Cooper's Thesaurus Linguae Latinae was published in 1584.

2, 42. *Passion*, deep sorrow and grief, as often in Shakespeare.

2, 45. After breakfast Sir Arthur intends to communicate to Mounchensey his purpose of sending Milliscent to the Nunnery.

3, 9. *to be in hand*, to be about.

3, 14. *read*, studied.

3, 38 seqq. The sense of these lines seems to be: If any other person should have offered to help me, I should not have cared for it, knowing that nobody can bring me comfort. Thy words, however, exercise some influence upon me, as I know thou art able to help me if thou wilt. But I feel sure that thou wilt not give up Milliscent, and therefore I should have preferred any other person to offer me his help; I should have believed him, but I cannot believe thee.

3, 49 seqq. The construction of this rather diffuse passage is: Come, Raymond, and make thy groning love .... leape, caper ... (l. 53), i. e. do not exhibit thy love in such a melancholy way, but in a more cheerful manner. — As ll. 51, 52, like l. 50, refer to *loue*, and contain an evident allusion to Cupid, the change of the gender (l. 51, 53) may easily be accounted for.

3, 52. *at hudman-blind*, i. e. with his eyes blind-folded as in the children's game now called blind-man's-buff. Cp. Haml. III. 4. 77

What devil was't
That thus hath cozened you at hoodman-blind.

3, 59. *in hugger-mugger*, in secrecy, clandestinely. Cp. Haml. IV. 5. 84, and Ford, 'Tis Pity she's a Whore, III. 1. (Works, ed. Hartley Coleridge, p. 35 a): *there is no way but to clap up a marriage in hugger-mugger* (quoted by Elze), and The Revenger's Tragedy V. (apud Dodsley, Old Plays, ed. Hazlitt, vol. V, p. 90): *and how quaintly he died, like a politician, in hugger-mugger.*

3, 65. *doe I bend in the hams?* Cp. Pericles IV. 2. 114 *The French knight that cowers i'the hams. Who? M. Veroles.*

3, 68. *to giue out*, to publish, proclaim.

3, 73. *to lanch*, to send a ship into the water, in a figurative sense here. Tieck translates: *die Alten, Eure Väter, | Gedenken thät'ge Beutel flott zu machen.*

3, 82. *to slubber*, to obscure or darken. Cp. Oth. I. 3. 227, and the First Part of Jeronimo (Dodsley, ed. Hazlitt vol. IV, p. 374): *The evening too begins to slubber day.*

3, 85. *spring*, springall, a youth, a lad.

3, 101. *a counterfeit*, a false coin; cp. Gentl. V. 4. 53 *thou counterfeit to thy true friend.*

3, 105 seq. Thou hast given me back to life, dear friend; my soul feels so free that neither time nor even death can lessen or alter my happiness.

3, 114 seq. What favour may Raymond expect at thy hands for the honour he renders to thee?

✓ 3, 123. *passe*, unfortunate state, predicament; cp. Lear III. 4. 65

   have his daughters brought him to this pass!

✓ 3, 143. *hollow*. The form *hollo* is also used by Shakespeare, Ven. 973

   she hears some huntsman hollo.

ACT II.

✓ 1, 7. *it tickles our Catastrophe.* The same expression occurs again V. 2. 10, and is used by Falstaff 2 H. IV., II. 1. 66:

   I'll tickle your Catastrophe.

1, 40. *The question is.* As similar incomplete constructions very often occur in familiar conversation, Mr. Hazlitt's reading *the question is good, neighbour B.* seems to be uncalled for.

✓ 1, 50. *Castilian*, 'a delicate courtier.

   Come, come, Castilian, skim the pusset curd,
   Shew thy queere substance, worthless, most absurd.'

(Quoted by Nares, s. v., from Marston's Satires, 1599.)

1, 52. 'His address to the smith, on reading the *little Geneva print*, was an equivoque on the redness of his eyes from having drunk too much, and the small type in which the Scriptures were printed in the common Genevan version' (Hazlitt). The English bible was printed several times at Geneva, first in 1560.

✓ 1, 55. *Hungarions*, a cant term for *hungry person*. Cp. Shak., M. W. I. 3. 23 *O base Hungarion wight.*

✓ 1, 60. *bosonians*, the same as *bezonians*, which is used twice by Shakespeare 2 H. IV., V. 3. 118; 2 H. VI., IV. 1. 134. The word comes from the Italian *bisogno* need, want, and means *a beggar.* — The sense of the line is: The keepers beg at my house and are quite dependent on me.

1, 61. *Gog* and *Magog*, originally two nations hostile to the Israelites; popular name for two colossal statues in the Guildhall, London.

1, 67. *the Cittizen of good fellowes*, in contrast with the preceding *a Boore, a Boore of the Country.*

✓ 2, 2. *with shalles.* A quibble on *shall*, shale, shell, and *shall*, denoting futurity. Nares, s. v., very aptly quotes, besides our passage, Churchyard, Challenge p. 153

   Thus all with shall or shalles ye shal be fed.

✓ 2, 6. *brangled*, confused, entangled.

✓ 2, 26. *orient*, bright, shining; cp. Shakespeare, Pilgr. 133 *bright, orient pearl.*

2, 40. *Were 't not for manhood sake.* But for the dignity of a gentleman of my age, I should not brave thee with mere words, but challenge thee with sword in hand.

2, 57. *soares*, soaring flight; thence, high-flown words, quarrel.

2, 68, 69. Addressing his father.

2, 82. *to fadge*, to go, proceed, succeed; cp. L.L.L. V. 1. 154, and Tw. N. II. 2. 34.

2, 84. Addressing R. Mounchensey.

2, 87. *fellowes of a handfull hie*, i. e. sprites. *hie*, high; *a handfull*, a palm, a measure of four inches. Cp. B. Jonson, Cynthia's Rev. III. 4:

> *Here stalks me by a proud and spangled sir*
> *That looks three handfuls higher than his foretop.*

(Quoted by Nares.)

3, 3. *the composure of weake frailtie meete.* As *composure* means 'the elements which compose s. t., the materials', it is not necessary to substitute *meets* (L) for the plural number *meete*.

3, 19 seq. Your absence will so waste his blood that his cheeks shall look quite pale.

3, 22. For *to waine*, to avert, to alienate, cp. 3 Henry VI., IV. 4. 17, and Tit. Andr. I. 1. 211.

3, 38. *your fathers may chance spie your parting.* The verb *to chance* is sometimes, though rarely, followed by the infinitive without *to*; cp. 2 H. IV., II. 1. 12 *It may chance cost some of us our liues*; Troil. I. 1. 26 *you may chance burn your lips* (Q), F *to burn*.

3, 63. *kept under. to keep under*, to restrain, detain, has here apparently an obscene sense; else *yet* at the beginning of the line can hardly be accounted for.

ACT III.

1, 7. *Holy matron, woman milde.* Apposition to *Daughter Marie.*

1, 22. *That* refers to *your* (l. 21): *you that so truely pay your tithe.* Cp. V. 2. 115.

1, 32. *buske.* 'The busk was thought very essential to the female figure. Marston, Scourge II. 7:

> *Her long slit sleeves, stiffe buske, puffe verdingall,*
> *Is all that makes her thus angelical.'*   Nares s. v.

1, 39. *the sacring Bell.* 'A small bell used in the Roman Catholic Church to call attention to the more solemn parts of the service of the mass.' Webster. The word also occurs Henry VIII., III. 2. 295.

1, 42. *Lattins*, Latin prayers or hymns.

1, 53. *mornings Masse.* Cp. *mornings' joy* Lucr. 1107, *morning's rest* Rom. V. 3. 189, *morning's dew* Tit. II. 3. 201, *a morning's holy office* Cymb. III. 3. 4.

1, 81. Cp. Per. IV. 4. 25: *Pericles, in sorrow all devoured.*

1, 87. *I, a poore innocent shee.* Cp. Tw. I. 5. 259 *the cruellest she.* It is, therefore, unnecessary to alter the punctuation as Hazlitt has done.

✓ 1, 90. *conscience*, thought, consideration; Haml. III. 1. 83

Thus conscience does make cowards of us all.

✓ 1, 95. *To thrust Mounchenseyes nose besides the cushion*, i. e. to impose upon M. Cp. the phrases *to miss the cushion, to be beside the cushion*. According to Nares, *cushion* was a term of archery, being a name for the mark at which the archers shot.

1, 101. Addressed to Harry Clare.

1, 111. *None only but* (Edd. *only, but*). *But only* as well as *only but* are often used for *only* or *but*. Cp. Merch. III. 5. 51 *in none only but parrots*.

✓ 2, 16. *my deere bosome*. Cp. the Shakespearian phrases *my dear heart, my dear blood, my dear soul*, in all of which *dear* has the signification of *inmost*.

2, 20. *Did you now know but how this test takes fire. but*, properly belonging to *know*, is attracted by the following sentence. A similar instance of attraction is Mcb. V. 8. 40

He only lived but till he was a man.

2, 81—87. The sense of the passage as we read it (l. 84 *Harry*) is: Peter Fabell, in the habit of Frier Hildersham, made his plot with the aid of Francke and Harry and with my own assistance, and *so*, i. e. in that disguise he conversed with Sir Arthur Clare.

✓ 2, 132. *vnbagd*, not pregnant. *to bag*, to become pregnant.

✓ 2, 137. *turne tippet*, to make a complete change, particularly used of a maid becoming a wife. The origin of the phrase is not clear. Cp. Ben Jonson, The Case is Altered III. 3. (ed. Gifford, vol. VI, p. 378 seq.): *You to turn tippet! fie, fie!* and Beaumont and Fletcher, Monsieur Thomas II. 2. 5 (ed. Darnley, vol. I, p. 472[b]): *You must turn tippet.* (Quoted by Nares.)

2, 141. *hees the onely man*. Cp. M. Ado III. 1. 92 *he is the onely man of Italy*.

2, 144. Cp. V. 1. 91 seqq.

✓ 2, 153. *To watch the coast be cleere*. The same proverbial expression occurs 1 H. VI., I. 3. 89 *see the coast cleared*.

✓ 2, 163. *tall*, lusty, sturdy. Shakespeare generally uses the word in an ironical or derisory sense; see Al. Schmidt, Shakespeare-Lexicon, s. v. But the contemporary writers often use it without ridiculing it as an affected term of fashion. Cp. Nares, s. v.

ACT IV.

✓ 1, 19. *A horse*, a machine upon which anything is supported by laying it across (Halliwell, Dict. of Arch. and Prov. Words, s. v. [3]). See, below, l. 121.

1, 32. The *&c.* means, of course, that Sir John repeats his old saying "We are all mortal; we'll live till we die, and be merry, and ther's an end." (Collier).

1, 44. *the stone Priest.* Cp. *a stone horse*, i. e. a horse not castrated.

1, 79. *goe vp the wind,* j. e. go against the wind. Cp. *down the wind*, in the direction of the wind.

2, 40. *mareterraneum skinker.* The Host seems to mean *mediterraneum skinker.* For *skinker*, tapster, drawer, see Nares s. v.

2, 71. *roomer*, an old sea term; *to go* or *put roomer*, to tack about before the wind. See Halliwell, Dict., s. v. *To cry roomer*, to give the command to tack about before the wind.

ACT V.

1, 28. *Ile firke him. to firk*, to beat, to drub; cp. H. V., IV. 4. 29 *I'll fer him, and firk him, and ferret him.*

1, 55, 56. The sense of the lines is: Tell me the plain truth, for your calling forbids all hypocrisy, nor need you be indulgent towards me (*nor beare with me*): I am quite prepared to hear and to bear the whole truth. Collier's conjecture, therefore, ingenious though it be, seems to be unnecessary.

1, 125. *Is not this the George?* In order to mislead the two knights, Fabell and his companions seem to have interchanged the signs of the two inns, and to have engaged Smug, in the disguise of Saint George, to stand over the door of the George. Only thus can we account for V. 2. 142 where Smug says *I will be Saint George again.* Cp., besides, ib. 144, 145. See Tieck, Alt-Englisches Theater II, p. 8.

2, 3. *Jenerts*, jennets; see the similar expression of the Host I. 2, 11 *my nimble Giberalters (gibber,* a bauky horse).

Ib. *bauke.* Steevens feels inclined to retain the original reading *banke.* 'The merry Host', he says, 'seems willing to assemble ideas expressive of trust and confidence. The old quartos begin the word *jenert* with a capital letter, and therefore we may suppose *Ienert's bank* to have been the shop of some banker, in whose possession money could be deposited with security. The Irish still say, *as sure as Burton's bank,* and our own countrymen *as sure as the bank of England.*' But even granting that there were country-banks in England as early as the end of the sixteenth century, which is by no means probable, we must own that we cannot make out the meaning of the expression in our passage. Quite as little are we satisfied by Mr. Hazlitt's conjecture *Ienert's back.* The word *bauk* which we have introduced into the text, is the ancient spelling of *balk* and is several times found in the old Edd. of Shakespeare (s. Al. Schmidt, Shak.-Lex., s. v.). For the use of *bauk* cp. *By reason of the contagion then in London, we balked the inns* Evelyn. (Quoted by Webster.).

Ib. *house.* The reading *horse* was probably influenced by the preceding *jenerts. house* was already conjectured by Nares, s. v.

Jenerts. As to the expression *my house, my castle,* cp. I. 1. 2 *Welcome good knight, to the George at Waltham, my free-hold, my tenements, goods and chattels.* By the reading, proposed by Mr. Hazlitt, *my house is my castle,* the construction of the whole passage seems to lose consistency.

2, 12. *the yellowes,* jaundice in horses; cp. Shak., Tam. III. 2. 54.

2, 16. *haue we Commedies in hand,* do we perform a comedy.

2, 26. *Sine Cerere et Baccho friget Venus.* Ter. Eun. 4, 5, 6.

2, 31. *Lusty Juventus* is the title of one of the oldest English Moral-Plays.

2, 46. *Storm,* be passionate, chafe.

2, 49. *to be humorous,* to act from caprice, cp. Span. Trag., Old Plays, ed. Hazlitt, vol. V, p. 31.

2, 57. *like a Cockatrices ege.* The cockatrice or basilisk was fabled to have so deadly an eye as to kill by its very look. Cp. Shak. Rom. III. 2. 45

> *Say thou but I,*
> *And that bare vowel I shall poison more*
> *Than the death-darting eye of cockatrice.*

2, 59. *skipper,* a thoughtless young fellow. Cp. Shak. Shr. II. 341 *skipper, stand back!*

2, 88. *sit thus long vpon their knees.* Milliscent and Mountchensey are kneeling before Clare.

2, 127. *Spindles noise. noise,* a company of musicians; cp. 2 H. IV., II. 4. 13 *find out Sneak's noise.*

EHRH. KARRAS, Printer, Halle.

PSEUDO-SHAKESPEARIAN PLAYS.

EDITED

BY

KARL WARNKE, Ph. D.

AND

LUDWIG PROESCHOLDT, Ph. D.

III. KING EDWARD III.

———————

HALLE:
MAX NIEMEYER.
1886.

KING EDWARD III.

REVISED AND EDITED

WITH INTRODUCTION AND NOTES

BY

KARL WARNKE, PH. D.

AND

LUDWIG PROESCHOLDT, PH. D.

HALLE:

MAX NIEMEYER.

1886.

A.257857

INTRODUCTION.

THE earliest edition of the Pseudo-Shakespearian play of King
Edward III. (A) was published in 1596, with the title: '*The Raigne
of King Edward the third.   As it hath bin sundrie times plaied about
the Citie of London.   London, Printed for Cuthbert Burby.   1596.*'
(Preserved in the British Museum; Press-mark C. 21. c. 50).[1])   A
second edition of the play (B) was printed in 1599 for the same
publisher and with the same title *(Imprinted at London by Simon
Stafford, for Cuthbert Burby.   And are to be sold at his shop neere
the Royall Exchange.   1599)*. (Preserved in the British Museum;
Press-mark C. 21. b. 40).[2])   Like most old plays, the *Editio princeps*
of Edward III. is very badly printed; there is scarcely a page in
it which is not disfigured by blunders and misprints.   The edition
of 1599 corrected part of these mistakes, but we need hardly add
that also B is far from being correctly printed; many misprints
passed from A into B, and many others were added in B.   B,
however, is not purely a reprint of A; it was intended to be a
revised edition.   Unfortunately he who revised the play had no
happy hand; for most of the alterations which he introduced into
the text are arbitrary and decidedly inferior to the readings of A.
It must be regretted therefore that modern editors should sometimes without any cogent reason have departed from A and given
the preference to the readings of the edition of 1599.

Most of the gross and palpable blunders exhibited both by
A and B were removed by Capell, who in 1760 edited Edward III.

---

[1]) The play was entered in the Stationers' Register on the first of
December 1595: '*Cutbert Burby.   Entred for his copie vnder the hands of
the wardens A book Intitled Edward the Third and the Blacke Prince, their
warres with King Iohn of Fraunce. . . . . vj^d.*' (Arber's Transscript III, p. 55).

[2]) According to the Stationers' Registers other editions would seem to
have followed in 1609, 1617, and 1625; but none of these is known to have
been preserved.

in 'Prolusions; or, Select Pieces of ancient Poetry. Compil'd with great Care from their several Originals, and offer'd to the Publick as Specimens of the Integrity that should be found in the Editions of worthy Authors. London. Printed for J. and R. Torson, in the Strand. 1760.' Capell kept what he had promised on the title-page; each scene of the play bears testimony how much care he took to give the play a form worthy of its contents. He first divided the piece into acts and scenes, added the *Dramatis Personæ*, and, which is more important, happily succeeded in correcting a great number of passages quite unintelligible in A and B. The age in which Capell lived, accounts for his sometimes overshooting the mark. Like Pope in his edition of Shakespeare, Capell, adapting the metre and grammar in Edward III. to the rules of his own time, often altered a word or a line which had been quite correctly printed in the old editions. Nor shall we be surprised to find that he did not scrupulously stick to A or B, but that he took indifferently the reading which he liked best. Mistakes, such as Capell would have thought them, are seldom to be met with in his edition (III. 3. 5 *tell me* om.). On the whole, every sensible reader must acknowledge that Capell's edition is comparatively speaking to be considered a good one, and that in many respects it is superior to all subsequent editions. None of the modern editors seem to have thought it necessary again to collate the old copies of the play; all of them entirely rely upon Capell and his notes.

In his edition of 'The Doubtful Plays of Shakespeare. London and New-York. s. a.', Tyrrell printed the play from Capell's edition, adding only some isolated conjectures of his own. But very few of these conjectures correct the reading of Capell and deserve to be introduced into the critical text of the play, viz. I. 1. 105, ib. 134, II. 2. 157. ·

To the reader of our own age the play has been made accessible by Prof. N. Delius' edition (Pseudo-shaksperesche Dramen, No. 1. Elberfeld, 1854). Delius' edition is based on Capell's Prolusions; where his text differs from that of Capell, it is most frequently owing to a strange mistake made by him. In a list of Various Readings added to his edition, Capell gives beside the *Varia lectio* of A and B a certain number of conjectural emendations which seemed to him very plausible, but not so well-founded

as to be embodied into the text of the play. In his Introductory
Notice Capell expressly says: 'he (the reader) will find at the end
of each poem all the other rejected readings of the editions made
use of; and, intermix'd with these, are some conjectural ones, being
such as were thought plausible, but not of force enough to demand
a place in the text. These latter readings have no mark given
them, the others are distinguish'd by the mark of the edition they
belong to.' Prof. Delius, having to all appearance not read that
notice, erroneously supposed *all* the readings contained in Capell's
list to have been drawn from some old edition, and consequently
adopted a great part of Capell's conjectures for his edition. Besides,
Delius, without giving any notice of it, altered Capell's text by
introducing a number of conjectures of his own. The text which
results from such a proceeding is of course by no means to be
trusted, and it is the less so, as the critical notes given ·by Delius
are scanty and inexact in the highest degree. As to the conjectural
readings proposed by Capell and adopted by Delius, only a few
of them seem to be incontestible, viz. I. 1. 39, I. 2. 104, I. 2. 153,
III. 2. 58, III. 3. 1, III. 3. 25; most of them, however, deserve no
place in the text of a critical edition. Of the conjectures made
by Delius, only five (I. 1. 36, I. 2. 159, II. 1. 57, II. 2. 40, II. 2. 117)
have been adopted by us.

Delius' edition has had the honour of being reprinted in the
'Leopold Shakspere' (p. 1037 — 1056) and in the Doubtful Plays
of William Shakespeare, edited by Max Moltke (Tauchnitz edition,
Vol. 1041). The former is a mere reprint of Delius' edition, into
which even obvious misprints have passed, cp. II. 1. 453 *same* f.
shame. Mr. Moltke, likewise, worked on Delius' edition, adopting,
now and then, some reading given by Delius in his *Varia Lectio*[1])
and inserting some few conjectures of his own.[2])

The latest modern edition of Edward III. has been published
by J. P. Collier in The Plays and Poems of W. Shakespeare, with
the purest text and briefest notes [including Edward III., The Two

---

[1]) Viz. II. 1. 184 *treasure* f. *treasurer*, II. 2. 103 *sweep* f. *beat*, ib. 124
objection f. *subjection*, III. 5. 36 *his green courage with those thoughts* f.
his courage with those grievous thoughts, IV. 4. 124 *wings* f. *strings*.

[2]) Viz. II. 1. 414 *environ'd* f. *inwir'd* (see ad loc.), ib. 418 *then* om., II.
2. 117 *fair rarities* f. *varieties*, ib. 158 *Arrive* f. *To arrive*, III. 2. 59 *Turned
aside* f. *Turned but aside*, IV. 4. 75 *your* f. *our*.

Noble Kinsmen, Mucedorus, and A Yorkshire Tragedy]. Maidenhead (completed in 1878). Limited to 58 Copies.' Mr. Collier, too, seems only to have made use of Capell's edition, and not to have consulted the old editions. Like Prof. Delius, he succeeded in correcting some lines of the play, viz. I. 2. 159, II. 1. 285, II. 2. 40; on the whole, however, he treated both the metre and the text of the play in quite an arbitrary and uncritical manner.

The play of Edward III. has been three times translated into German, first in 1836: Vier Schauspiele von Shakespeare, übersetzt von Ludwig Tieck. Stuttgart und Tübingen, 1836. From an essay of Hermann von Friesen (Shakespeare-Jahrbuch II, p. 64 seqq.) we learn that the four plays were translated not by Tieck, but by Wolf von Baudissin, and that Tieck only intended to accompany them with an introduction, which, however, was never published. The translations of Ortlepp (Nachträge zu Shakespeare's Werken, Stuttgart 1840, vol. II) and of Max Moltke (Leipzig, Universalbibliothek 685) rely in all essential points on that of Tieck-Baudissin.[1]

The greater part of Edward III. is based on Holinshed's Chronicle of England, the episode I, 2—II on Holinshed's Chronicle of Scotland and on Painter's Palace of Pleasure. With the exception of the scenes in which Villiers plays the principal part (IV. 1. 19—43, ib. 3. 1—56) and which the poet must have derived from some other source[2]), there is no reason to believe that the author of the play consulted any other book. We think it best to give the

---

[1] Ch. F. Weisse, the author of 'Eduard der Dritte, ein Trauerspiel in fünf Aufzügen' (Beytrag zum Deutschen Theater. Erster Theil. Zwote, verbesserte und vermehrte Auflage. Leipzig, 1765) appears not to have known the English play. His source was Rapin Thoyras' History of England. Cp. J. Minor, Ch. F. Weisse und seine Beziehungen zur deutschen Literatur des 18. Jahrhunderts, Innsbruck 1880, p. 206—208. — Whether there is an affinity or no between the Pseudo-Shakespearian 'Edward III.' and the tragedy of 'Edouard III.' by Gresset (translated into German, Wien 1758) and La Calprenède's 'Edouard III.' we are unable to say, as neither of the works have been accessible to us.

[2] The name of *Villiers* occurs in Holinshed as the name of a place, II, p. 641.

passages from which the facts were taken, here at full, with the acts and scenes which they illustrate.[1])

I. 1. 1 — 50 (Hol. II, 605; A. D. 1333): 'This yeare was the warre proclamed betwixt England and France, cheefely by the procurement of the lord Robert Dartois, a Frenchman, as then banished out of France, vpon occasion of a claime by him made vnto the earledome of Artois. This lord Robert after he was banished France, fled ouer vnto King Edward, who gladlie receiued him and made him earle of Richmond.'

(Ib., p. 611, 612): 'It is well knowne that Philip le Beau King of France had issue by his wife queene Jone three sons, Lewis surnamed Hutine, Philip Le Long, and Charles le Beau: also two daughters, the one dieing in hir infancie, and the other named Isabell liued, and was married vnto Edward the second of that name, king of England, who begot of hir this Edward the third, that made this claime. The three sonnes of the foresaid Philip le Beau reigned ech after other as kings of France . . . . (All three of them dying without leaving any heir) King Edward averred that the kingdome of France apperteined vnto him as lawfull heire, bicause that he alone was remaining of the kings stock, and touched his mothers father Philip le Beau, in the next degree of consanguinitie, as he that was borne of his daughter Isabell.'

I. 1. 56 seqq. According to Holinshed King Edward III. did homage to the French King for the dukedome of Guyenne. (II. p. 597; A. D. 1329) 'In the third yeare of his reigne about the Ascension-tide, King Edward went ouer into France, and coming to the French king Philip de Valois, as then being at Amiens, did there his homage vnto him for the duchie of Guien.'

I. 1. 121 — 138. For the King's campaign in Scotland, the author of the play seems to have made use of several accounts found in Holinshed. (V, p. 376) 'After this the governor [of King David] came to the castle of Lochindoris and laid siege to it, wherewithin was the countesse of Atholl, the wife of the late slaine earle Dauid. This woman hauing knowledge aforehand, that

---

1) We take the opportunity of expressing our thanks to the Administration of the University-Library at Göttingen for having favoured us with 'Holinshed's Chronicles of England, Scotland and Ireland. In six volumes. London 1807 seqq.', from which we give our quotations.

hir house should be besieged, had sent vnto the King of England
and to Edward Balioll for succours. The king of England now
doubting least all the strengths in Scotland, kept by such as were
his friends, would be lost without recouerie, if the same were not
the sooner rescued, he raised an armie of fortie thousand men,
and entering therewith into Scotland, came to the castle of Lochindoris aforesaid. The Scots that lay there at siege, vpon knowledge
had of his comming towards them, brake vp, and departed from
thence. Heerevpon, when he had refreshed the hold with new
men, munition, and vittels, he tooke the countesse foorth with him,
and passed with bloudie swoord thorough Murrey . . .'

I. 1. 134, 135. S. ad IV. 1. 1—18.

I. 1. 147—152 (V, p. 608). 'Thus we may perceiue that Flanders
rested wholie at king Edward's commandement.' ib. 'The aliance of
the earle of Heinault first procured the king of England all these
freends.' ib. 'There was sent to the emperour to procure his freend-
ship, from the king of England, the marques of Gulike . . . . The
duke of Gelderland . . . trauelled most earnestlie to procure him all
the freends within the empire that he could make.'

I. 2. 1—73 (V, p. 378). 'About the same time sir William
Montacute earle of Salisburie, togither with the earle of Arundell,
came into Scotland with a great power of men, and besieged the
castle of Dunbar, lieing at the same for the space of 22 weeks.
Within the said castell was the countesse hir selfe, surnamed blacke
Agnes of Dunbar, who shewed such manlie defense, that no gaine
was to be got anie waies forth at hir hands, so that in the end
they were constreined to raise their siege, and to depart without
speed of their purpose. It is said, that this countesse vsed manie
pleasant words in iesting and tawnting at the enimies dooings,
thereby the more to incourage hir souldiers.

The Earl of Douglas is very often mentioned in Holinshed,
f. i. II, p. 604: 'The Lord Wm Douglas still coasted the Englishmen,
doing to them what damage he might.' Likewise, the author of
the play found in Holinshed that the Earl of Warwick was sent
into Scotland (II., p. 606). Cp., besides, ib. p. 602 (A. D. 1334)
'then entering into Scotland, came to Roxborough where he repared
the castell which had beene aforetime destroied.'

ib. 94 seqq. The Countess of Salisbury is also mentioned in
Holinshed (II, p. 629): 'It chanced that King Edward finding

either the garter of the queene or of some lady with whom he was in loue (marginal note: The countes of Salisbury), being fallen from hir leg, stooped downe and tooke it vp, whereat diuerse of the nobles found matter to iest, and to talke their fansies merilie, touching the king's affection towards the woman, vnto whome he said, that if he liued, it should come to passe that most high honor should be giuen vnto them for the garter's sake: and therevpon shortlie after, he deuised and ordeined this order of the garter, with such a posie, wherby he signified that his nobles iudged otherwise of him than the truth was.'

The materials for the scenes following (l. 2 — II. 1 and 2) have been taken from Painter's Novel. But as the poet was indebted to it merely for the leading idea, not for any particulars of the episode, we think it sufficient only to give a summary of the contents of Painter's diffuse and prosy narrative.

In a war made by King Edward on King David of Scotland, the Scots lay siege to the castle of Roxborough, which is valiantly defended by the Countess of Salisbury. Being pressed hard by the besiegers, the Countess sends for help to King Edward. On hearing of his approach, the Scots speedily decamp; King Edward arrives and stays for some days in the Castle. Struck with the beauty and graces of the Countess, whose name is Ælips, he falls desperately in love with her, and endeavours to win her affections. All his proposals, however, are indignantly rejected by the Countess. Quite as little is she inveigled by a love-letter which the King, on his return to London, addresses to her. Meanwhile Earl Salisbury, the husband, and Earl Warwick, the father of the Countess, who have been kept prisoners in France, are released; the former, however, having long been ill, dies before coming home. When Warwick has arrived in London, the King induces him to intercede with the Countess in his favour. The old Earl who has sworn to help the king, without knowing for what purpose his assistance is required, keeps his word, and tries, not without many sighs and tears, to prevail upon his daughter to yield to the king. Highly gratified to see how firmly resolved she is not to deviate from the path of honour, he imparts her refusal to the king. Fallen into disfavour, he retires from the court and lives on his estates, leaving, however, his wife and daughter in London. Several times the King sends his secretary

to make the Countess change her mind; but seeing that her
chastity is not to be shaken by words, he resolves to make sure
of her by force. The mother, acquainted with the king's purpose,
and fearing that her whole family should have to suffer from his
disfavour, apparently succeeds in overpersuading her daughter.
Accompanied by the secretary, the two ladies repair to the Palace.
The King, delighted to see at length his wishes accomplished, leads
the Countess into his apartment. Here, however, she throws herself
at his feet, and presenting a knife to him, implores him rather to
kill her than deprive her of honour and chastity. The King,
overcome by the incorruptible sentiments and the steadfast character
of the Countess, changes his mind, and raising the lady from the
ground, kisses her and leads her out of the room. The whole
court being just assembled, Edward declares to have chosen the
Countess to be his queen, and the nuptial ceremony is instantly
performed by the Archbishop of York.

III. 1. Battle at Sluise (Hol. II, p. 614; A. D. 1340): 'The
French nauie laie betwixt Sluise and Blancbergh so that when the
king of England approched, either part descried other, and therewith prepared them to battell. The king of England staied, till
the sunne which at the first was in his face, came somewhat westward, and so had it vpon his backe, that it should not hinder the
sight of his people, and so therewith did set vpon his enimies with
great manhood, who likewise verie stoutlie incountered him, by
reason whereof issued a sore and deadlie fight betwixt them .'...
at length the Englishmen hauing the aduantage, not onelie of the
sunne, but also of the wind and tide, so fortunatlie that the French
fleet was driven into the streights in such wise that neither the
souldiers nor mariners could helpe themselues, in somuch that both
heauen, sea, and wind seemed all to haue conspired against the
Frenchmen . . .'

III. 3, 1—10 (Hol. II, p. 636): . . . 'at length by one of the
prisoners named Gobin de Grace, he (the king of England) was
told where he might passe with his armie ouer the riuer of Some,
at a foord in the same riuer, being hard in the bottome, and
verie shallow at an eb water . . . . When the king of England had
thus passed the riuer, he acquitted Gobin Agace and all his companie
of their ransomes, and gaue to the same Gobin an hundred nobles,
and a good horse, and so the king rode foorth as he did before.

III. 3. 219—226. (Hol. II, p. 637; A. D. 1346): 'Then he ordained three battels, in the first was the prince of Wales, and with him the earle of Warwike . . . *(not Audley)* . . . In the second battle was the earle of Northampton . . . *(not Derby)* . . . The third battell the king led himselfe.'

III. 4. 1—13. (Hol. II, p. 638; A. D. 1346): 'There were of Genowaies crosbowes to the number of twelue or fifteen thousand, the, which were commanded to go on before, and with their shot to begin the battell; but they were so werie with going on foot that morning six leagues armed with their crosbowes, that they said to their constables "We be not well vsed, in that we are commanded to fight this daie, for we be not in case to doo any great feat of armes, we haue more need of rest." These words came to the hearing of the earle of Alanson, who said "A man is well at ease to be charged with such a sort of rascals that faint and fail now at most need" .... When the Genowaies felt the arrowes persing their heads, armes and breasts, many of them cast downe their crosbowes, and cut the strings, and returned discomfited. When the French king saw them flee awaie, he said "Slea these rascals, for they will let and trouble us without reason."

III. 5. 10—56. (Hol. II, p. 639; A. D. 1346): 'They of that battell (the Prince's battle) had as then inough to doo, in somuch that some which were about him, as the earle of Northampton, and others sent to the king, where he stood aloft on a windmill hill,' requiring him to aduance forward, and come to their aid, they being as thus sore laid to of their enimies. The king hereupon demanded if his sonne were slaine, hurt or felled to the earth. "No (said the knight that brought the message), but he is sore matched." "Well (said the king) returne to him and them that sent you, and saie to them I will that this iournie be his, with the honor therof." With this answer the knight returned, which greatlie incouraged them to doo their best to win the spurs, being half abashed in that they had so sent to the king for aid."

III. 5. 61—100 (Hol. II, p. 639; A. D. 1346): 'Among other which died that daie, these I find registred by name as cheefest, Iohn king of Boheme' . . . . 'When the Frenchmen were clearelie ouercome, and those that were left aliue fled and gone, so that the Englishmen heard no more noise of them, king Edward came down from the hill (on the which he stood all that day with his

helmet still on his head) and going to the prince, imbraced him
in his armes, and kissed him, saiing: "Fair sonne, God send you
good perseuerance in this your prosperous beginning, you haue
noblie acquitted your selfe, you are well worthie to haue the gouern-
ance of a realme committed to your hands for your valiant doings."
The prince inclined himselfe to the earth in honouring his father,
as he best could. This done, they thanked God togither with their
souldiers for their good aduenture . . . . (ib. p. 640) . . . the king
ordered to search what the number was of them that were slaine,
and vpon the view taken, it was reported vnto him, that there were
found dead eleuen princes, foure score baronets, twelue hundred
knights, and more than thirtie thousand of the meaner sort.

IV. 1. 1—18 (Hol. II, p. 621; A. D. 1341): 'For whereas con-
tention arose betwixt one Charles of Blois and John earle of
Mountford, about the right to the duchie of Britaine; the earle of
Mountford, thinking that he had wrong offered him at the French
king's hands, who fauoured his aduersarie Charles de Blois, alied
himselfe with the king of England . . . . . (ib. p. 623) At length a
truce was taken for a time during the which the countess of Richmond (? *Mountford*) came ouer into England, to commune with
king Edward, touching the affaires of Britaine, who appointed sir
Robert Dartois, earle of Richmond, the earles of Salisburie, Pembroke . . . to go with her ouer into Britain.'

IV. 2. 7—35 (Hol. II, p. 640; A. D. 1346): 'When the said sir
John de Vienne (captain of Calis) saw the manner of the English
host, and what the king's intention was, he constreined all the
poore and meane people to depart out of the towne. The king
of England perceiuing that this was doone of purpose to spare
vittels, would not driue them backe againe to helpe to consume
the same, but rather pitied them; and therefore did not onelie
shew them so much grace to suffer them to passe through his
host, but also gaue them meat and drinke to dinner, and more-
ouer two pence sterling to euerie person.'

IV. 2. 37—61 (Hol. II, p. 643 seqq.; A. D. 1346): 'All this while
the siege continued still before Calis, and the French king amongst
other deuises which he imagined to raise the king of England
from it, procured the Scots to make warre into England, in somuch
that Dauid king of Scotland, notwithstanding the truce which
yet indured betwixt him and the king of England, vpon hope now

to doo some great exploit, by reason of the absence of king Edward, intangled then with the besieging of Calis, he assembled the whole puissance of his realme ... and with them entered into England, burning, spoiling, and wasting the countrie till he came as far as Durham. The lords of England that were left at home with the queene for the sure keeping and defense of the realme ... assembled an host of all such people as were able to beare armour, both preests and other. Their generall assemblie was appointed at Newcastell, and when they were all togither, they were to the number of 1200 men of armes, 3000 archers, and 7000 other, with the Welshmen, and issuing out of the towne, they found the Scots readie to come forward to incounter them .... The queene was there in person, and went from ranke to ranke, and incouragd hir people in the best manner she could, and that done she departed, committing them and their cause to God, the giuer of all victorie .... The king was taken in the field sore wounded, for he fought valiantly. He was prisoner to an esquier of Northumberland, who as soone as he had taken him, rode out of the field with him accompanied onlie with eight of his seruants, and rested not till he came to his owne castell where he dwelled, being thirtie miles distant from the place of the battell. The queene of England being certeinelie informed that the king of Scots was taken, and that John Copland had conveyed him out of the field, no man vnderstood to what place, she incontinentlie wrote to him, commanding him foorthwith to bring his prisoner king Dauid vnto hir presence: but John Copland wrote to hir againe for a determinate answer, that he would not deliuer his prisoner the said king Dauid vnto any person liuing, man or woman, except onelie to the king of England, his souereigne lord and master. Herevpon the queene wrote letters to the king, signifieng to him both of the happie victorie chanced to his people against the Scots, and also of the demeanour of John Copland, in deteining the Scotish king.'

IV. 2. 62 — 85 (Hol. II, p. 647 seq.; A. D. 1347): 'The French king perceiving he could not have his purpose, brake vp his host and returned to France, bidding Calis farewell. After that the French king with his host was once departed, without ministring anie succour to them within the towne, they began to sue for a parlee, which being granted, in the end they were contented to yeeld, and the king granted to receiue them and the towne on these conditions; that six of the cheefe burgesses of the towne should come foorth bareheaded, barefooted, and barelegged, and in their shirts, with halters about their necks, with the keies of the towne and castell in their hands, to submit themselues simplie to the kings will, and the residue he was contented to make mercie.'

IV. 3. 63—85 and IV..6. 9—17. (Hol., II, p. 665): 'Here is to be remembered that when this cardinall of Piergort was sent from the pope to trauell betwixt the parties for a peace to be had, and that the pope exhorted him verie earnestlie to shew his vttermost diligence and indeuour therein: at his setting foorth to go on that message, the said cardinall (as was said) made this answer: Most blessed father (said he) either we will persuade them to peace and quietnesse, either else shall the verie flintstones crie out of it. But this he spake not of himselfe, as it was supposed, but being a prelate in that time, he prophesied what should follow; for when the English archers had bestowed all their arrowes vpon their enimies, they tooke vp pebles from the place where they stood, being full of those kind of stones, and approching to their enimies, they drew the same with such violence on them, that lighting against their helmets, armor and targets, they made a great ringing noise, so that the cardinals prophesie was fulfilled, that he would either persuade a peace, or else the stones should crie out thereof.'

IV. 4. (Hol. II, p. 665; A. D. 1356): 'The prince offered to render into the kings hands all that he had woone in that voiage, as well townes as castels, and also to release all the prisoners, which he or any of his men had taken in that iournie: and further he was contented to haue been sworne not to beare armour against the French king within the terme of seuen yeares next following. But the French king would not agree therevnto: the vttermost that he would agree vnto, was this, that the prince and an hundred of his knights should yeeld themselues as prisoners vnto him, other-wise he would not haue the matter taken vp. . . . But the prince in no wise could be brought to any such vnreasonable condition.'

IV. 5. (Hol. II, p. 638, A. D. 1346: Cressy): 'Also at the same instant there fell a great raine and an eclipse with a terrible thunder, and before the raine, there came flieng ouer both armies a great number of crowes, for feare of the tempest comming: then

anon the aire began to wax cleare, and the sunne to shine faire
and bright, which was right in the Frenchmen's eies, and on the
Englishmen's backes . . .'

IV. 6. (Hol. II, p. 666; A. D. 1356): 'The vaward of the Frenchmen... began to disorder within a while, by reason of the shot of
the archers, togither with the helpe of the men of armes, amongst
whome in the forefront was the lord Iames Audeley, to performe
a vow which he had made, to be one of the first setters on . . . .
The noble prowesse of the said lord Iames Audley breaking through
the Frenchmens battell with the slaughter of many enimies was
that day most apparant. The loiall constancie of the noble earles
of Warwike and Suffolke, that fought so stoutlie, so earnestlie, and
so fiercelie, was right manifest. And the prince himselfe did not
onelie fulfill the office of a noble cheefteine, but also of a right
valiant and expert souldiour, attempting whatsoeuer any other
warriour would in such case have done.'

IV. 7. (Hol. II, p. 667): 'The prince of Wales . . . manfullie
assailed the maine battell of the Frenchmen, where the king himselfe was, who like a valiant prince would not flee, but fought
right manfullie: so that if the fourth part of his men had doone
halfe their parts as he did his, the victorie by likelihood had rested
(as Froissard saith) on his side: but he was forsaken by his three
sonnes, and of his brother the duke of Orleence, which fled out of
the battle with cleare hands. Finallie, after huge slaughter made
of those noblemen, and other which abode with him euen to the
end, he was taken, and so likewise was his yongest son Philip.'

IV. 8 and 9. 18—59. (Hol. II, p. 668): 'The prince gaue to the
lord Iames Audelie (who had receiued in the battell many sore
wounds) fiue hundred marks of yearelie reuenues assigned foorth
of his lands in England. The which gift the knight granted as
freelie as he had receiued it vnto foure of his esquiers, which in
the battell had beene euer attendant about his person, without
whose aid and valiant support he knew well that he had beene
slaine sundrie times in the same battell by his enimies, and therefore thought it a dutie of humanitie and gratitude to make them
amends with some temporall recompense that had saued his life,
than the which nothing is more deere . . . When the prince heard
that he had so doone, he meruelled What his meaning was thereby,
and caused him to be brought before his presence, and demanded

of him wherefore he had bestowed vpon him, and whether he thought that gift too meane for him or not. The lord Audelie so excused himselfe in extolling the good seruice doone to him by his esquiers, though he had so manie times escaped the dangers of death, that the prince did not onelie confirme the resignation of the fiue hundred marks, but gaue him fiue hundred marks more of like yearelie reuenues, in maner and forme as he had receiued the other.'

IV. 9. 1—17. Holinshed relates (II, p. 668): 'The prince made a great supper in his lodging that night to the French king, and to the most part of his nobles that were taken prisoners, and did all the honour that he could deuise to the king. And where he perceiued by his cheere and countenance, that his heart was full of pensiue greefe, carefull thought, and heauinesses, he comforted him in the best manner that he might.'

V. 1—3 and 64—96. (Hol. II, 645): 'King Edward immediatly by letters commanded Iohn Copland to repaire vnto him where he laie at siege before Calis, which with all conuenient speed he did, and there so excused himselfe of that which the queene had found hirselfe greeued with him, for deteining the king of Scots from hir, that the king did not onelie pardon him, but also gaue to him fiue hundred pounds sterling of yearelie rent, to him and to his heires bodie, commanding him yet vpon his returne into England to deliuer king Dauid vnto the queene, which he did, and so excused himselfe also vnto hir, that she was therewith satisfied and contented. Then the queene, after she had taken order for the safe keeping of the king of Scots, and good gouernement of the realme, tooke the sea and sailed ouer to the king hir husband still lieng before Calis.'

V. 4—59. (Hol. II, 647): 'This determinate resolution of king Edward being intimated to the commons of the towne, assembled in the market-place by the sound of the common bell before the capteine, caused manie a weeping eie amongst them: but in the end, when it was perceiued that no other grace would be obteined, six of the most wealthie burgesses of all the towne agreed to hazard their liues for the safeguard of the residue, and so according to the prescript order deuised by the king they went foorth to the gates, and were presented to the king, before whome they kneeled downe, offered to him the keies of the towne, and besought him to haue mercie upon them. But the king regarded them with a fell coun-

tenance, commanded stre ight that their heads should be striken off.
And although many of the noble men did make great intreatance
for them, yet would no grace be shewed, vntill the queene, being
great with child, came and kneeled downe before the king hir
husband, and with lamentable cheere and weeping eies intreated
so much for them, that finallie the kings anger was assuaged and
his rigor turned to mercie so that he gaue the prisoners vnto hir
to doo hir pleasure with them. Then the queene commanded
them to be brought into hir chamber, and caused the halters to
be taken from their necks, clothed them anew, gaue them their
dinner, and bestowing vpon ech of them six nobles, appointed them
to be conueied out of the host in safeguard, and set at libertie.'

None other of the so-called Pseudo-shakespearian plays has
so often been ascribed to England's greatest poet as King Edward III.
For the first time we find it attributed to Shakespeare in T. Goff's
Catalogue 1656. More than a hundred years later Capell took up
T. Goff's suggestion and printed Edward III. as 'a Play thought to
be writ by Shakespeare.' Far, however, from obtruding his hypothesis upon the reader, Capell unpretendingly says in the Introduction of the play: 'it must be confess'd that its being his work
is conjecture only, and matter of opinion, and the reader must
form one of his own, guided by what is now before him, and by
what he shall meet with in perusal of the piece itself.' With much
less reserve J. P. Collier stood up for Shakespeare's authorship in
his essay: 'King Edward III.: a historical play by William Shakespeare. An essay in vindication of Shakespeare's authorship of the
play.' (Privately printed; dated Maidenhead, March 14th, 1874.)
He even goes as far as to say at the end of his essay: 'I take
shame to myself that I could omit, in both my editions of Shakespeare, such a grand contribution to the series of our English
dramas as King Edward III.' [1]
In Germany Tieck seems to have been of opinion that the
play was composed by Shakespeare. Attributing plays of much

[1] In a letter addressed to the Athenæum (No. 2422, March 28, 1874,
p. 426) J. P. Collier set forth the same theory, in a somewhat abridged form,
but without adding any new arguments to it.

less intrinsic value to Shakespeare, he would certainly also have claimed Edward III. for his favorite poet, if he had got the opportunity of publishing the introduction which he had promised to add to Baudissin's translation. The subsequent translators, Ortlepp and Moltke, likewise think Shakespeare to have been the author of the play; neither of them, however, gives any reasons for his supposition. Moltke, it is true, promised in a postscript added to his translation to treat the question at large in his Shakespeare-Museum; but the latter ceased to exist, before any article in vindication of Shakespeare's authorship of our play had been published in it.

In the first edition of 'Shakespeare's Dramatische Kunst' Ulrici, judging only from Baudissin's translation of the play, was inclined to ascribe Edward III. to Shakespeare [1]); in the third edition of his book, however, having meanwhile read the English original, he no longer believes Shakespeare to have been the author of the play, though still freely allowing the great merits of which the play is possessed.

What were the reasons, we ask, which engaged Capell and Collier, the German translators, and for a time so eminent a critic as Ulrici, to attribute the play to Shakespeare?

The period into which our play leads us is among the most brilliant in English history. The victories obtained by King Edward in France, and the triumphs gained by his son the Black Prince over the French king must have filled the heart of every Englishman with pride and delight, and might well have tempted the pen of a poet like Shakespeare. The same sources, Holinshed and Painter, which so richly yielded for the Histories and Comedies, also afforded ample materials for the reign of King Edward III.

But not only the subject itself, but also the manner in which it is treated, reminds the reader of Shakespeare. In the first scenes the King appears to be bent only on prosecuting his rights in France and on delivering his country from the inroads of the

---

[1]) Ulrici's opinion was acceded to by Ch. Knight in his Pictorial Edition of Shakspere's Works, Doubtful Plays, p. 280 seqq.

treacherous Scot. The highest designs that ever king devised, are floating before his mind's eye: he will procure both the happiness and greatness of his country. But before destiny thinks him worthy of mastering his mighty foes, he must master himself and get the upperhand of his own unruly temper. The mighty King, whose very approach makes his enemies tremble, who appears to us as the bravest of the brave, plays quite an unworthy and unkingly part as soon as he leaves the path of honour and casts his eye on the wife of his vassal. He scolds at the drum which interrupts his love-sick musing; he prefers the company of his poet-secretary to that of his loyal generals; he lends no ear to the account of his ambassadors, and it is only for a moment that the aspect of his warlike son reminds him of his duty: no sooner does he hear the word Countess than he sinks back again into his shameful passion. True energy, however, and true greatness of mind will overcome all temptations. The virtue and chastity of the Countess form the bright star which leads the king back again to the way of honour and duty. Having conquered himself, Edward, truly great, may conquer others. The proud King of France and his overweening sons must feel the edge of Edward's sword: God gives the victory not to him who boasts of his own strength and confides in his own superior power, but to him whose cause is just and whose character has proved worthy of victory. And that indeed King Edward is worthy of victory, is well indicated at the end of the play by the mercy which he shows to the stubborn inhabitants of Calais. Thus, it will seem, the author has tried to show in his play that he only deserves to be crowned with success, and to become a master of others who strives to check his own passions, and to be a master of himself. There is no doubt that the same idea pervades a great number of the tragedies and historical plays of Shakespeare.[1]

Besides the king some other characters of the play are delineated in a manner which sufficiently proves that the author of King Edward III. was superior to the greater number of contemporary

---

[1] Mr. Furnivall (Leopold-Shakspere, p. CII) points out the double repetition of the leading idea of the King-and-Countess scene — a man won from intended baseness by the appeal of a nobler nature: first, Prince Charles of France by Villiers's appeal to him; second, King John of France by his son Prince Charles's appeal to him.

playwrights. The King's Son, the famous Black Prince, appears to us possessed with all those qualities which made him the darling prince of the English nation. Though he has just left his study and books, he is equal in valour and fearlessness to any knight who has passed his life in battle and slaughter. The battalions of the French surround him 'like emmets on a bank', and none is near to succour him; but his dauntless sword carves him a way and wins him a well-deserved knighthood. With his own hand he slays the mighty ally of the French, the king of Boheme; with his own hand he takes King John prisoner, and thus ends the long war. Though encompassed by the greatest dangers, the Prince, full of noble pride, rejects the dishonourable conditions proposed to him by the French king; but his heart bleeds when seeing Old Audley, his faithful companion, wounded to death, and in every way possible he endeavours to show him his high esteem and gratitude. Not only towards his friends but also towards his enemies Edward proves kind-hearted and humane: all those towns which willingly yield to his arms are spared by him, and only those which stubbornly make head against him must taste of the bitter fruit of war. On the height of glory and success the Prince does not forget that Heaven has chosen him to be his instrument, and humbly he acknowledges that God alone has guided his hand and sword. Only one feature seems not to be in unison with the character of the Prince as represented by our poet. When King John and his son have been taken prisoners, Prince Edward addresses them in a discourteous and even rude manner. This behaviour is the more surprising to us as according to Holinshed he did all in his power to pay his respect to the captive monarch, and to make him forget his misfortune.

The contrast between Edward and his adversaries is well set forth by the poet. All the virtues with which the king of England and the Black Prince are adorned, fall short in King John and his sons. As the cause for which they have taken up arms, is defective in itself, so their own and their soldiers' courage is far from being equal to the task. King Edward confides in God and his right, King John only trusts in his superior powers; the minds of the English rest unshaken by all vicissitudes of fortune, the French stand horror-stricken on hearing a mere prophesy. The English king and the Prince of Wales are loyal and equitable both

to their friends and enemies, the king of France eveu refuses to
ratify the word pawned by his own son. So indeed it seems but
just that the French king and his sons should be subdued by the
English.

Little is to be said of the generals and captains forming the
train of the two kings; in sentiment and even in language they
seem to be cast in the same mould; loyalty and courage are the
principles on which all of them regulate their doings.

With much more skill the poet has drawn the portrait of two
representatives of the English and French people. Copland, the
squire who refuses to give up his prisoner King David of Scotland
to any other person but to the king, is indeed a thoroughly
English character. His upright though stubborn behaviour must
deservedly have been applauded by the English public of the age
of Queen Elizabeth.

The episode in which Villiers plays the principal part has
not been taken from Holinshed. The poet doubtless added those
scenes, not only to set forth the mean character of the French
king, but also to represent the enemies of his nation as not wholly
devoid of honour and righteousness.

The talent of the author of our play, however, may best be
seen in the Countess-episode (I. 2 — IL 2). Out of the heroine of
a dull Italian novel he has formed a character which would certainly have done honour to any playwright of the age. The
Countess is indeed, as A. W. Ward (Engl. Dram. Lit., I, p. 457)
says, 'the true representative of high breeding united to moral
purity. Bright and courteous in word and demeanour, she is as
firm in her adherence to virtue as the prude who has no answer
but a shudder to the first suggestion of harm. She is the type
of what the king acknowledges her to be, when her constancy
has overcome his passion:

Arise, true English lady.'

It is true that also this episode is not without its drawbacks. We
shall hardly sympathize with the part the Earl of Warwick plays
as go-between between the king and his daughter, the Countess
of Salisbury. No right-minded person could ever have hit upon
Warwick's expedient in order to settle the conflict between honour
and duty. In Bandello's Novel first the Count and afterwards the
Countess simply advise their daughter to yield to the king; the

author of our play was well aware that such a character would not become the English stage; but trying to modify it, he did not succeed in giving it such a turn as to excite our sympathy.

But be this as it may, certain it is that the poet did not want power to fix and develop a character which he beheld before his mind's eye.

As to the diction of the play, it must be allowed that in a number of passages it rises above the pitch generally attained by the playwrights of the age (Cp. I. 1. 67 seqq., II. 2. 174 seqq., IV. 4. 40 seqq., IV. 5. 92 seqq.). It is more surprising that sometimes thoughts and expressions occurring in Shakespearian plays are also to be met with in King Edward III.[1]) Cp., e. g.,

I. 2. 131	*Now, in the Sunne alone it doth not lye,* *With light to take light from a mortall eye.*
and L. L. L. I. 1. 77	*Light, seeking light, doth light of light beguile.*
II. 1. 255 seqq.	*He that doth clip or counterfeit your stamp,* *Shall die, my Lord: And will your sacred selfe* *Comit high treason against the King of heauen,* *To stamp his Image in forbidden mettel,* *Forgetting your alleageance and your othe.*
and Meas. II. 4. 42	*It were as good* *To pardon him that hath from nature stolen* *A man already made, as to remit* *Their saucy sweetness, that do coin Heaven's image* *In stamps that are forbid.*
II. 1. 438	*The freshest summers day doth soonest taint* *The lothed carrion that it seemes to kisse.*
and Haml. II. 2. 181	*For if the sun breed maggots in a dead dog, being* *a good kissing carrion.*
IV. 4. 140	*If, then, we hunt for death, why do we feare it?* *If we feare it, why do we follow it?* *If we do feare, how can we shun it?* *If we do feare, with feare we do but aide* *The thing we feare, to seize on vs the sooner:* *If wee feare not, then no resolued proffer* *Can ouerthrow the limit of our fate;*

---

[1]) Cp., particularly, H. von Friesen's essay: Edward III., angeblich ein Stück von Shakespeare (Shakespeare-Jahrbuch II, p. 64).

For, whether ripe or rotten, drop we shall,
As we do drawe the lotterie of our doome.

and Jul. Cæs. II. 2. 32 *Cowards die many times before their deaths;*
The valiant never taste of death but once.
Of all the wonders that I yet have heard,
It seems to me most strange that men should fear;
Seeing that death, a necessary end,
Will come, when it will come.

IV. 9. 29 *My armes shall be thy grave.*

and 1H VI., IV. 7. 32 *Now my old arms are young John Talbot's grave.*

V. 1. 39 *Ah, be more milde vnto these yeelding men!*
It is a glorious thing to stablish peace,
And kings approch the nearest vnto God
By giuing life and safety vnto men.

and Merch. IV. 1. 192 *But mercy is above this sceptred sway,*
It is enthroned in the hearts of kings,
It is an attribute of God himself,
And earthly power doth then show likest God's,
When mercy seasons justice.

The line II. 1. 451 *Lillies, that fester, smel far worse then weeds* even literally occurs again in Shakespeare's Sonnets (94, 14), and the passage II. 2. 195 seqq.

Arise, true English Ladie; whom our Ile
May better boast of, then ever Romaine might
Of her, whose ransackt treasurie hath taskt
The vaine indeuor of so many pens

is considered by most critics as a direct allusion to Shakespeare's Lucrece.

Considering all these arguments we can hardly be astonished that Capell, the German translators, and Collier have felt inclined to ascribe the play to Shakespeare. And yet, though our play is certainly superior to many other contemporary pieces, and though some passages even directly remind the reader of Shakespeare, we are nevertheless of opinion that the whole of the play is such as to prevent us from adopting the hypothesis of Shakespeare's authorship.

The object which Shakespeare had in view in all his historical plays, was to represent the strife of human weakness and frailty against the unshaken decrees of fate. Thus he infused historical facts with new life, and interested his own age and all times in the destiny of his heroes; thus he succeeded in forming histories into tragedies. The author of Edward III., however, far from con-·ceiving the full meaning of history, was content skilfully to combine within the narrow limits of a play the most remarkable events of the reign of the great English king. His play is no more than a versified chronicle, and with the only exception of the king, not even an attempt is made to give the development of a character.

The sources from which Shakespeare invariably drew the subject of his historical plays were the chronicles of Holinshed and Hall; in none he made use of two sources so much opposed to each other as Painter's Novel is to Holinshed's Chronicle. The reign of King Edward is among the brightest chapters in English history; the names of the king and his warlike son are closely connected with the most splendid triumphs ever gained by the English people. It would indeed be surprising if Shakespeare, aware as he was of the dignity of history, should in drawing the picture of Edward III. have had recourse to an anecdote related by an Italian novelist. But even supposing he should have done so in the beginning of his dramatical career, he would certainly even then have more harmoniously interwoven the two plots with one another. Though there may indeed exist a sort of interior connexion between the episode and the principal plot, yet it appears more than doubtful whether the link joining the two parts was easily, if at all, discoverable by the play-going public of the age. The last three acts contain no more than two or three direct references to the main plot of the first two acts (III. 3.· 156 seq. and III. 5. 102); not even the names of the Countess, the heroine of the episode, and of Ludowick, the king's secretary, are mentioned again in the rest of the play. In most of his plays Shakespeare has united several actions into one: but in none is there so wide a chasm between them as in Edward III.

As to the composition of the principal plot, it is not to be denied that the author has selected with some skill the most important and interesting passages of Holinshed's chronicle, and it matters little that in some details he has thought fit to deviate from the strict course of history.[1]) But every attentive reader of the play must notice that the single scenes are not seldom as little internally connected as the two principal plots. Besides the progress of the play is sometimes impeded by a long narrative where we should have preferred to assist at the action itself. Add besides that most characters in the play suffer from a certain monotony, and that some of them, as Warwick and in some measure also the Prince of Wales, show real deficiencies such as never occur in Shakespeare.[2])

Nor does the general character of the style in our play speak in favour of Shakespeare's authorship. Mr. Furnivall is not wrong in saying (Leopold-Shakspere, p. C) that nearly all the characters talk in the same high exaggerated style. Isolated passages which remind the reader of Shakespeare, cannot be taken into account. First of all, we must not forget that some weak and trivial passages occur beside lines not unworthy of Shakespeare. Some phrases which are to be met with both in our play and in the genuine Works of Shakespeare belong neither to Shakespeare nor the author of Edward III., but to the age in which the plays were written, and it would not be difficult to gather the same or similar expressions from the works of other contemporary authors. But how are we to account for those two passages which to all appearance directly refer to Shakespeare? First, it is not beyond all doubt that, uncertain as the date of the play is, the passage (II. 2. 195) must needs have been written with respect to Shakespeare's poem.[3]) But even supposing that the line refers to it, it is, as Prof. Elze has already pointed out (Shakespeare-Jahrb. XIII, p. 79), highly improbable that Shakespeare should have called his poem, which we know had been very well received by his contemporaries[4]), a 'vain endeavour' of his pen. Much more

---

[1]) The war began in 1337 with King Philip of France. 1340 Naval Battle of Sluice. 1346 Battle of Crecy. 1346—1347 Siege of Calais. 1356 Battle of Poitiers against King John.

[2]) Also the lines II. 1. 194 seqq., 222 seqq. hardly agree with the character of the Countess, as intended by the poet. Cp. Friesen, l. c., p. 80.

[3]) The story of Lucrece was treated in a novel by Bandello-Painter which must have been known to the author of our play, in a ballad (Evans's Old Ballads, 1810, II, p. 301), and perhaps also in an early play.

[4]) *'The sweet witty soul of Ovid lives in mellifluous and honey-tongued Shakespeare. Witness his Venus and Adonis, his Lucreece, his sugared Sonnets among his private friends.'* Meres, Palladis Tamia, 1598.

likely it seems on the contrary that the author of King Edward III.,
envious of Shakespeare, should have somewhat depreciatingly have
alluded to the poem of his great rival. Neither can the line which
occurs again in the Sonnets, be considered as an absolutely cogent
argument. In no other instance has Shakespeare taken a verse
of one play to employ it in another one.[1]) From Meres, Palladis
Tamia 1598, we learn that Shakespeare's Sonnets, before being
published, were circulating among his private friends. So it may
well be supposed that the author of Edward III. should either
directly or indirectly have heard or read the verse in question
and have applied it in his play. Besides, the line, as H. von
Friesen rightly points out, agrees much better with the context of
the Sonnets than of the Play.

After all this, we are convinced that Shakespeare is not to
be regarded as the author of King Edward III. And indeed, bad
Shakespeare composed the play, it would be highly surprising that
neither Meres should have mentioned it, nor that the editors of
the first Folio-edition, though printing Love's Labour's Lost and
Romeo and Juliet after the quartos published by Cuthbert Burby
in 1598 and 1599 (through the reprint of 1609), should have ex-
cluded from their edition Edward III., published some years before
by the same Cuthbert Burby.

The best passages of the play, those perhaps which have
given rise to the hypothesis of Shakespeare's authorship, are to
be met with in the Countess-episode. There we find the greater
part of the locutions which remind the reader of Shakespeare;
there the allusion to Lucrece and the line from the Sonnets;
there lastly the character of the Countess, which is superior to all
the rest. No wonder, therefore, that part of the critics have felt
inclined to ascribe the episode at least to Shakespeare. This hypo-

---

'And Shakespeare, thou whose honey-flowing vein
Pleasing the world thy praises doth obtain,
Whose Venus and whose Lucreece, sweet and chaste,
Thy name in Fame's immortal book hath placed.'
R. Barnefield, Poems in Divers Humorous Persons, 1598.
 [1]) 2 H. VI., I. 1. 237 and III. 1. 86 cannot be taken into account.

thesis was started by Mr. Fleay, Academy 1874, April 25, p. 461 seqq.,
and Shakespeare Manual 1878, p. 303 seqq.

Mr. Fleay is of opinion that two hands have been at work in
the composition of the play. 'The two parts', he says, 'are distinctly different in general style and poetic power; they are also
clearly separated by metrical characteristics of the most pronounced
kind. They are equally distinguished by the use or disuse of
special words; and the personages common to the two portions
of the play — for example the Black Prince — have different
characters in those portions and are unequally developed.' All
these arguments, however, are merely indicated; only one — the
metrical test — is more at large developed by Mr. Fleay. As the
latter in many cases is important, we subjoin a table in which the
metrical peculiarities of our play have been set forth.

Act and Scene	Verse-lines	Rhyme-lines	Lines with double endings
I. 1	169	10	6
I. 2	166	50	11
II. 1	459	36	56
II. 2	212	8	21
III. 1	189	10	3
III. 2	75	6	3
III. 3	228	6	5
III. 4	13	1	—
III. 5	115	2	1
IV. 1	43	—	6
IV. 2	85	4	4
IV. 3	85	2	6
IV. 4	161	2	15
IV. 5	127	10	9
IV. 6	17	1	1
IV. 7	35	—	5
IV. 8	10	1	1
IV. 9	64	8	3
V.	243	4	4

On examining the list given above, we see, it is true, that
the total sum of rhymes is greater in the episode than in the
principal play. (Proportion of verse-lines to rhyme-lines in the

Independently of Mr. Fleay, Prof. A. W. Ward, A History of
English Dramatic Literature, 1875, I, p. 455 has come to a similar
conclusion. He even goes a step further than Mr. Fleay. In his
opinion, not only the episode is, both in language and characteri-
sation, not unworthy of Shakespeare, but also in the rest of the
play the learned Professor supposes a hand resembling Shake-
peare's, if not his own, to have been at work to relieve the mere
facts borrowed from the Chronicles. Prof. Ward thinks it not
impossible that Shakespeare 'made use of an earlier piece, introducing the entire episode of acts I and II, and modifying and
altering the substance of the entire play into its remaining acts.'
'But', he adds (p. 457) 'it is only for the first two acts that I
claim the honour of being recognised as wholly or at least substantially his. They are full of the conceits in which he indulged
in his earlier period; but they are conceits of so happy and thought-
ful a kind as not to contradict the theory suggested.' The same
remarks as we have made on Mr. Fleay's theory apply to Prof.
Ward's suggestion. Neither is it established that two authors have
been at work in the composition of our play, nor is there any
reason for supposing Shakespeare to have written part of the play.

In the third edition of 'Shakespeare's Dramatische Kunst'
Ulrici finds that both in style and composition Edward III. bears
a certain resemblance to Lodge's The Wounds of Civil War, and
thinks it not unlikely that Th. Lodge was the author of the play.
But as all external evidence is wanting, Ulrici himself gives his
suggestion as a mere guess, and indeed it seems hardly possible
ever to give a positive answer to the question as to the authorship of The Reign of King Edward III.

THE RAIGNE

OF

KING EDWARD THE THIRD.

DRAMATIS PERSONÆ.[1]

EDWARD III., *King of England.*
EDWARD, *Prince of Wales, his Son.*
Earl of WARWICK.
Earl of DERBY.
Earl of SALISBURY.
Lord AUDLEY.
Lord PERCY.
LODOWICK, EDWARD'S *Confident.*
SIR WILLIAM MOUNTAGUE.
SIR IOHN COPLAND.
Two Esquires, and a Herald.
ROBERT, *styling himself Earl, of*
  ARTOYS.
Earl of MOUNTFORD.
GOBIN DE GRAY.
IOHN, *King of France.*
CHARLES, *and* PHILIP, *his Sons.*
Duke of LORRAIN.

VILLIERS, *a French Lord.*
King of BOHEMIA } *Aids to King*
A Polish Captain }   *Iohn.*
Six Citizens
A Captain } *of Calais.*
A poor Inhabitant
Another Captain.
A Mariner.
Three Heralds.
Four Frenchmen.
DAVID, *King of Scotland.*
Earl DOUGLAS.
Two Scotch Messengers.

PHILIPPA, EDWARD'S *Queen.*
Countess of SALISBURY.
A French Woman.

Lords, and divers other Attendants;

Heralds, Officers, Soldiers etc.

Scene, dispersed; in ENGLAND, FLANDERS, *and* FRANCE.

---

[1] First add. by Cap.

ACT I.

SCENE I.

London. A Room of State in the Palace. Flourish.
Enter KING EDWARD, DERBY, PRINCE EDWARD, AUDLEY, *and* ARTOYS.

King. Robert of Artoys, banisht though thou be
From Fraunce, thy natiue Country, yet with vs
Thou shalt retayne as great a Seigniorie:
For we create thee Earle of Richmond heere.
And now goe forwards with our pedegree: 5
Who next succeeded Phillip le Bew?
   Art. Three sonnes of his, which all successively
Did sit vpon their fathers regall Throne,
Yet dyed, and left no issue of their loynes.
   King. But was my mother sister vnto those?   10
   Art. Shee was, my Lord; and onely Issabel
Was all the daughters that this Phillip had,
Whome afterward your father tooke to wife;
And from the fragrant garden of her wombe
Your gratious selfe, the flower of Europes hope,   15
Deriued is inheritor to Fraunce.
But note the rancor of rebellious mindes:
When thus the lynage of le Bew was out,
The French obscurd your mothers Priuiledge,
And, though she were the next of blood, proclaymed   20

ACT I. SCENE I. Stage-dir. First in Cap. *Enter* KING EDWARD, *attended;*
PRINCE OF WALES; WARWICK, DERBY; AUDLEY, ARTOIS, *and Others.* Cap.
and Del. — 6. *succeeded to* Coll. conj.; *Phillip of Bew* AB, corr. by Cap. —
7. *who all* Cap. prop.; *successefully* AB, corr. by Cap. — 17. *note*] *not* A. —
18. *of Bew* AB, *of le Beau* first Cap.

Iohn, of the house of Valoys, now their king:
The reason was, they say, the Realme of Fraunce,
Repleat with Princes of great parentage,
Ought not admit a gouernor to rule,
25 Except he be discended of the male;
And thats the speciall ground of their contempt,
Wherewith they study to exclude your grace:
But they shall finde that forged ground of theirs
To be but dusty heapes of brittile sande.
30 Perhaps it will be thought a heynous thing,
That I, a French man, should discouer this;
But heauen I call to recorde of my vowes:
It is not hate nor any priuate wronge,
But loue vnto my country and the right,
35 Prouokes my tongue, thus lauish in report.
You are the <u>lyneal</u> watchman of our peace,
And Iohn of Valoys indirectly climbes:
What then should subiects but imbrace their king?
And wherein may our duety more be seene,
40 Then stryuing to rebate a tyrants pride
And place the true shepheard of our comonwealth?
    King. This counsayle, Artoyes, like to fruictfull shewers,
Hath added growth vnto my dignitye;
And, by the fiery vigor of thy words,
45 Hot courage is engendred in my brest,
Which heretofore was <u>rakt</u> in ignorance,
But nowe doth mount with golden winges of fame,
And will approue faire Issabells discent
Able to yoak their stubburne necks with steele,
50 That spurne against my souereignety in France. [*Sound a horne.*
A messenger? — Lord Awdley, know from whence.

             Exit AUDLEY, *and returns.*

    Aud. The Duke of Lorrayne, hauing crost the seas,
Intreates he may haue conference with your highnes.

<hr>

    30. ART. *Perhaps* ,.. AB; ART. struck out by Cap. — 36. *watchmen*
AB, *watchman* Del. and Col. — 39. *And*] *Ah* AB, *And* proposed by Cap.
and adopted by Del. — 41. *And* om. by Cap. and subs. Edd. — 50. [*Cornet
within.*] mod. Edd. — 51. Stage-dir. add. by Tyr. and Del.

King. Admit him, Lords, that we may heare the newes.

Enter LORRAYNE.

Say, Duke of Lorrayne, wherefore art thou come?   ·   55
    Lor. The most renowned prince, King Iohn of France,
Doth greete thee, Edward, and by me commandes,
That, for so much as by his liberall gift
The Guyen Dukedome is entayld to thee,
Thou do him lowly homage for the same.   60
And, for that purpose, here I somon thee,
Repaire to France within these forty daies,
That there, according as the coustome is,
Thou mayst be sworne true liegeman to our king;
Or else thy title in that prouince dyes,   65
And hee himself will repossesse the place.
    King. See, how occasion laughes me in the face!
No sooner minded to prepare for France,
But straight I am inuited, — nay, with threats,
Vppon a penaltie, inioynd to come: 70
Twere but a childish part to say him nay. —
Lorrayne, returne this answere to thy Lord:
I meane to visit him as he requests;
But how? not seruilely disposd to bend,
But like a conquerer to make him bowe.   75
His lame vnpolisht shifts are come to light;
And trueth hath puld the visard from his face,
That sett a glosse vpon his arrogance.
Dare he commaund a fealty in mee?
Tell him, the Crowne that hee vsurpes, is myne,   80
And where he sets his foote, he ought to knele.
Tis not a petty Dukedome that I claime,
But all the whole Dominions of the Realme;
Which if with grudging he refuse to yeld,

    54. Stage-dir. *Enter a Messenger Lorrayne.* after l. 51 AB; *Exeunt
Lords. King takes his State. Re-enter Lords; with* LORRAIN, *attended.
Tyr. and Del.* — 64. *our*] *the* B and Edd. — 71. *foolish* B and Edd. —
76. *shists* A. — 78. *glasse* A; cp. *to set a gloss on* 1 H. VI., IV. 1. 103;
Tim. I. 2. 16.

85 Ile take away those borrowed plumes of his,
   And send him naked to the wildernes.
    Lor.   Then, Edward, here, in spight of all thy Lords,
   I doe pronounce defyaunce to thy face.
    Prince.   Defiance, French man? we rebound it backe,
90 Euen to the bottom of thy masters throat.
   And, be it spoke with reuerence of the king,
   My gratious father, and these other Lordes,
   I hold thy message but as scurrylous,
   And him that sent thee, like the lazy droane,
95 Crept vp by stelth vnto the Eagles nest;
   From whence weale shake him with so rough a storme,
   As others shalbe warned by his harme.
    War.   Byd him leaue off the Lyons case he weares,
   Least, meeting with the Lyon in the feeld,
100 He chaunce to teare him peecemeale for his pride.
    Art.   The soundest counsell I can giue his grace,
   Is to surrender ere he be constraynd.
   A voluntarie mischiefe hath lesse scorne,
   Then when reproch with violence is borne.
105   *Lor.*   Degenerate Traytor, viper to the place
   Where thou wast fostred in thine infancy,
   Bearest thou a part in this conspiracy?   [*He drawes his Sword.*
    King.   Lorraine, behold the sharpnes of this steele:
   Feruent desire that sits against my heart,   [*Drawing his.*
110 Is farre more thornie-pricking than this blade;
   That, with the nightingale, I shall be scard,
   As oft as I dispose my selfe to rest,
   Vntill my collours be displaide in Fraunce:
   This is thy finall Answere; so be gone.
115   *Lor.*   It is not that, nor any English braue,
   Afflicts me so, as doth his poysoned view,
   That is most false, should most of all be true. [*Exit* LORRAYNE,

<hr>

87. *spight*] *sight* prop. by Cap. and ad. by Del. — 105. *Regenerate*
AB and Cap., *Degenerate* Tyr. and Del. Col. says in a note: *Regenerate*
may be right, but most likely a misprint for *Degenerate*. In Rich. II., I. 1. 144.
Shakespeare has '*A recreant and most degenerate traitor*'. — 106. *was* A, —
108. Stage-dir. [*Drawing his.*] add. by Del. — 117. Stage-dir. wanting in
AB; mod. Edd. [*Exeunt Lorrain and Train.*].

King. Now, Lords, our fleeting Barke is vnder sayle;
Our gage is throwne, and warre is soone begun,
But not so quickely brought vnto an end.   120

Enter MOUNTAGUE.

But wherefore comes Sir William Mountague?
How stands the league betweene the Scot and vs?
Mount. Crackt and disseuered, my renowned Lord.
The treacherous King no sooner was informde
Of your withdrawing of your army backe,   125
But straight, forgetting of his former othe,
He made inuasion on the bordering Townes:
Barwicke is woon, Newcastle spoyld and lost,
And now the tyrant hath beguirt with seege
The Castle of Rocksborough, where inclosd   130
The Countes Salsbury is like to perish.
King. That is thy daughter, Warwicke, is it not?
Whose husband hath in Brittayne serud so long
About the planting of Lord Mountford there?
War. It is, my Lord.   135
King. Ignoble Dauid! hast thou none to greeue
But silly Ladies with thy threatning annes?
But I will make you shrinke your snailie hornes!
First, therefore, Audley, this shalbe thy charge,
Go leuie footemen for our warres in Fraunce;   140
And, Ned, take muster of our men at armes:
In euery shire elect a seuerall band.
Let them be Souldiers of a lustie spirite,
Such as dread nothing but dishonors blot;
Be warie therefore, since we do comence   145
A famous Warre, and with so mighty a nation.
Derby, be thou Embassador for vs
Unto our Father in Law, the Earle of Henalt:
Make him acquainted with our enterprise,

118. *Lord* AB, corr. by Cap. — 121, 122. Given to MOUN. in A. —
125. *your army*] *our army* B and Del. — 134. *Mounefort* AB and Cap.,
corr. by Tyr. — 139. *this shalbe*] *let this be* Col. — 146. *mighty nation*
Cap. and Tyr.

150 And likewise will him, with our owne allies
  That are in Flaunders, to solicite too
  The Emperour of Almaigne in our name.
  My selfe, whilst you are ioyntly thus employd,
  Will, with these forces that I haue at hand,
155 March, and once more repulse the trayterous Scot.
  But, Sirs, be resolute; we shal haue warres
  On euery side; and, Ned, thou must begin
  Now to forget thy study and thy bookes,
  And vre thy shoulders to an Armors weight.
160 *Prince.* As cheereful sounding to my youthfull spleene
  This tumult is of warres increasing broyles,
  As, at the Coronation of a king,
  The ioyfull clamours of the people are,
  When *Aue, Cæsar!* they pronounce alowd.
165 Within this schoole of honor I shal learne
  Either to sacrifice my foes to death,
  Or in a rightfull quarrel spend my breath.
  Then cheerefully forward, ech a seuerall way;
  In great affaires tis nought to use delay.   *[Exeunt.*

SCENE II.

ROXBOROUGH. *Before the Castle.*

Enter the COUNTESSE.

  Count. Alas, how much in vaine my poore eyes gaze
  For souccour that my soueraigne should send!
  Ah, cosin Mountague, I feare, thou wantst
  The liuely spirit, sharpely to solicit
5 With vehement sute the king in my behalfe:
  Thou dost not tell him, what a griefe it is
  To be the scornefull captiue to a Scot,
  Either to be wooed with broad vntuned othes,
  Or forst by rough insulting barbarisme:

---

153. *while* Col. — 155. *Scots* Cap. and subsequent Edd.
  SCENE II. Stage-dir. ROXBOROUGH. *Before the Castle.* add. by Cap.;
Enter COUNTESS OF SALISBURY, *and certain of her People, vpon the Walls.*
Cap. and subs. Edd. — 3. *A cosin* A; *wants* A. — 4. *spirirt* A.

Thou doest not tell him, if hc heere preuaile, 10
How much they will deride vs in the North,
And, in their vild, vnseuill, skipping giggs,
Bray foorth their Conquest and our ouerthrow
Euen in the barraine, bleake, and fruitlesse aire.

Enter DAUID, DOUGLAS, *and* LORRAINE.

I must withdraw, the euerlasting foe 15
Comes to the wall; Ile closely step aside,
And list their babble, blunt and full of pride.
   K. Da. My Lord of Lorrayne, to our brother of Fraunce
Commend vs, as the man in Christendome
That we most reuerence and intirely loue. 20
Touching your embassage, returne and say,
That we with England will not enter parlie,
Nor neuer make faire wether, or take truce;
But burne their neighbor townes, and so persist
With eager Roads beyond their Citie Yorke. 25
And neuer shall our bonny riders rest,
Nor rusting canker haue the time to eate
Their light-borne snaffles nor their nimble spurres,
Nor lay aside their Iacks of Gymould mayle,
Nor hang their staues of grayned Scottish ash 30
In peacefull wise vpon their Citie wals,
Nor from their buttoned tawny leatherne belts
Dismisse their byting whinyards, till your King
Cry out 'Enough, spare England now for pittie!'
Farewell, and tell him that you leaue vs here 35
Before this Castle; say, you came from vs,
Euen when we had that yeelded to our hands.
   Lor. I take my leaue, and fayrely will returne
Your acceptable greeting to my king.   [*Exit Lor.*
   King. Now, Duglas, to our former taske again, 40
For the deuision of this certayne spoyle.
   Dou. My liege, I craue the Ladie, and no more.

14. Stage-dir. *Enter* KING DAVID, *and Forces; with* DOUGLAS, LOR-
RAIN, *and Others.* Del. — 17. *rabble* B; [*Retiring behind the works.*]. Del.
— 20. *Whom* Cap. and Edd.; *must* A. — 25. *Rods* AB. — 27. *rust in
canker* AB, corr. by Cap. — 28. *spurre* A. — 38. *I* om. A.

King.   Nay, soft ye, sir, first I must make my choyse,
And first I do bespeake her for my selfe.

45   *Dou.*   Why then, my liege, let me enioy her iewels.

King.   Those are her owne, still liable to her,
And, who inherits her, hath those withall,

Enter a Scot in hast,

Mes.   My liege, as we were pricking on the hils,
To fetch in booty, marching hitherward,

50   We might discry a mighty host of men;
The sunne, reflicting on the armour, shewed
A field of plate, a wood of pikes aduanced.
Bethinke your highnes speedely herein :
An easie march within foure howres will bring

55   The hindmost rancke vnto this place, my liege.

King.   Dislodge, dislodge, it is the king of England.

Dou.   Iemmy, my man, saddle my bonny blacke.

King.   Meanst thou to fight, Duglas? we are to weake.

Dou.   I know it well, my liege, and therefore flie.

60   *Count.*   My Lords of Scotland, will ye stay and drinke?

King.   She mocks at vs; Duglas, I cannot endure it.

Count.   Say, good my Lord, which is he, must haue the Ladie,
And which, her iewels? I am sure, my Lords,
Ye will not hence, till you haue shard the spoyles,

65   *King.*   Shee heard the messenger, and heard our talke;
And now that comfort makes her scorne at vs.

Annother messenger.

Mes.   Arme, my good Lord! O, we are all surprisde!

Coun.   After the French embassador, my liege,
And tell him, that you dare not ride to Yorke;

70   Excuse it, that your bonnie horse is lame.

King.   She heard that too; intollerable griefe!
Woman, farewell! Although I do not stay . . . [*Exeunt Scots.*

---

43. *ye* om. B. — 47. Stage-dir. *Enter a Messenger hastily.* Del. —
52. *pickes* A. — 59. *flee* B and Edd. — 60. [*Rising from her concealment.*]
Del. — 61. *can't* Edd. — 62. *good* om. by Cap., Tyr., and Col. — 66. [*Enter
another messenger.*] Del. — 68. COUN. om. AB. — 71. *He* AB. — 72. *stay.*]
AB and Edd., *stay . . .*] Del.; [*Alarums. Exeunt Scots.*] Del.

Coun.   Tis not for feare, and yet you run away. —
O happie comfort, welcome to our house!
The confident and boystrous boasting Scot,   75
That swore before my walls they would not backe
For all the armed power of this land,
With facelesse feare that euer turnes his backe,
Turnd hence against the blasting North-east winde,
Vpon the bare report and name of Armes,   80

Enter MOUNTAGUE.

O Sommers day! See where my Cosin comes!
   Moun.   How fares my Aunt? Why, aunt, we are not Scots;
Why do you shut your gates against your friends?
   Coun.   Well may I giue a welcome, Cosin, to thee,
For thou comst well to chase my foes from hence.   85
   Moun.   The king himselfe is come in person hither;
Deare Aunt, discend, and gratulate his highnes.
   Coun.   How may I entertayne his Maiestie,
To shew my duety and his dignitie?   [*Exit, from above.*

Enter KING EDWARD, WARWICKE, ARTOYES, *with Others.*

   King.   What, are the stealing Foxes fled and gone,   90
Before we could vncupple at their heeles?
   War.   They are, my liege; but, with a cheereful cry,
Hot hounds, and hardie, chase them at the heeles.

Enter COUNTESSE.

   King.   This is the Countesse, Warwike, is it not?
   War.   Euen shee, my liege; whose beauty tyrants feare,   95
As a May blossome with pernitious winds,
Hath sullied, withered, ouercast, and donne.
   King.   Hath she been fairer, Warwike, then she is?

<hr>

76. *they*] *he* prop. by Cap. and ad. by Del. — 79. *againe* AB, *against*
prop. by Cap. and ad. by Del. — 80. *names* B; [*Enter Montague and Others.*]
Del. — 81. *Given to Moun.* in AB. — 82. *Why, aunt* first added by Cap. —
84. *coz* Col. — 89. [*Exit, from above.*] first add. by Cap.; [*Flourish. Enter . .*]
Del. — 93. *hunds* A; [*Re-enter Countess, attended.*] Del. — 95. *my* om. A;
tyrant's Cap., *tyrant* Del. — 96. *with*] *which* B and Col. — 97. *Have* Col.

War. My gratious King, faire is she not at all,
100 If that her selfe were by to staine her selfe,
     As I haue seene her when she was her selfe.
     King. What strange enchantment lurkt in those her eyes,
When they exceld this excellence they haue,
That now their dym declyne hath power to draw
105 My subiect eyes from persing maiestie,
     To gaze on her with doting admiration?
     Coun. In duetie lower then the ground I kneele,
And for my dul knees bow my feeling heart,
To witnes my obedience to your highnes,
110 With many millions of a subiects thanks
     For this your Royall presence, whose approch
     Hath driuen war and danger from my gate.
     King. Lady, stand vp; I come to bring thee peace,
How euer thereby I haue purchast war.
115   *Coun.* No war to you, my liege; the Scots are gone,
     And gallop home toward Scotland with their hate.
     King. Least, yeelding heere, I pyne in shamefull loue,
Come, weele persue the Scots; — Artoyes, away!
     Coun. A little while, my gratious soueraigne, stay,
120 And let the power of a mighty king
     Honor our roofe; my husband in the warres,
     When he shall heare it, will triumph for ioy;
     Then, deare my liege, now niggard not thy state:
     Being at the wall, enter our homely gate.
125   *King.* Pardon me, countesse, I will come no neare;
     I dreamde to night of treason, and I feare.
     Coun. Far from this place let vgly treason ly!
     King. No farther off, then her conspyring eye,
     Which shoots infected poyson in my heart,
130 Beyond repulse of wit or cure of Art.
     Now, in the Sunne alone it doth not lye,
     With light to take light from a mortall eye;
     For here two day-stars that myne eies would see

More then the Sunne, steales myne owne light from mee.
Contemplatiue desire, desire to be   135
In contemplation, that may master thee!
Warwike, Artoys, to horse and lets away!
    Coun.   What might I speake, to make my soueraigne stay?
    King.   What needs a tongue to such a speaking eie,
That more perswads then winning Oratorie?   140
    Coun.   Let not thy presence, like the Aprill sunne,
Flatter our earth, and sodenly be done.
More happie do not make our outward wall,
Then thou wilt grace our inner house withall.
Our house, my liege, is like a Country swaine,   145
Whose habit rude and manners blunt and playne
Presageth nought; yet inly beautified
With bounties riches and faire hidden pride.
For, where the golden Ore doth buried lie,
The ground, vndeckt with natures tapestrie,   150
Seemes barrayne, sere, vnfertill, fructles, dry;
And where the vpper turfe of earth doth boast
His pide perfumes and party-colloured cost,.
Delue there, and find this issue and their pride
To spring from ordure and corruptions side.   155
But, to make vp my all too long compare,
These ragged walles no testimonie are,
What is within; but, like a cloake, doth hide
From weathers Waste the vnder garnisht pride.
More gratious then my tearmes can, let thee be;   160
Intreat thy selfe to stay a while with mee.
    King.   As wise, as faire; what fond fit can be heard,
When wisedome keepes the gate as beauties gard? —
Countesse, albeit my busines vrgeth me,
Yt shall attend, while I attend on thee: 165
Come on, my Lords; heere will I host to night.   [*Exeunt.*

134. *steal* mod. Ed'd. — 144. *inward* B and Edd. — 153. *pide*] *pride*
AB, *proud* Edd., *pied* prop. by Cap. and ad. by Del.; *perfumes*] *presumes* B.
— 157. *testomie* A. — 159. *Waste*] *West* AB, *Waste* conj. by Del. and Col.

ACT II.

SCENE I.

The Same. Gardens of the Castle.

Enter LODOWICK.

    Lod. I might perceiue his eye in her eye lost,
His eare to drinke her sweet tongues vtterance,
And changing passion — like inconstant clouds
That rackt vpon the carriage of the windes
5 Increase and die — in his disturbed cheekes.
  Loe, when shee blusht, euen then did he looke pale,
As if her cheekes by some inchaunted power
Attracted had the cherie blood from his:
Anone, with reuerent feare when she grew pale,
10 His cheekes put on their scarlet ornaments;
  But no more like her oryentall red,
Then Bricke to Corrall or liue things to dead.
Why did he then thus counterfeit her lookes?
If she did blush, twas tender modest shame,
15 Being in the sacred presence of a King;
  If he did blush, twas red immodest shame,
To vaile his eyes amisse, being a king:
If she lookt pale, twas silly womans feare,
To beare her selfe in presence of a king;
20 If he lookt pale, it was with guiltie feare,
  To dote amisse, being a mighty king.
Then, Scottish warres, farewell; I feare twill prooue
A lingring English seege of peeuish loue.
Here comes his highnes, walking all alone.

Enter KING EDWARD.

25 *King.* Shee is growne more fairer far, since I came hither,
Her voice more siluer euery word then other,
Her wit more fluent. What a strange discourse

  ACT II. SCENE I. Stage-dir. add. by Cap. — 1. LOD.] LOR. A. —
4. *racke* A. — 10. *cheeke* A.B. — 15. *present* A. — 17. *waile* A.B; cp. Shak.
Ven. 956: *she vailed her eyelids*; Meas. V. 20: *vail your regard upon a
wronged maid.* — 25. *thither* A.

Vnfolded she of Dauid and his Scots!
'Euen thus', quoth she, 'he spake', and then spoke broad,
With epithites and accents of the Scot,   30
But somewhat better then the Scot could speake:
'And thus', quoth she, and answered then her selfe!
For who could speake like her? but she her selfe
Breathes from the wall an Angels note from Heauen
Of sweete defiance to her barbarous foes.   35
When she would talke of peace, me thinkes, her tong
Commanded war to prison; when of war,
It wakened Cæsar from his Romane graue,
To heare warre beautified by her discourse.
Wisedome is foolishnes but in her tongue;   40
Beauty a slander but in her faire face;
There is no summer but in her cheerefull lookes,
Nor frosty winter but in her disdayne.
I cannot blame the Scots that did besiege her,
For she is all the Treasure of our land;   45
But call them cowards, that they ran away,
Hauiug so rich and faire a cause to stay. —
Art thou there, Lodwicke? Giue me incke and paper!

  Lod. I will, my liege.

  King. And bid the Lords hold on their play at Chesse,   50
For wee will walke and meditate alone.

  Lod. I will, my soueraigne.   [*Exit* LODOWICK.

  King. This fellow is well read in poetrie,
And hath a lustie and perswasiue spirite:
I will acquaint him with my passion,   55
Which he shall shadow with a vaile of lawne,
Through which the Queene of beauties Queenes shall see
Her selfe the ground of my infirmitie.

     Enter LODWIKE.

  King. Hast thou pen, inke, and paper ready, Lodowike?
  Lod. Ready, my liege.   60

<hr>

 29. *spoke*] *spake* B and Edd., exc. Del. — 30. *Scots* Del. — 48. *Lodowicke* B and Edd. — 49. *liege*] *soueraigne* B and Edd. — 52. *soueraigne*]
liege B and Edd. Stage-dir. first in Cap. — 53. *well* om. B. — 57. *Queenes*]
Queen AB, corr. by Del. — 59. *Lodow.* B.

King. Then in the sommer-arber sit by me,
Make it our counsel-house or cabynet:
Since greene our thoughts, greene be the conuenticle,
Where we will ease vs by disburdning them.
65 Now, Lodwike, inuocate some golden Muse,
To bring thee hither an inchanted pen,
That may for sighes set downe true sighes indeed,
Talking of griefe, to make thee ready grone;
And when thou writest of teares, encouch the word
70 Before and after with such sweete laments,
That it may rayse drops in a Tarters eye,
And make a flynt-heart Sythian pytifull;
For so much moouing hath a Poets pen:
Then, if thou be a Poet, moue thou so,.
75 And be enriched by thy soueraignes loue.
For, if the touch of sweet concordant strings
Could force attendance in the eares of hel,
How much more shall the straine of poets wit
Beguile and rauish soft and humane myndes?
80   *Lod.* To whome, my Lord, shal I direct my stile?
    King. To one that shames the faire and sots the wise;
Whose bodie, as an abstract or a breefe,
Containes ech generall vertue in the worlde.
Better then bewtifull thou must begin;
85 Deuise for faire a fairer word then faire; .
And euery ornament that thou wouldest praise,
Fly it a pitch aboue the soare of praise.
For flattery feare thou not to be conuicted;
For, were thy admiration ten tymes more,
90 Ten tymes ten thousand more the worth exceeds
Of that thou art to praise, thy praises worth.
Beginne; I will to contemplat the while:
Forget not to set downe, how passionat,

65. *Lodowicke* B and Edd. — 68. *ready*] *really* conj. by Coll. —
71. *Torters* AB; *Tartar's* Cap. and subs. Edd. — 75. *soueraigne* A. —
77. *attention* conj. by Coll.; but cp. *Give attendance to reading* I. Tim. IV.
13; *Diligent attendance to instruction.* BARROW. Quoted by Webster. —
78. *straines* A and Del. — 79. *beguild* A. — 80. LOD.] LOR. A. — 82. *bodie
is an* AB; corr. by Cap. — 90. *the*] *thy* A. — 91. *thy*] *their* AB; corr. by Cap.
— 92 *Beginne I will* AB.

How hart-sicke, and how full of languishment,
Her beautie makes mee.   95
   Lod.   Write I to a woman?
   King.   What bewtie els could triumph ouer me,
Or who but women doe our loue-layes greet?
What, thinkest thou I did bid thee praise a horse?
   Lod. Of what condicion or estate she is,
Twere requisite that I should know, my Lord.   100
   King. Of such estate, that hers is as a throane,
And my estate the footstoole where shee treads:
Then maist thou iudge what her condition is,
By the proportion of her mightines.
Write on, while I peruse her in my thoughts. —   105
Her voice to musicke or the nightingale —:
To musicke euery sommer-leaping swaine
Compares his sunburnt louer when shee speakes;
And why should I speake of the nightingale?
The nightingale singes of adulterate wrong,   110
And that, compared, is too satyrical;
For sinne, though synne, would not be so esteemd,
But, rather, vertue sin, synne vertue deemd.
Her hair, far softer then the silke-wormes twist,
Like to a flattering glas, doth make more faire   115
The yelow Amber: — like a flattering glas
Comes in too soone; for, writing of her eies,
Ile say that like a glas they catch the sunne,
And thence the hot reflection doth rebounde
Against my brest, and burnes my hart within.   120
Ah, what a world of descant makes my soule
Vpon this voluntarie ground of loue! —
Come, Lodwick, hast thou turnd thy inke to golde?
If not, write but in letters Capitall
My mistres name, and it wil guild thy paper: 125
Reade, Lorde, reade;

95. *Writ* A. — 96. *triump on* A. — 99. Lod.] Lor. A. — 115. *to*] *as*
B and Edd., except Del. — 124—126. Two lines in AB, divided at *name* | and
reade | ; three lines in Cap. and Edd., ending at *capital,* | *name,* | *read.* | . — 124. *but
write* Col. — 126. '*Read, Lord, read.* So the old copies; but young Lodowick
was not a peer, and possibly it ought to run: *Read, lad, read*; or *lord* might
possibly be taken as an exclamation of impatience, *Read, lord! Read.*' Coll.
We have perhaps to read: *Read, Lodwick, read.*

Fill thou the emptie hollowes of mine eares
With the sweete hearing of thy poetrie.
   Lod. I haue not to a period brought her praise.
130   *King.* Her praise is as my loue, both infinit,
Which apprehend such violent extremes,
That they disdaine an ending period.
Her bewtie hath no match but my affection;
Hers more then most, myne most and more then more:
135 Hers more to praise, then tell the sea by drops,
Nay, more then drop the massie earth by sands,
And sand by sand print them in memorie:
Then wherefore talkest thou of a period
To that which craues vnended admiration?
140 Read, let vs heare.
   Lod. 'More faire and chast then is the queen of shades,' —
   King. That line hath two faults, grosse and palpable:
Comparest thou her to the pale queene of night,
Who, being set in darke, seemes therefore light?
145 What is she, when the sunne lifts vp his head,
But like a fading taper, dym and dead?
My loue shall braue the eye of heauen at noon,
And, being vnmaskt, outshine the golden sun.
   Lod. What is the other faulte, my soueraigne Lord?
150   *King.* Reade ore the line againe.
   Lod.   'More faire and chast'' —
   King. I did not bid thee talke of chastitie,
To ransack so the treasure of her minde;
For I had rather haue her chased then chast:
Out with the moone-line, I wil none of it;
155 And let me haue hir likened to the sun:
Say shee hath thrice more splendour then the sun,
That her perfections emulats the sunne,
That shee breeds sweets as plenteous as the sunne,
That shee doth thaw cold winter like the sunne,
160 That she doth cheere fresh sommer like the sunne,
That shee doth dazle gazers like the sunne;

137. *And said, by said,* AB; corr. by Cap. — 142. *line*] *loue* A, —
152. *treason* AB and Col., *treasure* Cap., Tyr., and Del. — 153. *I had*],
I would Col. — 157. *perfection* Cap. and mod. Edd.

Ańd, in this application to the sunne,
Bid her be free and generall as the sunne,
Who smiles vpon the basest weed that growes
As louinglie as on the fragrant rose.　　　165
Lets see what. followes that same moonelight line.
　　Lod.　'More faire and chast then is the queen of shades,
More bould in constancie' —
　　King.　In constancie! then who? ·
　　Lod.　　　.　　　`　　　　　'Then Iudith was.'
　　King.　O monstrous line!　Put in the next a sword,　　170
And I shall woo her to cut off my head.
Blot, blot, good Lodwicke!　Let vs heare the next.
　　Lod.　Theres all ·that yet is donne.
　　King.　I thancke thee then, thou hast don litle ill;
But what is don, is passing passing ill.　　175
No, let the Captaine talke of boystrous warr; ·
The prisoner, of immured darke constraint;
The; sick man best sets downe the pangs of death; ·
The man that starues, the sweetnes of a feast;
The frozen soule, the benefite of fire;.　　180
And euery griefe, his happie opposite:
Loue cannot sound well but in louers toungs;
Giue me the pen and paper, I will write.

Enter COUNTES.

But soft, here comes the treasurer of my spirit. —
Lodwick, thou knowst not how to draw a battell;　　185
These wings, these flankars, and these squadrons
Argue in thee defectiue discipline: ·
Thou shouldest haue placed this here, this other here.
　　Count.　Pardon my boldnes, my thrice gracious Lord;
Let my intrusion here be cald my duetie,　　190
That comes to see my soueraigne how he fares.
　　King.　Go, draw the same, I tell thee in what forme.

162. *to*] *of* Col. — 167. *queen*] *louer* AB; corr. by Cap. — 177. *emured*
AB. — 184. *treasure* B and Edd., except Del. — 186. *squadrons here* Cap.
and Tyr.; but *squadrons* must be read as a trisyllable. — 189. *Lords* AB;
corr. by Cap.

2*

    Lod. I go.   [*Exit* LODOWICK.

    Count. Sorry I am to see my liege so sad :

195 What may thy subiect do to driue from thee

    Thy gloomy consort, sullome melancholie?

    King. Ah, Lady, I am blunt and cannot strawe

The flowers of solace in a ground of shame : —

Since I came hither, Countes, I am wronged.

200   *Count.* Now God forbid that anie in my howse

Should thinck my soueraigne wrong! Thrice gentle King,

Acquaint me with your cause of discontent.

    King. How neere then shall I be to remedie?

    Count. As nere, my Liege, as all my womans power

205 Can pawne it selfe to buy thy remedy. ·

    · *King.* If thou speakst true, then haue I my redresse :

Ingage thy power to redeeme my Ioyes,

And I am ioyfull, Countes ; els I die.

    Count. I will, my Liege.

    King.   Sweare, Countes, that thou wilt.

210   *Count.* By heauen, I will.

    King. Then take thy selfe a litel waie aside,

And tell thy self, a king doth dote on thee :

Say that within thy power it doth lie

To make him happy, and that thou hast sworne

215 To giue him all the Ioy within thy power :

Do this, and tell me when I shall be happie.

    Count. All this is done, my thrice dread souereigne :

That power of loue, that I haue power to giue,

Thou hast with all deuout obedience ;

220 Inploy me how thou wilt in profe thereof.

    King. Thou hearst me saye that I do dote on thee.

    Count. Yf on my beauty, take yt if thou canst ;

Though litle, I do prise it ten tymes lesse :

If on my vertue, take it if thou canst ;

225 For vertues store by giuing doth augment :

    193. LoD.] LOR. A; Stage-dir. added by Cap. — 196. *Thy*] *This* B
and Edd., except Del. — 202. Given to *K. Edw.* in A; *your*] *theyr* A. —
209. *Counties* A. — 213. *it* first add. by Cap. — 214. *that* om. B. —
215. *him*] *me* Cap. and subs. Edd. — 217. Two lines in B, divided at *done.*

Be it on what it will, that I can giue
And thou canst take awaie, inherit it.
  King.   It is thy beautie that I woulde enioy.
  Count.   O, were it painted, I would wipe it off
And dispossesse my selfe, to giue it thee.   230
But, souereigne, it is souldered to my life:
Take one, and both; for, like an humble shaddow,
Yt hauntes the sunshine of my summers life.
  King.   But thou maist lend it me, to sport withall.
  Count.   As easie may my intellectual soule   235
Be lent awaie, and yet my bodie liue,
As lend my bodie, pallace to my soule,
Awaie from her, and yet retaine my soule.
My bodie is her bower, her Court, her abey,
And shee an Angell, pure, deuine, vnspotted: 240
If I should lend her house, my Lord, to thee,
I kill my poore soule, and my poore soule me.
  King.   Didst thou not swere to giue me what I would?
  Count.   I did, my liege, so, what you would, I could.
  King.   I wish no more of thee then thou maist giue: 245
Nor beg I do not, but I rather buie;
That is, thy loue; and for that loue of thine
In rich exchaunge I tender to thee myne.
  Count.   But that your lippes were sacred, my Lord,
You would prophane the holie name of loue.   250
That loue you offer me, you cannot giue;
For Cæsar owes that tribut to his Queene:
That loue you beg of me, I cannot giue;
For Sara owes that duetie to her Lord.
He that doth clip or counterfeit your stamp,   255
Shall die, my Lord: And will your sacred selfe
Comit high treason against the King of heauen,
To stamp his Image in forbidden mettel,
Forgetting your alleageance and your othe?

    230. *disposse* A. — 234. Continued to Coun. in A; *lend*] *leue* A. —
241. *lend*] *leaue* A. — 244. *liege*] *lord* Col. — 249. *o my lord* Cap., Tyr.,
and Del.; but *sacred* is used as a trisyllable. — 257. *'gainst* Cap. and subs.
Edd., except Del.

260 In violating mariage sacred law,
    You breake a greater honor then your selfe:
    To be a king is of a younger house
    Then to be maried; your progenitour, ·
    Sole-raigning Adam on the vniuerse,
265 By God was honored for a married man,
    But not by him annointed for a king.
    It is a pennalty to breake your statutes,
    Though not enacted with your highnes hand:
    How much more, to infringe the holy act,
270 Made by the mouth of God, seald with his hand?
    I know, my souereigne, in my husbands loue,
    Who now doth loyall seruice in his warrs,
    Doth but to try the wife of Salisbury,
    Whither shee will heare a wantons tale, or no;
275 Lest being therein guilty by my stay,
    From that, not from my liege, I tourne awaie.   [*Exit.*
    · *King.*   Whether is her bewtie by her words dyuine,
    Or are her words sweet chaplaines to her bewtie?
    Like as the wind doth beautifie a saile,
280 And as a saile becomes the vnseene winde,
    So doe her words her bewties, bewties wordes.
    O, that I were a honie-gathering bee,
    To beare the combe of vertue from this flower,
    And not a poison-sucking enuious spider,
285 To turne the iuce I take to deadlie venom!
    Religion is austere and bewty gentle;
    Too strict a gardion for so faire a ward!
    O, that shee were, as is the aire, to mee!
    Why, so she is; for, when I would embrace her,
290 This do I, and catch nothing but my selfe.
    I must enioy her; for I cannot beate
    With reason and reproofe fond loue awaie.

260. *secred* A. — 268. *with*] *by* Cap. and subs. Edd. — 269. *But how*
Col. — 281. *her bewties*] *her beauty* Cap., Tyr., and Del.; *bewties words*]
bewtie (y) words AB and subs. Edd., except Col. — 283. *this*] *his* AB and Del.
— 285. *iuce*] *vice* AB and Edd.; happily corr. by Col. — 287. *To stricke*
A, *Too strict* B and Edd.; *ward*] *weed* AB; corr. by Cap.

Enter WARWICKE.

Here comes her father: I will worke with him,
To beare my collours in this field of loue.
 War. How is it that my souereigne is so sad?   295
May I with pardon know your highnes griefe,
And that my old endeuor will remoue it,
It shall not comber long your maiestie.
 King. A kind and voluntary gift thou proferest,
That I was forwarde to haue begd of thee.   300
But, O thou world, great nurse of flatterie,
Whie dost thou tip mens tongues with golden words,
And peise their deedes with weight of heauie leade,
That faire performance cannot follow promise?
O, that a man might hold the hartes close booke   305
And choke the lauish tongue, when it doth vtter
The breath of falshood not carectred there!
 War. Far be it from the honor of my age,
That I should owe bright gould and render lead;
Age is a cynike, not a flatterer.   310
I saye againe, that, if I knew your griefe,
And that by me it may be lesned,
My proper harme should buy your highnes good.
 King. These are the vulger tenders of false men,
That neuer pay the duetie of their words.   315
Thou wilt not sticke to sweare what thou hast said;
But, when thou knowest my griefes condition,
This rash disgorged vomit of thy word
Thou wilt eate vp againe, and leaue me helples.
 War. By heauen, I will not, though your maiestie   320
Did byd me run vpon your sworde and die.
 King. Say that my greefe is no way medicinable
But by the losse and bruising of thine honour.
 War. Yf nothing but that losse may vantage you,
I would account that losse my vauntage too.   325
 King. Thinkst that thou canst vnswere thy oth againe?
 War. I cannot; nor I would not, if I could.

---

 299. *offerest* B and subs. Edd. — 310. *cyncke* A. — 311. *I if* A. —
314, 315. Continued to WAR. in A. — 325. *account*] *accomplish* A. —
326. *vnswere*] *answere* AB; cott. by Cap.

  King. But, if thou dost, what shal I say to thee?
  War. What may be said to anie periurd villaine,
330 That breaks the sacred warrant of an oath.
  King. What wilt thou say to one that breaks an othe?
  War. That hee hath broke his faith with God and man,
And from them both standes excommunicat.
  King. What office were it, to suggest a man
335 To breake a lawfull and religious vowe?
  War. An office for the deuill, not for man.
  King. That deuilles office must thou do for me,
Or breake thy oth and cancell all the bondes
Of loue and duetie twixt thy self and mee;
340 And therefore, Warwike, if thou art thy selfe,
The Lord and master of thy word and othe,
Go to thy daughter; and in my behalfe
Comaund her, woo her, win her anie waies,
To be my mistres and my secret loue.
345 I will not stand to heare thee make reply:
Thy oth breake hers, or let thy souereigne dye.   *[Exit.*
  War. O doting king! O detestable office!
Well may I tempt my self to wrong my self,
When he hath sworne me by the name of God
350 To breake a vowe, made by the name of God.
What, if I sweare by this right hand of mine
To cut this right hande off? The better waie
Were to prophaine the Idoll, then confound it:
But neither will I do; Ile keepe myne oath,
355 And to my daughter make a recantation
Of all the vertue I haue preacht to her:
Ile say, she must forget her husband Salisbury,
If she remember to embrace the king;
Ile say, an othe may easily be broken,
360 But not so easily pardoned, being broken;
Ile say, it is true charity to loue,
But not true loue to be so charitable;

  329. *to*] *of* Col. — 330. *breake* A. — 338. *and*] *or* AB and Edd. —
341. *thy*] *the* Col. — 346. *breakes* B. — 347 ss. Given to KING in A; *O det.*]
or det. AB; corr. by Cap. — 350. *by*] *in* Col. — 354. *my othe* B and Edd.

Ile say, his greatnes may beare out the shame,
But not his kingdome can buy out the sinne;
Ile say, it is my duety to perswade,   365
But not her honestie to giue consent.

Enter COUNTESSE.

See where she comes: Was neuer father had
Against his child an embassage so bad!
   Count. My Lord and father, I haue sought for you:
My mother and the Peeres importune you   370
To keepe in presence of his maiestie,
And do your best to make his highnes merrie.
   War. (*Aside.*) How shall I enter in this gracelesse errand?
I must not call her child; for wheres the father
That will in such a sute seduce his child?   375
Then, 'wife of Salisbury', shall I so begin?
No, hees my friend; and where is found the friend
That will doe friendship such indammagement?
(*To the Count.*) Neither my daughter nor my deare friends wife,
I am not Warwike, as thou thinkst I am,   380
But an atturnie from the Court of hell,
That thus haue housd my spirite in his forme,
To do a message to thee from the King.
The mighty king of England dotes on thee:
He that hath power to take away thy life,   385
Hath power to take thy honor; then consent
To pawne thine honor rather then thy life:
Honor is often lost and got againe,
But life, once gone, hath no recouerie.
The Sunne, that withers heye, doth nourish grasse;   390
The king, that would distaine thee, will aduance thee.
The Poets write that great Achilles speare
Could heale the wound it made: the morrall is,
What mighty men misdoo, they can amend.
The Lyon doth become his bloody iawes,   395

   371. *presence*] *promise* A. — 373 (*Aside.*) and 379. (*To the Count.*) not
in Edd. — 373. *arrant* AB. — 386. *thine* B and Edd. — 389. *doth*] *goth* A.

And grace his forragement by being milde,
When vassell feare lies trembling at his feete.
The king will in his glory hide thy shame;
And those that gaze on him to finde out thee,
400 Will loose their eie-sight, looking in the Sunne.
What can one drop of poyson harme the Sea,
Whose hugie vastures can digest the ill
And make it loose his operation?
The kings great name will temper thy misdeed's,
405 And giue the bitter potion of reproch
A sugred sweet and most delitious tast.
Besides, it is no harme to do the thing
Which without shame could not be left vndone.
Thus haue I in his maiesties behalfe
410 Apparaled sin in vertuous sentences,
And dwel vpon thy answere in his sute.
    Count. Vnnaturall beseege! woe me vnhappie,
To haue escapt the danger of my foes,
And to be ten times worse iniured by friends!
415 Hath he no meanes to stayne my honest blood,
But to corrupt the author of my blood
To be his scandalous and vile soliciter?
No maruell though the braunches be then infected,
When poyson hath encompassed the roote:
420 No maruell though the leprous infant dye,
When the sterne dame inuennometh the Dug.
Why then, giue sinne a pasport to offend,
And youth the dangerous reine of liberty:
Blot out the strict forbidding of the law,
425 And cancell euery cannon that prescribes
A shame for shame or pennance for offence.
No, let me die, if his too boystrous will

---

402. *vastnes* conj. by Col. — 404. *thy*] *their* AB and Col.; corr. by Cap.
— 405. *portion* A. — 409. *Then* Col. — 414. *inuierd* AB, *inwir'd* Del.;
Elze, Notes on Elizabethan Dramatists, II. p. 2, thinks *inuierd* to be possibly abbreviated from *environed,* as Max Moltke prints. — 418. *No marvel
then, though the branches be infected* Cap., Tyr., and Del.; *though the
branch be then inf.* Col.; *branches* may be read as a monosyllable, cp.
Abbott s. 471. — 423. *reigne* A.

Will haue it so, before I will consent
To be an actor in his gracelesse lust.
   War.   Why, now thou speakst as I would haue thee speake: 430
And marke how I vnsaie my words againe.
An honorable graue is more esteemd
Then the polluted closet of a king:
The greater man, the greater is the thing,
Be it good or bad, that he shall vndertake: 435
An vnreputed mote, flying in the Sunne,
Presents a greater substance then it is:
The freshest summers day doth soonest taint
The lothed carrion that it seemes to kisse:
Deepe are the blowes made with a mightie Axe: 440
That sinne doth ten times agreuate it selfe,
That is committed in a holie place:
An euill deed, done by authoritie,
Is sin and subbornation: Decke an Ape
In tissue, and the beautie of the robe   445
Adds but the greater scorne vnto the beast.
A spatious field of reasons could I vrge
Betweene his glory, daughter, and thy shame:
That poyson steweth worst in a golden cup;
Darke night seemes darker by the lightning flash;   450
Lillies, that fester, smel far worse then weeds;
And euery glory that inclynes to sin,
The shame is treble by the opposite.
So leaue I with my blessing in thy bosome;
Which then conuert to a most heauie curse,   455
When thou conuertest from honors golden name
To the blacke faction of bed-blotting shame!
   Count.   Ile follow thee; and when my minde turnes so,
My body sinke my soule in endles woo!   [*Exeunt.*

   448. *glory*] *gloomie* AB; corr. by Cap. — 453. *shame*] *same* Del. —
457, 459. *Exit.* Cap. and Del.

SCENE II.

The Same. A Room in the Castle.

Enter at one doore DERBY *from Fraunce, at an other doore* AUDLEY
with a Drum.

Der. Thrice noble Audley, well incountred heere!
How is it with our soueraigne and his peeres?
 Aud. Tis full a fortnight, since I saw his highnes,
What time he sent me forth to muster men;
5 Which I accordingly haue done, and bring them hither
In faire aray before his maiestie.
What newes, my Lord of Derby, from the Emperor?
 Der. As good as we desire: the Emperor
Hath yeelded to his highnes friendly ayd,
10 And makes our King leiuetenant-generall
In all his lands and large dominions:
Then *via* for the spacious bounds of Fraunce!
 Aud. What, doth his highnes leap to heare these newes?
 Der. I haue not yet found time to open them;
15 The king is in his closet, malcontent,
For what, I know not; but he gaue in charge,
Till after dinner none should interrupt him:
The Countesse Salisbury and her father Warwike,
Artoyes and all looke vnderneath the browes.
20 *Aud.* Vndoubtedly, then some thing is amisse. [*Trumpet within.*
 Der. The Trumpets sound, the king is now abroad.

Enter the KING.

 Aud. Here comes his highnes.
 Der. Befall my soueraigne all my soueraignes wish!
 King. Ah, that thou wert a Witch to make it so!
25 *Der.* The Emperour greeteth you. [*Presenting letters.*
 King. (*Aside.*) Would it were the Countesse!
 Der. And hath accorded to your highnes suite.

SCENE II. Stage-dir. add. by Cap.; *Enter Derby and Audley, meeting.*
Del. — 5. *hither* om. Cap. and Tyr. — 7. Given to KING EDW. in A. —
13. *this news* B and Edd., except Del. — 20. Stage-dir. added by Del. —
21. *Enter the* KING after l. 20 in AB and Edd., set aright by Del. —
22. AR. *Hhere* A. — 25. Stage-dir. added by Del. — 26 and 28. *Aside*
not in Edd.

King. (*Aside.*) Thou lyest, she hath not; but I would she had.
Aud. All loue and duety to my Lord the king!
King. Well, all but one is none: — What newes with you? 30
Aud. 1 haue, my liege, leuied those horse and foote
According to your charge, and brought them hither.
King. Then let those foote trudge hence vpon those horse
According to our discharge, and be gone. —
Darby,   35
Ile looke vpon the Countesse minde anone.
Dar. The Countesse minde, my liege?
King. 1 meane the Emperour: — leaue me alone.
Aud. What is in his mind?
Dar.   .   .   Lets leaue him to his humor. [*Exeunt.*
King. Thus from the harts aboundance speakes the tongue; 40
Countesse for Emperour: and indeed, why not?
She is as imperator ouer me
And I to her
Am as a kneeling vassaile, that obserues
The pleasure or displeasure of her eye.   45

Enter LODWIKE.

What saies the more then Cleopatras match
To Cæsar now?
Lod.   That yet, my liege, ere night
She will resolue your maiestie.   [*Drum within.*
King. What drum is this that thunders forth this march,
To start the tender Cupid in my bosome?   50
Poore shipskin, how it braules with him that beateth it!
Go, breake the thundring parchment bottome out,
And I will teach it to conduct sweet lynes.
Vnto the bosome of a heauenly Nymph;
For 1 will vse it as my writing paper,   55

32. *According as your* A. — 35, 36. One line in AB; Cap. and Edd. put *anon* in a line by itself. — 38. *Emperor's* Col. — 39. *What is his mind* A; *Exeunt.* AB, *Exeunt Derby and Audley.* Del. — 40. *aboundance*] *aboundant* AB, Cap. and Tyr., *abundance* Del. and Col. — 43, 44. One line in AB and Col. — 47. Col. ends the line at *liege.* — 48. Stage-dir. added by Del.

And so reduce him from a scoulding drum;
To be the herald and deare counsaile-bearer
Betwixt a goddesse and a mighty king.
Go, bid the drummer learne to touch the Lute,
60 Or hang him in the braces of his drum;
For now we thinke it an vnciuill thing,
To trouble heauen with such harsh resounds:
Away!   [Exit.
The quarrell that I haue requires no armes
65 But these of myne: and these shall meete my foe
In a deepe march of penytrable grones;
My eyes shall be my arrowes, and my sighes
Shall serue me as the vantage of the winde,
To wherle away my sweetest artyllerie.
70 Ah but, alas, she winnes the sunne of me,
For that is she her selfe; and thence it comes
That Poets tearme the wanton warriour blinde;
But loue hath eyes as iudgement to his steps,
Till too much loue'd glory dazles them. —

Enter LODWIKE.

75 How now?
 Lod. My liege, the drum that stroke the lusty march,
Stands with Prince Edward, your thrice valiant sonne.

Enter PRINCE EDWARD.

 King. I see the boy; oh, how his mothers face,
Modeld in his, corrects my straid desire,
80 And rates my heart, and chides my theeuish eie,
Who, being rich ennough in seeing her,
Yet seekes elsewhere: and basest theft is that
Which cannot cloke it selfe on pouertie. —
Now, boy, what newes?

62, 63. One line in AB; div. by Cap. — 63. (Stage-dir.) *Exit Lod.* B.
— 68. *ventage* Del. — 74. *two much* A. — Stage-dir. after l. 75 in AB;
set aright by Del. (*Re-enter* LODOWICK). — 77. *Enter* PRINCE. LODOWICK
retires to the door. Del. — 79. *Molded* B and Edd. — 83. *cloke*] *check*
Cap. and Edd., except Del.

Pr. Edw. I haue assembled, my deare Lord and father,   85
The choysest buds of all our English blood
For our affaires in Fraunce; and heere we come
To take direction from your maiestie.
    King. Still do I see in him deliniate
His mothers visage; those his eies are hers,   90
Who, looking wistely on me, make me blush:
For faults against them selues giue euidence;
Lust is a fire, and men like lanthornes show
Light lust within them selues euen through them selues.
Away, loose silkes of wauering vanitie!   95
Shall the large limmit of faire Brittanye
By me be ouerthrowne? and shall I not
Master this little mansion of my selfe?
Giue me an Armor of eternall steele!
I go to conquer kings; and shall I then   100
Subdue my selfe, and be my enimies friend?
It must not be. — Come, boy, forward, aduaunce!
Lets with our coullours sweete the Aire of Fraunce.

Enter LODWIKE.

    Lod. My liege, the Countesse with a smiling cheere
Desires accesse vnto your Maiestie.   105
    King. Why, there it goes! That verie smile of hers
Hath ransomed captiue Fraunce, and set the King,
The Dolphin, and the Peeres at liberty. —
Goe, leaue me, Ned, and reuell with thy friends. [*Exit* PRINCE.
Thy mother is but blacke, and thou, like her,   110
Dost put it in my minde how foule she is. —
Goe, fetch the Countesse hethor in thy hand,
And let her chase away those winter clouds;
For shee giues beautie both to heauen and earth. [*Exit* LODWIKE.

    87. *in*] *to* A and Del. — 91. *make*] *made* B and Edd., except Del. —
93. *Lust as a fire; and me like lanthorne show* AB, corrected by Cap. —
95. *of*] *or* A. — 96. *limits* Col.; *Brittayne* A. — 100. *shall I not then* AB;
not first om. by Cap. — 103. *sweete*] *sweep* Cap. and Tyr., *beat* Del., *sweat*
Col.; *sweet* seems to be = to *sweeten*. — *Enter Lodw.*] *Advancing from the
door and whispering him* Del. — 111. *if in*] *into* Cap. and Edd. —
113. *these* A.

115 The sin is more to hacke and hew poore men,
Then to embrace in an vnlawfull bed
The register of all varieties
Since Letherne Adam till this youngest howre.

Re-enter LODWIKE *with the* COUNTESSE.

King.   Goé, Lodwike, put thy hand into my purse,
120 Play, spend, giue, ryot, wast, do what thou wilt,
So thou wilt hence awhile and leaue me heere. [*Exit* LODOWICK.
Now, my soules plaiefellow, art thou come
To speake the more then heauenly word of yea
To my obiection in thy beautious loue?
125   *Count.*   My father on his blessing hath commanded —
  King.   That thou shalt yeeld to me?
  Count.   I, deare my liege, your due.
  King.   And that, my dearest loue, can be no lesse
Then right for right and tender loue for loue.
130   *Count.*   Then wrong for wrong and endles hate for hate.—
But, — sith I see your maiestie so bent,
That my vnwillingnes, my husbands loue,
Your high estate, nor no respect respected
Can be my helpe, but that your mightines
135 Will ouerbeare and awe these deare regards,
I bynd my discontent to my content,
And, what I would not, Ile compell I will,
Prouided that your selfe remoue those lets
That stand betweene your highnes loue and mine.
140   *King.*   Name them, faire Countesse, and, by heauen, I will.
  Count.   It is their liues that stand betweene our loue,
That I would haue chokt vp, my soueraigne.
  King.   Whose liues, my Lady?
  Count.   My thrice louing liege,

---

117. *rarieties* AB, *varieties* Del. and Col.; *fair rarities* Moltke. —
118. *till*] *to* Col. — 119. Stage-dir. as given by Del.; *Enter Countesse.* AB.
— 119. *thy purse* AB and Col. — 121. Stage-dir. add. by Cap. — 122. *and
art* Cap., Tyr., and Del. — 124. *subjection* Del., *abjection* Col. — 129. *tender*]
render AB and Col.; *tender* first in Cap. — 136. *I bend my discontent to thy
content* Col. — 140. *them*] *then* AB; corr. by Cap.

Your Queene and Salisbury, my wedded husband,
Who liuing haue that tytle in our loue,   145
That we cannot bestow but by their death.
   King.   Thy opposition is beyond our Law.
   Count.   So is your desire; If the law
Can hinder you to execute the one,
Let it forbid you to attempt the other.   150
I cannot thinke you loue me as you say,
Vnlesse you do make good what you haue sworne.
   King.   No more; thy husband and the Queene shall dye.
Fairer thou art by farre then Hero was,
Beardles Leander not so strong as I: 155
He swome an easie currauut for his loue,
But I will through a Hellespont of bloud,
To arryue at Cestus where my Hero lyes.
   Count.   Nay, youle do more; youle make the Ryuer too
With their hart-bloods that keepe our loue asunder,   160
Of which my husband and your wife are twayne.
   King.   Thy beauty makes them guilty of their death
And giues in euidence that they shall dye;
Vpon which verdict I, their Iudge, condemne them.
   Count. (*Aside.*) O periurde beautie, more corrupted Iudge!   165
When to the great Starre-chamber ore our heads
The vniuersall Sessions cals to count
This packing euill, we both shall tremble for it.
   King.   What saies my faire loue? is she resolude?
   Count.   Resolude to be dissolude; and, therefore, this: 170
Keepe but thy word, great king, and I am thine.
Stand where thou dost, Ile part a little from thee,
And see how I will yeeld me to thy hands.

---

148. *And so* Cap. and Edd. — 153 seqq. Continued to Coun. in A; *my queen*
Col. — 156. *for*] *to* Col. — 157. *through*] *throng* A; *a hellie* (*helly*) *spout
of bloud* AB, Cap. and Del.; *a Hellespont* was first proposed by Tyr. and
corroborated by Col. (Athenæum No. 2422, p. 426, March 28, 1874). —
158. *Arrive that Sestos* Cap., Tyr. and Col. — 160. *heart's blood* Col. —
165. (*Aside.*) not in Edd. — 167. *session* Cap. conj. — 168. *packing ill* Cap.
conj. — 169. *resolute* AB and Edd. — 170. Resolute AB; *Resolv'd* prop.
by Cap. and adopted by Del.

(Turning suddenly upon him, and showing two daggers.)
Here by my side doth hang my wedding-knifes:
175 Take thou the one, and with it kill thy Queene,
And learne by me to finde her where she lies;
And with this other Ile dispatch my loue,
Which now lies fast asleepe within my hart:
When they are gone, then Ile consent to loue.
180 Stir not, lasciuious king, to hinder me;
My resolution is more nimbler far,
Then thy preuention can be in my rescue,
And if thou stir, I strike; therefore stand still,
And heare the choyce that I will put thee to:
185 Either sweare to leaue thy most vnholie sute
And neuer henceforth to solicit me;
Or else, by heauen, this sharpe-pointed knyfe
Shall staine thy earth with that which thou wouldst staine,
My poore chast blood. (*Kneeling.*) Sweare, Edward, sweare,
190 Or I will strike and die before thee heere.
  King. Euen by that power I sweare, that giues me now
The power to be ashamed of my selfe,
I neuer meane to part my lips againe
In any words that tends to such a sute.
195 Arise, true English Ladie; whom our Ile
May better boast of, then euer Romaine might
Of her, whose ransackt treasurie hath taskt
The vaine indeuor of so many pens:
Arise; and be my fault thy honors fame,
200 Which after-ages shall enrich thee with.
I am awaked from this idle dreame; —
Warwike, my Sonne, Darby, Artoys, and Audley,
Braue warriours all, where are you all this while?

Enter all.
Warwike, I make thee Warden of the North:
205 Thou, Prince of Wales, and Audley, straight to Sea;

Scoure to New-hauen; some there staie for me:
My selfe, Artoys, and Darby wil through Flaunders,
To greete our friends there and to craue their aide.
This night will scarce suffice me to discouer
My follies seege against a faithfull louer; 210
For, ere the Sunne shal guildé the easterne skie,
Weele wake him with our marshall harmonie. [*Exeunt.*

ACT III.

SCENE I.

Enter KING IOHN OF FRAUNCE, *his two sonnes,* CHARLES OF NOR-
MANDIE, *and* PHILLIP, *and the* DUKE OF LORRAINE.

K. Iohn. Heere, till our Nauie of a thousand saile
Haue made a breakfast to our foe by Sea,
Let vs incampe, to wait their happie speede. —
Lorraine, what readines is Edward in?
How hast thou heard that he prouided is 5
Of marshiall furniture for this exployt?
Lor. To lay aside vnnecessary soothing,
And not to spend the time in circumstaunce,
Tis bruted for a certenty, my Lord,
That hees exceeding strongly fortified; 10
His subiects flocke as willingly to warre,
As if vnto a tryumph they were led.
Char. England was wont to harbour malcontents,
Blood-thirsty and seditious Catelynes,
Spend-thrifts, and such as gape for nothing else 15
But changing and alteration of the state;
And is it possible
That they are now so loyall in them selues?

211. *guilde*] *guide* AB; corr. by Cap. — 212. *martiall* B.
ACT III. SCENE I. — 2. *at sea* Col. — 6. *martiall* B. — 16. Read
alt'ration; change and Cap. and Edd. — 17, 18. One line in B; two lines
in Cap. and Edd., divided at *now.*

    Lor.   All but the Scot, who sollemnly protests,

20 As heeretofore I haue enformd his grace,

Neuer to sheath his Sword or take a truce.

    K. Iohn.   Ah, thats the anchredge of some better hope!

But, on the other side, to thinke what friends

King Edward hath retaynd in Netherland,

25 Among those euer-bibbing Epicures,

Those frothy Dutch men, puft with double-beer,

That drinke and <u>swill</u> in euery place they come,

Doth not a little aggrauate mine ire;

Besides, we heare, the Emperor conioynes,

30 And stalls him in his owne authoritie:

But, <u>all the</u> mightier that their number is,

The greater glory reapes the victory.

Some friends haue we beside domesticke power;

The sterne Polonian, and the warlike Dane,

35 The King of Bohemia, and of Cycelie,

Are all become confederates with vs,

And, as I thinke, are marching hither apace.   [*Drum within.*

But soft, I heare the musicke of their drums,

By which I gesse that their approch is neare.

Enter the KING OF BOHEMIA, *with* DANES, *and a Polonian Captaine,*
    with other soldiers, another way.

40   *King of Boh.*   King Iohn of Fraunce, as league and neigh-

Requires, when friends are any way distrest,   [borhood

I come to aide thee with my countries force.

    Pol. Cap.   And from great Musko, fearefull to the Turke,

And lofty Poland, nurse of hardie men,

45 I bring these seruitors to fight for thee,

Who willingly will venture in thy cause.

    K. Iohn.   Welcome, Bohemian King, and welcome all:

This your great kindnesse I will not forget.

    20. *his*] *your* Col. — 33. *drum stricke* A, *drumsticke* B, *domestick*
Cap. and Edd. — 35. *kings* Col.; *Boheme* Cap., Tyr., and Col., but read
Th' king. — 37. *hither apace*] *hitherward* Cap. and Tyr., but *hither*
is used as a monosyllable; Stage-dir. *Drum within* added by Del. —
40—43. Divided at *league,* | *any,* | *force.* | in B.

Besides your plentiful rewards in Crownes,
That from our Treasory ye shall receiue: 50
There comes a hare-braind Nation, deckt in pride,
The spoyle of whome will be a trebble gaine.
And now my hope is full, my ioy complete:
At Sea, we are as puissant as the force
Of Agamemnon in the Hauen of Troy;   55
By land, with Zerxes we compare of strength,
Whose souldiers drancke vp riuers in their thirst:
Then, Bayardlike, blinde, ouerweaning Ned,
To reach at our imperiall dyadem
Is either to be swallowed of the waues,   60
Or hackt a peeces when thou comest ashore.

Enter Marriner.

Mar.   Neere to the cost I haue discride, my Lord,
As I was busie in my watchfull charge,
The proud Armado of king Edwards ships:
Which, at the first, far off when I did ken,   65
Seemd as it were a groue of withered pines;
But, drawing neere, their glorious bright aspect,
Their streaming Ensignes, wrought of coulloured silke,
Like to a meddow full of sundry flowers,
Adornes the naked bosome of the earth: 70
Maiesticall the order of their course,
Figuring the horned Circle of the Moone:
And on the top-gallant of the Admirall
And likewise all the handmaides of his trayne
The Armes of England and of Fraunce vnite   75
Are quartred equally by Heralds art:
Thus, titely carried with a merrie gale,
They plough the Ocean hitherward amayne.
   K. Iohn. Dare he already crop the Flewer de Luce?
I hope, the hony being gathered thence,   80
He, with the spider, afterward approcht,

<hr>

49. *Beside* Cap. and Edd. — 52. *game* A and Del. — 62. MAR. om.
A; *discribde* A. — 73. *And* om. Cap. and Edd.; read *th' top.* — 75. *united*
Del. — 79. Continued to MAR. A.

Shall sucke forth deadly venom from the leaues. —
But wheres our Nauy? how are they prepared
To wing themselues against this flight of Rauens?

85 *Mar.* They, hauing knowledge, brought them by the scouts,
Did breake from Anchor straight, and, puft with rage
No otherwise then were their sailes with winde,
Made forth, as when the empty Eagle flies,
To satisfie his hungrie griping mawe.

90 *K. Iohn.* Theres for thy newes. Returne vnto thy barke;
And if thou scape the bloody strooke of warre
And do suruiue the conflict, come againe,
And let vs heare the manner of the fight. [*Exit* MARRINER.
Meane space, my Lords, tis best we be disperst

95 To seuerall places, least they chaunce to land:
First you, my Lord, with your Bohemian Troupes,
Shall pitch your battailes on the lower hand;
My eldest sonne, the Duke of Normandie,
Togeither with this aide of Muscouites,

100 Shall clyme the higher ground another waye;
Heere in the middle cost, betwixt you both,
Phillip, my yongest boy, and I will lodge.
So, Lords, be gon, and looke vnto your charge:
You stand for Fraunce, an Empire faire and large. [*Exeunt.*

105 Now tell me, Phillip, what is thy concept,
Touching the challenge that the English make?

  Phil. I say, my Lord, clayme Edward what he can,
And bring he nere so playne a pedegree,
Tis you are in possession of the Crowne,

110 And thats the surest poynt of all the Law:
But, were it not, yet ere he should preuaile,
Ile make a Conduit of my dearest blood,
Or chase those stragling vpstarts home againe.

  K. Iohn. Well said, young Phillip! Call for bread and Wine,
115 That we may cheere our stomacks with repast,

<hr>

83. *our*] *out* A. — 84. *flight*] *fleete* B. — 89. *satifie* A. — 90. *Thees* A,
There's B. — 93. [*Exit.*] A. — 104. [*Exeunt.*] after l. 103 in Qq. —
105. *thy concept*] *their concept* A, *thy conceite* B and Edd. — 111. *yet* om.
B. — 114. Divided at *bread* in B.

To looke our foes more sternely in the face.

A Table and Provisions brought in; King and his Son sit down to it.
Ordinànce afar off.

Now is begun the heauie day at Sea:
Fight, Frenchmen, fight; be like the fielde of Beares,
When they defend their younglings in their Caues!
Steer, angry Nemesis, the happie helme,   120
That, with the sulphur battels of your rage,
The English Fleete may be disperst and sunke.   [*Shot.*

   Phil.   O Father, how this eckoing Cannon-shot,
Like sweetest hermonie, disgests my cates!

   K. Iohn.   Now, boy, thou hearest what thundring terror tis, 125
To buckle for a kingdomes souerentie:
The earth, with giddie trembling when it shakes,
Or when the exalations of the aire
Breakes in extremitie of lightning flash,
Affrights not more then kings, when they dispose   130
To shew the rancor of their high-swolne harts.   [*Retreate.*
Retreate is sounded; one side hath the worse:
O, if it be the French! Sweete fortune, turne;
And, in thy turning, change the forward winds,
That, with aduantage of a fauoring skie,   135
Our men may vanquish, and the other flie!

Enter Marriner.

My heart misgiues: — say, mirror of pale death,
To whome belongs the honor of this day?
Relate, I pray thee, if thy breath will serue,
The sad discourse of this discomfiture.   140

   Mar.   I will, my Lord.
My gratious soueraigne, Fraunce hath tane the foyle,.

---

116. Stage-dir. add. by Cap.; *The battel heard, afarre off* AB (after l. 115).
— 120. *Stir* AB; corr. by Cap. — 121. *sulphur'd* Cap. and Edd., except Del.
— 124. *sweete* AB, *sweetest* first Cap. — 125. Div. at *thundring* in B. —
126. *To battle* Col. conj. — 129. *Break* Cap. and Edd. — 131. [*Retreate.*]
after l. 132 in Qq., corr. by Del. — 133. *it be* om. B. — 134. *froward*
B and Edd. — 135. *sauoring* A. — 136. *the other*] *thither* A, *th'other* B.
— 138. *the day* Col.

And boasting Edward triumphs with successe.
These Iron-harted Nauies,
145 When last I was reporter to your grace,
Both full of angry spleene, of hope, and feare,
Hasting to meete each other in the face,
At last conioynd; and by their Admirall
Our Admirall encountred manie shot:
150 By this, the other, that beheld these twaine
Giue earnest peny of a further wracke,
Like fiery Dragons tooke their haughty flight;
And, likewise meeting, from their smoky wombes
Sent many grym Embassadors of death.
155 Then gan the day to turne to gloomy night,
And darkenes did as wel inclose the quicke
As those that were but newly reft of life.
No leasure serud for friends to bid farewell;
And, if it had, the hideous noise was such,
160 As ech to other seemed deafe and dombe.
Purple the Sea, whose channel fild as fast
With streaming gore, that from the maymed fell,
As did her gushing moysture breake into
The crannied cleftures of the through-shot planks.
165 Heere flew a head, disseuered from the tronke,
There mangled armes and legs were tost aloft,
As when a wherle-winde takes the Summer-dust
And scatters it in middle of the aire.
Then might ye see the reeling vessels split,
170 And tottering sink into the ruthlesse floud,
Vntill their lofty tops were seene no more.
All shifts were tried, both for defence and hurt:
And now the effect of vallor and of fear,
Of resolution and of cowardize,
175 We liuely pictured; how the one for fame,
   The other by compulsion laid about:
Much did the *Nonpareille*, that braue ship;

<hr>

164. *cranny* AB. — 165. *dissuuered* A. — 169. *you* Col. — 173. *effects*
Cap. and Edd., except Del.; *fear*] *force* AB, corr. by Cap. — 174. *of a*
cowardize A. — 175. *We*] *Were* Cap. and Edd., except Del. — 177. *Nom*
fer illa AB, *Nonpareille* Cap., Tyr., and Del., *Nonperillo* Col.

So did the blacke-snake of Bullen, then which
A bonnier vessel neuer yet spred sayle.
But all in vaine; both Sunne, the Winde and tyde,   180
Reuolted all vnto our foemens side,
That we perforce were fayne to giue them way,
And they are landed. — Thus my tale is donne:
We haue vntimly lost, and they haue woone.

   K. Iohn.   Then rests there nothing, but with present speede 185
To ioyne our seueral forces al in one,
And bid them battaile, ere they rainge too farre.
Come, gentle Phillip, let vs hence depart;
This souldiers words haue perst thy fathers hart.   [*Exeunt.*

SCENE II.

Picardy: *Fields near* Cressi.

Enter two Frenchmen, a woman and two little Children meet them,
and other Citizens.

   One.   Wel met, my masters: How now? whats the newes?
And wherefore are ye laden thus with stuffe?
What, is it quarter-daie that you remoue,
And carrie bag and baggage too?

   Two.   Quarter-day? I, and quartering day, I feare: 5
Haue ye not heard the newes that flies abroad?

   One.   What newes?

   Three.   How the French Nauy is destroyd at Sea,
And that the English Armie is arriued.

   One.   What then?   10

   Two.   What then, quoth you? why, ist not time to flie,
When enuie and destruction is so nigh?

   One.   Content thee, man; they are farre enough from hence,
And will be met, I warrant ye, to their cost,
Before they breake so far into the Realme.   15

<hr>

178. *Boulogne* Cap. and Edd. — 180. *Wine* A. — 181. *foeman's* Col.
   Scene II. Stage-dir. Picardy. *Fields near* Cressi. add. by Cap.
— 2. *you* B and Edd. — 5. *quartering pay* A. — 11. *why, is not* Col.
— 12. *enemy* prop. by Cap. and adopted by Del.; *are* Col. — 14. *you* B
and Edd.

Two. I, so the Grashopper doth spend the time
In mirthfull iollitie, till Winter come;
And then too late he would redeeme his time,
When frozen cold hath nipt his carelesse head.
20 He, that no sooner will prouide a Cloake,
Then when he sees it doth begin to raigne,
May, peraduenture, for his negligence,
Be throughly washed, when he suspects it not.
We that haue charge and such a trayne as this,
25 Must looke in time, to looke for them and vs,
Least, when we would, we cannot be relieued.

 One. Belike, you then dispaire of all successe,
And thinke your Country will be subiugate.

 Three. We cannot tell; tis good to feare the worst.
30 *One.* Yet rather fight, then, like vnnaturall sonnes,
Forsake your louing parents in distresse.

 Two. Tush, they that haue already taken armes,
Are manie fearefull millions in respect
Of that small handfull of our enimies:
35 But tis a rightfull quarrell must preuaile;
Edward is sonne vnto our late kings sister,
Where Iohn Valoys is three degrees remoued.

 Woman. Besides, there goes a Prophesie abroad,
Published by one that was a Fryer once,
40 Whose Oracles haue many times prooued true;
And now he sayes, ‘The tyme will shortly come,
Whenas a Lyon, rowsed in the west,
Shall carrie hence the fluer-de-luce of France’:
These, I can tell yee, and such like surmises
45 Strike many french men cold vnto the heart.

Enter a Frenchman.

 Four. Flie, countrymen and cytizens of France!
Sweete-flowring peace, the roote of happie life,
Is quite abandoned and expulst the lande;

<hr>

16. *his time* Col. — 23. *thoroughly* Tyr. and Col. — 27. *then you* Col.;
all] *ill* AB. — 37. *When* Col.; *where* = *whereas*, as often in Shak.

Insted of whome ransack-constraining warre
Syts like to Rauens vppon your houses topps;   50
Slaughter aud mischiefe walke within your streets,
And, vnrestrained, make hauock as they passe;
The forme whereof euen now my selfe beheld
Vpon this faire mountaine whence I came.
For so far off as I directed mine eies,   55
I might perceaue five Cities all on fire,
Corne-fieldes and vineyards, burning like an ouen;
And, as the reaking vapour in the wind
Tourned but aside, I likewise might disserne
The poore inhabitants, escapt the flame,   60
Fall numberles vpon the souldiers pikes.
Three waies these dredfull ministers of wrath
Do tread the measures of their tragicke march;
Vpon the right hand comes the conquering king,
Vpon the lefte his hot vnbridled sonne,   65
And in the midst our nations glittering hoast;
All which, though distant, yet conspire in one,
To leaue a desolation where they come.
Flie therefore, Citizens, if you be wise,
Seeke out som habitation further off: 70
Here if you staie, your wives will be abused,
Your treasure sharde before your weeping eies;
Shelter your selues, for now the storme doth rise.
Away, away; me thinks, I heare their drums: —
Ah, wreched France, I greatly feare thy fall;   75
Thy glory shaketh like a tottering wall.   [*Exeunt.*

49. *which* Cap. conj.; *ransackt* AB, corr. by Cap. — 50. *raven-like
upon* prop. by Cap. and ad. by Del.; *on* Cap. and Edd.; *Ravens* is used as
a monosyllabe. — 54. *Now, upon* Cap., Tyr., and Del.; *fair* is used as a disyllable. — 55. *far as I did direct* Cap. and Edd.; *direct* Del.; *directed* to be
pron. *direct'd.* — 58. *leaking* AB, Cap., and Tyr.; *reeking* prop. by Cap.
and adopted by Del. and Col. — 59. *I tourned but aside* AB, *Turned aside*
Cap. and Tyr., *Ay turned but aside, I might* Cap. conj., *Turned but aside*
Del. and Col. — 65. *his*] *is* A. — 73. *Shelter you your selues* AB; *you*
first struck out by Cap. — 76. [*Exeunt.*] om. A.

SCENE III.

The Same. Drums.

Enter KING EDWARD, *and the* ERLE OF DARBY, *with Souldiors,
and* GOBIN DE GRAIE.

    King. Wheres the French man by whose cunning guidance
We found the shalow of this Riuer Some,
And had direction how to passe the sea?
    Gobin. Here, my good Lord.
5   *King.* How art thou calde? tell me thy name.
    Gobin. Gobin de Graie, if please your excellence.
    King. Then, Gobin, for the seruice thou hast done,
We here inlarge and giue thee liberty;
And, for a recompence, beside this good,
10   Thou shalt receiue fiue hundred markes in golde. —
I know not how, we should haue met our sonne,
Whom now in heart I wish I might behold.

Enter ARTOYES.

    Art. Good newes, my Lord; the prince is hard at hand,
And with him comes Lord Awdley and the rest,
15   Whome since our landing we could neuer meet.

Enter PRINCE EDWARD, LORD AWDLEY, *and Souldiers.*

    K. Edw. Welcome, faire Prince! How hast thou sped, my
Since thy arriual on the coaste of Fraunce?   [sonne,
    Pr. Edw. Succesfullie, I thanke the gratious heauens:
Some of their strongest Cities we haue wonne,
20   As Harflew, Lo, Crotaie, and Carentine,
And others wasted; leauing at our heeles
A wide apparent feild and beaten path,
For sollitarines to progresse in:

SCENE III. Stage-dir. *The same. Drums.* add. by Cap. — 1. *Where is* Cap. and Edd.; (*guide* AB and Edd.) *guidance* prop. by Cap. and adopted by Del. — 2. *riuer Sone* AB, *Somme* mod. Edd. — 5. *tell me* om. Cap. and Edd. — 6. *if it please* Col. — 9. *for recomp.* AB. — 13. Continued to KING in A. — 16. Two lines in B, divided at *Prince.* — 20. *As Harslen, Lie, Cratag, and Carentigne* AB. *As Harfleur, Lo, Crotage, and Carentan* Cap. and Edd. (*Loo .. Charenton* Col.).

Yet those that would submit, we kindly pardned;
But who in scorne refused our proffered peace,   25
Indurde the penaltie of sharpe reuenge.
   K. Edw.   Ah, Fraunce, why shouldest thou be thus obstinate
Agaynst the kind imbracement of thy friends?
How gently had we thought to touch thy brest
And set our foot vpon thy tender mould,   30
But that, in froward and disdainfull pride,
Thou, like a skittish and vntamed coult,
Dost start aside and strike vs with thy heeles?
But tel me, Ned, in all thy warlike course,
Hast thou not seene the vsurping king of Fraunce?   35
   Pr. Edw.   Yes, my good Lord, and not two howers ago,
With full a hundred thousand fighting men
Vppon the one side of the riuers banke;
I on the other; with his multitudes
I feard he would haue cropt our smaller power: 40
But happily, perceiuing your approch,
He hath withdrawen himselfe to Cressey plaines;
Where, as it seemeth by his good araie,
He meanes to byd vs battaile presently.
   K. Edw.   He shall be welcome; thats the thing we craue.   45

    Enter King Iohn, Dukes of Normandy, *and* Lorraine,
      King of Boheme, *yong* Phillip, *and Souldiers.*

   K. Iohn.   Edward, know, that Iohn, the true king of Fraunce,
Musing thou shouldst incroach vppon his land,
And, in thy tyranous proceeding, slay
His faithfull subiects, and subuert his Townes,
Spits in thy face; and in this manner folowing   50
Obraids thee with thine arrogant intrusion:

   25. *But*] *For* Edd.; *But* prop. by Cap. and adopted by Del.; *poffered*
A. — 27. *this* A. — 29. *gentle* B, Cap., and Tyr. — 31. *forward* Tyr. —
37. *an* B and Edd. — 38. *of*] *with* AB, *of (o')* Edd. — 39. *And on the
other; both his* AB, corr. by Cap.; *And I on the other* Col. — 40. *coped*
Col. conj. — 42. *Cressi'* Cap., *Crecy'* Tyr., *Cressi* Del. — 46. *Now,
Edward . . . Iohn, true* Cap. and Tyr. Read *th' true* and cp. l. 137. —
51. *thy* Col.

First, I condemne thee for a fugitiue,
A theeuish pyrate, and a needie mate,
One that hath either no abyding place,
55 Or else, inhabiting some barraine soile,
Where neither hearb or fruitfull graine is had,
Doest altogether liue by pilfering:
Next, insomuch thou hast infringed thy faith,
Broke leage and solemne couenant made with mee,
60 I hould thee for a false pernitious wretch:
And, last of all, although I scorne to cope
With one so much inferior to my selfe,
Yet, in respect thy thirst is all for golde,
Thy labour rather to be feared then loued,
65 To satisfie thy lust in either parte,
Heere am I come, and with me haue I brought
Exceding store of treasure, perle, and coyne.
Leaue therefore now to persecute the weake,
And, armed entring conflict with the armd,
70 Let it be seene, mongst other pettie thefts,
How thou canst win this pillage manfully.

   K. Edw. If gall or wormwood haue a pleasant tast,
Then is thy sallutation hony-sweete;
But as the one hath no such propertie,
75 So is the other most satiricall.
Yet wot how I regarde thy worthles tants:
If thou haue vttred them, to foile my fame
Or dym the reputation of my birth,
Know, that thy woluish barking cannot hurt;
80 If slylie to insinuate with the worlde,
And with a strumpets artifitiall line
To painte thy vitious and deformed cause,
Bee well assured, the counterfeit will fade,
And in the end thy fowle defects be seene;
85 But if thou didst it to prouoke me on,

60. *false*] *most* B and Edd., except Del.; Elze (I, p. 4) prop. *perfidious*
for *pernicious*. — 62. *such inf.* AB, *such an inf.* Del., *so much inf.* Cap.
and Tyr., *with one such,* [*so*] *inf.* Col. — 64. *They* A. — 66. *I haue* B and
Edd. — 77. *thou hast* Cap. conj.; *soil* prop. by Cap. and adopted by Del.
and Col. — 81. *line*] *hue* Col. conj., *lime* Elze (I, p. 5) conj.

As who should saie, I were but timerous
Or coldly negligent did need a spurre,
Bethinke thy selfe, how slacke I was at sea,
How since my landing I haue wonn no townes,
Entered no further but vpon the coast,   90
And there haue euer since securelie slept.
But if I haue bin otherwise imployd,
Imagin, Valoys, whether I intende
To skirmish, not for pillage, but for the Crowne
Which thou dost weare; and that I vowe to haue,   95
Or one of vs shall fall into his graue.

  Pr. Edw. Looke not for crosse inuectiues at our hands,
Or rayling execrations of despight:
Let creeping serpents, hid in hollow banckes,
Sting with theyr tongues; we haue remorseles swordes,   100
And they shall pleade for vs and our affaires.
Yet thus much, breefly, by my fathers leaue:
As all the immodest poyson of thy throat
Is scandalous and most notorious lyes,
And our pretended quarell is truly iust,   105
So end the battaile when we meet to daie:
May eyther of vs prosper and preuaile,
Or, luckles curst, receiue eternall shame!

  K. Edw. That needs no further question; and, I knowe,
His conscience witnesseth, it is my right. —   110
Therfore, Valoys, say, wilt thou yet resigne,
Before the sickle's thrust into the Corne,
Or that inkindled fury turne to flame?

  K. Iohn. Edward, I know what right thou hast in France;
And ere I basely will resigne my Crowne,   115
This Champion-field shall be a poole of bloode,
And all our prospect as a slaughter-house.

  Pr. Edw. I, that approues thee, tyrant, what thou art:
No father, king, or shepheard of thy realme,

Cham. Yes, sir; but M. Blague dwells ouer the way.

125   *Sir Ar.* Is not this the George? Before God, theres some
                                    [villany in this.

Cham. S'foote, our signe's remoou'd; this is strange!

                                    [*Exeunt.*

SCENE II.

Enter BLAGUE, *trussing his points.*

Host. Chamberlen, speake vp to the new lodgings, bid Nell
looke well to the bakt meats!

Enter SIR ARTHUR *and* SIR RAPH.

How now, my old Ienerts bauke my house, my castle, lie in
Waltham all night, and not vnder the Canopie of your host
5   Blagues house?

Sir Ar. Mine host, mine host, we lay all night at the George
   in Waltham; but whether the George be your fee-simple or no,
tis a doubtfull question. Looke vpon your signe!

Host. Body of Saint George, this is mine ouerthwart neigh-
10 bour hath done this to seduce my blind customers. Ile tickle
his catastrophe for this; if I do not indite him at next assises
for Burglary, let me die of the yellowes; for I see tis no
boote in these dayes to serue the good Duke of Norfolke. The
villanous world is turnd manger; one Iade deceiues another,
15 and your Ostler playes his part commonly for the fourth share.
Haue wee Commedies in hand, you whorson, villanous male
London letcher?

Sir Ar. Mine host, we haue had the moylingst night of it
that euer we had in our liues.

20   *Host.* Ist certaine?

---

124. *dwells* om. B. — 125. *before Ioue theres* D and the rest. — 126.
Foote D and the rest. — *Exeunt* om. Edd.

SCENE II. The scene is continued in Tieck. — 1—5. Divided at *lodg-
ings* | *meats* | *horse* | *not* | *house* in Edd. — 1. *speake*] *speed* L. — 2. *meat*
F and the rest; the stage-dir. *Enter* ... added by the pres. Edd. — 3. *my*
old Iennerts banke, my horse, my castle most Edd., *old jennet's back, my*
house [*Is*] *my castle* L. *house* for *horse* first conj. by Steevens. — 8. *doubt-*
full om. BD and the rest. — 10, 11. *to seduce ... for this* om. EFG. —
11. *at the next* D and the rest. — 12. *see it is* L. — 14. *mangy* L. —
17. *London-lecther* D, *London leether* E, *London-leather* FG. — 20. *Is it* F
and the rest.

Sir Raph. We haue bin in the Forrest all night almost.

Host. S'foot, how did I misse you? Hart, I was a-stealing a Bucke there.

Sir Ar. A plague on you; we were stayed for you.

Host. Were you, my noble Romanes? Why, you shall share;   25
the venison is a footing. *Sine Cerere & Baccho friget Venus*;
that is, theres a good breakfast prouided for a marriage thats
in my house this morning.

Sir Ar. A marriage, mine host?

Host. A coniunction copulatiue; a gallant match betweene   30
your daughter and M. Raymond Mountchensey, yong Iuuentus.

Sir Ar. How?

Host. Tis firme, tis done. Weele shew you a president i'th
Sir Raph. How? married?   [ciuill law for't.

Host. Leaue trickes and admiration. Theres a cleanely paire   35
of sheetes in the bed in the Orchard chamber, and they shall lie
there. What? Ile doe it; Ile serue the good Duke of Norfolke.

Sir Ar. Thou shalt repent this, Blague.

Sir Raph. If any law in England will make thee smart for
this, expect it with all seucrity.   40

Host. I renounce your defiance, if you parle so roughly.
Ile barracado my gates against you. Stand, faire bully; Priest,
come off from the rereward! What can you say now? Twas
done in my house; I haue shelter i'th Court for't. D'yee see yon
bay window? I serue the good Duke of Norfolk, and tis his lodg-   45
ing. Storm, I care not, seruing the good Duke of Norfolk. Thou
art an Actor in this, and thou shalt carry fire in thy face eternally.

Enter SMUG, MOUNTCHENSEY, HARRY CLARE, *and* MILLISCENT.

Smug. Fire, s'blood, theres no fire in England like your
Trinidado sack. Is any man heere humorous? We stole the
venison, and weele iustifie it: say you now!   50

---

21. Assigned to *Sir Ar.* in L. — 22. *Foote* D and the rest; *was stealing
of a* D and the rest. — 26. *Venere* BDEF. — 27. *there is* CFG and the rest;
that is CFG and the rest. — 31. *M.* (i. e. *Master*) om. L; *juvents* FG. —
33. *in the* F and the rest. — 36. *sheets on the bed* D and the rest; *bed on
the Orchard* B, *in Orchard Chamber* A. — 37. *I serue* D and the rest. —
43. *reward* EF. — 44. *in the* F and the rest. — 44, 45. *Dee see your bay*
A, *Doe see your bay* B, *Doe you see yon bay* D and the rest. — 48. *Fire,
nouns, ther's* D and the rest.

That neuer base affections enter there:
Fight and be valiant, conquer where thou comst!
185 Now follow, Lords, and do him honor too.
    Dar. Edward Plantagenet, prince of Wales,
As I do set this helmet on thy head,
Wherewith the chamber of·thy braine is fenst,
So may thy temples, with Bellonas hand,
190 Be still adornd with lawrell victorie:
Fight and be valiant, conquer where thou comst!
    Aud. Edward Plantagenet, prince of Wales,
Receiue this lance into thy manly hand;
Vse it in fashion of a brasen pen,
195 To drawe forth bloudie stratagems in France,
And print thy valiant deeds in honors booke:
Fight and be valiant, conquer where thou comst!
    Art. Edward Plantagenet, prince of Wales,
Hold, take this target, weare it on thy arme;
200 And may the view thereof, like Perseus shield,
Astonish and transforme thy gazing foes
To senselesse images of meger death:
Fight and be valiant, conquer where thou comst!
    K. Edw. Now wants there nought but knighthood, which
205 Wee leaue, till thou hast won it in the fielde.   [deferd
    Pr. Edw. My gratious father and yee forwarde peeres,
This, honor you haue done me, animates
And chears my greene yet scarse appearing strength
With comfortable good-presaging signes,
210 No otherwise then did ould Iacobes wordes,
Whenas he breathed his blessings on his sonnes.
These hallowed giftes of yours when I prophane,
Or vse them not to glory of my God,
To patronage the fatherles and poore,
215 Or for the benefite of Englands peace,
Be numbe my ioynts, waxe feeble both mine armes,

188. *thy*] *this* AB; corr. by Cap. — 189. *with*] *by* Cap. prop. —
193. *manlike* B and Edd. — 197. *conquer*] *vanquish* A. — 204. Two
lines in B, divided at *nought*. — 206. Prefix PR. EDW. om. in A. — 216. *Be-
numb* Tyr.

Wither my hart, that, like a saples tree,
I may remayne the map of infamy.
   K. Edw.   Then thus our steelde Battailes shall be rainged:
The leading of the vawarde, Ned, is thyne;   220
To dignifie whose lusty spirit the more,
We temper it with Audleys grauitie,
That, courage and experience ioynd in one,
Your manage may be second vnto none:
For the mayne battells, I will guide my selfe;   225
And, Darby, in the rereward march behind.
That orderly disposd and set in ray,
Let vs to horse; and God graunt vs the daye!   [*Exeunt.*

SCENE IV.

The Same.

Alarum.   Enter a many French men flying.
After them PRINCE EDWARD, *running.   Then enter*
KING IOHN *and* DUKE OF LORAINE.

   K. Iohn.   Oh, Lorrain, say, what meane our men to fly?
Our nomber is far greater then our foes.
   Lor.   The garrison of Genoaes, my Lorde,
That came from Paris, weary with their march,
Grudging to be so soddenly imployd,   5
No sooner in the forefront tooke their place,
But, straite retyring, so dismaide the rest,
As likewise they betook themselues to flight,
In which, for hast to make a safe escape,
More in the clustering throng are prest to death,   10
Then by the ennimie, a thousandfold.
   K. Iohn.   O haplesse fortune! Let vs yet assay,
If we can counsell some of them to stay.   [*Exeunt.*

<hr>

219. *thus*] *this* A; *battle* Col.
   SCENE IV. Stage-dir. *The same.* add. by Cap. — 5. *so* add. by
Cap. — 10. *throng*] *through* B. — 13. *Exeunt.* om. A.

SCENE V.

The Same.

Enter KING EDWARD *and* AUDLEY.

K. Edw.　Lord Audley, whiles our sonne is in the chase,
Withdraw your powers vnto this little hill,
And heere a season let vs breath our selues.
　　Aud.　I will, my Lord.　　　　　[*Exit.　Sound Retreat.*
5　　*K. Edw.*　Iust dooming heauen, whose secret prouidence
To our grosse iudgement is inscrutable,
How are we bound to praise thy wondrous works,
That hast this day giuen way vnto the right,
And made the wicked stumble at them selues!

Enter ARTOYS.

10　　*Art.*　Rescue, King Edward!　Rescue for thy sonne!
　　K. Edw.　Rescue, Artoys? what, is he prisoner,
Or by violence fell beside his horse?
　　Art.　Neither, my Lord; but narrowly beset
With turning Frenchmen, whom he did persue,
15　As tis impossible that he should scape,
Except yor highnes presently descend.
　　K. Edw.　Tut, let him fight; we gaue him armes to day,
And he is laboring for a knighthood, man.

Enter DERBY.

　　Dar.　The Prince, my Lord, the Prince! oh, succour him!
20　Hees close incompast with a world of odds!
　　K. Edw.　Then will he win a world of honor too,
If he by vallour can redeeme him thence;
If not, what remedy? we haue more sonnes
Then one, to comfort our declyning age.

Re-enter AUDLEY.

25　　*Aud.*　Renowned Edward, giue me leaue, I pray,
To lead my souldiers where I may releeue
Your Graces sonne, in danger to be slayne.

SCENE V. Stage-dir. *The same.* add. by Cap. — 2. *our* A; cp. l. 26.
— 10. ART. om. in A. — 12. *Or else* Cap. and Edd., but *Or* may be read
as a disyllable; *fell'd* Anonymus conj. in Col. — 15. *it is* B. — 24. *declying* B.

The snares of French, like Emmets on a banke,
Muster about him; whilst he, Lion-like,
Intangled in the net of their assaults,   30
Frantiquely wrends, and bytes the wouen toyle:
But all in vaine, he cannot free him selfe.
　K. Edw.　Audley, content; I will not haue a man,
On paine of death, sent forth to succour him:
This is the day, ordaynd by desteny,   35
To season his courage with those greeuous thoughts,
That, if he breaketh out, Nestors yeares on earth
Will. make him sauor still of this exployt.
　Dar.　Ah, but he shall not liue to see those dayes.
　K. Edw.　Why, then his Epitaph is lasting prayse.   40
　Aud.　Yet, good my Lord, tis too much wilfulnes,
To let his blood be spilt, that may be saude.
　K. Edw.　Exclayme no more; for none of you can tell
Whether a borrowed aid will serue, or no;
Perhapps, he is already slayne or tane.   45
And dare a Falcon when shees in her flight,
And cuer after sheele be haggard-like:
Let Edward be deliuered by our hands,
And still, in danger, heele expect the like;
But if himselfe himselfe redeeme from thence,   50
He wil haue vanquisht cheerefull death and feare,
And euer after dread their force no more,
Then if they were but babes or Captiue slaues.
　Aud.　O cruell Father! Farewell, Edward, then!
　Dar.　Farewell, sweete Prince, the hope of chiualry!   55
　Art.　O, would my life might ransome him from death!
　K. Edw.　But soft, me thinkes I heare　　*[Sound Retreat.*
The dismall charge of Trumpets loud retreat.
All are not slayne, I hope, that went with him;
Some will returne with tidings, good or bad.   60

　　36. *his green courage with those thoughts* Cap. and Edd., except Del.
— 37. *if he breathe out Nestors yeares on earth,* prop. by Cap. and
adopted by Del. and Col. — 41. *my good* Col. — 47. *huggard* A. —
56. Omitted by Col. — 57. *Forbear, my lords; — but soft* Cap. and Tyr.;
Stage-dir. added by Del.

Enter PRINCE EDWARD *in tryumph, bearing in his hande his shiuered*
Launce, and the KING OF BOHEME, *borne before, wrapt in the Collours.*
They runne and imbrace him.

Aud.   O ioyfull sight! victorious Edward liues!
Dar.   Welcome, braue Prince!
K. Edw.   Welcome, Plantagenet!
Pr. Edw.   [*kneele and kisse his fathers hand.*]
    First hauing donne my duety as beseemed,
65 Lords, I regreet you all with harty thanks.
  And now, behold, after my winters toyle,
  My paynefull voyage on the boystrous sea
  Of warres deuouring gulphes and steely rocks,
  I bring my fraught vnto the wished port,
70 My Summers hope, my trauels sweet reward:
  And heere, with humble duety, I present
  This sacrifice, this first fruit of my sword,
  Cropt and cut downe euen at the gate of death,
  The king of Boheme, father, whome I slue;
75 Whose thousands had intrencht me round about,
  And laye as thicke vpon my battered crest,
  As on an Anuell, with their ponderous glaues:
  Yet marble courage still did vnderprop;
  And when my weary armes, with often blowes,
80 Like the continuall laboring Wood-mans Axe
  That is enioynd to fell a load of Oakes,
  Began to faulter, straight I would remember
  My gifts you gaue me, and my zealous vow,
  And then new courage made me fresh againe,
85 That, in despight, I carud my passage forth,
  And put the multitude to speedy flyght.
  Lo, thus hath Edwards hand fild your request,
  And done, I hope, the duety of a knight.

72. *the first* Col. — 74. *Bohemia* B and Del. — 75. *Whom you said*
AB, *Whose thousands* Cap. and Edd., *Who you said* Col., *Who you saw*
Anonymus in Col. — 76. *laid* Anon. in Col. — 82. *remember*] *recouer* AB,
corr. by Cap.; Col. prints the line: *Would recover, straight I would remember.*
— 85. *craud* A. — 87. *this* A; *has* Col.

K. Edw.   I, well thou hast deserud a knight-hood, Ned!
And, therefore, with thy sword, yet reaking warme   90
[*His Sword borne by a Soldier.*
With blood of those that sought to be thy bane,
Arise, Prince Edward, trusty knight at armes:
This day thou hast confounded me with ioy,
And proude thy selfe fit heire vnto a king.
Pr. Edw.   Here is a note, my gratious Lord, of those   95
That in this conflict of our foes were slaine:
Eleuen Princes of esteeme, Foure score
Barons, a hundred and twenty knights,
And thirty thousand common souldiers;
And, of our men, a thousand.   100
K. Edw.   Our God be praised! Now, Iohn of Fraunce, I hope,
Thou knowest King Edward for no wantonesse,
No loue - sicke cockney, nor his souldiers iades.
But which way is the fearefull king escapt?
Pr. Edw.   Towards Poyctiers, noble father, and his sonnes. 105
K. Edw.   Ned, thou and Audley shall pursue them still;
Myselfe and Derby will to Calice streight,
And there begyrt that Hauen-towne with seege.
Now lies it on an vpshot; therefore strike,
And wistlie follow, whiles the game's on foote.   110
What Picture's this?
Pr. Edw.   A Pellican, my Lord,
Wounding her bosome with her crooked beak,
That so her nest of young ones may be fed
With drops of blood that issue from her hart;
The motto *Sic et vos*, 'and so should you'.   [*Exeunt.* 115

<hr>

90. *wreaking* B; Stage - dir. after l. 86 in A. — 91. *that*] *who* Col.;
fought] AB and Edd., *sought* Tyr. and Col. — 92. *in arms* Col. —
97—100. Three lines in AB, div. at *Barons* |, *thousand* |, *thousand* |. —
98. *Barons, and Earls; a hundred twenty knights* Cap., Tyr., and Col.;
and hundred Tyr.; *hundred* used as a trisyllable. — 99. *private souldiers* B,
Cap. and Col. — 101. Prefix K. EDW. om. in A. — 101, 102. Div. at *France*
in B. — 111. *is this* B. — 113. *might* A. — 115. *Exeunt* om. B.

ACT IV.

SCENE I.

Bretagne.   Camp of the English.

Enter LORD MOUNTFORD *with a Coronet in his hande; with him the*
EARLE OF SALISBURY.

  Moun. My Lord of Salisbury, since by your aide
 Mine ennemie Sir Charles of Bloys is slaine,
 And I againe am quietly possest
 In Brittaines Dukedome, knowe that I resolue,
5 For this kind furtherance of your king and you,
 To sweare allegeance to his maiesty:
 In signe whereof receiue this Coronet,
 Beare it vnto him, and, withall, mine othe,
 Neuer to be but Edwards faithful friend.
10 *Sal.* I take it, Mountfort: Thus, I hope, ere long
 The whole Dominions of the Realme of Fraunce
 Wilbe surrendred to his conquering hand. [*Exit* MOUNTFORD.
 Now, if I knew but safely how to passe,
 I would at Calice gladly meete his Grace,
15 Whether, I am by letters certified,
 Yet he intends to haue his host remooude.
 It shal be so, this pollicy will serue: —
 Ho, whose within? Bring Villiers to me.

Enter VILLIERS.

 Villiers, thou knowest, thou art my prisoner,
20 And that I might for ransome, if I would,
 Require of thee a hundred thousand Francks,
 Or else retayne and keepe thee captiue still:
 But so it is, that for a smaller charge
 Thou maist be quit, and if thou wilt thy selfe.

  ACT IV. SCENE I. Stage-dir. *Bretagne. Camp of the English.*
add. by Cap. — 1. *our* A. — 8. *my* B and Edd. — 12. *Exit* A, om. in
B, *Exit Mountford* Cap. — 14. *at*] *to* AB; corr. by Cap. — 16. *Yet*] *That*
Cap. and Edd. — 21. *a*] *an* B and Edd. — 24. *an if* Cap. and Edd.

And this it is: Procure me but a pasport   25
Of Charles, the Duke of Normandy, that I
Without restraint may haue recourse to Callis
Through all the Countries where he hath to do;
Which thou maist easely obtayne, I thinke,
By reason I haue often heard thee say,   30
He and thyself were students once together:
And then thou shalt be set at libertie.
How saiest thou? wilt thou vndertake to do it?
  Vil.   I will, my Lord; but I must speake with him.
  Sal.   Why, so thou shalt; take Horse, and post from hence: 35
Onely before thou goest, sweare by thy faith,
That, if thou canst not compasse my desire,
Thou wilt returne my prisoner backe againe;
And that shalbe sufficient warrant for thee.
  Vil.   To that condition I agree, my Lord,   40
And will vnfaynedly performe the same.   *[Exit.*
  Sal.   Farewell, Villiers. —
This once I meane to trie a French mans faith.   *[Exit.*

SCENE II.

Picardy.   The English Camp before Calais.

Enter KING EDWARD *and* DERBY, *with Souldiers.*

  K. Edw.   Since they refuse our profered league, my Lord,
And will not ope their gates, and let vs in,
We will intrench our selues on euery side,
That neither vituals nor supply of men
May come to succour this accursed towne: 5
Famine shall combate where our swords are stopt.

Enter sixe poore Frenchmen.

  Der.   The promised aid, that made them stand aloofe,
Is now retirde and gone an other way:

31. *thyself*] *thou* AB, corr. by Cap.; *That he and thou* prop. by Cap.;
wert B. — 32. *thou*] *thyself* Col. — 39. *thee*] *mee* AB; corr. by Cap. —
43. *Thus* AB and Edd., *This* prop. by Cap. and adopted by Del.
  SCENE II. Stage-dir. add. by Cap. — 2. *their*] *the* B and Edd. —
6. Stage-dir. behind l. 9 in Cap. and Edd.; *six*] *some* Cap. and Edd.

It will repent them of their stubborne will.
10 But what are these poore ragged slaues, my Lord?
    K. Edw. Aske what they are; it seemes, they come from Callis.
    Der. You wretched patterns of dispayre and woe,
What are you, liuing men or glyding ghosts,
Crept from your graues to walke vpon the earth?
15 *Poore.* No ghosts, my Lord, but men that breath a life
Farre worse then is the quiet sleepe of death:
Wee are distressed poore inhabitants,
That long haue been deseased, sicke, and lame;
And now, because we are not fit to serue,
20 The Captayne of the towne hath thrust vs foorth,
That so expence of victuals may be saued.
    K. Edw. A charitable deed, no doubt, and worthy praise!
But how do you imagine then to speed?
We are your enemies; in such a case
25 We can no lesse but put ye to the sword,
Since, when we proffered truce, it was refusde.
    Poore. And if your grace no otherwise vouchsafe,
As welcome death is vnto vs as life.
    K. Edw. Poore silly men, much wrongd and more distrest!
30 Go, Derby, go, and see they be relieud;
Command that victuals be appoynted them,
And giue to euery one fiue Crownes a peece:
                    [*Exeunt* DERBY *and* FRENCHMEN.
The Lion scornes to touch the yeelding pray,
And Edwards sword must flesh it selfe in such
35 As wilfull stubbornnes hath made peruerse.

Enter LORD PEARSIE.

Lord Persie! welcome: whats the newes in England?
    Per. The Queene, my Lord, commends her to your Grace,
And from hir highnesse and the Lord viceregent

---

11. Two ll. in B, div. at *seemes.* — 12. *partners* B. — 13. *ye* B and
Edd. — 22. *no doubt* om. Cap., Tyr., Del. — 25. *you* B and Edd. — 27. *An
if* Cap. and Edd. — 30. *Good Derby* Cap. prop. — 32. Stage-dir. add.
by Cap. — 34. *fresh* AB, *flesh* conj. by Del. and Col. — 37. *comes heere*
AB; corr. by Cap. — 38. *vice-gerent* Del.

I bring this happie tidings of successe:
Dauid of Scotland, lately vp in armes,   40
Thinking, belike, he soonest should preuaile,
Your highnes being absent from the Realme,
Is, by the fruitfull seruice of your peeres
And painefull trauell of the Queene her selfe,
That, big with child, was euery day in armes,   45
Vanquisht, subdude, and taken prisoner.

   K. Edw.   Thanks, Persie, for thy newes, with all my hart!
What was he, tooke him prisoner in the field?

   Per.   A Squire, my Lord; Iohn Copland is his name:
Who since, intreated by her Maiestie,   50
Denies to make surrender of his prize
To anie but vnto your grace alone;
Whereat the Queene is greouously displeasd.

   K. Edw.   Well, then weele haue a Pursiuaunt dispatcht,
To summon Copland hither out of hand,   55
And with him he shall bring his prisoner king.

   Per.   The Queene's, my Lord, her selfe by this at Sea,
And purposeth, as soone as winde will serue,
To land at Callis, and to visit you.

   K. Edw.   She shall be welcome; and, to wait her comming,   60
Ile pitch my tent neere to the sandy shore.

Enter a French Caplayne.

   Capt.   The Burgesses of Callis, mighty king,
Haue by a counsell willingly decreed
To yeeld the towne and Castle to your hands,
Vpon condition, it will please your grace   65
To graunt them benefite of life and goods.

   K. Edw.   They wil so!   Then, belike, they may command,
Dispose, elect, and gouerne as they list.
No, sirra, tell them, since they did refuse
Our princely clemencie at first proclaymed,   70

<hr>

43. *faithfull* B and Edd. — 49. *A Esquire* A. — 54. *dispatch* A. —
57. *Queene my Lord* A; *The queen, my lord, herself's by* Cap. prop. —
61. Stage-dir. *French* add. by Del. — 62. Prefix CAPT. om. in A.

They shall not haue it now, although they would;
I will accept of nought but fire and sword,
Except, within these two daies, sixe of them,
That are the welthiest marchaunts in the towne,
75 Come naked, all but for their linnen shirts,
With each a halter hangd about his necke,
And prostrate yeeld themselues, vpon their knees,
To be afflicted, hanged, or what I please;
And so you may informe their masterships.

                          [*Exeunt* K. EDWARD *and* PERCY.

80 *Cap.* Why, this it is to trust a broken staffe:
Had we not been perswaded, Iohn our king
Would with his armie haue releeud the towne,
We had not stood vpon defiance so:
But now tis past that no man can recall,
85 And better some do go to wrack then all.   [*Exit.*

SCENE III.

Poitou. Fields near Poitiers. The French camp; Tent of the Duke of Normandy.

Enter CHARLES OF NORMANDY *and* VILLIERS.

    Charles. I wounder, Villiers, thou shouldest importune me
For one that is our deadly ennemie.
    Vil. Not for his sake, my gratious Lord, so much
Am I become an earnest aduocate,
5 As that thereby my ransome will be quit.
    Charles. Thy ransome, man? why, needest thou talke of that?
Art thou not free? and are not all occasions,
That happen for aduantage of our foes,
To be accepted of, and stood vpon?
10   *Vil.* No, good my Lord, except the same be iust;
For profit must with honor be comixt,
Or else our actions are but scandalous.

73. *this* B. — 79. (Stage-dir.) K. EDWARD *and* PERCY add. by Del.
SCENE III. Stage-dir. as given by Cap. — 8. *of*] *on* prop. by Cap.
and adopted by Del.; *of our*] *over* Col. conj. — 9. *unstood upon* Cap. prop.

But, letting passe these intricate obiections,
Wilt please your highnes to subscribe, or no?
  Charles.   Villiers, I will not, nor I cannot do it;   15
Salisbury shall not haue his will so much,
To clayme a pasport how it pleaseth himselfe.
  Vil.   Why, then I know the extremitie, my Lord;
I must returne to prison whence I came.
  Charles.   Returne? I hope thou wilt not;   20
What bird that hath escapt the fowlers gin,
Will not beware how shees insnard againe?
Or, what is he, so senceles and secure,
That, hauing hardely past a dangerous gulfe, .
Will put him selfe in perill there againe?   25
  Vil.   Ah, but it is mine othe, my gratious Lord,
Which I in conscience may not violate,
Or else a kingdome should not draw me hence.
  Charles.   Thine othe? why, that doth bind thee to abide:
Hast thou not sworne obedience to thy Prince?   30
  Vil.   In all things that vprightly he commands:
But either to perswade or threaten me,
Not to performe the couenant of my word,
Is lawlesse, and I need not to obey.
  Charles.   Why, is it lawfull for a man to kill,   35
And not, to breake a promise with his foe?
  Vil.   To kill, my Lord, when warre is once proclaymd,
So that our quarrel be for wrongs receaude,
No doubt, is lawfully permitted vs:
But, in an othe, we must be well aduisd,   40
How we do sweare; and, when we once haue sworne,
Not to infringe it, though we die therefore:
Therefore, my Lord, as willing I returne,
As if I were to flie to paradise.
  Charles.   Stay, my Villiers; thine honorable minde   45
Deserues to be eternally admirde.
Thy sute shalbe no longer thus deferd;

17. *please* prop. by Cap. and adopted by Del. — 20. *Villiers* add. at
the end of the line by Cap. and Edd. — 22. *be ware* Cap. and Del. — 26. *my
othe* B and Edd. — 45. *thy* B and Edd.

Giue me the paper, Ile subscribe to it:
And, where tofore I loued thee as Villiers,
50 Heereafter Ile embrace thee as my selfe;
Stay, and be still in fauour with thy Lord.
    Vil. I humbly thanke your grace; I must dispatch,
And send this pasport first vnto the Earle,
And then I will attend your highnes pleasure.
55   *Charles.* Do so, Villiers; — and Charles, when he hath neede,
Be such his souldiers, howsoeuer he speed! [*Exit* VILLIERS.

Enter KING IOHN.

    K. Iohn. Come, Charles, and arme thee; Edward is intrapt,
The Prince of Wales is falne into our hands,
And we haue compast him, he cannot scape.
60   *Charles.* But will your highnes fight to-day?
    K. Iohn. What else, my son? hees scarse eight thousand
And we are three score thousand at the least.   [strong,
    Charles. I haue a prophecy, my gratious Lord,
Wherein is written, what successe is like
65 To happen vs in this outragious warre;
It was deliuered me at Cresses field
By one that is an aged Hermyt there.
[*Reads*] 'When fethered foul shal make thine army tremble,
            And flint-stones rise and breake the battell-ray,
70   Then thinke on him that doth not now dissemble;
              For that shalbe the haples dreadfull day:
            Yet, in the end, thy foot thou shalt aduance
            As farre in England as thy foe in Fraunce.'
    K. Iohn. By this it seemes we shalbe fortunate:
75 For as it is impossible that stones
Should euer rise and breake the battaile-ray,
Or airie foule make men in armes to quake,   ·
So is it like, we shall not be subdude:
Or say this might be true, yet in the end,
80 Since he doth promise we shall driue him hence

58. *has* Col. — 61. Two ll. in B, div. at *sonne;* Cap. prop. *To day!
What else, my son.* — 66. *Crecy'* Tyr., *Cressi'* Del. — 68. [*Reads*] add.
by Cap.

And forrage their Countrie as they haue don ours,
By this reuenge that losse will seeme the lesse.
But all are fryuolous fancies, toyes, and dreames:
Once we are sure we haue insnard the sonne,
Catch we the father after how we can.   [*Exeunt.* 85

SCENE IV.

The same.   The English Camp.

Enter PRINCE EDWARD, AUDLEY, *and others.*

Pr. Edw.   Audley, the armes of death embrace vs round,
And comfort haue we none, saue that to die;
We pay sower earnest for a sweeter life.
At Cressey field our Clouds of Warlike smoke
Chokt vp those French mouths and disseuered them: 5
But now their multitudes of millions hide,
Masking as twere, the beautious burning Sunne,
Leauing no hope to vs, but sullen darke
And eielesse terror of all-ending night.
   Aud.   This suddaine, mightie, and expedient head   10
That they haue made, faire Prince, is wonderfull.
Before vs in the vallie lies the king,
Vantagd with all that heauen and earth can yeeld;
His partie stronger battaild then our whole:
His sonne, the brauing Duke of Normandie,   15
Hath trimd the Mountaine on our right hand vp
In shining plate, that now the aspiring hill
Shewes like a siluer quarrie or an orbe,
Aloft the which the Banners, bannarets,
And new-replenisht pendants cuff the aire   20
And beat the windes, that for their gaudinesse
Struggles to kisse them: on our left hand lies
Phillip, the younger issue of the king,
Coting the other hill in such arraie,

25   That all his guilded vpright pikes do seeme
Streight trees of gold, the pendants leaues;
And their deuice of Antique heraldry,
Quartred in collours, seeming sundry fruits,
Makes it the Orchard of the Hesperides:

30   Behinde vs too the hill doth beare his height,
For like a halfe Moone, opening but one way,
It rounds vs in; there at our backs are lodgd
The fatall Crosbowes, and the battaile there
Is gouernd by the rough Chattillion.

35   Then thus it stands: the valleie for our flight
The king binds in; the hils on either hand
Are proudly royalized by his sonnes;
And on the Hill behind stands certaine death
In pay and seruice with Chattillion.

40   *Pr. Edw.*   Deathes name is much more mightie then his deeds;
Thy parcelling this power hath made it more.
As many sands as these my hands can hold,
Are but my handful of so many sands;
Then, all the world, and call it but a power,

45   Easely tane vp, and quickly throwne away:
But if I stand to count them sand by sand,
The number would confound my memorie,
And make a thousand millions of a taske,
Which briefelie is no more, indeed, then one.

50   These quarters, squadrons, and these regiments,
Before, behinde vs, and on either hand,
Are but a power: When we name a man,
His hand, his foote, his head hath seuerall strengthes;
And being al but one selfe instant strength,

55   Why, all this many, Audely, is but one,
And we can call it all but one mans strength.
He that hath farre to goe, tels it by miles;
If he should tell the steps, it kills his hart:

The drops are infinite, that make a floud,
And yet, thou knowest, we call it but a Raine.   60
There is but one Fraunce and one King of Fraunce,
That Fraunce hath no more kings; and that same king
Hath but the puissant legion of one king,
And we haue one: Then apprehend no ods,
For one to one is faire equalitie.   65

Enter an Herald from KING IOHN.

What tidings, messenger? be playne and briefe.

   Her.   The king of Fraunce, my soueraigne Lord and master,
Greeteth by me his fo, the Prince of Wales:
If thou call forth a hundred men of name,
Of Lords, Knights, Squires, and English gentlemen,   70
And with thyselfe and those kneele at his feete,
He straight will fold his bloody collours vp,
And ransome shall redeeme liues forfeited;
If not, this day shall drinke more English blood,
Then ere was buried in our Bryttish earth.   75
What is the answere to his profered mercy?

   Pr. Edw.   This heauen, that couers Fraunce, containes the
That drawes from me submissiue orizons;   [mercy
That such base breath should vanish from my lips,
To vrge the plea of mercie to a man,   80
The Lord forbid! Returne, and tell thy king,
My tongue is made of steele, and it shall beg
My mercie on his coward <u>burgonet</u>;
Tell him, my colours are as red as his,
My men as bold, our English armes as strong;   85
Returne him my defiance in his face.

   Her.   I go.   [*Exit.*

Enter another Herald.

   Pr. Edw.   What newes with thee?

   Her.   The Duke of Normandie, my Lord and master,
Pittying thy youth is so ingirt with perill,

<hr>

61. *and* first add. by Cap. — 68. *Greets by me* AB, *Greets thus by
me* Cap., Tyr., and Del., *Greeteth by me* Col. — 69. *cull forth* Col. conj.;
an B and Edd.; *hundreth* B. — 70. *Esquires* A. — 75. *your* conj. in Col.
— 81 *thy*] *the* A. — 87. [*Exit.*] om. A; *Herald* (Stage-dir.) add. by Del.

5

90 By me hath sent a nimble-ioynted iennet,
 As swift as euer yet thou didst bestride,
 And therewithall he counsels thee to flie;
 Else death himself hath sworne that thou shalt die.
  Pr. Edw. Back with the beast vnto the beast that sent him!
95 Tell him, I cannot sit a cowards horse;
 Bid him to-daie bestride the iade himselfe;
 For I will staine my horse quite ore with bloud,
 And double guild my spurs, but I will catch him;
 So tell the carping boy, and get thee gone. [*Exit Herald.*

Enter another Herald.

100 *Her.* Edward of Wales, Phillip, the second sonne
 To the most mightie christian king of France,
 Seeing thy bodies liuing-date expird,
 All full of charitie and christian loue,
 Commends this booke, full fraught with holy prayers,
105 To thy faire hand, and, for thy houre of lyfe,
 Intreats thee that thou meditate therein,
 And arme thy soule for hir long iourney towards.
 Thus haue I done his bidding, and returne.
  Pr. Edw. Herald of Phillip, greet thy Lord from me:
110 All good that he can send, I can receiue;
 But thinkst thou not, the vnaduised boy
 Hath wrongd himselfe in thus far tendering me?
 Haply he cannot praie without the booke,
 — I thinke him no diuine extemporall —,
115 Then render backe this common place of prayer,
 To do himselfe good in aduersitie;
 Besides he knows not my sinnes qualitie,
 And therefore knowes no praiers for my auaile;
 Ere night his praier may be to praie to God,
120 To put it in my heart to heare his praier.
 So tell the courtly wanton, and be gone.
  Her. I go.   [*Exit Herald.*

<hr>

99. *capring* A; [*Exit Herald.*] and *Herald* after *another* add. by Del.
— 104. *holy* add. by Cap. and Tyr. — 112. *thus*] *this* A; *farre* B. —
113. *Happily* A. — 122. [*Exit Herald.*] om. A.

Pr. Edw. How confident their strength and number makes
Now, Audley, sound those siluer winges of thine, [them! —
And let those milke-white messengers of time 125
Shew thy times learning in this dangerous time.
Thyselfe art bruis'd and bit with many broiles,
And stratagems forepast with yron pens
Are texted in thine honorable face;
Thou art a married man in this distresse, 130
But danger wooes me as a blushing maide:
Teach me an answere to this perillous time.
  Aud. To die is all as common as to liue:
The one in choice, the other holds in chase;
For, from the instant we begin to liue, 135
We do pursue and hunt the time to die:
First bud we, then we blow, and after seed,
Then, presently, we fall; and, as a shade
Followes the bodie, so we follow death.
If, then, we hunt for death, why do we feare it? 140
If we feare it, why do we follow it?
If we do feare, how can we shun it?
If we do feare, with feare we do but aide
The thing we feare, to seize on vs the sooner:
If wee feare not, then no resolued proffer 145
Can ouerthrow the limit of our fate;
For, whether ripe or rotten, drop we shall,
As we do drawe the lotterie of our doome.
  Pr. Edw. Ah, good olde man, a thousand thousand armors
These words of thine haue buckled on my backe: 150
Ah, what an idiot hast thou made of lyfe,
To seeke the thing it feares! and how disgrast
The imperiall victorie of murdring death,
Since all the liues, his conquering arrowes strike,
Seeke him, and he not them, to shame his glorie! 155
I will not giue a pennie for a lyfe,
Nor halfe a halfepenie to shun grim death,

<hr>

124. *strings* Del. — 127. *bruis'd*] *busic* AB, corr. by Cap.; *bit*] *bent*
Cap. and Tyr. — 129. *texed* B, Cap., and Tyr. — 141. *Or, if we* Cap. and
Tyr. — 142. Om. in Cap. and Edd. — 151. *thou hast made* Col.

5*

Since for to liue is but to seeke to die,
And dying but beginning of new lyfe.
160 Let come the houre when he that rules it will!
To liue or die I hold indifferent.   [*Exeunt.*

SCENE V.

The same.   The French Camp.

Enter KING IOHN *and* CHARLES.

K. Iohn.   A sodaine darknes hath defast the skie,
The windes are crept into their caues for feare,
The leaues moue not, the world is husht and still,
The birds cease singing, and the wandring brookes
5 Murmure no wonted greeting to their shores;
Silence attends some wonder and expecteth
That heauen should pronounce some prophecie:
Where or from whome proceeds this silence, Charles?
   Charles.   Our men, with open mouthes and staring eyes,
10 Looke on each other, as they did attend
Each others wordes, and yet no creature speakes;
A tongue-tied feare hath made a midnight houre,
And speeches sleepe through all the waking regions.
   K. Iohn.   But now the pompeous Sunne, in all his pride,
15 Lookt through his golden coach vpon the worlde,
And, on a sodaine, hath he hid himselfe,
That now the vnder-earth is as a graue,
Darke, deadly, silent, and vncomfortable.   [*A clamor of rauens.*
Harke, what a deadly outcrie do I heare?
20   *Charles.*   Here comes my brother Phillip.
   K. Iohn.   All dismaid:

Enter PHILLIP.

What fearefull words are those thy lookes presage?
   Phil.   A flight, a flight!

SCENE V. Stage-dir. added by Cap. — 3. *wood* prop. by Cap. and
adopted by Del. — 8. *Whence* prop. by Cap. and adopted by Del. — 19. *a*
om. B. — 20. [*Enter* PHILLIP.] add. by Del. — 20, 21. *All dismaid* . . .
presage one line in A, two lines in B, divided at *words; All dismaid* put
in a line by itself in mod. Edd.

K. Iohn.   Coward, what flight? thou liest, there needs no
Phil.   A flight.   [flight.

K. Iohn.   Awake thy crauen powers, and tell on   25
The substance of that verie feare indeed,
Which is so gastly printed in thy face:
What is the matter?

Phil.   A flight of vgly rauens
Do croke and houer ore our souldiers heads,
And keepe in triangles and cornerd squares,   30
Right as our forces are imbatteled;
With their approach there came this sodain fog,
Which now hath hid the airie floor of heauen
And made at noone a night vnnaturall
Vpon the quaking and dismaied world: 35
In briefe, our souldiers haue let fall their armes,
And stand like metamorphosd images,
Bloudlesse and pale, one gazing on another.

K. Iohn.   I, now I call to mind the prophesie,
But I must giue no enterance to a feare. —   40
Returne, and harten vp those yeelding soules:
Tell them, the rauens, seeing them in armes,
So many faire against a famisht few,
Come but to dine vpon their handieworke
And praie vpon the carrion that they kill: 45
For when we see a horse laid downe to die,
Although he be not dead, the rauenous birds
Sit watching the departure of his life;
Euen so these rauens for the carcases
Of those poore English, that are markt to die,   50
Houer about, and, if they crie to vs,
Tis but for meate that we must kill for them.
Awake, and comfort vp my souldiers,
And sound the trumpets, and at once dispatch
This litle busines of a silly fraude.   [*Exit* PHILIP. 55

26. *The very substance of that feare* prop. by Cap. and adopted by
Del. — 33. *floor*] *flower* AB. — 41. *these* AB. — 47. *he be* add. by Cap.,
Tyr., and Del. — 50. *these* B. — 55. [*Exit Prince.*] A.

Another noise. SALISBURY *brought in by a French Captaine.*

    Cap. Behold, my liege, this knight and fortie mo,
Of whom the better part are slaine and fled,
With all indeuor sought to breake our rankes,
And make their waie to the incompast prince:
60 Dispose of him as please your maiestie.
    K. Iohn. Go, and the next bough, souldier, that thou seest,
Disgrace it with his bodie presently;
For I do hold a tree in France too good
To be the gallowes of an English theefe.
65   *Sal.* My Lord of Normandie, I haue your passe
And warrant for my safetie through this land.
    Charles. Villiers procurd it for thee, did he not?
    Sal. He did.
    Charles. And it is currant, thou shalt freely passe.
70   *K. Iohn.* I, freely to the gallows to be hangd,
Without deniall or impediment: —
Awaie with him!
    Charles. I hope your highnes will not so disgrace me,
And dash the vertue of my seale at armes:
75 He hath my neuer-broken name to shew,
Carectred with this princely hand of mine;
And rather let me leaue to be a prince
Than break the stable verdict of a prince:
I doo beseech you, let him passe in quiet.
80   *K. Iohn.* Thou and thy word lie both in my command;
What canst thou promise that I cannot breake?
Which of these twaine is greater infamie,
To disobey thy father or thyselfe?
Thy word, nor no mans, may exceed his power;
85 Nor that same man doth neuer breake his worde,
That keepes it to the vtmost of his power.
The breach of faith dwels in the soules consent:
Which if thyselfe without consent doo breake,
Thou art not charged with the breach of faith.
90 Go, hang him: for thy lisence lies in mee,
And my constraint stands the excuse for thee.

56. *more* mod. Edd. — 73—79. Given to VIL. in A.

Charles.   What, am I not a soldier in my word?
Then, armes, adieu, and let them fight that list!
Shall I not giue my girdle from my wast,
But with a gardion I shall be controld,   95
To saie, I may not giue my things awaie?
Vpon my soule, had Edward, prince of Wales,
Ingagde his word, writ downe his noble hand
For all your knights to passe his fathers land,
The roiall king, to grace his warlike sonne,   100
Would not alone safe conduct giue to them,
But with all bountie feasted them and theirs.
   K. Iohn.   Dwelst thou on presidents? Then be it so!
Say, Englishman, of what degree thou art.
   Sal.   An Earle in England, though a prisoner here,   105
And those that knowe me, call me Salisburie.
   K. Iohn.   Then, Salisburie, say whether thou art bound.
   Sal.   To Callice, where my liege, King Edward, is.
   K. Iohn.   To Callice, Salisburie? Then to Callice packe,
And bid the king prepare a noble graue,   110
To put his princely sonne, blacke Edward, in.
And as thou trauelst westward from this place,
Some two leagues hence there is a loftie hill,
Whose top seemes toplesse, for the imbracing skie
Doth hide his high head in her azure bosome;   115
Vpon whose tall top when thy foot attaines,
Looke backe vpon the humble vale beneath,
Humble of late, but now made proud with armes,
And thence behold the wretched prince of Wales,
Hoopt with a band of yron round about.   120
After which sight, to Callice spurre amaine,
And saie, the prince was smoothered, and not slaine:
And tell the king, this is not all his ill;

102. Elze (Notes I, 10) suggests to read *bounty'd = bounty had.* But
see Shak. Cor. IV. 6. 35: *We should by this, to all our lamentation, If he
had gone forth consul, found it so,* and Dekker, Shoemakers' Holiday III. 3. 61:
The puling girle Would willingly accepted Hammons loue. — 107. *whither* B.
— 112. *westwards* Tyr. — 116. *Unto* prop. by Cap. and adopted by Del.
— 117. *below* Cap. and Edd. — 120. *bond* A.

For I will greet him, ere he thinkes I will.
125 Awaie, be gone; the smoake but of our shot
  Will choake our foes, though bullets hit them not. *[Exit.*

SCENE VI.

The same. A Part of the Field of Battle.
Alarum. Enter Prince Edward *and* Artoys.

 Art. How fares your grace? are you not shot, my Lord?
 Pr. Edw. No, deare Artoys; but choakt with dust and
And stept aside for breath and fresher aire. [smoake,
 Art. Breath then, and too it againe! The amazed French
5 Are quite distract with gazing on the crowes;
 And, were our quiuers full of shafts againe,
 Your grace should see a glorious day of this: —
 O, for more arrowes! Lord, that's our want.
 Pr. Edw. Courage, Artoys! a fig for feathered shafts,
10 When feathered foules doo bandie on our side!
 What need we fight, and sweate, and keepe a coile,
 When railing crowes outscolde our aduersaries?
 Vp, vp, Artoys! The ground itselfe is armd
 With fire-containing flint; command our bowes
15 To hurle awaie their pretie-colored Ew,
 And to it with stones: Awaie, Artoys, awaie!
 My soule doth prophesie we win the daie. *[Exeunt.*

SCENE VII.

The same. Another Part of the Field of Battle.
Alarum. Enter King Iohn.

 K. Iohn. Our multitudes are in themselues confounded,
Dismayed, and distraught; swift-starting feare

126. [Exit.] om. B.
Scene VI. Stage-dir. add. by Cap. — 4. *to't* Cap. and Edd. —
8. *that is* Cap. and Edd. — 14. *With* om. AB and Del. — 16. *to't* Cap.
and Edd.
Scene VII. No scene marked in Edd. — 1. K. Iohn om. A.

Hath buzd a cold dismaie through all our armie,
And euerie pettie disaduantage promptes
The feare-possessed abiect soul to flie. 5
Myselfe, whose spirit is steele to their dull lead,
What with recalling of the prophesie,
And that our natiue stones from English armes
Rebell against vs, finde myselfe attainted
With strong surprise of weake and yeelding feare. 10

Enter CHARLES.

Charles. Fly, father, flie! the French do kill the French,
Some, that would stand, let driue at some that flie;
Our drums strike nothing but discouragement,
Our trumpets sound dishonor and retire;
The spirit of feare, that feareth nought but death, 15
Cowardly workes confusion on itselfe.

Enter PHILLIP.

Phil. Plucke out your eies, and see not this daies shame!
An arme hath beate an armie; one poore Dauid
Hath with a stone foild twentie stout Goliahs;
Some twentie naked staruelings, with small flints, 20
Hath driuen backe a puisant host of men,
Araid and fenst in all accoutrements.
K. Iohn. Mordieu, they quoit at vs, and kill vs up;
No lesse than fortie thousand wicked elders
Haue fortie leane slaues this daie stoned to death. 25
Charles. O, that I were some other countryman!
This daie hath set derision on the French,
And all the world will blurt and scorne at vs.
K. Iohn. What, is there no hope left?
Phil. No hope, but death, to burie vp our shame. 30
K. Iohn. Make vp once more with me; the twentieth part
Of those that liue, are men inow to quaile
The feeble handfull on the aduerse part.

---

11. CHARLES om. A. — 17. PHIL. om. A. — 21. *Haue* B and Edd. —
22 (*accomplements* (AB and Edd. — 23. *quait* AB. — 28. *wilt* A.

Charles.   Then charge againe: if heauen be not opposd,
35 We cannot loose the daie.

    K. Iohn.   On, awaie!   [*Exeunt.*

SCENE VIII.

The same.   Another Part of the Field of Battle.

Enter AUDLEY, *wounded, and rescued by two squires.*

    Esq.   How fares my Lord?
    Aud.   Euen as a man may do,
That dines at such a bloudie feast as this.
    Esq.   I hope, my Lord, that is no mortall scarre.
    Aud.   No matter, if it be; the count is cast,
5 And, in the worst, ends but a mortall man.
Good friends, conuey me to the princely Edward,
That in the crimson brauerie of my bloud
I may become him with saluting him.
Ile smile, and tell him, that this open scarre
10 Doth end the haruest of his Audleys warre.   [*Exeunt.*

SCENE IX.

The same.   The English Camp.

Enter PRINCE EDWARD, KING IOHN, CHARLES, *and all,*

with Ensignes spred.

Retreat sounded.

    Pr. Edw.   Now, Iohn in France, and lately Iohn of France,
Thy bloudie Ensignes are my captiue colours;
And you, high-vanting Charles of Normandie,

---

35. *On, on, away* Cap., Tyr., and Del.

    SCENE VIII.   No new scene in Edd. (Stage-dir.) *The same — Battle*
not in Edd.; *Esquires* B.

    SCENE IX.   Stage-dir. add. by Cap.

That once to-daie sent me a horse to flie,
Are now the subiects of my clemencie. 5
Fie, Lords, is it not a shame that English boies,
Whose early daies are yet not worth a beard,
Should in the bosome of your kingdome thus,
One against twentie, beate you vp together?
    K. Iohn. Thy fortune, not thy force, hath conquerd vs. 10
    Pr. Edw. An argument that heauen aides the right.

          Enter ARTOYS *with* PHILLIP.

See, see, Artoys doth bring with him along
The late good counsell-giuer to my soule!
Welcome, Artoys; and welcome, Phillip, too:
Who now of you or I haue need to praie? 15
Now is the prouerbe verified in you,
'Too bright a morning breeds a louring daie.'

      Sound Trumpets. Enter AUDLEY.

But say, what grym discoragement comes heere!
Alas, what thousand armed men of Fraunce
Haue writ that note of death in Audleys face? 20
Speake, thou that wooest death with thy careles smile,
And lookst so merrily vpon thy graue,
As if thou wert enamored on thyne end,
What hungry sword hath so bereaud thy face,
And lopt a true friend from my louing soule? 25
    Aud. O Prince, thy sweet bemoaning speech to me
Is as a morneful knell to one dead-sicke.
    Pr. Edw. Deare Audley, if my tongue ring out thy end,
My armes shalbe thy graue: What may I do
To win thy life, or to reuenge thy death? 30
If thou wilt drinke the blood of captyue kings,
Or that it were restoritiue, command
A Health of kings blood, and Ile drinke to thee;

<hr>

6. *is't not* B and Edd. — 12. *bring along with him* Cap., Tyr., and
Col. — 23. *thy* B and Edd., except Del. — 24. *bewreath'd* Col. — 26. *becoming* A. — 29. *thy*] *the* A. — 33. *Heath* AB.

If honor may dispence for thee with death,
35 The neuer-dying honor of this daie
Share wholie, Audley, to thyselfe, and liue.
  Aud. Victorious Prince, — that thou art so, behold
A Cæsars fame in kings captiuitie —,
If I could hold dym death but at a bay,
40 Till I did see my liege thy royall father,
My soule should yeeld this Castle of my flesh,
This mangled tribute, with all willingnes,
To darkenes, consummation, dust, and Wormes.
  Pr. Edw. Cheerely, bold man! thy soule is all too proud
45 To yeeld her Citie for one little breach;
Should be diuorced from her earthly spouse
By the soft temper of a French man's sword?
Lo, to repaire thy life, I giue to thee
Three thousand Marks a yeere in English land.
50 *Aud.* I take thy gift, to pay the debts I owe:
These two poore Squires redeemd me from the French
With lusty and deer hazzard of their liues:
What thou hast giuen me, 1 giue to them;
And, as thou louest me, Prince, lay thy consent
55 To this bequeath in my last testament.
  Pr. Edw. Renowned Audley, liue, and haue from mee
This gift twise doubled to these Squires and thee:
But liue or die, what thou hast giuen away
To these and theirs shall lasting freedome stay.
60 Come, gentlemen, I will see my friend bestowed
Within an easie Litter; then weele martch
Proudly toward Callis, with tryumphant pace,
Vnto my royall father, and there bring
The tribut of my wars, faire Fraunce his king.   [*Exeunt.*

---

  40. *loyall* AB. — 46. *She'ld* Del. — 51. *Esquires* AB. — 53. *given to me* Cap. and Edd. — 57. *Esquires* AB. — 60. *Ile see* B and Edd. — 64. *France's king* Cap. and Edd.

ACT V.

Picardy. The English Camp before Calais.

Enter KING EDWARD, QUEEN PHILLIP, DERBY, *soldiers.*

K. Edw. No more, Queene Phillip, pacifie yourselfe;
Copland, except he can excuse his fault,
Shall finde displeasure written in our lookes.
And now vnto this proud resisting towne!
Souldiers, assault; I will no longer stay, 5
To be deluded by their false delaies;
Put all to sword, and make the spoyle your owne.

*Enter sixe Citizens in their shirts, bare-foote, with halters about
their necks.*

All. Mercy, King Edward! mercie, gratious Lord!
K. Edw. Contemptuous villaines, call ye now for truce?
Mine eares are stopt against your bootelesse cryes: — 10
Sound drums; [*allarum*] draw threatning swords!
1. *Cit.* Ah, noble Prince, take pittie on this towne,
And heare vs, mightie king!
We claime the promise that your highnes made;
The two daies respit is not yet expirde, 15
And we are come with willingnes to beare
What tortering death or punishment you please,
So that the trembling multitude be saued.
K. Edw. My promise? Well, I do confesse as much:
But I require the cheefest Citizens 20
And men of most account that should submit;
You, peraduenture, are but seruile groomes,
Or some fellonious robbers on the Sea,
Whome, apprehended, law would execute,
Albeit seuerity lay dead in vs: 25
No, no, ye cannot ouerreach vs thus.

ACT V. Stage-dir. add. by Cap. — *Enter sixe Citizens &c.* before l. 1
in B and Edd. — 11. *drums, allarum, draw* AB, corr. by Cap. — 12 seqq. Given
to ALL in Edd. — 12, 13. Two ll. in modern Edd., divided at *Prince.* —
20. *requir'd* prop. by Cap. and adopted by Del.

    2. *Cit.* The Sun, dread Lord, that in the western fall
Beholds vs now low-brought through miserie,
Did in the Orient purple of the morne
30 Salute our comming forth, when we were knowne;
Or may our portion be with damned fiends.
    K. Edw. If it be so, then let our couenant stand
We take possession of the towne in peace:
But, for yourselues, looke you for no remorse;
35 But, as imperiall iustice hath decreed,
Your bodies shalbe dragd about these wals,
And after feele the stroake of quartering steele:
This is your dome; — go, souldiers, see it done.
    Queen. Ah, be more milde vnto these yeelding men!
40 It is a glorious thing to stablish peace,
And kings approch the nearest vnto God
By giuing life and safety vnto men:
As thou intendest to be king of France,
So let her people liue to call thee king;
45 For what the sword cuts down or fire hath spoyld,
Is held in reputation none of ours.
    K. Edw. Although experience teach vs this is true,
That peacefull quietnes brings most delight,
When most of all abuses are controld,
50 Yet, insomuch it shalbe knowne that we
As well can master our affections
As conquer other by the dynt of sword,
Phillip, preuaile; we yeeld to thy request:
These men shall liue to boast of clemencie,
55 And, tyrannie, strike terror to thyselfe.
    2. *Cit.* Long liue your highnes! happy be your reigne!
    K. Edw. Go, get you hence, returne vnto the towne,
And if this kindnes hath deserud your loue,
Learne then to reuerence Edward as your king. — [*Exeunt Citizens.*
60 Now, might we heare of our affaires abroad,

---

30. Elze (Notes &c. I, 11) supposes two verses to the following effect
to have dropped out: *To be the chiefest men of all our town; Of this, my
sovereign lord, be well assured.* — 31. *friends* Cap. — 33. *of this town*
Col. — 38. *doom* B. — 44. *her*] *thy* B. — 52. *others* Col.

We would, till glomy Winter were ore-spent,
Dispose our men in garrison a while.
But who comes heere?

Enter COPLAND *and* KING DAUID.

Der. Copland, my Lord, and Dauid, King of Scots.
K. Edw. Is this the proud presumtious Squire of the North, 65
That would not yeeld his prisoner to my Queen?
Cop. I am, my liege, a Northern Squire indeed,
But neither proud nor insolent, I trust.
K. Edw. What moude thee then, to be so obstinate
To contradict our royall Queenes desire? 70
Cop. No wilfull disobedience, mightie Lord,
But my desert and publike law of armes:
I tooke the king myselfe in single fight,
And, like a souldier, would be loath to loose
The least preheminence that I had won. 75
And Copland straight vpon your highnes charge
Is come to Fraunce, and, with a lowly minde,
Doth vale the bonnet of his victory:
Receiue, dread Lord, the custome of my fraught,
The wealthie tribute of my laboring hands, 80
Which should long since haue been surrendred vp,
Had but your gratious selfe bin there in place.
Queen. But, Copland, thou didst scorne the kings command,
Neglecting our commission in his name.
Cop. His name I reuerence, but his person more; 85
His name shall keepe me in allegeance still,
But to his person I will bend my knee.
K. Edw. I praie thee, Phillip, let displeasure passe;
This man doth please mee, and I like his words:
For what is he that will attempt great deeds, 90
And loose the glory that ensues the same?
All riuers haue recourse vnto the Sea,
And Coplands faith relation to his king.

62, 63. One line in B. — 64. *Sots* B. — 65. *Esquire* AB. — 67. *Northen*
A, *Northren* B; *Esquire* AB. — 69. K. EDW. om. B. — 72. *of]* at A. —
78. *vaile* B. — 90. *attmpt* A; *high* Cap. and Edd.

Kneele therefore downe: now rise, King Edwards knight;
95 And, to maintayne thy state, I freely giue
Fiue hundred marks a yeere to thee and thine.

Enter SALISBURY.

Welcome, Lord Salisburie: what news from Brittaine?
    Sal. This, mightie king: the Country we haue won,
And Iohn de Mountfort, regent of that place,
100 Presents your highnes with this Coronet,
Protesting true allegeaunce to your Grace.
    K. Edw. We thanke thee for thy seruice, valiant Earle;
Challenge our fauour, for we owe it thee.
    Sal. But now, my Lord, as this is ioyful newes,
105 So must my voice be tragicall againe,
And I must sing of dolefull accidents.
    K. Edw. What, haue our men the ouerthrow at Poitiers?
Or is our sonne beset with too much odds?
    Sal. He was, my Lord: and as my worthlesse selfe
110 With fortie other seruiceable knights,
Vnder safe conduct of the Dolphins seale,
Did trauaile that way, finding him distrest,
A troupe of Launces met vs on the way,
Surprisd, and brought vs prisoners to the king,
115 Who, proud of this, and eager of reuenge,
Commanded straight to cut off all our heads:
And surely we had died, but that the Duke,
More full of honor then his angry syre,
Procurd our quicke deliuerance from thence;
120 But, ere we went, 'Salute your king', quoth hee,
'Bid him prouide a funerall for his sonne,
To day our sword shall cut his thred of life;
And, sooner then he thinkes, weele be with him,
To quittance those displeasures he hath done.'
125 This said, we past, not daring to reply;
Our harts were dead, our lookes diffusd and wan.
Wandring at last we clymd vnto a hill,

From whence, although our griefe were much before,
Yet now to see the occasion with our eies
Did thrice so much increase our heauines.   130
For there, my Lord, oh, there we did descry
Downe in a vallie how both armies laie:
The French had cast their trenches like a ring,
And euery Barricados open front
Was thicke imbost with brasen ordynaunce;   135
Heere stood a battaile of ten thousand horse,
There twise as many pikes in quadrant wise,
Here Crosbowes, arm'd with deadly-wounding darts:
And in the midst, like to a slender poynt
Within the compasse of the horison,   140
As twere a rising bubble in the sea,
A Hasle-wand amidst a wood of Pynes,
Or as a beare fast chaind vnto a stake,
Stood famous Edward, still expecting when
Those doggs of Fraunce would fasten on his flesh.   145
Anon the death-procuring knell begins:
Off goe the Cannons, that, with trembling noyse,
Did shake the very Mountayne where they stood;
Then sound the Trumpets clangor in the aire,
The battailes ioyne: and, when we could no more   150
Discerne the difference twixt the friend and fo,
So intricate the darke confusion was,
Away we turnd our watrie eies with sighs,
As blacke as pouder fuming into smoke.
And thus, I feare, vnhappie haue I told   155
The most vntimely tale of Ewards fall.

   Queen.   Ah me! is this my welcome into Fraunce?
Is this the comfort that I lookt to haue,
When I should meete with my belooued sonne?
Sweete Ned, I would, thy mother in the sea   160
Had been preuented of this mortall griefe!

   K. Edw.   Content thee, Phillip; tis not teares will serue,
To call him backe, if he be taken hence:

   138. *Crosbowes and deadly* AB, corr. by Cap.; *armed, deadly* Col. —
148. *we stood* prop. by Cap. — 149. *clangors* Cap. and Edd.

Comfort thy selfe, as I do, gentle Queene,
165 With hope of sharpe, vnheard-of, dyre reuenge. —
He bids me to prouide his funerall,
And so I will; but all the Peeres in Fraunce
Shall mourners be, and weepe out bloody teares,
Vntill their emptie vaines be drie and sere:
170 The pillers of his hearse shall be their bones;
The mould that couers him, their Cities ashes;
His knell, the groning cryes of dying men;
And, in the stead of tapers on his tombe,
An hundred fiftie towers shall burning blaze,
175 While we bewaile our valiant sonnes decease.

After a flourish, sounded within, enter an Herald.

Her. Reioyce, my Lord; ascend the imperial throne!
The mightie and redoubted prince of Wales,
Great seruitor to bloudie Mars in armes,
The Frenchmans terror, and his countries fame,
180 Triumphant rideth like a Romane peere,
And, lowly at his stirop, comes afoot
King Iohn of France, together with his sonne,
In captiue bonds; whose diadem he brings
To crowne thee with, and to proclaime thee king.
185 *K. Edw.* Away with mourning, Phillip, wipe thine eies; —
Sound, Trumpets, welcome in Plantaginet!

Enter PRINCE EDWARD, KING IOHN, PHILLIP, AUDLEY, ARTOYS.

K. Edw. As things, long lost, when they are found again,
So doth my sonne reioyce his fathers heart,
For whom euen now my soule was much perplext.
190 *Queen.* Be this a token to expresse my ioy,   [*Kisse him.*
For inward passions will not let me speake.
Pr. Edw. My gracious father, here receiue the gift,
                    [*Presenting him with K. Iohn's crown.*

170. *their*] *his* AB and Edd., except Del. — 171. *Citie* AB, Cap. and
Tyr., *city's* Col., *cities'* Del. — 174. *fiftie*] *lofty* Col. — 192. [*Presenting
him &c.*] add. by Del.

This wreath of conquest and reward of warre,
Got with as mickle perill of our liues,
As ere was thing of price before this daie;   195
Install your highnes in your proper right:
And, herewithall, I render to your hands
These prisoners, chiefe occasion of our strife.

   K. Edw. So, Iohn of France, I see you keepe your word;
You promist to be sooner with our selfe   200
Then we did thinke for, and tis so indeed:
But, had you done at first as now you do,
How many ciuill townes had stoode vntoucht,
That now are turnd to ragged heaps of stones!
How many peoples liues mightst thou haue saud,   205
That are vntimely sunke into their graues!

   K. Iohn. Edward, recount not things irreuocable;
Tell me what ransome thou requirest to haue.

   K. Edw. Thy ransome, Iohn, hereafter shall be known:
But first to England thou must crosse the seas,   210
To see what intertainment it affords;
Howere it fals, it cannot be so bad,
As ours hath bin since we ariude in France.

   K. Iohn. Accursed man! of this I was fortolde,
But did misconster what the prophet told.   215

   Pr. Edw. Now, father, this petition Edward makes
To thee, whose grace hath bin his strongest shield,
That, as thy pleasure chose me for the man
To be the instrument to shew thy power,
So thou wilt grant that many princes more,   220
Bred and brought vp within that little Isle,
May still be famous for lyke victories!
And, for my part, the bloudie scars I beare,
The wearie nights that I haue watcht in field,
The dangerous conflicts I haue often had,   225
The fearefull menaces, were proffered me,
The heate and cold and what else might displease,
I wish were now redoubled twentiefold;
So that hereafter ages, when they reade

230 The painfull traffike of my tender youth,
    Might thereby be inflamd with such resolue,
    As not the territories of France alone,
    But likewise Spain, Turkie, and what countries els
    That iustly would prouoke faire Englands ire,
235 Might, at their presence, tremble and retire.
        K. Edw.   Here, English Lordes, we do proclaime a rest,
    An interceasing of our painfull armes:
    Sheath vp your swords, refresh your weary lims,
    Peruse your spoiles; and, after we haue breathd
240 A daie or two within this hauen-towne,
    God willing, then for England weele be shipt;
    Where, in a happie houre, I trust, we shall
    Arriue, three kings, two princes, and a queene.
                        [*Flourish.   Exeunt omnes.*

    232. *territory* Cap. prop. — 237. *An*] *And* Del.; *intercession* A. —
243. *Flourish. Exeunt omnes,* add. by Del.

THE END.

NOTES.

ACT I.

1, 12. Grammar seems to require *daughter;* cp. *thou art all my child,* i. e. my only child, All's III. 2. 71.

1, 36. *lyneal,* directly descending, hereditary, as often in Shakespeare.

1, 41. Read *th' true.* Capell was doubtless induced by the metre to strike out *And* (l. 41); the construction, however, is: *stryuing to rebate and* [*to*] *place . . .,* the participle *stryuing* referring to *our* (l. 39): *when may we show our duty more than in striving* &c. — As to *place,* establish in an office, cp. *this yellow slave will place thieves and give them title* Tim. IV. 3. 35; *if I can place thee, I will* Per. IV. 6. 204.

1, 46. *rakt,* i. e. *rackt,* tormented; cp. *racked with deep despair* Milton (quoted by Webster).

1, 76. *lame,* cp. *lame of sense* Oth. I. 3. 63, *most lame and impotent conclusion* ib. II. 1. 162.

1, 85. Cp. *we'll pull his plumes* 1 H. VI., III. 3. 7, *Ajax employed plucks down Achilles' plumes* Troil. I. 3. 386.

1, 90. Cp. *until it had returned These terms of treason doubled down his throat* Rich. II., I. 1. 57.

1, 98. *Lyon's case,* the lion's skin. This passage corroborates Wint. IV. 4. 844: *though my case be a pitiful one, I hope I shall not be flayed out of it.* Cp., besides, *The man that once did sell the lion's skin While the beast lived, was killed with hunting him.* H. V., IV. 3. 93.

1, 134. *plant,* to install, to invest. Cp. *Anointed, crowned, planted many years* Rich. II., IV. 127; *to plant unrightful kings* ib. V. 1. 63.

1, 159 *vre,* i. e. *inure* (not Shak.) *The French soldiers have from their youth been practised and ured in feats of arms.* Sir Th. More (quoted by Webster).

2, 7. *scornefull,* in a passive sense, as Lucr. 520 *So thy surviving husband shall remain The scornful mark of every open eye.*

2, 12. *skipping*, wanton. Cp. *so skipping a dialogue* Tw. I. 5. 214, *thy skipping spirit* Merch. II. 2. 196.

2, 23. *to make fair weather*, to conciliate oneself, Ado I. 3. 25, K. John V. 1. 21, 2 H VI., V. 1. 30.

2, 29. *Gymould*, consisting of links or rings: *And in their pale dull mouths the gimmal'd* (Old Edd. *Jymold*) *bit Lies foul with chewed grass* H. V., IV. 2. 49.

2, 33. *whinyard*, a sword or hanger. Nares · quotes, besides our passage, The Wits, O. Pl. VIII. 412 *This deboshed whinyard I will reclaim to comely bow and arrow.*

2, 75, 76. *Scot . . . they.* Cp. Troil. V. 3. 40 — 42 *When many times the captive Grecian falls, Even in the fan and wind of your fair sword, You bid them rise and live.*

2, 81. *O Sommers day*, o lucky hit. Cp. the common phrase *as one shall see in a summer's day*, Mids. I. 2. 89, H. V., III. 6. 67, ·ib. IV. 8. 23.

2, 96. Constr.: *As a May-blossom [is sullied] with pernitious winds.*

2, 104 seq. The sense is: to take piercing majesty from my eyes and to make them gaze on her with doting admiration.

2, 125. *no near*, i. e. no nearer. The old form of the comparative is often to be met with in Shakespeare.

2, 131. Cp. *Light seeking light doth light of light beguile* L. L. L., l. 1. 77, *by light we lose light* ib. V. 2. 376.

2, 153. *pide perfumes*, cp. *daisies pied* L. L. L., V. 2. 904. — *cost*, ornament, pomp.

ACT II.

1, 2. *to drinke.* The infinitive with *to* is often put in the second of two clauses (*and to*) after verbs which, according to modern grammar, would reject *to.* Cp. *Makes both my body pine, and soul to languish* Per. I. 2. 31, *And let them all encircle him about, And, fairy-like, to pinch the unclean knight* M. Wiv. IV. 4. 56. (Abbott, s. 250). On the other hand, cp. *still losing when I saw myself to win* Sonn. 119, 4; *To see great Hercules whipping a gig, And profound Solomon to tune* (some Edd. *tuning*) *a jig, And Nestor play at push-pin with the boys* L. L. L., IV. 3. 167 — 9.

1, 4. The verb belonging to *rack*, floating vapour, cloud, is only once used by Shakespeare in an intransive sense, *the racking clouds*, i. e. the fleeting clouds 3 H VI., II. 1. 27.

1, 29. It seems doubtful whether the poet intended a contrast between *spake* and *spoke*, both forms being very common in Elizabethan writers. Perhaps *spoke* is a mere misprint for *spake* (B).

1, 57. *queen of queens* L. L. L., IV. 3. 41; H. VIII., II. 4. 141; III. 2. 95. The reading of AB *queen* for *queens* is a misprint, *s* having dropped out before *s* in *shall*.

1, 68. *ready grone.* Cp. K. John II. 211 *ready mounted are they* (i. e. *the cannons*); Webster quotes: *we ourselves will go ready armed before the children of Isaac* Num. XXXII, 17. In both these instances, it is true, *ready* (adv.) is added to a participle, not to an infinitive.

1, 71. *Tarters.* As in Marlowe's Tamburlaine the word always appears in the form *Tarter*, we have thought *Torter* to be a misprint for *Tarter*.

1, 72. *flynt-heart*, i. e. flint-hearted.

1, 107. *sommer-leaping. to leap*, to be desirous, to rejoice; cp. below II. 2. 13 *What, doth his highnes leap to heare these news.* As to the composition of the word, cp. *the summer-swelling flower*, i. e. growing up in summer, Gent. II. 4. 162.

1, 122. *voluntarie*, spontaneous; cp. *voluntary dotage of some mistress* Oth. IV. 1. 27.   •

1, 127. Cp. *the hollow of thine ear* Rom. III. 5. 3.

1, 143 seqq. Cp. Rom. II. 2. 4:

> *Arise, fair sun, and kill the envious moon,*
> *Who is already sick and pale with grief*
> *That thou, her maid, art far more fair than she.*

1, 179—181. These lines are not in conformity either with the preceding or the following lines.

1, 184. *treasurer* (A). Painter, p. 186ᵃ: *to you that like a faithfull keeper and only treasurer of my heart, you may by some shining blame of pitte bring* &c. *treasure* was apparently introduced by B only for the sake of metre.

1, 186. We have not thought it necessary to alter *flankars* (AB), because the form *flankard*, though in another signification, also occurs.

1, 187. *discipline*, military skill, as often in Shak.

1, 235. Cp. *men indued with intellectual sense and souls.* Err. II. 1. 22.

1, 255 seqq. Cp. Meas. II. 4. 43.

> *It were as good*
> *To pardon him, that hath from nature stolen*
> *A man already made, as to remit*
> *Their saucy sweetness, that do coin Heaven's image*
> *In stamps that are forbid.*

1, 281. The reading *bewties* (twice) seems to be corroborated by passages as: *one that composed your beauties* Mids. I. 1. 48, *I might in virtues, beauties ... exceed account* Merch. III. 2. 158.

1, 284. Cp. *thy spiders that suck up thy venom.* Rich. II., III. 2. 14.

1, 296. Constr. *If I may . . . . and that* (= if) *my old endeuor* &c. As to the use of *that* cp. Sonn. 39, 13 *Were it not thy sour leisure gave sweet leave To entertain the time . . . And that thou teachest how to make one twain.*

1, 353. It would be better not to keep the oath rendered by my right hand (*prophane the Idoll*) than to have my hand cut off (*than confound it*).

1, 361. She would indeed do a favour to the love of the king, but would not bear true love to her husband.

1, 392. Cp. 2 H. VI., V. 1. 99 seqq:

> *these brows of mine,*
> *Whose smile and frown, like to Achilles' spear,*
> *Is able with the change to kill and cure.*

('alluding to Telephus cured by the dust scraped from Achilles' spear, by which he had been wounded.' Al. Schmidt.).

1, 396. Cp. *And he* (the lion) *from forage will incline to play.* L. L. L., IV. 1. 93.

1, 402. Though *vastures* may be a misprint for *vastness* (Collier), yet it may be an English form like *verdure, ordure.*

1, 404. *thy misdeeds.* Though the reading of the old editions *their misdeeds* is not devoid of sense, we have adopted Capell's conjecture on account of l. 398, which contains the same idea.

1, 412. We are unable to quote another passage in which *besiege* is used as a noun.

1, 414. Pron. *inj'rèd.* We think it impossible that *inuierd* should be an abbreviation from *environed*, which, besides, would be much too weak an expression to be used here by the Countess. *inwired*, prop. by Delius, is not to be found in any dictionary, and can therefore not be introduced into the text.

1, 438. Cp. Haml. II. 2. 181: *For if the sun breeds magots in a dead dog, being a good kissing carrion . . .*

1, 451. The same line occurs Shak. Sonn. 94, 14. See Introduction, p. xxx.

2, 10. The spelling *leiuetenant* is not to be altered, as it proves the pronunciation of the word.

2, 13. *to leap*, to be desirous; cp. *our master will leap to be his friend* Ant. III. 13. 51 and Per. V. 3. 45 *my heart leaps to be gone into my mother's bosom.*

2, 42—43. These lines are possibly to be printed as one line (AB) and to be read: *She's as | imp'ra | tor o | ver me | and I | to her* Cp. supra l. 5, and II. 1. 417.

2, 56. *him* i. e. him that beats the drum.

2, 64. The same quibble perhaps Gentl. V. 4. 57: *I'll woo you like a soldier, at arms' end.* ‾

2, 83. 'which cannot use poverty as a pretext.'

2, 117. *rarieties*, the reading of the old editions, is quite an incongruous formation and probably only a misprint for *varieties*, which in our passage agrees very well with the preceding *register*. Shakespeare uses *variety* in a similar sense when speaking of Cleopatra, Ant. II. 2. 240: *Age cannot wither her, nor custom stale Her infinite variety.*

2, 118. *Letherne Adam.* Elze, Notes II, p. 3, thinks *letherne* to be O. E. *leper, liper, leperand = nequam, malus*, vile, hateful. But as *lether* in this signification is not to be met with in Elizabethan English, and as, besides, Adam, in our context at least, can hardly be called *nequam, malus*, we incline to adopt Mr. Furnivall's explanation (Transactions of the New Shakspere Society Dec. 9, 1881, p. 10; Academy, July 22, 1882) who supposes the expression to be equivalent to 'Adam clad in skins.' This explanation is supported by Genesis III. 21: *'Unto Adam also and to his wife did the Lord God make coats of skin and clothed them'*, and particularly by Shak. Err. IV. 3. 13 *the picture of old Adam* ('meaning the bailiff because the buff he wore resembled the native buff of Adam' Al. Schmidt, s. v.)

2, 124. *objection*, suit, request.

2, 136. 'I render my discontent subject to my submission, to my resignation.' As to *content*, cp. Rich. II., V. 2. 38 *To whose high will we bound our calm contents.*

2, 137. The sense of the somewhat irregular construction is: 'I will compel myself willingly to do what I would not like to do.'

2, 143. There is no reason to read with Elze *my thrice loved lord*, the present participle (gerund) often having the meaning of a passive participle. See Abbott, s. 372, and cp. Ant. III. 13. 77: *his all-obeying breath*, i. e. obeyed by all, Lucr. 993: *his unrecalling crime.* *loving* = beloved, kind, affectionate, friendly, very often occurs in Shakespeare: *my loving subjects* K. John II. 203, *my friends and loving countrymen* 1 H VI., III. 1. 137, *most loving liege* Rich. II., I. 1. 21. See Al. Schmidt, s. v. *unrecalling* and *love*.

2, 168. *packing*, deceitful. Cp. *here's packing to deceive us all* Shr. V. 1. 121.

2, 169, 170. As a quibble is doubtless intended between *Resolude* and *dissolude*, we have adopted Capell's conjecture (l. 170), and have, besides, introduced the same word in l. 169. The error is easily to be accounted for, as the printer or corrector tried to give the first line the regular number of syllables, and consequently wrote *Resolute* also in l. 170.

2, 197. Commonly taken for an allusion to Shakespeare's Lucrece (p. in 1594). The story of Lucrece was also in Painter's Palace of Pleasure, and there seems to have existed a drama about the same subject.

ACT III.

1, 19 seqq. These lines are addressed to Charles; Collier's proposal to read *your* for *his* l. 20 is therefore unnecessary.

1, 27. *swill*, to drink greedily; cp. Rich. III., V. 2. 9 *The boar that swills your warm blood like wash.*

1, 30. *stall*, install, invest; cp. Rich. III., I. 3. 206 *decked in thy rights as thou art stalled in mine.*

1, 97. *on the lower hand;* cp. *on the upper hand* R. III., IV. 4. 37.

1, 126. *to buckle*, to join in close fight, as often in Shak.

1, 176. *lay about*, to fall to work with might and main, to do one's best, especially in fighting. Troil. I. 2. 58: *he'll lay about him to-day.*

2, 12. *envy*, malice, ill-will, as often in Shakespeare, f. i. *you turn the good we offer into envy* H. VIII., III. 1. 113.

3, 1. As we don't know any other instance in which *guide* is = guiding, guidance, we have thought it best to adopt Cap.'s proposal.

3, 6. In Holinshed's Chronicle the French guide is called *Gobin de Grace.*

3, 20. We have printed the names as given by Holinshed.

3, 77. *to foile my fame.* Cp. *And must not foil the precious note of it* (the crown) *with a base slave* Cymb. II. 3. 126 (M. Edd. *soil*).

3, 81. Elze (Notes I, 5) proposes to read *lime* f. *line*, but he gives no instance for the use of *lime* = paint. As to *line*, cp. As III. 2. 97 *all the pictures fairest lined are but black to Rosalind.*

3, 113. *that* supplies the place of *Before* (l. 112) and *turne* is the subjunctive mood. The construction was not understood and consequently altered by B.

3, 155. *wantoness* (= wanton) occurs again III. 5. 102 (not Shak.).

3, 161. *resty-stiffe*, stiff with too much rest, cp. Cymb. III. 6. 34: *when resty sloth finds the down pillow hard.*

3, 175. *tipe*, distinguishing mark, sign, badge; H. VIII., I. 3. 31: *tall stockings, short blistered breeches, and those types of travel.*

✓ 3, 190. *laurel*, adjectively used also by Shakespeare, *laurel victory* Ant. I. 3. 100.

✓ 3, 214. *to patronage* twice in Shakespeare 1 H. VI., III. 1. 48 and III. 4. 32.

✗ 5, 12. *fell* = fallen, Tit. II. 4. 50, Tim. IV. 3. 265, Lear IV. 6. 54.

5, 36. *those* = such.

✓ 5, 37. *breaketh out*, forces his way.   Cp. K. John V. 6. 24: *broke out to acquaint you with this evil.*   The construction of l. 38, in Capell's reading, is quite unintelligible.

✓ 5, 79. *often*, adjectively used; cp. *my often rumination* As IV. 1. 19.

✓ 5, 109. *upshot*, final issue, conclusion Tw. IV. 2. 76: *I cannot pursue this sport to the upshot.*

ACT IV.

✓ 1, 16. *Yet* = now, by this time (Germ. jetzt); cp. H. V., III. 3. 1: *How yet resolves the governor of the town.*

2, 34. Cp. 1 H. IV., V. 4. 133: *full bravely hast thou fleshed thy maiden sword,* 1 H. VI., IV. 7. 36: *did flesh his puny sword in Frenchmen's blood.*

3, 8. As Shakespeare uses much more frequently *to make* (*take*) *advantage of* than *to take advantage on*, it seems unnecessary to alter with Capell and Delius *of* into *on*.

✓ 4, 5. *mouths*, i. e. moths.

4, 44, 45.   Cp. *So Beauty blemished once* (*is*) *for ever lost* P. P. 13. See Abbott, s. 403.

4, 75. *in our Bryttish earth*, in Britanny (?). *in your Brittish earth*, as proposed in Collier, seems to be too gross a hyperbole.

✓ 4, 83. *burgonet*, close fitting helmet, used by Shakespeare only 2. H. VI., V. 1. 200, 204, 208; Ant. I. 5. 24.

4, 124. *siluer wings.* "Perhaps the writer was thinking of the Homeric ἔπεα πτερόεντα. Silver refers to the sweetness of Audley's eloquence. Milk-white messengers are his grey locks which have brought with them experience." W. G. S. (i. e. W. G. Stone, Leopold-Shakspere, Introd., p. C.).

4, 134. 'Whichsoever we may choose, either life or death, the one holds the other in chase: for life hunts after death, and death prosecutes life.'

4, 140 seqq.   Cp. Jul. Cæsar II. 2. 32:
Cowards die many times before their deaths,
The valiant never taste of death but once.
Of all the wonders that I yet have heard,
It seems to me most strange that men should fear,

> *Seeing that death, a necessary end,*
> *Will come when it will come.*

7, 22. As *accomplements* is not given in the dictionaries, we have preferred to read *accoutrements*.

7, 24. *elders*, unusually = old soldiers.

8, 7. *brauery*, splendor, finery; cp. *with scarp and fans and double change of bravery* Shr. IV. 3. 57.

9, 5. *Are.* The construction is not quite exact, but the sense is clear.

9, 26. The reading of A *becoming* might perhaps quite as well have been retained.

9, 32. *that* = if; cp. note ad II. 1. 296.

9, 37, 38. The captivity of the king will procure thee a Cæsar's fame.

ACT V.

39. Cp. Shak. Merch. IV. 1. 192:

> *But mercy is above this sceptred sway;*
> *It is enthroned in the hearts of Kings,*
> *It is an attribute to God himself;*
> *And earthly power doth then show likest God's,*
> *When mercy seasons justice.*

124. *to quittance* occurs in Shakespeare only 1 H. VI., II. 1. 14.

154. Cp. *black despair* 2 H. VI., III. 3. 23, R. III., II. 2. 36., and *saw sighs reek from you* L. L. L., IV. 3. 140, *he furnaces the thick sighs from him* Cymb. I. 6. 67, *love is a smoke raised with the fume of sighs* Rom. I. 1. 196.

EHRHARDT KARRAS, Printer, Halle.

PSEUDO-SHAKESPEARIAN PLAYS.

EDITED

BY

KARL WARNKE, PH. D.

AND

LUDWIG PROESCHOLDT, PH. D.

IV. THE BIRTH OF MERLIN

HALLE:

MAX NIEMEYER.

1887.

THE BIRTH OF MERLIN.

REVISED AND EDITED

WITH INTRODUCTION AND NOTES

BY

KARL WARNKE, PH. D.

AND

LUDWIG PROESCHOLDT, PH. D.

––––––––

HALLE:

MAX NIEMEYER.

1887.

A.257858

INTRODUCTION.

In 1662 Kirkman the bookseller published a drama with the title '*The Birth of Merlin: Or, the Childe hath found his Father: As it hath been several times Acted with great applause. Written by William Shakespear, and William Rowley. Placere cupio. London: Printed by Tho: Johnson for Francis Kirkman, and Henry Marsh, and are to be sold at the Princes Arms in Chancery Lane. 1662.'* [London, British Museum, C. 34. l. 7]. As the play seems not to have been mentioned before, and as Kirkman gives us no notice of the copy from which he had it printed, we neither know when *The Birth of Merlin* was first performed, nor on what authority the publisher attributed it to Shakespeare and Rowley. In all appearance Kirkman simply reprinted the play from an old edition. Grammar and versification bear distinctly the stamp of the age of Queen Elizabeth or King James I. Besides, if Kirkman had chosen to alter the text, he would certainly not have printed the whole of the play as prose, but would have tried to re-establish the verse-lines, in which the play originally must have been written.

The play was edited again by H. Tyrrell (The Doubtful Plays of Shakespeare, London, 1851, pp. 411—443), and, somewhat later, quite independently of Tyrrell's edition, by Delius (Pseudo-shakspearesche Dramen, vol. II., Elberfeld, 1856).[1]) Both editors took pains to correct the text which, though not so corrupt as that of many other contemporary plays, yet exhibits a certain number of passages to which the critic's knife must be applied. Both editors, however, overshot their mark by modernizing the grammar of the play and by introducing into it a great many alterations which for the most part are quite uncalled for. Tyrrell, besides, gives no various readings at all; the list of various readings

---

1) Delius' edition was without any corrections or additions reprinted by Max Moltke, Tauchnitz-edition, vol. 1041, p. 279—352.

exhibited by Delius, is far from being exhaustive. Thus, we hope, a new edition of the interesting play will be welcomed by all the friends of Elizabethan literature.

Professor Elze has devoted some of his Notes on Elizabethan Dramatists (Halle, 1880—1886) to our play, viz. vol. I., No. II—VI, and vol. II., No. CI. These emendations as well as the corrections and alterations of the precedent editors have been carefully pointed out by us in the footnotes of our edition.

The title-page of *The Birth of Merlin* bears the names of Shakespeare and Rowley. All that is known about the life of W. Rowley, is summed up by A. W. Ward, History of English Dramatic Literature, vol. II., p. 134 seq. 'William Rowley (who has been confounded not only with his namesake Samuel, but with another Rowley of the name of Ralph) is mentioned as an actor of the Duke of York's company in the year 1610, but already in 1607 he had produced, together with Day and Wilkins, a play *The Travailes of the Three English Brothers* (the brothers Shirley)[1]. In 1613 he was a leading member in the same (now the Prince of Wales') company; in 1637 he married; and nothing further is known of his life (except that he acted in one of his plays and in a mask by Middleton). A tradition handed down by Langbaine records that he was 'beloved by those great men, Shakespeare, Fletcher, and Jonson'.' W. Rowley's extant plays are *A New Wonder, A Woman Never Vext* (a comedy, pr. 1632), *All's Lost by Lust* (a tragedy, pr. 1633), *A Match at Midnight* (a comedy, pr. 1633), *A Shoemaker a Gentleman* (a comedy, pr. 1638). Besides Rowley wrote together with Massinger *The Parliament of Love* (licensed for the stage 1624); together with Fletcher *The Maid in the Mill* (first acted 1623), also, according to Dyce, *The Queen of Corinth* (produced between 1616 and 1619) and *The Bloody Bro-ther* (written after 1624); together with Middleton *A Fair Quarrel* (pr. 1617), *The World tossed at Tennis* (pr. 1620), *The Changeling* (acted 1623), *The Spanish Gipsey* (pr. 1653); together with Dekker and Ford *The Witch of Edmonton* (pr. 1658); together with Web-

---

[1] Considering the dates of Rowley's other compositions, it must be doubtful whether *The Old Law*, the title-page of which bears the names of Rowley, Middleton, and Massinger, was in fact composed as early as 1599, as Steevens, on the evidence of a passage in the play, feels inclined to suppose.

ster *A Cure for a Cuckold* (pr. 1661, by Kirkman), and *The Thra-cian Wonder* (pr. 1661, by Kirkman)[1]). As after all this W. Rowley was a favorite and well-known author of the age, it may well be that Kirkman, who attributed several plays to him, is right to say that he was also the author of *The Birth of Merlin*. But whether Shakespeare had a hand in the composition of this play, is an assertion which seems far less plausible.

Kirkman's intimation has, as far as we see, only been adopted by Tieck; all other critics, particularly Ulrici (Shakespeare's Dramatische Kunst vol. III., p. 109 seq.) and A. W. Ward (l. c., vol. I., p. 468 seq.) are of opinion that Shakespeare cannot be supposed to have had any share in our play. *The Birth of Merlin* was the first play read and copied by Tieck, when he first came to London in 1817. Twelve years afterwards he made the drama, together with other plays, known to his own countrymen by publishing a translation of it in his Shakespeare's Vorschule, Leipzig, 1829, vol. II., p. 219—366[2]). In the introductory pages preceding his translation, Tieck gives an analysis of the play, in which he sets forth all that may be said in favour of it. And indeed, it must be allowed that the author of the play, whoever he may have been, had some of the qualities requisite to a dramatic poet. The plot is on the whole well conducted; the scenes are full of action and dramatic life; the characters, particularly Prince Uter and Jane the Mother of Merlin, are somewhat skilfully shadowed forth. All those qualities, however, may be freely allowed to a great number of anonymous plays of the age, without entitling us to ascribe them to Shakespeare. And we are, it will seem, the less permitted to attribute even part of *The Birth of Merlin* to England's great poet, as the play shows deficiencies not to be met with in Shakespeare's genuine works.

In *The Birth of Merlin*, as in many other plays of the period, two stories form the groundwork on which the action of the drama is raised. But far from being skilfully intertwined with each other and melted into one, these two plots are not even externally con-nected with each other; the tragical fate of King Aurelius and

---

[1]) Cp. Delius, l. c., p. VI. seq.

[2]) The play was again translated into German by H. Döring (Gotha, 1833; 2nd ed. 1840), and by E. Ortlepp, Nachträge zu Shakespeare, vol. I., pp. 177—290.

the accession of his brother Uter Pendragon have no relation whatever to the episode in which the two daughters of the Earl of Chester play the principal part. It is hardly to be supposed that Shakespeare, who in his own works most harmoniously blended two or more stories into one, should not have been aware of the chasm gaping between the two plots of the play.

Likewise the characters in *The Birth of Merlin* would have taken quite a different turn, if touched up by Shakespeare's pen. At the time at which apparently our play was written, Shakespeare was composing his most consummate works, such as *Lear*, *Macbeth*, and *Coriolanus*. At that epoch he would certainly not have been contented with such poor and shallow characters as the Hermit and Earl Edol are in our play. Nor would he, as A. W. Ward rightly points out, have omitted the opportunity of revealing more psychological depth in the conflict of the Prince between duty and passion. And, last, not least, Shakespeare would certainly have succeeded in forming out of the renowned Merlin a figure more dramatic and more interesting than the Merlin of our play. Though it is true that the character of the marvellous boy-prophet is not destitute of a certain genuine freshness and briskness, yet the author of the play seems to have made use of him for no higher purpose than the gratification of the groundlings. Even admitting that the scenes grouped around Merlin, his hell-born father, and the Clown are due to Rowley's pen, it is quite improbable that in a play, written, though only in part, by Shakespeare, the character from which the whole play is named, should take so very little part in the action of it, as Merlin does. All that Merlin performs is to foretell their fate to the King, to Vortiger, and the Prince. And he foretells it invariably in the same manner, always conjuring up more or less frightful apparitions and shows of demons, dragons, and kings. 'The design of our dramatist', to use the words of A. W. Ward, 'seems to have fallen short of the poetic conception of a poetic theme, while his execution, though vigorous, is so coarse as to give a burlesque air to much of his drama. Shakspere at least would never have taken part in a work which after so rude and coarse a fashion ventured on the same kind of ground as that familiar to his own airy step' (l. c., vol. I., p. 469).

In most of the so-called Pseudo-Shakespearian Plays, particularly in *The Two Noble Kinsmen* and *King Edward III.*, the editors and commentators have been able to point out a number of passages and phrases which remind the reader of Shakespeare. Nothing of the kind is to be found in *The Birth of Merlin*. Throughout the play the language is either rough and homebred, or stilted and artificial; the verse, too, is uneven and far from showing Shakespeare's happy hand. Surely, no unbiassed reader will, in the absence of all external arguments, be disposed only from internal evidence to ascribe the play to Shakespeare. And indeed, Tieck himself seems to have been of opinion that the play, as it is, is not quite worthy of Shakespeare's genius, since he concludes his essay with the words: 'Had Shakespeare completed the play by himself, it is not to be doubted that we should be indebted to him for a production far superior to *The Birth of Merlin*.'

We are sorry to have to state that in spite of our researches we have not succeeded in discovering the special source from which the contents, especially the comic scenes, of our play have been taken. Let us hope that we are more successful, when we have the opportunity of consulting again the rich collections of the British Museum.

THE BIRTH OF MERLIN:

OR,

THE CHILDE HATH FOUND HIS FATHER.

DRAMATIS PERSONÆ.

AURELIUS, *King of Brittain.*

VORTIGER, *King of the Welsh Brittains.*

VTER PENDRAGON *the Prince, Brother to* AURELIUS.

DONOBERT, *a Nobleman, and Father to* CONSTANTIA *and* MODESTIA.

The Earl of GLOSTER, *and Father to* EDWYN.

EDOLL, *Earl of Chester, and General to* KING AURELIUS.

CADOR, *Earl of Cornwal, and Suitor to* CONSTANTIA.

EDWYN, *Son to the Earl of* GLOSTER, *and Suitor to* MODESTIA.

TOCLIO *and* OSWOLD, *two Noblemen.*

MERLIN *the Prophet.*

ANSELME *the Hermit, after Bishop of Winchester.*

CLOWN, *brother to* IONE, *mother of* MERLIN.

SIR NICHODEMUS NOTHING, *a Courtier.*

THE DEVIL, *father of* MERLIN.

OSTORIUS, *the Saxon General.*

OCTA, *a Saxon Nobleman.*

PROXIMUS, *a Saxon Magician.*

Two Bishops.

Two Saxon Lords.

Two of EDOLS *Captains.*

Two Gentlemen.

A little Antick Spirit.

ARTESIA, *Sister to* OSTORIUS *the Saxon General.*

CONSTANTIA *and* MODESTIA } *Daughters to* DONOBERT.

IONE GOE-TOO'T, *Mother of* MERLIN.

A Waiting-woman to ARTESIA.

LUCINA, *Queen of the Shades.*

The Scene: BRITTAIN.

Dramatis Personæ. *Vortiger, King of Brittain* A and Del., *Vortiger, King of Wales* Tyr.; cp. IV. 1. *Vortiger, King of the Welsh Brittains.*

ACT I.

SCENE I.

A Room in the Castle of Lord DONOBERT.

Enter DONOBERT, GLOSTER, CADOR, EDWIN, CONSTANTIA,
and MODESTIA.

Cador. You teach me language, sir, as one that knows
The Debt of Love I owe unto her Vertues;
Wherein like a true Courtier I have fed
My self with hope of fair Success, and now
Attend your wisht consent to my long Suit.   5
   Dono. Believe me, youthful Lord,
Time could not give an opportunity
More fitting your desires, always provided,
My Daughters love be suited with my Grant.
   Cador. 'Tis the condition, sir, her Promise seal'd.   10
   Dono. Ist so, Constantia?
   Const. I was content to give him words for oathes;
He swore so oft he lov'd me —
   Dono. That thou believest him?
   Const. He is a man, I hope.   15
   Dono. That's in the trial, Girl.
   Const. However, I am a woman, sir.
   Dono. The Law's on thy side then: sha't have a Husband,
I, and a worthy one. Take her, brave Cornwal,
And make your happiness great as our wishes.   20

   The whole of the play, the rhyme-couplets only excepted, being printed
as prose in A, we shall only indicate the passages in which we differ from
the division of lines as adopted by Delius.
   ACT I. SCENE I. Stage - dir. add. by Tyr. — 2. *their Vertues* A and
Edd. — 13. *me* —] *me.* A and Edd. — 20. *your*] *our* A and Edd. Tieck:
So schön sei euer Glück wie unsre Wünsche.

Cador.   Sir, I thank you.

Glost.   Double the fortunes of the day, my Lord,
And crown my wishes too: I have a son here,
Who in my absence would <u>protest</u> no less
25   Unto your other Daughter.

Dono.   Ha, Gloster, is it so? what says Lord Edwin?
Will she protest as much to thee?

Edwin.   Else must she want some of her Sisters faith, Sir.

Modest.   Of her credulity much rather, Sir:
30   My Lord, you are a Soldier, and methinks
The height of that Profession should diminish
All heat of Loves desires,
Being so late employ'd in blood and ruine.

Edwin.   The more my Conscience tyes me to repair
35   The worlds losses in a new succession.

Modest.   Necessity, it seems, ties your affections then,
And at that rate I would unwillingly
Be thrust upon you; a wife is a dish soon cloys, sir.

Edwin.   Weak and diseased appetites it may.

40   *Modest.*   Most of your making have dull stomacks, sir.

Dono.   If that be all, Girl, thou shalt quicken him;
Be kinde to him, Modestia: Noble Edwin,
Let it suffice, what's mine in her, <u>speaks yours</u>;
For her consent, let your fair suit go on,
45   She is a woman, sir, and will be won.

Edwin.   You give me comfort, sir.

Enter TOCLIO.

Dono.   Now, Toclio?

Toclio.   The King, my honor'd Lords, requires your presence,
And calls a Councel for return of answer
Unto the parling enemy, whose Embassadors
50   Are on the way to Court.

Dono.   So suddenly?
Chester, it seems, has ply'd them hard at war,
They sue so fast for peace, which by my advice

---

35. *worlds* may be read as a disyllable. — 42. *Modesta* A. — 46. *Enter*
TOCLIO after l. 45 in A.

They ne're shall have, unless they leave the Realm.
Come, noble Gloster, let's attend the King.
It lies, sir, in your Son to do me pleasure,   55
And save the charges of a Wedding-Dinner;
If you'l make haste to end your Love-affairs,
One cost may give discharge to both my cares. [*Exit* DONO.,

    Edwin. I'le do my best.   ·GLOSTER.
    Cador. Now, Toclio, what stirring news at Court?   60
    Toclio. Oh, my Lord, the Court's all fill'd with rumor, the
City with news, and the Country with wonder, and all the
bells i'th' Kingdom must proclaim it, we have a new Holy-day
a coming.
    Const. A holy-day! for whom? for thee?   65
    Toclio. Me, Madam! 'sfoot! I'de be loath that any man
should make a holy-day for me yet:
In brief, 'tis thus: There's here arriv'd at Court,
Sent by the Earl of Chester to the King,
A man of rare esteem for holyness,   70
A reverent Heremit, that by miracle
Not onely saved our army,
But without aid of man o'rethrew
The pagan Host, and with such wonder, sir,
As might confirm a Kingdom to his faith.   75
    Edwin. This is strange news, indeed; where is he?
    Toclio. In conference with the King, that much respects him.
    Modest. Trust me, I long to see him.
    Toclio. Faith, you will find no great pleasure in him, for

---

66—67. Elze, Notes on Elizabethan Dramatists, vol. 1., Halle, 1880, p. 2.
considers these two lines as verse, dividing them at *man,* and proposing to read
for my sake instead of *for me.* It may however well be that Toclio only
delivers the account about the Hermit in verse. A similar case occurs
II. 1. 9 seqq. — 72 seqq. Elze, l. c., regulates the lines: *Not only saved our
army, but without* | THE *aid of man o'erthrew the pagan host* | *And with
such wonder, sir, as might confirm* | *A kingdom to his faith.* But as Shak.
says *with aid of s. b.* (3 H. VI., II. 1. 147, 2 H. VI., IV. 5. 4, Haml. IV. 1. 33),
we seem not to be permitted to add *the* in the phrase *without aid of s. b.*;
besides the separation of *without* from *the aid,* and of *confirm* from *kingdom*
sounds at any rate harsh to the ear. As to *without,* cp. Cor. III. 3. 133
That won you without blows. In l. 73 a foot is wanting, as in many other
lines of our play.

80 ought that I can see, Lady. They say he is half a Prophet
   too: would he could tell me any news of the lost Prince,
   there's twenty Talents offer'd to him that finds him.
       Cador. Such news was breeding in the morning.
       Toclio. And now it has birth and life, sir. If fortune bless
85 me, I'le once more search those woods where then we lost
   him; I know not yet what fate may follow me.   [*Exit.*
       Cador. Fortune go with you, sir. Come, fair Mistriss,
   Your Sister and Lord Edwin are in game,
   And all their wits at stake to win the Set.
90   *Const.* My sister has the hand yet; we had best leave them:
   She will be out anon as well as I,
   He wants but cunning to put in a Dye. [*Exit* CADOR, CONST.
       Edwin. You are a cunning Gamester, Madam.
       Modest. It is a desperate Game, indeed, this Marriage,
95 Where there's no winning without loss to either.
       Edwin. Why, what but your perfection, noble Lady,
   Can bar the worthiness of this my suit?
   If so you please I count my happiness
   From difficult obtaining, you shall see
100 My duty and observance.
       Modest. There shall be place to neither, noble sir;
   I do beseech you, let this mild Reply
   Give answer to your suit: for here I vow,
   If e're I change my Virgin-name, by you
105 It gains or looses.
       Edwin.   My wishes have their crown.
       Modest. Let them confine you then,
   As to my promise you give faith and credence.
       Edwin. In your command my willing absence speaks it. [*Exit.*
       Modest. Noble and vertuous: could I dream of Marriage,
110 I should affect thee, Edwin. Oh, my soul,
   Here's something tells me that these best of creatures,
   These models of the world, weak man and woman,
   Should have their souls, their making, life, and being,
   To some more excellent use: if what the sense

       104. *name by you,* | *It* A and Edd. — 105. *theircr own* A, *their own*
   Tyr. — 107. *As to my promise, you give faith and credence* A and Edd.

Calls pleasure were our ends, we might justly blame 115
Great natures wisdom, who rear'd a building
Of so much art and beauty to entertain
A guest so far incertain, so imperfect:
If onely speech distinguish us from beasts,
Who know no inequality of birth or place, 120
But still to fly from goodness: oh, how base
Were life at such a rate! No, no, that power
That gave to man his being, speech and wisdom,
Gave it for thankfulness. To him alone
That made me thus, may I thence truly know, 125
I'le pay to him, not man, the love I owe. [*Exit.*

SCENE II.

The British Court.

Flourish Cornets. Enter AURELIUS *King of Brittain,* DONOBERT,
GLOSTER, CADOR, EDWIN, TOCLIO, OSWOLD, *and Attendants.*

Aur. No tiding of our brother yet? 'Tis strange,
So ne're the Court, and in our own Land too,
And yet no news of him: oh, this loss
Tempers the sweetness of our happy conquests
With much untimely sorrow. 5
Dono. Royal sir,
His safety being unquestion'd, you should to time
Leave the redress of sorrow. Were he dead,
Or taken by the foe, our fatal loss
Had wanted no quick Herald to disclose it.
Aur. That hope alone sustains me, 10
Nor will we be so ingrateful unto heaven
To question what we fear with what we enjoy.
Is answer of our message yet return'd
From that religious man, the holy Hermit,
Sent by the Earl of Chester to confirm us 15

116. A so-called syllable-pause-line. — 125. *whence* A and Tyr.,
thence Del.
     SCENE II. *The British Court* add. by Tyr. — 6. *you* wanting in A
and Edd.

In that miraculous act? For 'twas no less:
Our Army being in rout, nay, quite o'rethrown,
As Chester writes, even then this holy man,
Arm'd with his cross and staff, went smiling on,
20   And boldly fronts the foe; at sight of whom
The Saxons stood amaz'd: for, to their seeming,
Above the Hermit's head appear'd such brightness,
Such clear and glorious beams, as if our men
March't all in fire; wherewith the Pagans fled,
25   And by our troops were all to death pursu'd.
     Glost. 'Tis full of wonder, sir.
     Aurel. Oh, Gloster, he's a jewel worth a Kingdom.
Where's Oswold with his answer?
     Oswold. 'Tis here, my Royal Lord.
30   *Aurel.* In writing? will he not sit with us?
     Oswold. His Orizons perform'd, he bad me say,
He would attend with all submission.
     Aurel. Proceed to councel then; and let some give order,
The Embassadors being come to take our answer,
35   They have admittance. Oswold, Toclio,
Be it your charge! — [*Exeunt* OSWOLD *and* TOCLIO] And now,
The holy councel of this reverend Hermit: [my Lords, observe
[*Reads*] 'As you respect your safety, limit not
That onely power that hath protected you;
40   Trust not an open enemy too far,
He's yet a looser, and knows you have won;
Mischiefs not ended are but then begun.
                              ANSELME *the Hermit.*'
     Dono. Powerful and pithie, which my advice confirms:
No man leaves physick when his sickness slakes,
45   But doubles the receipts: the word of Peace
Seems fair to blood-shot eyes, but being appli'd
With such a medicine as blinds all the sight
Argues desire of Cure, but not of Art.
     Aurel. You argue from defects; if both the name

<hr>

22. *Hermit head* A. — 30. Two lines in Del., div. at *writing.* —
36. Stage-dir. add. by Tyr. — 42. *then but* Tyr. — 48. *not knowledge of
Art* Tyr.

And the condition of the Peace be one,   50
It is to be prefer'd, and in the offer,
Made by the Saxon, I see nought repugnant.
 Glost. The time of truce requir'd for thirty days,
Carries suspicion in it, since half that space
Will serve to strength their weakned Regiments.   55
 Cador. We in less time will undertake to free
Our Country from them.
 Edwin.   Leave that unto our fortune.
 Dono. Is not our bold and hopeful General
Still Master of the field, their Legions faln,
The rest intrencht for fear, half starv'd, and wounded,   60
And shall we now give o're our fair advantage?
'Fore heaven, my Lord, the danger is far more
In trusting to their words then to their weapons.

Enter OSWOLD.

 Oswold. The embassadors are come, sir.
 Aurel.   Conduct them in!
We are resolv'd, my Lords: since policy fail'd   65
In the beginning, it shall have no hand
In the conclusion.
That heavenly power that hath so well begun
Their fatal overthrow, I know, can end it:
From which fair hope my self will give them answer.   70

Flourish Cornets. Enter ARTESIA *with the Saxon Lords.*

 Dono. What's here? a woman Orator?
 Aurel. Peace, Donobert! — Speak, what are you, Lady?
 Artes. The sister of the Saxon General,
Warlike Ostorius the East Angles King;
My name Artesia, who in terms of love   75
Brings peace and health to great Aurelius,
Wishing she may return as fair a present
As she makes tender of.

55. *Regiment* A, *Regiments* Tyr. — 56. *We*] *Who* A and Edd. —
62. *Force heaven* A, corr. by Tyr. — 74. *Anglese* A. — 77. *she*] *the army* Tyr.

   Aurel. The fairest present e're mine eyes were blest with! —
80 Command a chair there for this Saxon Beauty: —
Sit, Lady, we'l confer: your warlike brother
Sues for a peace, you say?
   Arles. With endless love unto your State and Person.
   Aurel. Ha's sent a moving Orator, believe me. —
85 What thinkst thou, Donobert? ·
   Dono. Believe me, sir, were I but young agen,
This gilded pill might take my stomack quickly.
   Aurel. True, thou art old: how soon we do forget
Our own defects! Fair damsel, — oh, my tongue
90 Turns Traitor, and will betray my heart — sister to
Our enemy: — 'sdeath, her beauty mazes me,
I cannot speak if I but look on her. —
What's that we did conclude?
   Dono. This, Royal Lord —
   Aurel.   Pish, thou canst not utter it: —
95 Fair'st of creatures, tell the King your Brother,
That we, in love — ha! — and honor to our Country,
Command his Armies to depart our Realm.
But if you please, fair soul — Lord Donobert,
Deliver you our pleasure.
   Dono.   I shall, sir:
100 Lady, return, and certifie your brother —
   Aurel. Thou art too blunt and rude! return so soon?
Fie, let her stay, and·send some messenger
To certifie our pleasure.
   Dono.   What meanes your Grace?
   Aurel. To give her time of rest to her long Journey;
105 We would not willingly be thought uncivil.
   Arles. Great King of Brittain, let it not seem strange,
To embrace the Princely Offers of a friend,
Whose vertues with thine own, in fairest merit,
Both States in Peace and Love may now inherit.
110   *Aurel.* She speakes of Love agen!
Sure, 'tis my fear, she knows I do not hate her.
   Arles. Be, then, thy self, most great Aurelius,

79. *presence* Tyr.

And let not envy nor a deeper sin
In these thy Councellors deprive thy goodness
Of that fair honor, we in seeking peace			115
Give first to thee, who never used to sue
But force our wishes. Yet, if this seem light,
Oh, let my sex, though worthless your respect,
Take the report of thy humanity,
Whose mild and vertuous life loud fame displayes,			120
As being o'recome by one so worthy praise.
   Aurel. She has an Angels tongue. — Speak still.
   Dono. This flattery is gross, sir; hear no more on't. —
Lady, these childish complements are needless;
You have your answer, and believe it, Madam,			125
His Grace, though yong, doth wear within his breast
Too grave a Councellor to be seduc't
By smoothing flattery or oyly words.
   Artes. I come not, sir, to wooe him.
   Dono. 'Twere folly, if you should; you must not wed him.			130
   Aurel. Shame take thy tongue! Being old and weak thy self,
Thou doat'st, and looking on thine own defects,
Speak'st what thou'dst wish in me. Do I command
The deeds of others, mine own act not free?
Be pleas'd to smile or frown, we respect neither:			135
My will and rule shall stand and fall together.
Most fair Artesia, see the King descends
To give thee welcome with these warlike Saxons,
And now on equal terms both sues and grants:
Instead of Truce, let a perpetual League			140
Seal our united bloods in holy marriage;
Send the East Angels King this happy news,
That thou with me hast made a League for ever,
And added to his state a friend and brother.
Speak, dearest Love, dare you confirm this Title?			145
   Artes. I were no woman to deny a good
So high and noble to my fame and Country.

---

   115. *honor. We* Del. — 116. *use* A and Del, *used* Tyr. — 131 seqq. added
to Dono.'s words (l. 130) A. Tyr. puts *Shame take thy tongue* twice: *wed him,
Shame take thy tongue.* Aur. *Shame take thy tongue! Bring* &c. — 132. *thy*
Tyr. — 146. *to deny so high and noble a proposal to my fame and country* Tyr.

    Aurel. Live, then, a Queen in Brittain.

    Glost. He meanes to marry her.

150   *Dono.* Death! he shall marry the devil first!

Marry a Pagan, an Idolater?

    Cador. He has won her quickly.

    Edwin. She was woo'd afore she came, sure,

Or came of purpose to conclude the Match.

155   *Aurel.* Who dares oppose our will? My Lord of Gloster,

Be you Embassador unto our Brother,

The Brother of our Queen Artesia;

Tell him, for such our entertainment looks him,

Our marriage adding to the happiness

160 Of our intended joys; mans good or ill

In this like waves agree, come double still.

Enter HERMIT.

Who's this? the Hermit? Welcome, my happiness!

Our Contries hope, most reverent holy man,

I wanted but thy blessing to make perfect

165 The infinite sum of my felicity.

    Hermit. Alack, sweet Prince, that happiness is yonder,

Felicity and thou art far asunder;

This world can never give it.

    Aurel. Thou art deceiv'd: see here what I have found,

170 Beauty, Alliance, Peace, and strength of Friends,

All in this all exceeding excellence:

The League's confirm'd.

    Hermit. With whom, dear Lord?

    Aurel. With the great Brother of this Beauteous woman,

175 The Royal Saxon King.

    Hermit.   Oh, then I see,

And fear thou art too near thy misery.

What magick could so linck thee to this mischief?

By all the good that thou hast reapt by me,

Stand further from destruction.

180   *Aurel.* Speak as a man, and I shall hope to obey thee.

    158. *Tell him as such our entertainment looks for him* Tyr.

Hermit.   Idolatress, get hence! fond King, let go:
Thou hugst thy ruine and thy Countries woe.
   Dono.   Well spoke, old Father; too him, bait him soundly.
Now, by heavens blest Lady, I can scarce keep patience.
   1. *Saxon Lord.*   What devil is this?   185
   2. *Saxon Lord.*   That cursed Christian, by whose hellish charmes
Our army was o'rethrown.
   Hermit.   Why do you dally, sir? Oh, tempt not heaven;
Warm not a serpent in your naked bosom:
Discharge them from your Court.   190
   Aurel.   Thou speak'st like madness!
Command the frozen shepherd to the shade,
When he sits warm i'th' Sun; the fever-sick
To add more heat unto his burning pain:
These may obey, 'tis less extremity
Then thou enjoynst to me. Cast but thine eye   195
Upon this beauty, do it, I'le forgive thee,
Though jealousie in others findes no pardon;
Then say thou dost not love; I shall then swear
Th'art immortal and no earthly man.
Oh, blame then my mortallity, not me.   200
   Hermit.   It is thy weakness brings thy misery,
Unhappy Prince.
   Aurel.   Be milder in thy doom.
   Hermit.   'Tis you that must indure heavens doom, which faln   ? *E.M.*
Remembers just.
   Artes.   Thou shalt not live to see it. — How fares my Lord? 205
If my poor presence breed dislike, great Prince,
I am no such neglected soul, will seek
To tie you to your word.
   Aurel.   My word, dear Love! may my Religion,
Crown, State, and Kingdom fail, when I fail thee.   210
Command Earl Chester to break up the camp
Without disturbance to our Saxon friends;
Send every hour swift posts to hasten on
The King her Brother, to conclude this League,

   181. *Idolaters* A. — 195. *eyes* Tyr. — 198. *love me* A, *love like me*
Tyr., *love* Del. — 206. *breeds* Tyr.

215 This endless happy Peace of Love and Marriage;
    Till when provide for Revels, and give charge
    That nought be wanting which may make our triumphs
    Sportful and free to all. If such fair blood
    Ingender ill, man must not look for good. [*Ex. all but*
                                        Heremit. Florish.

                Enter MODESTIA, *reading in a book.*

220   *Mod.* How much the oft report of this blest Hermit
    Hath won on my desires; I must behold him:
    And sure this should be he. Oh, the world's folly,
    Proud earth and dust, how low a price bears goodness!
    All that should make man absolute, shines in him.
225 Much reverent Sir, may I without offence
    Give interruption to your holy thoughts?
        Hermit. What would you, Lady?
        Mod. That which till now ne're found a language in me:
    I am in love.
        Her.   In love? with what?
        Mod.   With vertue.
230   *Her.* There's no blame in that.
        Mod. Nay, sir, with you, with your Religious Life,
    Your Vertue, Goodness, if there be a name
    To express affection greater, that,
    That would I learn and utter: Reverent Sir,
235 If there be any thing to bar my suit,
    Be charitable and expose it; your prayers
    Are the same Orizons which I will number.
    Holy Sir,
    Keep not instruction back from willingness,
240 Possess me of that knowledge leads you on
    To this humility; for well I know,
    Were greatness good, you would not live so low.
        Her. Are you a Virgin?
        Mod. Yes, Sir.
245   *Her.* Your name?
        Mod. Modestia.

    217. *make* A, *will make* Tyr., *may make* Del. — 219. *men* Tyr. —
233. *that*] *than that word* Del. — 246. *Modesta* A.

Her. Your name and vertues meet, a Modest Virgin:
Live ever in the sanctimonious way
To Heaven and Happiness.   There's goodness in you,
I must instruct you further.   Come, look up,   250
Behold yon firmament: there sits a power,
Whose foot-stool is this earth.   Oh, learn this lesson,
And practise it: he that will climb so high,
Must leave no joy beneath to move his eye.

Mod. I apprehend you, sir: on Heaven I fix my love,   255
Earth gives us grief, our joys are all above;
For this was man in innocence naked born,
To show us wealth hinders our sweet return.   [*Exeunt.*

A C T II.

SCENE I.

A Forest.

Enter Clown and his sister great with childe.

Clown. Away! follow me no further, I am none of thy brother.
What, with Childe? great with Childe, and knows not whose
the Father on't!   I am asham'd to call thee Sister.

Joan. Believe me, Brother, he was a Gentleman.

Clown. Nay, I believe that; he gives arms, and legs too,   5
and has made you the Herald to blaze 'em.   But, Joan,
Joan, sister Joan, can you tell me his name that did it?
how shall we call my Cousin, your bastard, when we have it?

Joan. Alas, I know not the Gentlemans name, Brother!
I met him in these woods, the last great hunting;   10
He was so kinde and proffer'd me so much,
As I had not the heart to ask him more.

Clown. Not his name? why, this showes your Country
-breeding now; had you been brought up i'th' City, you'd

<hr>

254. *leave*] *let* Tyr.; but *leave* is often almost = to let, to suffer,
cp. *you barely leave our thorns to prick ourselves* All's IV. 2. 19, and see
Al. Schmidt, Sh.-L., s. v. *leave* 8). — 254 and 258. *Exit*] corr. by Tyr.
    ACT II. SCENE I. *A Forest.* add. by Tyr. — 2. *know* Tyr. — 8. *name*
Del. — 9—12. Not printed as verse in A and Edd., cp. ad I. 1. 66. —
14. *breeding. Now, had* Del.

15 have got a Father first, and the childe afterwards: Hast
thou no markes to know him by?

    Joan. He had most rich Attire, a fair Hat and Feather,
a gilt Sword, and most excellent Hangers.

    Clown. Pox on his Hangers, would he had bin gelt for his labor.

20   *Joan.* Had you but heard him swear, you would have thought —

    Clown. I, as you did. Swearing and lying goes together
still. Did his Oathes get you with Childe, we shall have a
roaring Boy then, yfaith. Well, sister, I must leave you.

    Joan. Dear brother, stay, help me to finde him out,

25 I'le ask no further.

    Clown. 'Sfoot, who should I finde? who should I ask for?

    Joan. Alas, I know not, he uses in these woods,
And these are witness of his oathes and promise.

    Clown. We are like to have a hot suit on't, when our

30 best witness's but a Knight a'th' Post.

    Joan. Do but enquire this Forrest, I'le go with you;
Some happy fate may guide us till we meet him.

    Clown. Meet him? and what name shall we have for him,
when we meet him? 'Sfoot, thou neither knowst him nor

35 canst tell what to call him. Was ever man tyr'd with such a
business, to have a sister got with childe, and know not who
did it? Well, you shall see him, I'le do my best for you,
Ile make Proclamation; if these Woods and Trees, as you say,
will bear any witness, let them answer. Oh yes: If there be

40 any man that wants a name, will come in for conscience sake,
and acknowledge himself to be a Whore-Master, he shall have
that laid to his charge in an hour, he shall not be rid on in
an age; if he have Lands, he shall have an heir; if he have
patience, he shall have a wife; if he have neither Lands nor

45 patience, he shall have a Whore. So ho, boy, so ho, so, so.

    [*Within*] *Prince Vter.* So ho, boy, so ho, illo ho, illo ho.

    Clown. Hark, hark, sister, there's one hollows to us; what
a wicked world's this, a man cannot so soon name a whore,
but a knave comes presently: and see where he is; stand

50 close a while, sister.

35. *tied* Tyr. — 39. *Oyes* Del. — 46. *boy*] *by* A, corr. by Tyr.

Enter PRINCE VTER.

Prince. How like a voice that Eccho spake, but oh,
My thoughts are lost for ever in amazement.
Could I but meet a man to tell her beauties,
These trees would bend their tops to kiss the air
That from my lips should give her praises up.   55
  Clown. He talks of a woman, sister.
  Joan. This may be he, brother.
  Clown. View him well; you see, he has a fair Sword, but
his Hangers are faln.
  Prince. Here did I see her first, here view her beauty: 60
Oh, had I known her name, I had been happy.
  Clown. Sister, this is he, sure; he knows not thy name
neither. A couple of wise fools yfaith, to get children, and
know not one another.
  Prince. You weeping leaves, upon whose tender cheeks 65
Doth stand a flood of tears at my complaint,
And heard my vows and oathes —
  Clown. Law, Law, he has been a great swearer too; tis he,
  Prince. For having overtook her.   [sister.
As I have seen a forward blood-hound strip   70
The swiftest of the cry, ready to seize
His wished hopes, upon the sudden view,
Struck with astonishment, at his arriv'd prey,
Instead of seizure stands at fearful bay;
Or like to Marius soldiers, who, o'retook,   75
The eye-sight killing Gorgon at one look
Made everlasting stand: so fear'd my power,
Whose cloud aspir'd the Sun, dissolv'd a shower.
Pigmalion, then I tasted thy sad fate,
Whose Ivory picture and my fair were one: 80
Our dotage past imagination,
I saw and felt desire —
  Clown. Pox a your fingering! did he feel, sister?
  Prince.   But enjoy'd not.

<hr>

51. *spoke, but ah* Tyr. — 63. *either* Del. — 64. *not know* Tyr. —
67. *And*] *You* Del. — 71. *swifter* A and Edd. — 75. *whom o'ertook* Del. —
82. *not*] *now* A, corr. by Tyr. and Del.

Oh fate, thou hadst thy days and nights to feed
85 On calm affection; one poor sight was all,
Converts my pleasure to perpetual thrall:
Imbracing thine, thou lostest breath and desire,
So I, relating mine, will here expire.
For here I vow to you, mournful plants,
90 Who were the first, made happy by her fame,
Never to part hence, till I know her name.

    Clown. Give me thy hand, sister, *The Childe has found
his Father.* This is he, sure, as I am a man; had I been a
woman, these kind words would have won me, I should have
95 had a great belly too, that's certain. Well, I'le speak to him.
— Most honest and fleshly-minded Gentleman, give me your
hand, sir.

    Prince. Ha, what art thou, that thus rude and boldly darest
Take notice of a wretch so much ally'd ˙
100 To misery as I am?

    Clown. Nay, Sir, for our aliance, I shall be found to be a
poor brother-in-Law of your worships. The Gentlewoman you
spake on, is my sister: you see what a clew she spreads; her
name is Joan Go-too't, I am her elder, but she has been at
105 it before me; 'tis a woman's fault. — Pox a this bashfulness!
come forward, Jug, prethee, speak to him.

    Prince. Have you e're seen me, Lady?

    Clown. Seen ye? ha, ha! It seems she has felt you too.
Here's a young Go-too't a coming, sir; she is my sister; we
110 all love to Go-too't, as well as your worship. She's a Maid
yet, but you may make her a wife, when you please, sir.

    Prince. I am amaz'd with wonder: Tell me, woman,
What sin have I comitted worthy this?

    Joan. Do you not know me, sir?

115   *Prince.* Know thee! as I do thunder, hell, and mischief;
Witch, scullion, hag!

    Clown. I see, he will marry her; he speaks so like a
husband.

    87. *losest* Tyr. — 89. *you, ye mournful* Tyr. and Del. Read *mournful*
as three syllables. — 98. *rudely* Tyr. — Div. at *boldly | wretch | am* by Del.
— 110. *she's scarce a* Tyr. — 113. *I*] *you* A and Del., corr. by Tyr. —
116. *wicth* A; *stallion* A, *scullion* Del. The same misprint occurs in Q 2 (1604) of
Hml. II, 2. 616.

Prince.   Death! I will cut their tongues out for this blasphemy.
Strumpet, villain, where have you ever seen me?   120
   Clown.   Speak for your self, with a pox to ye.
   Prince.   Slaves, Ile make you curse your selves for this temp-
   Joan.   Oh, sir, if ever you did speak to me,   [tation.
It was in smoother phrase, in fairer language.
   Prince.   Lightning consume me, if I ever saw thee.   125
My rage o'reflowes my blood, all patience flies me. [*Beats her.*]
   Clown.   Hold, I beseech you, sir, I have nothing to say to you.
   Joan.   Help, help! murder, murder!

Enter TOCLIO *and* OSWOLD.

   Toclio.   Make haste, Sir, this way the sound came, it was a wood.
   Oswold.   See where she is, and the Prince, the price of all 130
our wishes.
   Clown.   The prince, say ye? ha's made a poor Subject of
me, I am sure.
   Toclio.   Sweet Prince, noble Vter, speak, how fare you, sir?
   Oswold.   Dear sir, recal your self; your fearful absence   135
Hath won too much already on the grief
Of our sad King, from whom our laboring search
Hath had this fair success in meeting you.
   Toclio.   His silence and his looks argue distraction.
   Clown.   Nay, he's mad, sure, he will not acknowledge my 140
sister, nor the childe neither.
   Oswold.   Let us entreat your Grace along with us;
Your sight will bring new life to the King your Brother.
   Toclio.   Will you go, sir?
   Prince.   Yes, any whether; guide me, all's hell, I see;   145
Man may change air, but not his misery.   [*Exit* PRINCE,
   Joan.   Lend me one word with you, sir.   TOCLIO.
   Clown.   Well said, sister, he has a Feather, and fair Hangers
too, this may be he.
   Oswold.   What would you, fair one?   150
   Joan.   Sure, I have seen you in these woods ere this.

 Oswold. Trust me, never; I never saw this place,
Till at this time my friend conducted me.
 Joan. The more's my sorrow then.
155 *Oswold.* Would I could comfort you.
I am a Bachelor, but it seems you have
A husband, you have been fouly o'reshot else.
 Clown. A woman's fault, we are all subject to go to't, sir.

      Enter Toclio.

 Toclio. Oswold, away; the Prince will not stir a foot without
160 *Oswold.* I am coming. Farewell, woman.   [you.
 Toclio. Prithee, make haste.   [*Exit* Oswold.
 Joan. Good sir, but one word with you, ere you leave us.
 Toclio. With me, fair soul?
 Clown. Shee'l have a fling at him too; the Childe must
165 have a Father.
 Joan. Have you ne'er seen me, sir?
 Toclio. Seen thee? 'Sfoot, I have seen many fair faces in
my time. Prithee, look up, and do not weep so. Sure, pretty
wanton, I have seen this face before.
170 *Joan.* It is enough, though you ne're see me more. [*Sinks down.*
 Toclio. 'Sfoot, she's faln. This place is inchanted, sure;
look to the woman, fellow.   [*Exit.*
 Clown. Oh, she's dead, she's dead! As you are a man,
stay and help, sir. — Joan, Joan, sister Joan, why, Joan Go
175 -too't, I say; will you cast away your self, and your childe,
and me too? what do you mean, sister?
 Joan. Oh, give me pardon, sir; 'twas too much joy
Opprest my loving thoughts; I know you were
Too noble to deny me — ha! Where is he?
180 *Clown.* Who, the Gentleman? he's gone, sister.
 Joan. Oh! I am undone then! Run, tell him I did
But faint for joy; dear brother, haste, why dost thou stay?
Oh, never cease, till he give answer to thee.
 Clown. He: which he? what do you call him, tro?

<hr>

 161. Stage-dir. not in A and Edd. — 168seqq. Printed as verse, div.
at *thee | time | so | before.* Del. — 170. *your,* corr. by Tyr. and Del. —
171. Div. at *fallen* Del. — 178. *thought* Del. — 181. *run and tell* Tyr.

Joan. Unnatural brother! 185
Shew me the path he took, why dost thou dally?
Speak, oh, which way went he?
  Clown. This way, that way, through the bushes there.
  Joan. Were it through fire,
The Journey's easie, winged with sweet desire. [*Exit.* 190
  Clown. Hey day, there's some hope of this yet. Ile follow
her for kindreds sake; if she miss of her purpose now, she'l
challenge all she findes, I see; for if ever we meet with a
two-legd creature in the whole Kingdom, the Childe shall
have a Father, that's certain. [*Exit.* 195

SCENE II.

An Ante-chamber at the British Court.

Loud Musick. Enter two with the Sword and Mace, CADOR, EDWIN,
two Bishops, AURELIUS, OSTORIUS, *leading* ARTESIA *Crown'd,* CON-
STANCIA, MODESTIA, OCTA, PROXIMUS *a Magician,* DONOBERT,
GLOSTER, OSWOLD, TOCLIO; *all pass over the Stage. Manet* DONOBERT,
GLOSTER, EDWIN, CADOR.

  Dono. Come, Gloster, I do not like this hasty Marriage.
  Gloster. She was quickly wooed and won: not six days since
Arrived an enemy to sue for Peace,
And now crown'd Queen of Brittain; this is strange.
  Dono. Her brother too made as quick speed in coming, 5
Leaving his Saxons and his starved Troops,
To take the advantage, whilst 'twas offer'd.
'Fore heaven, I fear the King's too credulous;
Our Army is discharg'd too.
  Gloster. Yes, and our General commanded home. 10
Son Edwin, have you seen him since?
  Edwin. He's come to Court, but will not view the presence,
Nor speak unto the King; he 's so discontent
At this so strange aliance with the Saxon,
As nothing can perswade his patience. 15

  186—187. Div. at *took* by Del. — 192. *she'd* Del.
    SCENE II. *An Antechamber at the British Court* add. by Tyr. —
  1. *Come, Gloster* put in a line by itself Del.

Cador. You know, his humor will indure no check,
No, if the King oppose it:
All crosses feeds both his spleen and his impatience;
Those affections are in him like powder,
20 Apt to inflame with every little spark,
And blow up all his reason.
    Gloster. Edol of Chester is a noble Soldier.
    Dono. So is he, by the Rood, ever most faithful
To the King and Kingdom, how e're his passions guide him.

    Enter EDOLL *with Captains.*

25   *Cador.* See where he comes, my Lord.
    Omnes. Welcome to Court, brave Earl.
    Edol. Do not deceive me by your flatteries:
Is not the Saxon here? the Legue confirm'd?
The Marriage ratifi'd? the Court divided
30 With Pagan Infidels? the least part Christians,
At least in their Commands? Oh, the gods!
It is a thought that takes away my sleep,
And dulls my senses so I scarcely know you:
Prepare my horses, Ile away to Chester.
35   *Capt.* What shall we do with our Companies, my Lord?
    Edol. Keep them at home to increase Cuckolds,
And get some Cases for your Captainships;
Smooth up your brows, the wars has spoil'd your faces,
And few will now regard you.
40   *Dono.* Preserve your patience, Sir.
    Edol. Preserve your Honors, Lords, your Countries Safety,
Your Lives and Lands from strangers. What black devil
Could so bewitch the King, so to discharge
A Royal Army in the height of conquest,
45 Nay, even already made victorious,
To give such credit to an enemy,
A starved foe, a stragling fugitive,
Beaten beneath our feet, so low dejected,

---

17. ? *Not even if.* — 18. *crosses* used as a monosyllable; *feed* Tyr.
and Del.; *both*] *but* Del. — 36. ? *Cuckolds with.* — 38. *have* Tyr. — 48. *love
dejected* A, corr. by Tyr. and Del.

So servile, and so base, as hope of life
Had won them all to leave the Land for ever?   50
    Dono. It was the Kings will.
    Edol. It was your want of wisdom,
That should have laid before his tender youth
The dangers of a State, where forain Powers
Bandy for Soveraignty with Lawful Kings;   55
Who being settled once, to assure themselves,
Will never fail to seek the blood and life
Of all competitors.
    Dono. Your words sound well, my Lord, and point at safety,
Both for the Realm and us; but why did you,   60
Within whose power it lay, as General,
With full Commission to dispose the war,
Lend ear to parly with the weakned foe?
    Edol. Oh, the good Gods!
    Cador. And on that parly came this Embassie.   65
    Edol. You will hear me?
    Edwin. Your letters did declare it to the King,
Both of the Peace, and all Conditions,
Brought by this Saxon Lady, whose fond love
Has thus bewitched him.   70
    Edol. I will curse you all as black as hell,
Unless you hear me; your gross mistake would make
Wisdom herself run madding through the streets,
And quarrel with her shadow. Death!
Why kill'd ye not that woman?   75
    Dono. Glost.   Oh, my Lord!
    Edol. The great devil take me quick, had I been by,
And all the women of the world were barren,
She should have died, ere he had married her
On these conditions.
    Cador. It is not reason that directs you thus.   80
    Edol. Then have I none, for all I have directs me.
Never was man so palpably abus'd,
So basely marted, bought and sold to scorn.
My Honor, Fame, and hopeful Victories,

        63. *the*] *your* Tyr. — 81. *then I have* Tyr.

85 The loss of Time, Expences, Blood, and Fortunes,
   All vanisht into nothing.
      Edwin.   This rage is vain, my Lord:
   What the King does, nor they nor you can help.
      Edol.   My Sword must fail me then.
90   *Cador.*   'Gainst whom will you expose it?
      Edol.   What's that to you? 'gainst all the devils in hell,
   To guard my country.
      Edwin.   These are airy words.
      Edol.   Sir, you tread too hard upon my patience.
      Edwin.   I speak the duty of a Subjects faith,
95 And say agen, had you been here in presence,
   What the king did, you had not dar'd to cross it.
      Edol.   I will trample on his Life and Soul that says it.
      Cador.   My Lord!
      Edwin.   Come, come.
      Edol.   Now, before heaven —
      Cador.   Dear Sir!
      Edol.   Not dare? thou liest beneath thy lungs.
100   *Gloster.*   No more, son Edwin.
      Edwin.   I have done, sir; I take my leave.
      Edol.   But thou shalt not, you shall take no leave of me, Sir.
      Dono.   For wisdoms sake, my Lord —
      Edol.   Sir, I'le leave him, and you, and all of you,
105 The Court and King, and let my Sword and friends
   Shuffle for Edols safety: stay you here,
   And hug the Saxons, till they cut your throats,
   Or bring the Land to servile slavery.
   Such yokes of baseness Chester must not suffer!
110 Go, and repent betimes these foul misdeeds,
   For in this League all our whole Kingdome bleeds,
   Which Ile prevent, or perish.   [*Exit* EDOL, CAPT.
      Glost.   See how his rage transports him!
      Cador.   These passions set apart, a braver soldier
115 Breathes not i'th' world this day.
      Dono.   I wish his own worth do not court his ruine.
   The King must Rule, and we must learn to obay,
   True vertue still directs the noble way.

90. *oppose* Del. (*expose* = to lay bare). — 102. *thou shall* A.

SCENE III.

Hall of state in the Palace.

Loud Musick. Enter AURELIUS, ARTESIA, OSTORIUS, OCTA,
PROXIMUS, TOCLIO, OSWOLD, *Hermit.*

Aurel. Why is the Court so dull? me thinks, each room
And angle of our Palace should appear
Stuck full of objects fit for mirth and triumphs,
To show our high content. Oswold, fill wine!
Must we begin the Revels? Be it so, then!   5
Reach me the cup: Ile now begin a Health
To our lov'd Queen, the bright Artesia,
The Royal Saxon King, our warlike brother.
Go and command all the whole Court to pledge it.
Fill to the Hermit there! Most reverent Anselme,   10
Wee'l do thee Honor first, to pledge my Queen.
  Her. I drink no healths, great King, and if I did,
I would be loath to part with health to those
That have no power to give it back agen.
  Aurel. Mistake not, it is the argument of Love   15
And Duty to our Queen and us.
  Artes. But he ows none, it seems.
  Her. I do to vertue, Madame. Temperate minds
Covets that health to drink, which nature gives
In every spring to man; he that doth hold   20
His body but a Tenement at will,
Bestows no cost, but to repair what's ill:
Yet if your healths or heat of Wine, fair Princess,
Could this old frame or these cras'd limbes restore,
Or keep out death or sickness, then fill more,   25
I'le make fresh way for appetite; if no,
On such a prodigal who would wealth bestow?
  Ostorius. He speaks not like a guest to grace a wedding.

Enter TOCLIO.

  Artes. No, sir, but like an envious imposter.
  Octa. A Christian slave, a Cinick.   30

Ostor. What vertue could decline your Kingly spirit
To such respect of him whose magick spells
Met with your vanquisht Troops, and turn'd your Arms
To that necessity of fight, which, through dispair
35 Of any hope to stand but by his charms,
Had been defeated in a bloody conquest?
    Octa. 'Twas magick, hellbred magick did it, sir,
And that's a course, my Lord, which we esteem
In all our Saxon Wars unto the last
40 And lowest ebbe of servile treachery.
    Aurel. Sure, you are deceiv'd, it was the hand of heaven
That in his vertue gave us victory.
Is there a power in man that can strike fear
Thorough a general camp, or create spirits
45 In recreant bosoms above present sense?
    Ostor. To blind the sense there may, with apparition
Of well arm'd troops, which in themselves are air,
Form'd into humane shapes, and such that day
Were by that Sorcerer rais'd to cross our fortunes.
50 *Aurel.* There is a law tells us that words want force
To make deeds void; examples must be shown
By instances alike, ere I believe it.
    Ostor. 'Tis easily perform'd, believe me, sir:
Propose your own desires, and give but way
55 To what our Magick here shall straight perform,
And then let his or our deserts be censur'd.
    Aurel. We could not wish a greater happiness
Then what this satisfaction brings with it.
Let him proceed, fair brother.
    Ostor.   He shall, sir.
60 Come, learned Proximus, this task be thine:
Let thy great charms confound the opinion
This Christian by his spells hath falsly won.
    Prox. Great King, propound your wishes, then,

---

34. *which through*] *which the* A, *which but for the* Tyr., *when the*
Del. As to the use of *through,* cp. 1H. IV., III. 2. 124 *thou art like enough,*
through vassal fear, to fight against me, and Cymb. V. 3. 61 *some falling*
merely through fear. — 47. *which in*] *within* A, corr. by Tyr., but not
by Del.

What persons, of what State, what numbers, or how arm'd,
Please your own thoughts; they shall appear before you.   65
   Aurel. Strange art! What thinkst thou, reverent Hermit?
   Her. Let him go on, sir.
   Aurel. Wilt thou behold his cunning?
   Her. Right gladly, sir; it will be my joy to tell,
That I was here to laugh at him and hell.   70
   Aurel. I like thy confidence.
   Artes. His sawcy impudence! — Proceed to th'trial.
   Prox. Speak your desires, my Lord, and be it placed
In any angle underneath the Moon,
The center of the Earth, the Sea, the Air,   75
The region of the fire, nay, hell itself,
And I'le present it.
   Aurel. Wee'l have no sight so fearful, onely this:
If all thy art can reach it, show me here
The two great Champions of the Trojan War,   80
Achilles and brave Hector, our great Ancestor,
Both in their warlike habits, Armor, Shields,
And Weapons then in use for fight.
   Prox. 'Tis done, my Lord, command a halt and silence,
As each man will respect his life or danger.   85
Armel, Plesgeth!

Enter Spirits.

   Spirits. Quid vis?
   Prox. Attend me!
   Aurel. The Apparition comes; on our displeasure,
Let all keep place and silence. [*Within Drums beat Marches.* 90

     Enter Proximus, *bringing in* Hector, *attir'd and arm'd
after the Trojan manner, with Target, Sword, and Battel-ax, a
Trumpet before him, and a Spirit in flame colours with a Torch;
at the other door* Achilles *with his Spear and Falchon, a Trumpet,
and a Spirit in black before him; Trumpets sound alarm, and they
manage their weapons to begin the Fight: and after some Charges,
the Hermit steps between them, at which seeming amaz'd the spirits
tremble.*   [*Thunder within.*

  Prox. What ·means this stay, bright Armel, Plesgeth?
Why fear you and fall back?
Renew the Alarums, and enforce the Combat,
Or hell or darkness circles you for ever.
95 *Arm.* We dare not.
  Prox. Ha!
  Plesgeth. Our charms are all dissolv'd: Armel, away!
'Tis worse then hell to us, whilest here we stay. *[Exit all.*
  Herm. What! at a Non-plus, sir? command them back,
                 [for shame!
100 *Prox.* What power o're-aws my Spells? Return, you
Armel, Plesgeth, double damnation seize you! [Hell-hounds!
By all the Infernal powers, the prince of devils
Is in this Hermits habit: what else could force
My Spirits quake or tremble thus?
105 *Her.* Weak argument to hide your want of skill:
Does the devil fear the devil, or war with hell?
They have not been acquainted long, it seems.
Know, misbelieving Pagan, even that Power,
That overthrew your Forces, still lets you see,
110 He onely can controul both hell and thee.
  Prox. Disgrace and mischief! Ile enforce new charms,
New spells, and spirits rais'd from the low Abyss
Of hells unbottom'd depths.
  Aurel.   We have enough, sir;
Give o're your charms, wee'l finde some other time
115 To praise your Art. I dare not but acknowledge
That heavenly Power my heart stands witness to:
Be not dismaid, my Lords, at this disaster,
Nor thou, my fairest Queen: we'l change the Scene
To some more pleasing sports. Lead to our Chamber. —
120 How ere in this thy pleasures finde a cross,
Our joy's too fixed here to suffer loss.
  Toclio. Which I shall adde to, sir, with news I bring:
The Prince, your Brother, lives.
  Aurel. Ha!

---

  93. *Alarms* A, corr. by Del. — 98. *while* Tyr. — *Exeunt Spirits*
Tyr. and Del. — 119. *our*] *your* A and Edd.

120 how ere *sc.* however

Toclio. And comes to grace this high and heaven-knit Mar- 125
Aurel. Why dost thou flatter me, to make me think   [riage.
Such happiness attends me?

Enter PRINCE VTER *and* OSWOLD.

Toclio. His presence speaks my truth, sir.
Dono. 'Fore me, 'tis he: look, Gloster.
Glost. A blessing beyond hope, sir.   130
Aurel. Ha, 'tis he: welcome, my second Comfort.
Artesia, Dearest Love, it is my Brother,
My Princely Brother, all my Kingdom's hope:
Oh, give him welcome, as thou lov'st my health.
Artes. You have so free a welcome, sir, from me,   135
As this your presence has such power, I swear,
O're me, a stranger, that I must forget
My Countrey, Name, and Friends, and count this place
My Joy and <u>Birthright</u>.
Prince. 'Tis she! 'tis she, I swear! oh, ye good gods, 'tis she! 140
That face within those woods where first I saw her,
Captived my senses, and thus many months
Bar'd me from all society of men.
How came she to this place?
Brother Aurelius, speak that Angel's name,   145
Her heaven-blest name, oh, speak it quickly, sir.
Aurel. It is Artesia, the Royal Saxon Princess.
Prince. A woman, and no Deity, no feigned shape,
To mock the reason of admiring sense,
On whom a hope as low as mine may live,   150
Love, and enjoy, dear Brother, may it not?
Aurel. She is all the Good or Vertue thou canst name,
My Wife, my Queen.
Prince. Ha! your wife!
Artes. Which you shall finde, sir, if that time and fortune 155
May make my love but worthy of your tryal.
Prince. Oh!
Aurel. What troubles you, dear Brother?

Why with so strange and fixt an eye dost thou
160 Behold my Joys?
   Artes.   You are not well, sir.
   Prince.   Yes, yes. — Oh, you immortal powers,
Why has poor man so many entrances
For sorrow to creep in at, when our sense
165 Is much too weak to hold his happiness?
Oh, say, I was born deaf: and let your silence
Confirm in me the knowing my defect;
At least be charitable to conceal my sin,
For hearing is no less in me, dear Brother.
170   *Aurel.*   No more!
I see thou art a Rival in the Joys
Of my high Bliss. Come, my Artesia;
The Day's most prais'd when 'tis ecclipst by Night,
Great Good must have as great Ill opposite.
175   *Prince.*   Stay, hear but a word; yet now I think on't,
This is your Wedding-night, and were it mine,
I should be angry with least loss of time.
   Artes.   Envy speaks no such words, has no such looks.
   Prince.   Sweet rest unto you both.
180   *Aurel.*   Lights to our Nuptial Chamber.
   Artes.   Could you speak so,
I would not fear how much my grief did grow.
   Aurel.   Lights to our Chamber; on, on, set on!
          [Exeunt. Manet Prince.
   Prince.   'Could you speak so,
I would not fear how much my grief did grow.'
185 Those were her very words; sure, I am waking,
She wrung me by the hand, and spake them to me
With a most passionate affection.
Perhaps she loves, and now repents her choice,
In marriage with my brother. Oh, fond man,
190 How darest thou trust thy Traitorous thoughts, thus to
Betray thy self? 'twas but a waking dream,
Wherein thou madest thy wishes speak, not her,

  183. *Exeunt all except the Prince* Tyr. — 184. *griefs* A, corr. by Del. —
190. *Traitors* A.

In which thy foolish hopes strives to prolong
A wretched being. So sickly children play
With health-lov'd toys, which for a time delay,   195
But do not cure the fit. Be, then, a man,
Meet that destruction which thou canst not flie.
From not to live, make it thy best to die,
And call her now, whom thou didst hope to wed,
Thy brothers wife. Thou art too nere akin,   200
And such an act above all name's a sin
Not to be blotted out; heaven pardon me!
She's banisht from my bosom now for ever.
To lowest ebbes men justly hope a flood;
When vice grows barren, all desires are good.   205

Enter Waiting Gentlewoman with a Jewel.

Gent. The noble Prince, I take it, sir?
Prince. You speak me, what I should be, Lady.
Gent. Know, by that name, sir, Queen Artesia greets you.
Prince. Alas, good vertue, how is she mistaken!
Gent. Commending her affection in this Jewel, sir.   210
Prince. She binds my service to her: ha! a Jewel, 'tis
A fair one, trust me, and methinks, it much
Resembles something I have seen with her.
Gent. It is an artificial crab, Sir.
Prince. A creature that goes backward.   215
Gent. True, from the way it looks.
Prince. There is no moral in it aludes to her self?
Gent. 'Tis your construction gives you that, sir;
She's a woman.
Prince. And, like this, may use her legs and eyes   220
Two several ways.
Gent.   Just like the Sea-crab,
Which on the Mussel prayes, whilst he bills at a stone.
Prince. Pretty in troth. Prithee, tell me, art thou honest?
Gent. I hope I seem no other, sir.
Prince. And those that seem so, are sometimes bad enough. 225

193. *strive* Tyr. and Del. — 197. No stop behind *Flie* (flie from) in
Del. — 222. *mistle* Del. — 221—2, 226—30, 232—3, 237—38 are printed as
prose by Del.

Gent. If they will accuse themselves for want of witness,
Let them, I am not so foolish.
    Prince.   I see th'art wise.
Come, speak me truly: What is the greatest sin?
    Gent. That which man never acted; what has been done
230 Is as the least, common to all as one.
    Prince. Dost think thy Lady is of thy opinion?
    Gent. She's a bad Scholar else; I have brought her up,
And she dares owe me still.
    Prince. I, 'tis a fault in greatness, they dare owe
235 Many, ere they pay one. But darest thou
Expose thy scholar to my examining?
    Gent. Yes, in good troth, sir, and pray put her to't too;
'Tis a hard lesson, if she answer it not.
    Prince. Thou know'st the hardest.
240   *Gent.* As far as a woman may, sir.
    Prince. I commend thy plainness.
When wilt thou bring me to thy Lady?
    Gent. Next opportunity I attend you, sir.
    Prince. Thanks, take this, and commend me to her.
245   *Gent.* Think of your Sea-crab, sir, I pray.   [*Exit.*
    Prince. Oh, by any means, Lady. —
What should all this tend to?
If it be Love or Lust that thus incites her,
The sin is horrid and incestuous;
250 If to betray my life, what hopes she by it?
Yes, it may be a practice 'twixt themselves,
To expel the Brittains and ensure the State
Through our destructions; all this may be
Veil'd with a deeper reach in villany,
255 Then all my thoughts can guess at; — however,
I will confer with her, and if I finde
Lust hath given Life to Envy in her minde,
I may prevent the danger: so men wise
By the same step by which they fell, may rise;
260 Vices are Vertues, if so thought and seen,
And Trees with foulest roots branch soonest green.   [*Exit.*

247. *shall* Tyr. — 253. *destruction* Tyr. — 254. *valid* A, *veil'd* Del.

ACT III.

SCENE I.

Before the Palace of King AURELIUS.
Enter Clown and his Sister.

Clown. Come, sister, thou that art all fool, all mad woman.
Joan. Prithee, have patience, we are now at Court.
Clown. At Court! ha, ha, that proves thy madness: was
there ever any woman in thy taking travel'd to Court for a
husband? 'Slid, 'tis enough for them to get children, and   5
the City to keep 'em, and the Countrey to finde Nurses:
every thing must be done in his due place, sister.
Joan. Be but content a while; for, sure, I know
This Journey will be happy. Oh, dear brother,
This night my sweet Friend came to comfort me;   10
I saw him and embrac't him in mine arms.
Clown. Why did you not hold him, and call me to help you?
Joan. Alas, I thought I had been with him still,
But when I wak't —
Clown. A pox of all Loger-heads! then you were but in   15
a Dream all this while, and we may still go look him. Well,
since we are come to Court, cast your Cats eyes about you,
and either finde him out you dreamt on, or some other, for
Ile trouble my self no further.

Enter DONOBERT, CADOR, EDWIN, *and* TOCLIO.

See, see, here comes more Courtiers; look about you, come;   20
pray, view 'em all well; the old man has none of the marks
about him, the other have both Swords and Feathers: what
thinkest thou of that tall yong Gentleman?
Joan. He much resembles him; but, sure, my friend,
Brother, was not so high of stature.   25
Clown. Oh, beast, wast thou got a childe with a short thing too?
Dono. Come, come, Ile hear no more on't: Go, Lord Edwin,
Tell her, this day her sister shall be married

ACT III. SCENE I. *Before the Palace of King Aurelius* add. by Tyr. —
1. *that* om. by Tyr. and Del. — 15. *Ah pox* A. — 22. *both*] *but* Del. —
26. *got with child* Tyr.

To Cador, Earl of Cornwal; so shall she
30 To thee, brave Edwin, if she'l have my blessing.
      Edwin.   She is addicted to a single Life,
She will not hear of Marriage.
      Dono.   Tush, fear it not: go you from me to her,
Use your best skill, my Lord, and if you fail,
35 I have a trick shall do it: haste, haste about it.
      Edwin.   Sir, I am gone;
My hope is in your help more then my own.
      Dono.   And worthy Toclio, to your care I must
Commend this business
40 For Lights and Musick, and what else is needful.
      Toclio.   I shall, my Lord.
      Clown.   We would intreat a word, sir.   Come forward, sister.
                              [*Exit* DONO., TOC., CADOR.
      Edwin.   What lackst thou, fellow?
      Clown.   I lack a father for a childe, sir.
45   *Edwin.*   How! a God-father?
      Clown.   No, sir, we mean the own father: it may be you,
sir, for any thing we know; I think the childe is like you.
      Edwin.   Like me! prithee, where is it?
      Clown.   Nay, 'tis not born yet, sir, 'tis forth coming; you
50 see, the childe must have a father: what do you think of
my sister?
      Edwin.   Why, I think, if she ne're had husband, she's a
whore, and thou a fool. Farewell.   [*Exit.*
      Clown.   I thank you, sir. Well, pull up thy heart, sister;
55 if there be any Law i'th' Court, this fellow shall father it,
'cause he uses me so scurvily.   There's a great Wedding
towards, they say; we'l amongst them for a husband for thee.

              Enter SIR NICODEMUS *with a letter.*

If we miss there, Ile have another bout with him that abus'd
me.   See, look, there comes another Hat and Feather, this
60 should be a close Letcher, he's reading of a Love-letter.
      Sir Nic.   Earl Cador's Marriage, and a Masque to grace it.
So, so!

57. *among* Tyr.

This night shall make me famous for Presentments. '—
How now, what are you?

Clown. A couple of Great-Brittains, you may see by our 65
bellies, sir.

Sir Nic. And what of this, sir?

Clown. Why, thus the matter stands, sir: There's one of your
Courtiers Hunting Nags has made a Gap through another
mans Inclosure. Now, sir, here's the question, who should be 70
at charge of a Fur-bush to stop it?

Sir Nic. Ha, ha, this is out of my element: the Law must end it.

Clown. Your worship says well; for, surely, I think some
Lawyer had a hand in the business, we have such a trouble-
som Issue.   75

Sir Nic. But what's thy business with me now?

Clown. Nay, sir, the business is done already, you may
see by my sisters belly.

Sir Nic. Oh, now I finde thee. This Gentlewoman, it
seems, has been humbled.   80

Clown. As low as the ground would give her leave, sir,
and your Worship knows this: though there be many fathers
without children, yet to have a childe without a father, were
most unnatural.

Sir Nic. That's true, ifaith, I never heard of a childe yet 85
that e're begot his father.

Clown. Why, true, you say wisely, sir.

Sir Nic. And therefore I conclude, that he that got the
childe, is without all question the father of it.

Clown. I, now you come to the matter, sir; and our suit 90
is to your Worship for the discovery of this father.

Sir Nic. Why, lives he in the Court here?

Joan. Yes, sir, and I desire but Marriage.

Sir Nic. And does the knave refuse it? Come, come, be
merry, wench; he shall marry thee, and keep the childe too, 95
if my Knighthood can do any thing. I am bound by mine
Orders to help distressed Ladies, and can there be a greater
injury to a woman with childe, then to lack a father for't?
I am asham'd of your simpleness. Come, come, give me a

99. *your* om. Del.

100 Courtiers Fee for my pains, and Ile be thy Advocate my
self, and justice shall be found; nay, Ile sue the Law for it;
but give me my Fee first.

    Clown. If all the money I have i'th' world will do it, you
shall have it, sir.

105   *Sir Nic.* An Angel does it.

    Clown. Nay, there's two, for your better eyesight, sir.

    Sir Nic. Why, well said! Give me thy hand, wench, Ile
teach thee a trick for all this, shall get a father for thy
childe presently, and this it is, mark now: You meet a man,
110 as you meet me now, thou claimest Marriage of me, and
layest the childe to my charge; I deny it: pish, that's
nothing, hold thy Claim fast, thy word carries it, and no Law
can withstand it.

    Clown. Ist possible?

115   *Sir Nic.* Past all opposition; her own word carries it. Let
her challenge any man, the childe shall call him Father;
there's a trick for your money now.

    Clown. Troth, Sir, we thank you, we'l make use of your
trick, and go no further to seek the childe a Father, for
120 we challenge you, Sir: sister, lay it to him, he shall marry
thee, I shall have a worshipful old man to my brother.

    Sir Nic. Ha, ha, I like thy pleasantness.

    Joan. Nay, indeed, Sir, I do challenge you.

    Clown. You think we jest, sir?

125   *Sir Nic.* I, by my troth, do I. I like thy wit yfaith, thou
shalt live at Court with me; didst never here of Nicodemus
Nothing? I am the man.

    Clown. Nothing? 'slid, we are out agen. Thou wast never
got with childe with nothing, sure?

130   *Joan.* I know not what to say.

    Sir Nic. Never grieve, wench, show me the man, and pro-
cess shall fly out.

    Clown. 'Tis enough for us to finde the children, we look
that you should finde the Father, and therefore either do us
135 justice, or we'l stand to our first challenge.

    106. *better sight* Tyr. — 111. *push* A, corr. by Tyr. and Del. —
112. *words carries* A, *words carry* Tyr., *word carries* Del. — 119. *the
childe* om. Tyr. — 128. *wert* Tyr.

Sir Nic.   Would you have justice without an Adversary?
Unless you can show me the man, I can do you no good in it.

   Clown.   Why, then I hope you'l do us no harm, sir; you'l restore

   Sir Nic.   What, my Fee? marry, Law forbid it!   [my money.
Finde out the party, and you shall have justice,   140
Your fault clos'd up, and all shall be amended,
The Childe his Father, and the Law-suit ended.   [*Exit.*

   Clown.   Well, he has deserv'd his Fee, indeed, for he has
brought our suit to a quick end, I promise you, and yet the
Childe has never a Father; nor we have no more mony to 145
seek after him.   A shame of all lecherous placcats! Now you
look like a Cat had newly kitten'd; what will you do now,
tro? Follow me no further, lest I beat your brains out.

   Joan.   Impose upon me any punishment,
Rather then leave me now.   150

   Clown.   Well, I think I am bewitched with thee; I cannot
finde in my heart to forsake her.   There was never sister
would have abus'd a poor brother as thou hast done; I am
even pin'd away with fretting, there's nothing but flesh and
bones about me.   Well, and I had my money agen, it were 155
some comfort.   Hark, sister, does it not thunder?   [*Thunder.*

   Joan.   Oh yes, most fearfully: What shall we do, brother?

   Clown.   Marry, e'en get some shelter, ere the storm catch us:
away, let's away, I prithee.

   *Enter the Devil in mans habit, richly attir'd, his feet and his
                        head horrid.*

   Joan.   Ha, 'tis he! Stay, brother, dear brother, stay.   160

   Clown.   What's the matter now?

   Joan.   My love, my friend is come; yonder he goes.

   Clown.   Where, where? show me where; Ile stop him, if
the devil be not in him.

   Joan.   Look there, look yonder!   165
Oh, dear friend, pity my distress,

For heaven and goodness, do but speak to me.
    Devil. She calls me, and yet drives me headlong from her.
Poor mortal, thou and I are much uneven,
170 Thou must not speak of goodness nor of heaven,
If I confer with thee; but be of comfort:
Whilst men do breath, and Britains name be known,
The fatal fruit thou bear'st within thy womb,
Shall here be famous till the day of doom.
175   *Clown.* 'Slid, who's that talks so? I can see nobody.
    Joan. Then art thou blind or mad. See where he goes,
And beckons me to come; oh, lead me forth,
I'le follow thee in spight of fear or death.   [*Exit.*
    Clown. Oh brave! she'l run to the devil for a husband;
180 she's stark mad, sure, and talks to a shaddow, for I could
see no substance: Well, I'le after her; the childe was got by
chance, and the father must be found at all adventure. [*Exit.*

SCENE II.

The Porch of a Church.

Enter HERMIT, MODESTIA, *and* EDWIN.

    Mod. Oh, reverent sir, by you my heart hath reacht
At the large hopes of holy Piety,
And for this have I craved your company,
Here in your sight religiously to vow
5 My chaste thoughts up to heaven, and make you now
The witness of my faith.
    Her. Angels assist thy hopes.
    Edwin. What meanes my Love? thou art my promis'd wife.
    Mod. To part with willingly what friends and life
10 Can make no good assurance of.
    Edwin. Oh, finde remorse, fair soul, to love and merit,
And yet recant thy vow.
    Mod. Never:
This world and I are parted now for ever.
15   *Her.* To finde the way to bliss, oh, happy woman,

---

173. *fruit*] *print* Del. — 176. *thou art* Tyr.
SCENE II. *The Porch of a Church* add. by Tyr. — 3. *have* add. by Del.

Th'ast learn'd the hardest Lesson, well I see.
Now show thy fortitude and constancy:
Let these thy friends thy sad departure weep,
Thou shalt but loose the wealth thou couldst not keep.
My contemplation calls me, I must leave ye.   20
    Edwin. O, reverent Sir, perswade not her to leave me.
    Her. My Lord, I do not, nor to cease to love ye;
I onely pray her faith may fixed stand;
Marriage was blest, I know, with heavens own hand. [*Exit.*
    Edwin. You hear him, Lady, 'tis not a virgins state,   25
But sanctity of life, must make you happy.
    Mod. Good sir, you say you love me; gentle Edwin,
Even by that love I do beseech you, leave me.
    Edwin. Think of your fathers tears, your weeping friends,
Whom cruel grief makes pale and bloodless for you.   30
    Mod. Would I were dead to all.
    Edwin.   Why do you weep?
    Mod. Oh, who would live to see
How men with care and cost seek misery?
    Edwin. Why do you seek it then? What joy, what pleasure
Can give you comfort in a single life?   35
    Mod. The contemplation of a happy death,
Which is to me so pleasing that I think
No torture could divert me: What's this world,
Wherein you'd have me walk, but a sad passage
To a dread Judgement-Seat, from whence even now   40
We are but bail'd, upon our good abearing,
Till that great Sessions come, when Death, the Cryer,
Will surely summon us and all to appear,
To plead us guilty or our bail to clear?
What musick's this?   [*Soft Musick.* 45

    Enter two Bishops, DONOBERT, GLOSTER, CADOR, CONSTANCIA,
                        OSWOLD, TOCLIO.

    Edwin. Oh, now resolve, and think upon my love!
This sounds the Marriage of your beauteous sister,

    16. *lesson well, I see* Del. — 21. *her not* Tyr. — 25. *virgin state* Tyr. —
30. *bloodless all for* Tyr. — 42. *that*] *those* Tyr. — 45. Stage-dir. *Bishops, Edwin, Don.* corr. by Tyr.

Vertuous Constancia, with the noble Cador.
Look, and behold this pleasure.
50 *Mod.* Cover me with night,
It is a vanity not worth the sight.
 Dono. See, see, she's yonder.
Pass on! Son Cador, Daughter Constancia,
I beseech you all, unless she first move speech,
55 Salute her not. — Edwin, what good success?
  Edwin. Nothing as yet, unless this object take her.
  Dono. See, see, her eye is fixt upon her sister;
Seem careless all, and take no notice of her: —
On afore there; come, my Constancia.
60 *Mod.* Not speak to me, nor dain to cast an eye
To look on my despised poverty?
I must be more charitable; — pray, stay, Lady,
Are not you she whom I did once call sister?
  Const. I did acknowledge such a name to one,
65 Whilst she was worthy of it, in whose folly,
Since you neglect your fame and friends together,
In you I drown'd a sisters name for ever.
  Mod. Your looks did speak no less.
  Glost. It now begins to work, this sight has moved her.
70 *Dono.* I knew this trick would take, or nothing.
  Mod. Though you disdain in me a sister's name,
Yet charity, me thinks, should be so strong
To instruct ere you reject. I am a wretch,
Even follies instance, who perhaps have er'd,
75 Not having known the goodness bears so high
And fair a show in you; which being exprest,
I may recant this low despised life,
And please those friends whom I have mov'd to grief.
  Cador. She is coming, yfaith; be merry, Edwin.
80 *Const.* Since you desire instruction, you shall have it.
What is 't should make you thus desire to live
Vow'd to a single life?
  Mod. Because I know I cannot flie from death.

<hr>

53. *Pass on son Cador. Daughter* A and Edd. — 59. *on there afore*
Tyr. — 70. *know* A and Del., *knew* Tyr. — 78 *have* add. by Del.

Oh, my good sister, I beseech you, hear me:
This world is but a Masque, catching weak eyes   85
With what is not our selves but our disguise,
A Vizard that falls off, the Dance being done,
And leaves Deaths Glass for all to look upon;
Our best happiness here lasts but a night,
Whose burning Tapers makes false Ware seem right.   90
Who knows not this, and will not now provide
Some better shift before his shame be spy'd,
And knowing this vain world at last will leave him,
Shake off these robes that help but to deceive him!
   Const.   Her words are powerful, I am amaz'd to hear her! 95
   Dono.   Her soul's inchanted with infected Spells.
Leave her, best Girl; for now in thee
Ile seek the fruits of Age, Posterity. —
Out o' my sight! sure, I was half asleep
Or drunk, when I begot thee.   100
   Const.   Good sir, forbear.   What say you to that, sister?
The joy of children, a blest Mothers Name?
Oh, who without much grief can loose such Fame?
   Mod.   Who can enjoy it without sorrow rather?
And that most certain where the joy's unsure,   105
Seeing the fruit that we beget, endure
So many miseries, that oft we pray
The Heavens to shut up their afflicted day;
At best we do but bring forth Heirs to die,
And fill the Coffins of our enemy.   110
   Const.   Oh, my soul!
   Dono.   Hear her no more, Constantia,
She's sure bewitcht with Error; leave her, Girl.
   Const.   Then must I leave all goodness, sir: away,
Stand off, I say.
   Dono.   How's this?   115
   Const.   I have no father, friend, no husband now;
All are but borrowed robes, in which we masque
To waste and spend the time, when all our Life
Is but one good betwixt two Ague-days,

    90. *make* Tyr. — 119. *between* Tyr.

120 Which from the first ere we have time to praise,
A second Fever takes us: Oh, my best sister,
My souls eternal friend, forgive the rashness
Of my distemper'd tongue; for how could she,
Knew not her self, know thy felicity,
125 From which worlds cannot now remove me?
        Dono. Art thou mad too, fond woman? What's thy meaning?
        Const. To seek eternal happiness in heaven,
Which all this world affords not.
        Cador. Think of thy Vow, thou art my promis'd Wife.
130   *Const.* Pray, trouble me no further.
        Omnes.   Strange alteration!
        Cador. Why do you stand at gaze, you sacred Priests?
You holy men, be equal to the Gods,
And consummate my Marriage with this woman.
        Bishop. Her self gives barr, my Lord, to your desires
135 And our performance; 'tis against the Law
And Orders of the Church to force a Marriage.
        Cador. How am I wrong'd! Was this your trick, my Lord?
        Dono. I am abus'd past sufferance;
Grief and amazement strive which Sense of mine
140 Shall loose her being first. Yet let me call thee Daughter.
        Cador. Me, Wife.
        Const. Your words are air, you speak of want to wealth,
And wish her sickness, newly rais'd to health.
        Dono. Bewitched Girls, tempt not an old mans fury,
145 That hath no strength to uphold his feeble age,
But what your sights give life to. Oh, beware,
And do not make me curse you.
        [Kneel.] Mod. Dear father,
Here at your feet we kneel, grant us but this,
150 That, in your sight and hearing, the good Hermit
May plead our Cause; which, if it shall not give
Such satisfaction as your Age desires,
We will submit to you.
        Const.   You gave us life;
Save not our bodies, but our souls, from death.

        124. *Who knew* Tyr.

Dono. This gives some comfort yet: Rise with my blessings. — 155
Have patience, noble Cador, worthy Edwin;
Send for the Hermit that we may confer.
For, sure, religion tyes you not to leave
Your careful Father thus; if so it be,
Take your content, and give all grief to me.   [*Exeunt.* 160

SCENE III.

A cave in the Forest.

Thunder and Lightning; Enter Devil.

Devil.   Mix light and darkness; earth and heaven dissolve,
Be of one piece agen, and turn to Chaos;
Break all your works, you powers, and spoil the world,
Or, if you will maintain earth still, give way
And life to this abortive birth now coming,   5
Whose fame shall add unto your Oracles.
Lucina, Hecate, dreadful Queen of Night,
Bright Proserpine, be pleas'd for Ceres love,
From Stigian darkness summon up the Fates,
And in a moment bring them quickly hither,   10
Lest death do vent her birth and her together.   [*Thunder.*
Assist, you spirits of infernal deeps,
Squint-ey'd Erictho, midnight Incubus,
Rise, rise to aid this birth prodigious.

Enter Lucina and the three Fates.

Thanks, Hecate; hail, sister to the Gods!   15
There lies your way, haste with the Fates, and help,
Give quick dispatch unto her laboring throws,
To bring this mixture of infernal seed
To humane being;   [*Exeunt Fates.*
And to beguile her pains, till back you come,   20
Anticks shall dance and Musick fill the room. —   [*Dance.*
Thanks, Queen of Shades.

160. *Take you content* Del.
    SCENE III. *A Cave in the Forest* add. by Tyr. — 8. *from Ceres* Tyr. —
20. *beguil* A.

Lucina. Farewel, great servant to th'infernal King.
In honor of this childe, the Fates shall bring
25 All their assisting powers of Knowledge, Arts,
Learning, and Wisdom, all the hidden parts
Of all-admiring Prophecy, to fore-see
The event of times to come. His Art shall stand
A wall of brass to guard the Brittain Land.
30 Even from this minute, all his Arts appears
Manlike in Judgement, Person, State, and years.
Upon his brest the Fates have fixt his name,
And since his birthplace was this forrest here,
They now have nam'd him *Merlin Silvester.*

35   *Devil.* And Merlin's name in Brittany shall live,
Whilst men inhabit here or Fates can give
Power to amazing wonder; envy shall weep,
And mischief sit and shake her ebbone wings,
Whilst all the world of Merlins magick sings.   [*Exit.*

SCENE IV.

The Forest.

Enter Clown.

Clown. Well, I wonder how my poor sister does, after
all this thundering; I think she's dead, for I can hear no
tidings of her. Those woods yields small comfort for
her; I could meet nothing but a swinherds wife, keeping
5 hogs by the Forestside, but neither she nor none of her sowes
would stir a foot to help us; indeed, I think she durst not
trust her self amongst the trees with me, for I must needs
confess I offer'd some kindness to her. Well, I would fain
know what's become of my sister. If she have brought me
10 a yong Cousin, his face may be a picture to finde his
Father by. So ho! sister Joan, Joan Go-too't, where art
thou?

Joan. (within). Here, here, brother, stay but a while, I
come to thee.

26. *and* add. by Del. — 30. *Art* Tyr. — 35. *Brittain* A.
SCENE IV. *The Forest* add. by Tyr. — 3. *These* Tyr.; *yield* Tyr. and
Del.; *for*] *to* Tyr. — 7. *amongst*] *under* Tyr. — 11. *so oh* A.

Clown.   O brave! she's alive still, I know her voice, she   15
speaks, and speaks cherfully, methinks.   How now, what
Moon-calf has she got with her?

Enter JOAN *and* MERLIN *with a Book.*

Joan.   Come, my dear Merlin, why dost thou fix thine eye
So deeply on that book?
  Merlin.   To sound the depth
Of Arts, of Learning, Wisdom, Knowledge.   20
  Joan.   Oh, my dear, dear son,
Those studies fits thee when thou art a man.
  Merlin.   Why, mother, I can be but half a man at best,
And that is your mortality; the rest
In me is spirit; 'tis not meat, nor time,   25
That gives this growth and bigness; no, my years
Shall be more strange then yet my birth appears.
Look, mother, there's my Uncle.
  Joan.   How doest thou know him, son? thou never sawst him.
  Merlin.   Yet I know him, and know the pains he has taken   30
for ye, to finde out my Father. — Give me your hand, good Uncle.
  Clown.   Ha, ha, I'de laugh at that, yfaith.   Do you know me, sir?
  Merlin.   Yes, by the same token that even now you kist the
swinherds wife i'th' woods, and would have done more, if she
would have let you, Uncle.   35
  Clown.   A witch, a witch, a witch, sister! Rid him out of
your company, he is either a witch or a conjurer; he could
never have known this else.
  Joan.   Pray, love him, brother, he is my son.
  Clown.   Ha, ha, this is worse then all the rest yfaith; by   40
his beard, he is more like your husband.   Let me see, is your
great belly gone?
  Joan.   Yes, and this the happy fruit.
  Clown.   What, this Hartichoke? A Childe born with a beard
on his face?   45
  Merlin.   Yes, and strong legs to go, and teeth to eat.

     19. *depths of art* Tyr. — 22. *fit* Tyr. and Del. — 30. *Yet*] *Yes* Del.

Clown. You can nurse up your self, then? There's some
charges sav'd for Soap and Candle. 'Slid, I have heard of
some that has been born with teeth, but never none with
50 such a talking tongue before.

Joan. Come, come, you must use him kindly, brother;
Did you but know his worth, you would make much of him.

Clown. Make much of a Moncky? This is worse then *Tom
Thumb*, that let a fart in his Mothers belly; a Childe to
55 speak, eat, and go the first hour of his birth, nay, such a
Baby as had need of a Barber before he was born too,
why, sister, this is monstrous, and shames all our kindred.

Joan. That thus 'gainst nature and our common births
He comes thus furnisht to salute the world,
60 Is power of Fates, and gift of his great father.

Clown. Why, of what profession is your father, sir?

Merlin. He keeps a Hot-house i'th' Low-Countries; will
you see him, sir?

Clown. See him? why, sister, has the childe found his father?
65 *Mer.* Yes, and Ile fetch him, Uncle.   [*Exit.*

Clown. Do not Uncle me, till I know your kindred. Fore
my conscience, some Baboon begot thee. — Surely, thou art
horribly deceived, sister, this Urchin cannot be of thy breeding; I shall be asham'd to call him cousin, though his father
70 be a Gentleman.

Enter MERLIN *and* DEVIL.

Merlin. Now, my kinde Uncle, see:
The Childe has found his Father, this is he.

Clown. The devil it is; ha, ha, is this your sweet-heart,
sister? have we run through the Countrey, haunted the City,
75 and examin'd the Court to finde out a Gallant with a Hat
and Feather, and a silken Sword, and golden Hangers, and
do you now bring me to a Ragamuffin with a face like a
Frying-pan?

Joan. Fie, brother, you mistake, behold him better.

49. *have been* Tyr. — 54. *that . . . belly* om. Tyr. — 66. *for* A and
Del., *fore* Tyr.

Missing Page

Missing Page

To meet bold Edol, their stern General,
That now, contrary to the Kings command,   25
Hath re-united all his cashier'd Troops,
And this way beats his drums to threaten us.
   Octa.   Then our Plot is discover'd.
   Ostor.   Come, th'art a fool, his Army and his life
Is given unto us: where is the Queen my sister?   30
   Octa.   In conference with the Prince.
   Ostor.   Bring the Guards nearer, all is fair and good;
Their Conference, I hope, shall end in blood.   [*Exeunt.*

SCENE VI.

A Room in the Palace.
Enter PRINCE *and* ARTESIA.

   Artes.   Come, come, you do but flatter;
What you term Love, is but a Dream of blood,
Wakes with injoying, and with open eyes
Forgot, contemn'd, and lost.
   Prince.   I must be wary, her words are dangerous. —   5
True, we'l speak of Love no more, then.
   Artes.   Nay, if you will, you may;
'Tis but in jest, and yet so children play
With fiery flames, and covet what is bright,
But, feeling his effects, abhor the light.   10
Pleasure is like a Building, the more high,
The narrower still it grows; Cedars do dye
Soonest at top.
   Prince.   How does your instance suit?
   Artes.   From Art and Nature to make sure the root,   15
And lay a fast foundation, ere I try
The incertain Changes of a wavering Skie.
Make your example thus. — You have a kiss, —
Was it not pleasing?
   Prince.   Above all name to express it.

   28. *Plot's* A.
   SCENE VI. No new scene in Edd. — 14. *instanced* A, corr. by Tyr.
and Del.

20   *Artes.* Yet now the pleasure's gone,
And you have lost your joys possession.
    Prince. Yet when you please, this flood may ebb again.
    Artes. But where it never ebbs, there runs the main.
    Prince. Who can attain such hopes?
25   *Artes.* Ile show the way to it, give you
A taste once more of what you may enjoy.   [*Kiss.*
    Prince. Impudent whore! —
I were more false than Atheism can be,
Should I not call this high felicity.
30   *Artes.* If I should trust your faith, alas, I fear,
You soon would change belief.
    Prince. I would covet Martyrdom to make't confirm'd.
    Artes. Give me your hand on that you'l keep your word?
    Prince. I will.
35   *Artes.* Enough: Help, husband, king Aurelius, help!
Rescue betraid Artesia!
    Prince. Nay, then 'tis I that am betraid, I see;
Yet with thy blood Ile end thy Treachery.
    Artes. How now? what troubles you? Is this you, sir,
40 That but even now would suffer Martyrdom
To win your hopes, and is there now such terror
In names of men to fright you? nay, then I see
What mettle you are made on.
    Prince. Ha! was it but tryal? then I ask your pardon:
45 What a dull slave was I to be so fearful! —
Ile trust her now no more, yet try the utmost. —
I am resolved, no brother, no man breathing,
Were he my bloods begetter, should withhold
Me from your love; I 'd leap into his bosom,
50 And from his brest pull forth that happiness
Heaven had reserved in you for my enjoying.
    Artes. I, now you speak a Lover like a Prince! —
Treason, treason!
    Prince. Agen?
55   *Artes.* Help, Saxon Princes: Treason!

    25. *you*] *me* A and Edd. — 32. *make it* Tyr., but read *I'd.* — 51. Om.
by Tyr.

Enter OSTORIUS, OCTA *&c.*

Ostor.　Rescue the Queen: strike down the Villain.

Enter EDOL, AURELIUS, DONOBERT, CADOR, EDWIN, TOCLIO,
　　　　OSWOLD, *al the other door.*

Edol.　Call in the Guards: the Prince in danger! —
Fall back, dear Sir, my brest shall buckler you.
　　Aurel.　Beat down their weapons!
　　Edol.　Slave, wert thou made of brass, my sword shall bite thee.　60
　　Aurel.　Withdraw, on pain of death!　Where is the Traitor?
　　Artes.　Oh, save your life, my Lord; let it suffice,
My beauty forc't mine own captivity.
　　Aurel.　Who did attempt to wrong thee?
　　Prince.　　　　　　　　　　　　　　　　Hear me, Sir.
　　Aurel.　Oh, my sad soul! wast thou?　　　　　　　65
　　Artes.　Oh, do not stand to speak; one minutes stay
Prevents a second speech for ever.
　　Aurel.　Make our Guards strong:
My dear Artesia, let us know thy wrongs
And our own dangers.　　　　　　　　　　　70
　　Artes.　The Prince your brother, with these Brittain Lords,
Have all agreed to take me hence by force
And marry me to him.
　　Prince.　The Devil shall wed thee first:
Thy baseness and thy lust confound and rot thee!　75
　　Artes.　He courted me even now, and in mine ear
Sham'd not to plead his most dishonest love
And their attempts to seize your sacred person,
Either to shut you up within some prison,
Or, which is worse, I fear, to murther you.　　　80
　　Omnes Brittains.　'Tis all as false as hell.
　　Edol.　And as foul as she is.
　　Artes.　You know me, Sir?
　　Edol.　　　　　　　　　　Yes, Deadly Sin, we know you,
And shall discover all your villany.
　　Aurel.　Chester, forbear!　　　　　　　　　85

　　　　66. *not slay* Tyr. — 81. *'tis false as* Tyr.

　　　　　　　　　　　　　　　　4*

Ostor. Their treasons, sir, are plain:
Why are their Souldiers lodg'd so near the Court?
    Octa. Nay, why came he in arms so suddenly?
    Edol. You fleering Anticks, do not wake my fury.
90   *Octa.* Fury?
    Edol. Ratsbane, do not urge me.
    Artes. Good sir, keep farther from them.
    Prince. Oh, my sick heart!
She is a witch by nature, devil by art.
95   *Aurel.* Bite thine own slanderous tongue; 'tis thou art false,
I have observ'd your passions long ere this.
    Ostor. Stand on your guard, my Lord, we are your friends,
And all our Force is yours.
    Edol. To spoil and rob the Kingdom.
    Aurel.   Sir, be silent.
100   *Edol.* Silent! how long? till Doomsday? shall I stand by,
And hear mine Honor blasted with foul Treason,
The State half lost, your life endangered,
And yet be silent?
    Artes. Yes, my blunt Lord, unless you speak your Treasons.
105 Sir, let your Guards, as Traitors, seize them all,
And then let tortures and devulsive racks
Force a confession from them.
    Edol. Wilde-fire and Brimstone eat thee! Hear me, sir!
    Aurel. Sir, Ile not hear you.
    Edol.   But you shall! Not hear me?
110 Were the worlds Monarch, Cesar, living, he should hear me.
I tell you, Sir, these serpents have betraid
Your Life and Kingdom: does not every day
Bring tidings of more swarms of lowsie slaves,
The offal fugitives of barren Germany,
115 That land upon our Coasts, and by our neglect
Settled in Norfolk and Northumberland?
    Ostor. They come as Aids and Safeguards to the King.
    Octa. Has he not need, when Vortiger's in arms,
And you raise Powers, 'tis thought, to joyn with him?

---

102. *and your life endanger'd, yet* A and Edd. — 110. Two lines in
Del., div. at *he.* — 113. *knaves* Tyr. — 115. *and have by* Tyr.

Edol. Peace, you pernicious Rat.   120
Dono.   Prithee, forbear.
Edol. Away, suffer a gilded rascal,
A low-bred despicable creeper, an insulting Toad,
To spit his poison'd venome in my face!
Octa. Sir, sir!
Edol. Do not reply, you Cur; for, by the Gods,   125
Tho' the Kings presence guard thee, I shall break all patience,
And, like a Lion rous'd to spoil, shall run
Foul-mouth'd upon thee, and devour thee quick. —
Speak, sir, will you forsake these scorpions,
Or stay till they have stung you to the heart?   130
Aurel. Y'are traitors all. This is our wife, our Queen:
Brother Ostorius, troop your Saxons up,
We'l hence to Winchester, and raise more powers,
To man with strength the Castle Camilot. —
Go hence, false men, joyn you with Vortiger,   .   135
The murderer of our brother Constantine:
We'l hunt both him and you with dreadful vengeance.
Since Brittain fails, we'l trust to forrain friends,
And guard our person from your traitorous ends.
          [*Exeunt* Aurel., Ostor., Octa, Artes., Toc., Osw.
Edwin. He's sure bewitch't.
Glost.   What counsel now for safety? 140
Dono. Onely this, sir: with all the speed we can,
Preserve the person of the King and Kingdom.
Cador. Which to effect, 'tis best march hence to Wales,
And set on Vortiger before he joyn
His Forces with the Saxons.   145
Edwin. On, then, with speed for Wales and Vortiger!
That tempest once o'reblown, we come, Ostorius,
To meet thy traiterous Saxons, thee and them,
That with advantage thus have won the King,
To back your factions and to work our ruines.   150
This, by the Gods and my good Sword, I'le set
In bloody lines upon thy Burgonet.   [*Exeunt.*

    133. *and* not in A and Edd. — 137. *vengance* A. — 140. *bewitch* A,
corr. by Tyr. and Del. — 144. *joins* Tyr. — 150. *ruin* Tyr.

ACT IV.

SCENE I.

Before a Ruined Castle in Wales.

Enter CLOWN, MERLIN, *and a little antick Spirit.*

Mer. How now, Uncle? Why do you search your pockets so? Do you miss any thing?

Clown. Ha! Cousin Merlin, I hope your beard does not overgrow your honesty; I pray, remember, you are made up
5   of sisters thread, I am your mothers brother, whosoever was your father.

Mer. Why, wherein can you task my duty, Uncle?

Clown. Your self or your page it must be, I have kept no other company, since your mother bound your head to my
10   Protectorship; I do feel a fault of one side; either it was that Sparrowhawk, or a Cast of Merlins, for I finde a Covey of Cardecus sprung out of my pocket.

Mer. Why, do you want any money, Uncle? Sirrah, had you any from him?

15   *Clown.* Deny it not, for my pockets are witness against you.

Spirit. Yes, I had, to teach you better wit to look to it.

Clown. Pray, use your fingers better, and my wit may serve as it is, sir.

Mer. Well, restore it.

20   *Spirit.* There it is.

Clown. I, there's some honesty in this; 'twas a token from your invisible Father, Cousin, which I would not have to go invisibly from me agen.

Mer. Well, you are sure you have it now, Uncle?

25   *Clown.* Yes, and mean to keep it now from your pages filching fingers too.

Spirit. If you have it so sure, pray show it me agen.

Clown. Yes, my little juggler, I dare show it. Ha, cleanly conveyance agen! Ye have no invisible fingers, have ye? 'Tis
30   gone, certainly.

Spirit. Why, sir, I toucht you not.

Mer. Why, look you, Uncle, I have it now. How ill do
you look to it. Here, keep it safer.

Clown. Ha, ha, this is fine, yfaith. I must keep some other
company, if you have these slights of hand.   35

Mer. Come, come, Uncle, 'tis all my Art which shall not
offend you, sir, onely I give you a taste of it to show you
sport.

Clown. Oh, but 'tis ill jesting with a mans pocket, tho'.
But I am glad to see your cunning, Cousin, for now will I   40
warrant thee a living till thou diest. You have heard the
news in Wales here?

Mer. Uncle, let me prevent your care and counsel,
'Twill give you better knowledge of my cunning.
You would prefer me now, in hope of gain,   45
To Vortiger, King of the Welsh Brittains,
To whom are all the <u>Artists</u> summon'd now,
That seeks the secrets of futurity,
The Bards, the Druids, Wizards, Conjurers,
Not an Aruspex with his whisling spells,   50
No Capnomancer with his musty fumes,
No Witch or Juggler, but is thither sent,
To calculate the strange and fear'd event
Of his prodigious Castle, now in building,
Where all the labors of the painful day   55
Are ruin'd still i'th' night, and to this place
You would have me go.

Clown. Well, if thy mother were not my sister, I would
say she was a witch that begot thee; but this is thy father,
not thy mother wit. Thou hast taken my tale into thy mouth,   60
and spake my thoughts before me; therefore away, shuffle thy
self amongst the Conjurers, and be a made man before thou
comest to age.

Mer. Nay, but stay, Uncle, you overslip my dangers:
The Prophecies and all the cunning Wizards   65
Have certifi'd the king that this his Castle

Can never stand, till the foundation's laid
With Mortar temper'd with the fatal blood
Of such a childe whose father was no mortal.

70   *Clown.* What's this to thee? If the devil were thy father,
was not thy mother born at Carmarden? Diggon for that,
then; and then it must be a childes blood, and who will
take thee for a childe with such a beard of thy face? Is
there not diggon for that too, Cousin?

75   *Mer.* I must not go: lend me your ear a while,
I'le give you reasons to the contrary.

Enter two Gentlemen.

1. *Gent.* Sure, this is an endless piece of work the king has
sent us about!

2. *Gent.* Kings may do it, man; the like has been done to
80 finde out the Unicorn.

1. *Gent.* Which will be sooner found, I think, then this
fiend-begotten childe we seek for.

2. *Gent.* Pox of those Conjurers that would speak of such
a one, and yet all their cunning could not tell us where to
85 finde him.

1. *Gent.* In Wales they say assuredly he lives; come, let's
enquire further.

Mer. Uncle, your perswasions must not prevail with me:
I know mine enemies better then you do.

90   *Clown.* I say, th'art a bastard then, if thou disobey thine
Uncle. Was not Joan Go-too't, thy mother, my sister? If
the devil were thy father, what kin art thou to any man
alive, but Bailys and Brokers? and they are but brothers in
Law to thee neither.

95   1. *Gent.* How's this? I think we shall speed here.

2. *Gent.* I, and unlook't for too. Go near and listen to them.

Clown. Hast thou a beard to hide it? Wilt thou show
thy self a childe? Wilt thou have more hair then wit? Wilt
thou deny thy mother, because no body knows thy father?
100 Or shall thine Uncle be an ass?

86. *said* Tyr. — 96. *ne're* A. — 97. *Wilt then* Del.

1. *Gent.*   Bless ye, friend: pray, what call you this small
Gentlemans name?

Clown.   Small, sir? a small man may be a great Gentleman;
his father may be of an ancient house, for ought we know, sir.

2. *Gent.*   Why, do you not know his father?   105

Clown.   No, nor you neither, I think, unless the devil be in ye.

1. *Gent.*   What is his name, sir?

Clown.   His name is my Cousin, sir; his education is my
sisters son, but his maners are his own.

Mer.   Why ask ye, Gentlemen? my name is Merlin.   110

Clown.   Yes, and a Goshawk was his father, for ought we
know; for I am sure his mother was a Wind-sucker.

2. *Gent.*   He has a mother, then?

Clown.   As sure as I have a sister, sir.

1. *Gent.*   But his father you leave doubtful.   115

Clown.   Well, Sir, as wise men as you doubt, whether he
had a father or no?

1. *Gent.*   Sure, this is he we seek for.

2. *Gent.*   I think no less: and, sir, we let you know the
King hath sent for you.   120

Clown.   The more childe he; and he had bin rul'd by me,
he should have gone before he was sent for.

1. *Gent.*   May we not see his mother?

Clown.   Yes, and feel her too, if you anger her; a devilish
thing, I can tell ye, she has been. Ile go fetch her to ye. [*Exit.* 125

2. *Gent.*   Sir, it were fit you did resolve for speed,
You must unto the King.

Mer.   My service, sir,
Shall need no strickt command, it shall obey
Most peaceably; but needless 'tis to fetch
What is brought home. My journey may be staid,   130
The King is coming hither
With the same quest you bore before him; hark,
This drum will tell ye.   [*Within Drums beat a low March.*

1. *Gent.*   This is some cunning indeed, sir.

Florish.   Enter VORTIGER, *reading a letter,* PROXIMUS,
with Drum and Soldiers, &c.

135   *Vort.*   Still in our eye your message, Proximus,
We keep to spur our speed:
Ostorius and Octa we shall salute
With succor against Prince Vter and Aurelius,
Whom now we hear incamps at Winchester.
140 There's nothing interrupts our way so much
As doth the errection of this fatal Castle,
That spite of all our Art and daily labor
The night still ruines.
      Prox.   As erst I did affirm, still I maintain,
145 The fiend-begotten childe must be found out,
Whose blood gives strength to the foundation;
It cannot stand else.

        Enter CLOWN *and* JOAN, *joining* MERLIN.

      Vort.   Ha! Is't so?
Then, Proximus, by this intelligence
He should be found: speak, is this he you tell of?
150   *Clown.*   Yes, Sir, and I his Uncle, and she his mother.
      Vort.   And who is his father?
      Clown.   Why, she his mother can best tell you that, and
yet I thinke the childe be wise enough, for he has found his
father.
155   *Vort.*   Woman, is this thy son?
      Joan.   It is, my Lord.
      Vort.   What was his father? Or where lives he?
      Mer.   Mother, speak freely and unastonisht;
That which you dar'd to act, dread not to name.
160   *Joan.*   In which I shall betray my sin and shame.
But since it must be so, then, know, great King,
All that my self yet knows of him is this:
In pride of blood and beauty I did live,
My glass the Altar was, my face the Idol;
165 Such was my peevish love unto my self,
That I did hate all other; such disdain

      139. *encamp'd* Del. — 141. *famous Castle* Tyr. — 147. *Enter* CLOWN
and JOAN, MERLIN A.

Was in my scornful eye that I suppos'd
No mortal creature worthy to enjoy me.
Thus with the Peacock I beheld my train,
But never saw the blackness of my feet;   170
Oft have I chid the winds for breathing on me,
And curst the Sun, fearing to blast my beauty.
In midst of this most leaprous disease,
A seeming fair young man appear'd unto me,
In all things suiting my aspiring pride,   175
And with him brought along a conquering power,
To which my frailty yielded; from whose embraces
This issue came; what more he is, I know not.
    Vort. Some Incubus or Spirit of the night
Begot him then, for, sure, no mortal did it.   180
    Mer. No matter who, my Lord; leave further quest,
Since 'tis as hurtful as unnecessary
More to enquire: Go to the cause, my Lord,
Why you have sought me thus?
    Vort. I doubt not but thou knowst; yet, to be plain,   185
I sought thee for thy blood.
    Mer. By whose direction?
    Prox. By mine;
My art infallible instructed me,
Upon thy blood must the foundation rise   190
Of the Kings building, it cannot stand else.
    Mer. Hast thou such leisure to enquire my Fate,
And let thine own hang careless over thee?
Knowst thou what pendclous mischief roofs thy head,
How fatal, and how sudden?   195
    Prox. Pish!
Bearded abortive, thou foretel my danger? —
My Lord, he trifles to delay his own.
    Mer. No, I yield my self: and here before the King
Make good thine Augury, as I shall mine.   200
If thy fate fall not, thou hast spoke all truth,
And let my blood satisfie the Kings desires:
If thou thy self wilt write thine Epitaph,

    185. *I have no doubt* Del. — 189. *infalable* A.

Dispatch it quickly, there's not a minutes time
205 Betwixt thee and thy death.   [*A stone falls and kills Proximus.*
    Prox. Ha, ha, ha!
    Mer. I, so thou mayest die laughing.
    Vort. Ha! This is above admiration. Look, is he dead?
    Clown. Yes, sir, here's brains to make morter on, if you'l
210 use them. — Cousin Merlin, there's no more of this stone fruit
ready to fall, is there? I pray, give your Uncle a little fair
warning.
    Mer. Remove that shape of death. And now, my Lord,
For clear satisfaction of your doubts, Merlin will show
215 The fatal cause that keeps your Castle down,
And hinders your proceedings.
Stand there, and by an apparition see
The labor and the end of all your destiny.
Mother and Uncle, you must be absent.
220   *Clown.* Is your father coming, Cousin?
    Mer. Nay, you must be gone.
    Joan. Come, you'l offend him, brother.
    Clown. I would fain see my brother i'law; if you were
married, I might lawfully call him so.
            [*Exeunt* JOAN *and* CLOWN. MERLIN *strikes his wand.*
              Thunder and Lightning; two Dragons appear, a
              White and a Read; they fight a while, and pause.
225   *Vort.* What means this stay?
    Mer. Be not amaz'd, my Lord, for on the victory,
Of loss or Gain, as these two Champions ends,
Your fate, your life, and kingdom, all depends;
Therefore observe it well.
230   *Vort.* I shall. Heaven be auspicious to us.
      [*Thunder: The two Dragons fight agen, and the White*
    Dragon drives off the Red.

---

204. *time*] *space* Tyr. — 205. *'twixt* A; *and death* Tyr. Elze, Notes,
Vol. II, p. 1 supposes ll. 209 and 210 to form one verse; but we must not
forget that lines with three or four feet very often occur in our play. —
215. *your fatal Castle* A, corr. by Tyr. and Del. — 218. *and end* A and
Edd. — 224. *Exeunt Joan and Clown.* om. A. — 225. Om. by Tyr.; *stay.*
Elze, 1. c. II, p. 2 proposes to read *play,* but *stay* directly refers to the
preceding stage-dir. *and pause.*

Vort.   The conquest is on the white Dragons part.
Now, Merlin, faithfully expound the meaning.
   Mer.   Your Grace must then not be offended with me.
   Vort.   It is the weakest part I found in thee,
To doubt of me so slightly.   Shall I blame   235
My prophet that foretells me of my dangers?
Thy cunning I approve most excellent.
   Mer.   Then know, my Lord, there is a dampish Cave,
The nightly habitation of these Dragons,
Vaulted beneath where you would build your Castle,   240
Whose enmity and nightly combats there
Maintain a constant ruine of your labors.
To make it more plain, the Dragons, then,
Your self betoken and the Saxon King;
The vanquisht Red is, sir, your dreadful Emblem.   245
   Vort.   Oh, my fate!
   Mer.   Nay, you must hear with patience, Royal sir.
You slew the lawful King Constantius:
'Twas a red deed, your Crown his blood did cement.
The English Saxon, first brought in by you   250
For aid against Constantius brethren,
Is the white horror who now, knit together,
Have driven and shut you up in these wilde mountains; .
And though they now seek to unite with friendship,
It is to wound your bosom, not embrace it,   255
And with an utter exstirpation
To rout the Brittains out, and plant the English.
Seek for your safety, Sir, and spend no time
To build the airy Castles; for Prince Vter,
Armed with vengeance for his brothers blood,   260
Is hard upon you.   If you mistrust me,
And to my words crave witness, sir, then know,
Here comes a messenger to tell you so.   *[Exeunt.*

Enter Messenger.

   Mes.   My Lord!   Prince Vter!
   Vort.   And who else, sir?   265

---

   234. *Is it* Del.; *I have found* Tyr. — 242. *of our labour* Tyr. —
257. *To rout*] *Drive* Tyr. — 262. *craves* A, corr. by Tyr. and Del.

Mes.   Edol, the great General.

Vort.   The great Devil!   They are coming to meet us.

Mes.   With a full power, my Lord.

Vort.   With a full vengeance

They mean to meet us; so we are ready

270 To their confront.   At full march, <u>double footing</u>,

We'l loose no ground, nor shall their numbers fright us:

If it be Fate, it cannot be withstood;

We got our Crown so, be it lost in blood.   [*Exeunt.*

SCENE II.

Open Country in Wales.

Enter PRINCE VTER, EDOL, CADOR, EDWIN, TOCLIO,
with Drum and Soldiers.

Prince.   Stay, and advice; hold, drum!

Edol.   Beat, slave!   Why do you pause?

Why make a stand? where are our enemies?

Or do you mean we fight amongst our selves?

5   *Prince.*   Nay, noble Edol,

Let us here take counsel, it cannot hurt,

It is the surest Garison to safety.

Edol.   Fie on such slow delays!   So fearful men,

That are to pass over a flowing river,

10   Stand on the bank to parly of the danger,

Till the tide rise, and then be swallowed.

Is not the King in field?

Cador.   Proud Vortiger, the Traitor, is in field.

Edwin.   The Murderer and Usurper.

15   *Edol.*   Let him be the devil, so I may fight with him.

For heavens love, sir, march on!

Oh, my patience! will you delay,

Untill the Saxons come to aid his party?   [*A Tucket.*

Prince.   There's no such fear: prithee, be calm a while.

270. *As full* A and Tyr.; *confront, at full march double footing.* Del.
SCENE II.   *Open Country in Wales.* add. by Tyr. — 5—6. One line
in Del. — 6.   Read *Let's here | take coun | sel, it | can't hurt,* or *coun | sel,
— | it can | not hurt |.* Elze, Notes I, p. 2. proposes to read *Let us take
counsel here.* — 11. *then*] *they* Tyr. — 15—16. Div. at *devil* Del.

Hark! It seems by this, he comes or sends to us.   20
    Edol. If it be for parly, I will drown the summons,
If all our drums and hoarseness choke me not.

Enter Captain.

    Prince. Nay, prithee, hear. — From whence art thou?
    Cap. From the King Vortiger.
    Edol. Traitor, there's none such: Alarum, drum, strike, slave, 25
Or, by mine honor, I will break thy head,
And beat thy drumsticks both about thine ears.
    Prince. Hold, noble Edol,
Let's hear what Articles he can inforce.
    Edol. What articles or what conditions   30
Can you expect to value half your wrong,
Unless he kill himself by thousand tortures,
And send his carcase to appease your vengeance
For the foul murder of Constantius,
And that 's not a tenth part neither.   35
    Prince. 'Tis true,
My brothers blood is crying to me now,
I do applaud thy counsel: hence, be gone! — [*Exit Captain.*
We'l hear no parly now but by our swords.
    Edol. And those shall speak home in death-killing words: 40
Alarum to the fight; sound, sound the Alarum.   [*Exeunt.*

SCENE III.

A Field of Battle.

   Alarum. Enter EDOL, *driving all* VORTIGERS *Force before him,*
      then exit. Enter PRINCE VTER *pursuing* VORTIGER.

    Vort. Dost follow me?
    Prince.   Yes, to thy death I will.
    Vort. Stay, be advis'd;
I would not be the onely fall of Princes,
I slew thy brother.

---

    22. *me* twice in A and Tyr. — 25—27. Div. at *such | honor | both |
ears* Del. — 27. *drums heads* A, corr. by Del. — 38. *your counsel* Tyr., *thy
counsels* Del.
    SCENE III. *A Field of Battle* add. by Tyr. — 1. *the death* Tyr. —
3. *It would* Del.

5   *Prince.* Thou didst,
Black Traitor, and in that vengeance I pursue thee.
     Vort.   Take mercy for thy self, and flie my sword,
Save thine own life as satisfaction,
Which here I give thee for thy brothers death.
10   *Prince.* Give what's thine own: a Traitors heart and head,
That 's all thou art right Lord of. The Kingdom
Which thou usurp'st, thou most unhappy Tyrant,
Is leaving thee; the Saxons which thou broughtst
To back thy usurpations, are grown great,
15   And where they seat themselves, do hourly seek
To blot the Records of old Brute and Brittains
From memory of men, calling themselves
Hingest-men, and Brittain Hingest-land, that no more
The Brittain name be known: all this by thee,
20   Thou base destroyer of thy Native Countrey.

Enter EDOL.

     Edol. What, stand you talking? Fight!
     Prince. Hold, Edol.
     Edol. Hold out, my sword,
And listen not to King or Princes word;
25   There's work enough abroad, this task is mine.   [*Alarum.*
     Prince. Prosper thy Valour, as thy Vertues shine. [*Exeunt.*

SCENE IV.

Another Part of the Field of Battle.

Enter CADOR *and* EDWIN.

     Cador. Bright Victory her self fights on our part,
And, buckled in a golden Beaver, rides
Triumphantly before us.
     Edw. Justice is with her,
5   Who ever takes the true and rightful cause.
Let us not lag behinde them.

7. *flee* Tyr. — 18. *Brittain* om. in A and Edd. — 21. *are you*
Tyr.; *Fight* printed as stage-dir. in A; Tyr. omitting *fight* adds [*He
attacks Vort.*].
SCENE IV. No new scene in Tyr.

Enter PRINCE.

Cador. Here comes the Prince. How goes our fortunes, Sir?
Prince. Hopeful and fair, brave Cador.
Proud Vortiger, beat down by Edols sword,
Was rescu'd by the following multitudes,   10
And now for safety's fled unto a Castle
Here standing on the hill: but I have sent
A cry of hounds as violent as hunger,
To break his stony walls; or, if they fail,
We'l send in wilde fire to dislodge him thence,   15
Or burn them all with flaming violence.   [*Exeunt.*

SCENE V.

Another Part of the Field.

Blazing Star appears.

Florish Trumpets. *Enter* PRINCE VTER, EDOL, CADOR, EDWIN,
TOCLIO, *with Drum and Soldiers.*

Prince. Look, Edol: still this fiery exalation shoots
His frightful horors on th'amazed world;
See, in the beam that's 'bout his flaming ring,
A Dragons head appears, from out whose mouth
Two flaming <u>flakes</u> of fire stretch East and West.   5
Edol. And see, from forth the body of the Star
Seven smaller blazing streams directly point
On this affrighted kingdom.
Cador. 'Tis a dreadful Meteor.
Edwin. And doth portend strange <u>fears.</u>   10
Prince. This is no Crown of Peace; this angry fire
Hath something more to burn then Vortiger;
If it alone were pointed at his fall,
It would pull in his blasing Piramids
And be appeas'd, for Vortiger is dead.   15
Edol. These never come without their large effects.

7. *go* Del. — 14. *strong walls* Tyr. — 16. *with all* Tyr.
SCENE V. *Another Part of the Field.* add. by Tyr. — 1. *Look, Edol*
put by Elze (Notes I., p. 3) in a line by itself. — 3. *that 'bout* A and Del.,
corr. by Tyr. — 5. *flames] snakes* Tyr. — 14. *his] its* Tyr.

90 By me hath sent a nimble-ioynted iennet,
As swift as euer yet thou didst bestride,
And therewithall he counsels thee to flie;
Else death himself hath sworne that thou shalt die.
    Pr. Edw. Back with the beast vnto the beast that sent him!
95 Tell him, I cannot sit a cowards horse;
Bid him to-daie bestride the iade himselfe;
For I will staine my horse quite ore with bloud,
And double guild my spurs, but I will catch him;
So tell the carping boy, and get thee gone.   *[Exit Herald.*

Enter another Herald.

100   *Her.* Edward of Wales, Phillip, the second sonne
To the most mightie christian king of France,
Seeing thy bodies liuing-date expird,
All full of charitie and christian loue,
Commends this booke, full fraught with holy prayers,
105 To thy faire hand, and, for thy houre of lyfe,
Intreats thee that thou meditate therein,
And arme thy soule for hir long iourney towards.
Thus haue I done his bidding, and returne.
    Pr. Edw. Herald of Phillip, greet thy Lord from me:
110 All good that he can send, I can receiue;
But thinkst thou not, the vnaduised boy
Hath wrongd himselfe in thus far tendering me?
Haply he cannot praie without the booke,
— I thinke him no diuine extemporall —,
115 Then render backe this common place of prayer,
To do himselfe good in aduersitie;
Besides he knows not my sinnes qualitie,
And therefore knowes no praiers for my auaile;
Ere night his praier may be to praie to God,
120 To put it in my heart to heare his praier.
So tell the courtly wanton, and be gone.
    Her. I go.   *[Exit Herald.*

99. *capring* A; [*Exit Herald.*] and *Herald* after *another* add. by Del.
— 104. *holy* add. by Cap. and Tyr. — 112. *thus*] *this* A; *farre* B. —
113. *Happily* A. — 122. [*Exit Herald.*] om. A.

Pr. Edw. How confident their strength and number makes
Now, Audley, sound those siluer winges of thine,   [them.—
And let those milke-white messengers of time   125
Shew thy times learning in this dangerous time.
Thyselfe art bruis'd and bit with many broiles,
And stratagems forepast with yron pens
Are texted in thine honorable face;
Thou art a married man in this distresse,   130
But danger wooes me as a blushing maide:
Teach me an answere to this perillous time.
  Aud. To die is all as common as to liue:
The one in choice, the other holds in chase;
For, from the instant we begin to liue,   135
We do pursue and hunt the time to die:
First bud we, then we blow, and after seed,
Then, presently, we fall; and, as a shade
Followes the bodie, so we follow death.
If, then, we hunt for death, why do we feare it?   140
If we feare it, why do we follow it?
If we do feare, how can we shun it?
If we do feare, with feare we do but aide
The thing we feare, to seize on vs the sooner:
If wee feare not, then no resolued proffer   145
Can ouerthrow the limit of our fate;
For, whether ripe or rotten, drop we shall,
As we do drawe the lotterie of our doome.
  Pr. Edw. Ah, good olde man, a thousand thousand armors
These words of thine haue buckled on my backe: 150
Ah, what an idiot hast thou made of lyfe,
To seeke the thing it feares! and how disgrast
The imperiall victorie of murdring death,
Since all the liues, his conquering arrowes strike,
Seeke him, and he not them, to shame his glorie!   155
I will not giue a pennie for a lyfe,
Nor halfe a halfepenie to shun grim death,

Since for to liue is but to seeke to die,
And dying but beginning of new lyfe.
160 Let come the houre when he that rules it will!
To liue or die I hold indifferent.   *[Exeunt.*

SCENE V.

The same. The French Camp.

Enter KING IOHN *and* CHARLES.

K. Iohn. A sodaine darknes hath defast the skie,
The windes are crept into their caues for feare,
The leaues moue not, the world is husht and still,
The birds cease singing, and the wandring brookes
5 Murmure no wonted greeting to their shores;
Silence attends some wonder and expecteth
That heauen should pronounce some prophecie:
Where or from whome proceeds this silence, Charles?
 Charles. Our men, with open mouthes and staring eyes,
10 Looke on each other, as they did attend
Each others wordes, and yet no creature speakes;
A tongue-tied feare hath made a midnight houre,
And speeches sleepe through all the waking regions.
 K. Iohn. But now the pompeous Sunne, in all his pride,
15 Lookt through his golden coach vpon the worlde,
And, on a sodaine, hath he hid himselfe,
That now the vnder-earth is as a graue,
Darke, deadly, silent, and vncomfortable. *[A clamor of rauens.*
Harke, what a deadly outcrie do I heare?
20 *Charles.* Here comes my brother Phillip.
 K. Iohn.   All dismaid:

Enter PHILLIP.

What fearefull words are those thy lookes presage?
 Phil. A flight, a flight!

K. Iohn. Coward, what flight? thou liest, there needs no
Phil. A flight. [flight.

K. Iohn. Awake thy crauen powers, and tell on 25
The substance of that verie feare indeed,
Which is so gastly printed in thy face:
What is the matter?

Phil. A flight of vgly rauens
Do croke and houer ore our souldiers heads,
And keepe in triangles and cornerd squares, 30
Right as our forces are imbatteled;
With their approach there came this sodain fog,
Which now hath hid the airie floor of heauen
And made at noone a night vnnaturall
Vpon the quaking and dismaied world: 35
In briefe, our souldiers haue let fall their armes,
And stand like metamorphosd images,
Bloudlesse and pale, one gazing on another.

K. Iohn. I, now I call to mind the prophesie,
But I must giue no enterance to a feare. — 40
Returne, and harten vp those yeelding soules:
Tell them, the rauens, seeing them in armes,
So many faire against a famisht few,
Come but to dine vpon their handieworke
And praie vpon the carrion that they kill: 45
For when we see a horse laid downe to die,
Although he be not dead, the rauenous birds
Sit watching the departure of his life;
Euen so these rauens for the carcases
Of those poore English, that are markt to die, 50
Houer about, and, if they crie to vs,
Tis but for meate that we must kill for them.
Awake, and comfort vp my souldiers,
And sound the trumpets, and at once dispatch
This litle busines of a silly fraude. [*Exit* PHILIP. 55

26. *The very substance of that feare* prop. by Cap. and adopted by
Del. — 33. *floor*] *flower* AB. — 41. *these* AB. — 47. *he be* add. by Cap.,
Tyr., and Del. — 50. *these* B. — 55. [*Exit Prince.*] A.

Prince.   Thanks, Edol, we imbrace the name and title,
And in our Sheild and Standard shall the figure
Of a Red Dragon still be born before us,
To fright the bloody Saxons.   Oh, my Aurelius,
160 Sweet rest thy soul; let thy disturbed spirit
Expect revenge, think what it would, it hath:
The Dragon's coming in his fiery wrath.   *[Exeunt.*

ACT V.

SCENE I.

A barren Waste, a huge Rock appearing.
Thunder, then Musick.

Enter JOAN *fearfully,* THE DEVIL, *following her.*

Joan.   Hence, thou black horror!   Is thy lustful fire
Kindled agen? Not thy loud-throated thunder
Nor thy adulterate infernal Musick
Shall e're bewitch me more.   Oh, too too much
5   Is past already!
    Devil.   Why dost thou fly me?
I come a Lover to thee to imbrace
And gently twine thy body in mine arms.
    Joan.   Out, thou Hell-hound!
10   *Devil.*   What hound so e're I be,
Fawning and sporting as I would with thee,
Why should I not be stroakt and plaid withal?
Willt thou not thank the Lion might devour thee,
If he shall let thee pass?
    Joan.   Yes, thou art he;
15   Free me, and Ile thank thee.
    Devil.   Why, whither wouldst?
I am at home with thee, thou art mine own,
Have we not charge of family together?
Where is your son?
    Joan.   Oh, darknesse cover me!
    Devil.   There is a pride which thou hast won by me,

ACT V. SCENE I. *A barren . . . appearing.* add. by Tyr. — 3. *adul-*
terous Tyr. — 9. *thou* om. Tyr. — 12. *not* I Tyr.

The mother of a fame, shall never die.   20
Kings shall have need of written Chronicles
To keep their names alive, but Merlin none;
Ages to ages shall like Satellites
Report the wonders of his name and glory,
While there are tongues and times to tell his story.   25
    Joan. Oh, rot my memory before my flesh,
Let him be called some hell- or earth-bred monster,
That ne're had hapless woman for a mother!
Sweet death, deliver me! Hence from my sight!
Why shouldst thou now appear? I had no pride   30
Nor lustful thought about me, to conjure
And call thee to my ruine, whenas at first
Thy cursed person became visible.
    Devil. I am the same I was.
    Joan.   But I am chang'd.
    Devil. Agen Ile change thee to the same thou wert,   35
To quench my lust. — Come forth, by thunder led,
My Coajutors in the spoils of mortals.   [*Thunder.*

Enter Spirits.

Claspe in your Ebon arms that prize of mine,
Mount her as high as palled Hecate;
And on this rock Ile stand to cast up fumes   40
And darkness o're the blew-fac'd firmament:
From Brittain and from Merlin Ile remove her,
They ne're shall meet agen.
    Joan. Help me some saving hand!
If not too late, I cry: Let mercy come!   45

Enter MERLIN.

    Mer. Stay, you black slaves of night, let loose your hold,
Set her down safe, or by th'infernal Stix,
Ile binde you up with exorcisms so strong,
That all the black <u>pentagoron</u> of hell
Shall ne're release you. Save your selves and vanish!   50
                        [*Exeunt Spirits.*

    22. *name* Tyr. — 23. *Sabalists* A and Tyr., corr. by Del. — 28. *for his mother* Tyr. — 36. *quench to* A. — 37. *spoil* Tyr. — 38. (Stage-dir.) *Spirit* A. —50. *you* A, corr. by Tyr. and Del.

Devil. Ha! What's he?

Mer. The Childe has found his Father. Do you not know me?

Devil. Merlin!

Joan. Oh, help me, gentle son!

55 *Mer.* Fear not, they shall not hurt you.

Devil. Relievest thou her to disobey thy father?

Mer. Obedience is no lesson in your school;

Nature and kind to her commands my duty;

The part that you begot was against kinde,

60 So all I ow to you, is to be unkind.

Devil. Ile blast thee, slave, to death, and on this rock

Stick thee as an eternal Monument.

Mer. Ha, ha, thy power's too weak; what art thou, devil,

But an inferior lustful Incubus,

65 Taking advantage of the wanton flesh,

Wherewith thou dost beguile the ignorant?

Put off the form of thy humanity,

And cral upon thy speckled belly, serpent,

Or Ile unclasp the jaws of Acheron,

70 And fix thee ever in the local fire.

Devil. Traitor to hell! Curse that I e're begot thee!

Mer. Thou didst beget thy scourge. Storm not, nor stir,

The power of Merlins Art is all confirm'd

In the Fates decretals. Ile ransack hell,

75 And make thy masters bow unto my spells.

Thou first shalt taste it, — [*Thunder and Lightning in the Rock.*

Tenibrarum precis, devitiarum et infirorum Deus, hunc Incu-

bum in ignis eterni abisum accipite, aut in hoc carcere tenebroso

in sempiternum astringere mando.

[*The Rock incloses him.*

80 So! there beget earthquakes or some noisom damps,

For never shalt thou touch a woman more. —

How chear you, mother?

Joan. Oh, now my son is my deliverer,

Yet I must name him with my deepest sorrow.

[*Alarum afar off.*

51. *What is* Del. — 52. Two lines in Del. — 62. *as* add. by Del. —
75. *master* Tyr.; *spell* Del. — 76. *shall* A. — 77. *precis*] *princeps* prop.
by Elze, Notes I., p. 3. -- 80. *some* om. Del.

Mer.   Take comfort now: past times are ne're recal'd,   85
I did forsee your mischief, and prevent it.
Hark, how the sounds of war now call me hence
To aid Pendragon that in battail stands
Against the Saxons, from whose aid
Merlin must not be absent. Leave this soyl,   90
And Ile conduct you to a place retir'd,
Which I by art have rais'd, call'd Merlins Bower.
There shall you dwell with solitary sighs,
With grones and passions, your companions,
To weep away this flesh you have offended with,   95
And leave all bare unto your aierial soul.
And when you die, I will erect a Monument
Upon the verdant Plains of Salisbury,
No King shall have so high a sepulchre,
With pendulous stones that I will hang by art,   100
Where neither Lime nor Morter shalbe us'd,
A dark Enigma to the memory,
For none shall have the power to number them,
A place that I will hallow for your rest,
Where no Night-hag shall walk, nor Ware-wolf tread: 105
There Merlins Mother shall be sepulcher'd.   [*Exeunt.*

SCENE II.

The British Camp.

Enter Donobert, Gloster, *and* Hermit.

Dono.   Sincerely, Gloster, I have told you all:
My Daughters are both vow'd to Single Life,
And this day gone unto the Nunnery,
Though I begot them to another end,
And fairly promis'd them in Marriage,   5
One to Earl Cador, t'other to your son,
My worthy friend, the Earl of Gloster.
Those lost, I am lost: they are lost, all's lost.
Answer me this, then: Is't a sin to marry?

---

10   *Hermit.* Oh no, my Lord.

Dono. Go to, then, Ile go no further with you;
I perswade you to no ill, perswade you, then,
That I perswade you well.

    Gloster. 'Twill be a good Office in you, sir.

Enter CADOR *and* EDWIN.

15   *Dono.* Which since they thus neglect,
My memory shall lose them now for ever. —
See, see, the Noble Lords, their promis'd Husbands!
Had Fate so pleas'd, you might have call'd me Father.

    Edwin. Those hopes are past, my Lord; for even this minute
20 We saw them both enter the Monastery,
Secluded from the world and men for ever.

    Cador. 'Tis both our griefs we cannot, Sir.
But from the King take you the Times joy from us:
The Saxon King Ostorius slain and Octa fled,
25 That Woman-fury, Queen Artesia,
Is fast in hold, and forc't to re-deliver
London and Winchester, which she had fortifi'd,
To Princely Vter, lately styl'd Pendragon,
Who now triumphantly is marching hither
30 To be invested with the Brittain Crown.

    Dono. The joy of this shall banish from my breast
All thought that I was Father to two Children,
Two stubborn Daughters, that have left me thus.
Let my old arms embrace, and call you Sons;
35 For, by the Honor of my Fathers House,
I'le part my estate most equally betwixt you.

    Edwin, Cador. Sir, y'are most noble.

Flor. Tromp. Enter EDOL *with Drum and Colours,*
OSWOLD *bearing the Standard,* TOCLIO *the Shield, with
the Red Dragon pictur'd in'em, two* BISHOPS *with the
Crown,* PRINCE VTER, MERLIN, ARTESIA *bound,* GUARD,
and CLOWN.

    Prince. Set up our Sheild and Standard, noble Soldiers.

<hr>

    11. *I will* Del. — 19. *past, my Lord, for ever; this* Tyr. — 23. ? *take the.*
— 30. *British Crown* Tyr. — 37. *you are* Tyr. and Del.

We have firm hope that, tho' our Dragon sleep,
Merlin will us and our fair Kingdom keep.   40
   Clown.   As his Uncle lives, I warrant you.
   Glost.   Happy Restorer of the Brittains fame,
Uprising Sun, let us salute thy glory:
Ride in a day perpetual about us,
And no night be in thy thrones zodiack.   45
Why do we stay to binde those Princely browes
With this Imperial Honor?
   Prince.   Stay, noble Gloster!
That monster first must be expel'd our eye,
Or we shall take no joy in it.
   Dono.   If that be hindrance, give her quick Judgement,   50
And send her hence to death; she has long deserv'd it.
   Edol.   Let my Sentence stand for all: take her hence,
And stake her carcase in the burning Sun,
Till it be parcht and dry, and then fley off
Her wicked skin, and stuff the pelt with straw   55
To be shown up and down at Fairs and Markets,
Two pence a piece to see so foul a Monster,
'Twill be a fair monopoly, and worth the begging.
   Artes.   Ha, ha, ha!
   Edol.   Dost laugh, Erictho?   60
   Artes.   Yes, at thy poor invention,
Is there no better torturemonger?
   Dono.   Burn her to dust.
   Artes.   That's a Phœnix death, and glorious.
   Edol.   I, that's too good for her.
   Prince.   Alive she shall be buried, circled in a wall,   65
Thou murdress of a King, there starve to death.
   Artes.   Then Ile starve death when he comes for his prey,
And i'th' mean time Ile live upon your curses.
   Edol.   I, 'tis diet good enough; away with her!
   Artes.   With joy, my best of wishes is before,   70
Thy brother's poison'd, but I wanted more.   *[Exit.*

   39. *fair hope* Tyr. — 49. *Or else we take* Tyr. — 57. *piece.   To see*
Del. — 58. *'Twill] will* A and Edd.; *and worth the begging* om. Tyr. —
64. *to* A. — 65. *Alive* put in a line by itself by Del. — 69. *diet* om. Del..

Prince. Why does our Prophet Merlin stand apart,
Sadly observing these our Ceremonies,
And not applaud our joys with thy hid knowledge?
75 Let thy divining Art now satisfie
Some part of my desires; for well I know,
'Tis in thy power to show the full event,
That shall both end our Reign and Chronicle.
Speak, learned Merlin, and resolve my .fears,
80 Whether by war we shal expel the Saxons,
Or govern what we hold with beauteous peace
In Wales and Brittain?
    Mer. Long happiness attend Pendragons Reign!
What Heaven decrees, fate hath no power to alter:
85 The Saxons, sir, will keep the ground they have,
And by supplying numbers still increase,
Till Brittain be no more. So please your Grace,
I will in visible apparitions
Present you Prophecies which shall concern
90 Succeeding Princes which my Art shall raise,
Till men shall call these times the latter days.
    Prince. Do it, my Merlin,
And Crown me with much joy and wonder.

Merlin *strikes. Hoeboys. Enter a King in Armour, his
Sheild quarter'd with thirteen Crowns. At the other door
enter divers Princes who present their Crowns to him at
his feet, and do him homage; then enters Death and strikes
        him; he, growing sick, Crowns* Constantine. [*Exeunt.*
    Mer. This King, my Lord, presents your Royal Son,
95 Who in his prime of years shall be so fortunate,
That thirteen several Princes shall present
Their several Crowns unto him, and all Kings else
Shall so admire his fame and victories,
That they shall all be glad,
100 Either through fear or love, to do him homage;
But death, who neither favors the weak nor valiant,
In the middest of all his glories soon shall seize him,

97. *unto*] *to* Tyr. — 101. *favours neither* Tyr.

Scarcely permitting him to appoint one
In all his purchased Kingdoms to succeed him.
   Prince. Thanks to our Prophet   105
For this so wish'd for satisfaction ;
And hereby now we learn that always Fate
Must be observ'd, what ever that decree:
All future times shall still record this Story,
Of Merlin's learned worth and Arthur's glory.   110

[Exeunt Omnes.

THE END.

NOTES.

ACT I.

1, 10. Her promise already ratified this condition.

1, 24. *protest*, i. e. declare his love; cp. Wiv. III. 5. 75: *after we had embraced, kissed and protested*, and Cæs. I. 2. 74: *to stale with ordinary oaths my love to every new protester.*

1, 40. *dull stomacks*, i. e. weak appetite. Tieck: '*Viel eurer Art sind nur von schwachem Hunger.*'

1, 43. *speaks yours*, i. e. declares itself yours. Cp. Wint. I. 2. 178: *we are yours in the garden*, i. e. we are at your service.

1, 44, 45. Cp. Tit. Andr. II. 1. 82, 83:

> *She is a woman, therefore may be woo'd*
> *She is a woman, therefore may be won.*

1, 90 seqq. Tieck:

> '*Die Schwester ist im Vorteil noch; kommt, lasst sie,*
> *Sie wird nicht minder schnell als ich verlieren,*
> *Ihm fehlt nur Kunst die Würfel zu regieren.*'

1, 106. Your wishes must put some restraint on you, if you give faith and credence to my promise. The punctuation of A (*then, as to my promise, you give faith and promise?*), adopted by Edd., is void of all sense.

2, 1. Though the form *tiding* does not occur in Shakespeare, we have not altered it, as it is not uncommon in Middle English; cp. Skeat, Etym. Dict., s. v.

2, 38, 39. The only Power, i. e. God, who has discomfited the enemy, should not be limited; you should pursue your victory, and not treat with the enemy.

2, 42. If mischiefs are not quite uprooted and destroyed, they will soon reappear with new vigour; if the vanquished enemy is spared by the conqueror, he will soon grow mischievous again. Tieck:

> *'Beschränkt nicht, liebt ihr eure Sicherheit,*
> *Die hohe Macht, die euch allein beschirmte,*
> *Traut einem offenen Feinde nicht zu sehr,*
> *Noch ist er im Verlust, ihr habt gewonnen,*
> *Sonst endet Unheil nicht, ist nur begonnen.'*

2, 45. Tieck: *'das Wort des Friedens*
> *Ist blut'gen Augen schön, doch angewendet*
> *Mit Pflastern, durch die das Gesicht erblindet,*
> *Zeigt wen'ge Kunst, wenn auch der Heilung Wunsch.'*

2, 56. Tieck: *'Man kann gewiss in wen'ger Zeit von ihnen*
> *Das Land befrein.'*

But it would perhaps be better to give ll. 56 and 57 *(Who* (not
We) in less time will undertake to free Our country from them?) to
Aurelius and not to *Cador.*

2, 79. Aurelius evidently repeats the expression used by
Artesia; Tyrrell's conjecture is, therefore, to be rejected.

2, 86. If I were but young again, I am sure this gilded pill
would take my appetite quickly, I should have no appetite to taste
it; whereupon the king replies: To be sure, you are old, and you
have quite forgotten the defects of your own youth. As for *to take
one's stomach,* cp. 1 H. IV., II. 3. 44: *what is't that takes from thee
thy stomach?* Tieck seems to be mistaken in translating:

> *'Wär' ich nur wieder jung, die gold'ne Pille*
> *Begehrte wohl mein Magen leicht.'*

2, 118. Tieck:
> *'Lass mich als Weib, so unwert ich auch bin,*
> *Die Nachricht bringen deiner Menschlichkeit,*
> *Des milde Tugend Fama laut verkündet,*
> *Und der die Völker sich in Liebe bindet.'*

2, 121. *As being* &c is loosely annexed to *Take the report of
thy humanity* l. 119, = that we are overcome &c.

2, 134. And do I act mine own (deeds) not free. As to *free*
= freely, cp. H. VIII., II. 1. 82: *I as free forgive you as I would
be forgiven;* and Mcb. II. 1. 19: *which else should free have
wrought.*

2, 158 seqq. The sense of the passage, which is perhaps somewhat corrupt, seems to be: Tell him that our entertainment expects
him as such (i. e. as brother), and that our marriage will add to
our joys and happiness; the good or evil qualities of man and
woman, like two waves, get united and doubled by marriage (*in
this*). Tieck:

> *'Sagt ihm welch' grosse Freud' ihn hier erwartet,*
> *Und wie mein Glück der Ehebund vermehrt,*

> *Wie jede Freude mir nun doppelt helle*
> *Im Spiegel dieser wollustreichen Welle.'*

2, 58. *sweet* often applied to heaven and celestial things.
Cp. IV. 5. 160: *Sweet rest thy soul.*

ACT II.

1, 5. Tieck: *'Denn er armiert und beint auch dazu, und braucht dich zum Herold, seine Armatur kund zu geben.'* As to *blaze* = proclaim like a herald, cp. 2 H. VI., IV. 10. 76: *thou shalt wear it* (the blood) *as a herald's coat, to emblaze the honour that thy master got.*

1, 27. *uses*, i. e. is accustomed to go, frequents. *He useth every day to a merchant's house where I serve water.* B. Jonson (Quoted by Webster.).

1, 30. *Knight of the Post*, a man who gained his living by giving false evidence on trials or false bail (Nares, s. v.), is here comically applied by the Clown to the trees of the forest which his sister had called to witness.

1, 39. *Oh yes*, i. e. *oyez*, hear ye, give attention, the usual introduction of a publication of the public crier. (Al. Schmidt, Shakespeare-Lexicon, s. v.).

1, 53. i. e. to relate her beauties to him (*Fänd' ich hier wen, die Schön' ihm zu beschreiben.* Tieck.).

1, 67. Though the construction is somewhat inexact, it does not seem necessary to read *you* for *and.*

1, 69. Tieck: '*Weil ich sie fand und doch verlor.*'

1, 75 seqq. These lines seem to refer to one of two adventures related by Plutarch, Life of Marius, ch. 39 and ch. 45. A soldier was sent by the magistrates of the town of Minturnæ into Marius' bedroom, in order to kill him. But on seeing Marius' face, and on hearing his voice, the soldier, frightened out of his wits, threw away his sword and fled from the house. — In ch. 45 Plutarch relates that Marius once sent some warriors with the order to kill Anthony the orator. When the soldiers found Anthony in his chamber, 'they beganne to encorage one another to kill him, not one of them having the harte to laye handes uppon him. For Anthonyes tongue was as sweete as a Sirene, and had such an excellent grace in speaking that when he begann to speake vnto the souldiers, and to pray them to saue his life: there was not one of them so hard hearted, as once to touch him, no not onely to looke him in the face, but looking downewardes, fell a weeping.' See North's Plutarch, ed. 1579, p. 477.

1, 78. Tieck: *'Zur Sonne strebt der Dunst, wird Regenflut.*'

1, 98. *rude and boldly* = rudely and boldly, as often in Shak.

√ 1, 103. Cp. All's I. 3. 188: *you have wound a goodly clew.*

√ 1, 106. *Jug*, a diminutive of Joan, also occurs Lr. I. 4. 245: *Whoop, Jug, I love thee.*

1, 110. As *maid* is = girl (*is there a maid with child by him?* Meas. I. 2. 92), Tyrrell's conjecture is quite uncalled for.

1, 127. We are to suppose that the Prince turns to the Clown, in order to beat him too.

√ 1. 157. *overshot*, exceeded in shooting, blundering. Cp. H. V., III. 7. 134: *'tis not the first time you were overshot.*

√ 2. 12. *the presence*, i. e. the court. Cp. H. VIII., IV. 2. 37: *i' the presence he would say untruths*, i. e. before the king and his court.

2, 13. *discontent*, i. e. discontented.

√ 2, 15. *perswade his patience.* Cp. Hml. IV. 5. 168: *hadst thou thy wits and didst persuade revenge?* and 3 H. VI., III. 3. 176: *sends me a paper to persuade me patience.*

2, 31. It would perhaps be better to write *With Pagan Infidels, the least part Christians*, for the sense seems to be: The court is divided with pagan Infidels, who are equal to the christians, if not in number, at least in authority and influenc *(in their commands).*

2, 37. Your commissions are not worth anything, you may inclose and keep them. Tieck: '*Schlafmützen schafft euch an anstatt der Helme.*'

2, 49. They had already resolved to leave the country, hoping by that means to preserve their lives.

2, 51, 52. These two lines may be considered as a blank-verse (l. 52 *'Twas*).

2, 71, *as black as hell.* Cp. John IV. 3. 121: *thou'rt damned as black, nay, nothing is so black.*

2, 83. For the proverbial phrase *bought and sold* (our German *verraten und verkauft*) cp. Err. III. 1. 72, John V. 4. 10, 1 H. VI., IV. 4. 13, Rich. III., V. 3. 305, Troil. II. 1. 51.

2, 90. Cp. *to be exposed against the warring winds* Lr. IV. 7. 32, where Ff. and modern Edd. read *opposed.*

2, 111. *all our whole Kingdome*, cp. II. 3. 9: *all the whole Court.*

3, 30. Cp. Cæs. IV. 3. 133: *how vilely doth this cynic rhyme.*

3, 45. *above present sense*, i. e. without their perceiving any thing directly by the eye.

3, 46. *there may*, scil. be such a power.

3, 86. We have not been able to discover the names of the two spirits elsewhere.

√ 3, 139. *birthright*, i. e. patrimony, inheritance.

3, 150. *on whom* refers to *woman*, l. 148.

3, 195. *health-loved*, i. e. loved when they were in a state of health.

3, 198. Tieck: '*Du kannst nicht leben, stirb mit keckem Mut.*'
The use of the infinitive with *to* after a preposition is very surprising;
it may be compared with passages as *For to have this absolute
power of Dictator they added never to be afraid to be deposed*, i. e.
for to to have &c. North's Plutarch 611 (Quoted by Abbott, § 355).

3, 205. If we see our vicious thoughts and actions miscarry,
we turn from vice, and only endeavour to do what is good.

3, 222. *Mussel*, i. e muscle, a bivalvular shell-fish (Cp. Tp. I.
2. 463).

3, 257. *Envy* = malice, as often in Shak.

ACT III.

1, 146. *placcats*. 'Placket, probably a stomacher (according
to some a petticoat, or the opening in it.' A. Schmidt, Shak.-Lex.,
s. v. Cp. LLL. III. 186: *Dread prince of plackets* and Lr. III. 4. 100:
keep thy hand out of plackets.

2, 22. *nor to cease*, i. e. nor do I persuade you to cease.

2, 42. Cp. Wint. III. 2. 1: *this sessions even pushes against our
heart.*

2, 65. The regular construction being interrupted by l. 66
in you (l. 67) takes up again *in whose folly.*

2, 75. *goodness*, i. e. happiness, good fortune.

2, 84 seqq. Tieck:

> '*Ich bitte, theure Schwester, hör' mich an:*
> *Die Welt ist Maskenspiel, nicht was ich bin,*
> *Nur meine Larve täuscht den schwachen Sinn.*
> *Die Larve fällt, sobald der Tanz vollbracht,*
> *Und alle schaun dann in des Todes Nacht.*
> *Das Glück, es überlebt den Abend nicht,*
> *Wo Falsches ächt scheint bei der Kerzen Licht.*
> *Wer dies erkennt, sucht edlere Gewande,*
> *Die ihn bedecken vor der Blösse Schande.*
> *Er weiss, die Welt flieht ihn in kurzer Zeit,*
> *Und wirft es ab, dies täuschend bunte Kleid.*'

2, 104. Tieck:

> '*Ist dies ein Quell nicht ewig neuer Sorgen?*
> *Wie ungewiss sind diese Mutterfreuden!*
> *Die wir geboren, sehn wir oftmals leiden*
> *So manche Not, dass wir zum Himmel flehn,*
> *Er mög' ihr frühes End' uns lassen sehn.*
> *Auch glücklich, raubt der Tod doch, was uns freute,*
> *So steuern wir zu unsers Feindes Beute.*'

2, 116. Tieck:

> '*Nicht Freunde, Vater, Gatten hab' ich nun.*
> *Geborgte Maskenkleider sind es nur,*
> *Worin wir schwärmen; unser Leben ist*
> *Ein freier Tag nur zwischen Fieberbrennen,*
> *Und eh' [wir] diesen nur geniessen können,*
> *Rafft uns ein zweites Fieber hin. O Schwester!*
> *Du meiner Seele Trost, vergieb den Hohn.*
> *Wie konnte die, (ich muss dich Vorbild nennen)*
> *Die sich nicht kannte, wohl dein Glück erkennen?*
> *Von ihm soll nun die Welt mich nicht mehr trennen.*'

2, 120. *Which* refers to *one good* (l. 119). The construction is: Ere we, away from the ague-day, have time to praise the good day.

3, 11. *vent*, apparently = scent. This passage seems to corroborate the explanation of *it (war) is sprightly walking, audible, and full of vent*, Cor. IV. 5. 238, as given in Edinb. Rev., Oct. 1872. *vent*, in both the passages, is a technical term of sportsmen for scent, and *full of scent* means full of eager excitement, as a dog scenting any thing, full of pluck and courage. S. Al. Schmidt, Shak.-Lex., s. v. *vent* 5.

5, 80. *Or are mine eyes matches?* The sense seems to be: or are my eyes indeed equal to each other, so that both of them always see the same thing? Cp. Spens. F. Q., IV. 1. 28:

> *Als as she double spake, so heard she double,*
> *With matchlesse eares, deformed and distort.*

5, 103. Tieck: '*Von Seiten der Mutter stammt sie von den Willigs in Suffolk ab, aber unser eigentliches Stammschloss ist Brings-herein und Lassnichtlos.*' *Layton-Buzzard*, i. e. Lay it on, Buzzard, was perhaps a technical term of hunting.

5, 107. Tieck: '*Seine Ahnherrn stammen aus Höllenbrodel in Wales.*'

5, 18. Upon such a hazardous sea that the least miscarriage shall ruin me.

5, 25. For *contráry*, cp. Wint. V. 1. 45, John IV. 2. 198, Tim. IV. 3. 144, Hml. III. 2. 221.

6, 3. *Wakes with injoying*, i. e. that awakes, that ceases to be as soon as we will enjoy it. Tieck:

> '*Was ihr Liebe nennt,*
> *Ist nur ein Traum, der beim Genuss entschwindet.*'

6, 60. Cp. Wiv. II. 1. 136: *I have a sword, and it shall bite thee,* and Rich. II., I. 3. 303, Lr. V. 3. 276.

6, 63. My own beauty made me as it were his prisoner. Tieck:

'*Die eigne Schönheit brachte mir Gefahr.*'

6, 65. *O my sad soul.* Tieck: '*O meine Ahnung.*' Cp. LLL. V.
2. 741: *entreat out of a new-sad soul* and Ado V. 1. 42: *my soul
doth tell me Hero is belied.*

6, 95. Cp. 3 H. VI., I. 4. 41: *view this face, and bite thy tongue
that slanders him with cowardice.*

6, 108. Cp. *fire and brimstone!* Tw. II. 5. 56, Oth. III. 1. 245.

ACT IV.

1, 11. *Sparrow-hawk,* i. e. the little Antick Spirit.

1, 12. *Cardecu.* 'Quart d'écu, the quarter of a crown, i. e. fifteen
pence, or thereabouts.' Nares, s. v.

1, 29. *conveyance,* dishonest practice, trickery; cp. 3 H. VI., III.
3. 160: *Till I make King Lewis behold thy sly conveyance and thy
Lord's false love.*

1, 47. *Artist,* scholar, as also sometimes in Shakespeare.

1, 71. *Diggon.* ? = *dig on.* Tieck: '*Darauf berufe dich nur.
Dann soll es ja auch eines Kindes Blut sein, und wer wird dich mit
deinem langen Bart wol für ein Kind halten? Ist das nicht Grund
genug, Vetter?*'

1, 94. *neither* follows *but* by way of enforcing it. Cp. Merch.
III. 5. 9: *and that is but a kind of bastard hope neither.*

1. 112. *Wind-sucker* (the name of the kestrel, a species of
kite) seems to have been a denomination for a wanton woman.
As to the tropical use of the word, cp. Ben Jonson, Silent Woman,
Act I.: *Did you ever hear such a wind-sucker as this? Or such a
rook as the other?* (Quoted by Nares, *s. v.*)

1, 139. As to the construction, which is altered by Delius, cp:
John IV. 2, 165: *whom they say is killed to-night,* Cymb. I. 4, 137
whom in constancy you think stands so safe.

1, 174. *a seeming fair young man,* i. e. he who was in appearance a fair young man.

1, 194. Cp. Lr. III. 4, 69: *All the plagues that in the pendulous
air hang fated o'er men's faults.*

1, 227. 'There is no doubt some corruption in [this] line, but
it baffles my endeavours to detect and mend it.' Elze, Notes I,
p. 2. It seems to be best to consider *Of* as a corruption of *on,*
as it often occurs; cp. *such a beard of thy face,* supra IV. 1, 73,
Pox of those Conjurers, ib. 83. Also Tieck seems to have understood the passage in this way:

> '*an diesem Kampf,*
> *Am Sieg und Fall, der diesem wird gegeben,*
> *Hängt euer Schicksal, euer Reich und Leben.*'

1, 270. *double footing*, i. e. taking double steps; another expression for *at full march*.

2, 16. These lines might also be divided:

> *For heavens love, sir, march on! — Oh, my patience!*
> *Will you delay untill the Saxons come*
> *To aid his party?*

3, 3. The sense is: I should not like to be the only man that brings princes to fall. Tieck: '*Nicht aller Fürsten Blut will ich vergiessen.*'

5, 5. As to the use of *flakes*, cp. Lr. IV. 7, 30: *these white flakes*, i. e. this white hair.

5, 10. *fears*, i. e. fearful objects, as Rom. IV. 3, 50: *environed with all these hideous fears.*

5, 18. *Pithon*, i. e. Pythian.

5, 50. 51. The construction is inexact, *in it* being pleonastic after *from which*: we gather from thy tears that there is much sorrow in it, or, that much sorrow will come from it.

5, 112. The sense is: with the title of Monarch of the West.

5, 161. *think it hath*, i. e. shall have the revenge which it would like to have.

ACT V.

1, 49. *Pentagoron* and *local fire*, (l. 70) cabalistic expressions, the exact meaning of which is not intelligible to us.

1, 77. *precis.* We have not adopted Elze's conjecture, because *precis*, in cabalistic language, seems to have been an expression for *God*; cp. Doctoris Iohannis Fausti Magicae Naturalis et Innaturalis Erster Theil. Passau 1505, p. 11: *O Adonay, precis, Christe, Ahischca*; p. 54: *apraecis Diabolam.* [*precis* from *prex, preces* = deprecation?].

1, 94. *passion*, i. e. sorrow.

1, 96. Tieck: '*Und deinen Geist vom Ird'schen zu befrei'n.*' to leave s. t. bare to, i. e. to abandon, to surrender to. Cp. *left me bare to weather* Cymb. III. 3. 64, *left me naked to mine enemies* H. VIII., III. 2. 458.

1, 100. *pendulous*, cp. supra IV. 1. 194.

2, 11 seqq. The difficult passage seems to be an exclamation addressed to the daughters: Go to, then; I shall live without you

(Cp. Merch. I. 2. 97: *I shall make shift to go without him*). But you may be persuaded that I only persuaded you well. Tieck:

> '*So sei's! Ich sehe sie nicht wieder,*
> *Zum Uebel überred' ich nicht, sagt ihnen*
> *Dass ich ja nur das Gute stets begehrte.*
> GL. *Ihr thut daran ein gutes Werk.*'

2, 22. scil. *to call you father.*

√ 2, 70. *is before*, i. e. goes before, is performed before.

EHRHARDT KARRAS, Printer, Halle.

Principien der Sprachgeschichte von **Hermann Paul.** 2. Aufl.
1886. 8. 9,00.

Sammlung kurzer Grammatiken germanischer Dialekte.
Herausgegeben von **Wilhelm Braune.** 8.

Bis jetzt sind erschienen:

A. In der Hauptreihe:

Bd. I. **Gotische Grammatik** mit einigen Lesestücken und Wortverzeichnis von Wilhelm Braune. 3. Aufl. 1887. *ℳ* 2,40.

Bd. II. **Mittelhochdeutsche Grammatik** von Hermann Paul. 2. Aufl. 1884. *ℳ* 2,60.

Bd. III. **Angelsächsische Grammatik** von Eduard Sievers. 2. Aufl. 1886. *ℳ* 4,20.

Bd. IV. Altnordische Grammatik 1. **Altisländische und altnorwegische Grammatik** unter Berücksichtigung des Urnordischen von Adolf Noreen. 1884. *ℳ* 3,80.

Bd. V. **Althochdeutsche Grammatik** von Wilhelm Braune. 1886. *ℳ* 4,60.

B. In der Ergänzungsreihe:

Bd. I. **Nominale Stammbildungslehre** der altgermanischen Dialekte von Friedrich Kluge. 1886. *ℳ* 2,60.

Neudrucke deutscher Litteraturwerke des XVI. und XVII. Jahrhunderts (herausgegeben von Prof. Dr. W. Braune in Giessen). No. 1—67. à 60 Pf.

 1. Martin Opitz, Buch von der deutschen Poeterei. (1624.)
 2. Johann Fischart, Aller Praktik Grossmutter. (1572.)
 3. Andreas Gryphius, Horribilicribrifax. Scherzspiel. (1663.)
 4. M. Luther, An den christlichen Adel deutscher Nation. (1520.)
 5. Johann Fischart, Der Flöhhaz. (1573.)
 6. Andreas Gryphius, Peter Squenz. Schimpfspiel. (1663.)
7—8. Das Volksbuch vom Doctor Faust. (1587.)
 9. J. B. Schupp, Der Freund in der Not. (1657.)
10—11. Lazarus Sandrub, Delitiæ historicæ et poeticæ. (1618.)
12—14. Christian Weise, Die drei ärgsten Erznarren. (1673.)
 15. J. W. Zinkgref, Auserlesene Gedichte deutsch. Poeten. (1624.)
16—17. Joh. Lauremberg, Niederdeutsche Scherzgedichte. 1652. Mit Einleitung, Anmerkungen und Glossar von W. Braune.
 18. M. Luther, Sendbrief an Leo X. Von der Freiheit eines Christenmenschen. Warum des Papsts Bücher verbrannt seien. Drei Reformationsschriften aus dem Jahre 1520.
19—25. H. J. Chr. v. Grimmelshausen, Der abenteuerliche Simplicissimus. Abdr. d. ältesten Originalausgabe (1669.)
26—27. Hans Sachs, Sämmtliche Fastnachtspiele in chronolog. Ordnung n. d. Originalen hersg. von Edmund Goetze. 1. Bändchen.
 28. M. Luther, Wider Hans Worst. (1541.)
 29. Hans Sachs, Der hürnen Seufrid, Tragoedie in 7 Acten.
 30. Burk. Waldis, Der verlorne Sohn, ein Fastnachtspiel. (1527.)
31—32. Hans Sachs, Fastnachtspiele hersg. von E. Goetze. 2.
 33. Barth. Krüger, Hans Clawerts Werckliche Historien. (1587.)
34—35. Caspar Scheidt, Friedrich Dedekinds Grobianus. (1551.)
 36. Hayneccius, Hans Pfriem Meister Kecks. Komödie. (1582.)

37—38. Andreas Gryphius, Sonn- und Feiertags-Sonette. (1639 und 1663.) Herausg. von Dr. Heinrich Welti.

39—40. Hans Sachs, Fastnachtspiele herausg. von E. Goetze. 3.

41. Das Endinger Judenspiel. Herausg. von K. v. Amira.

42—43. Hans Sachs, Fastnachtspiele herausg. von E. Goetze. 4.

44—47. Die Gedichte des Königsberger Dichterkreises aus Alberts Arien und musikalischer Kürbshütte (1638—1650) herausgeg von L. H. Fischer.

48. Heinrich Albert. Musikbeilagen zu den Gedichten des Königsberger Dichterkreises, hg. von Rob. Eitner.

49. Burk. Waldis' Streitgedichte gegen Herzog Heinrich d. Jüngern von Braunschweig. Herausgeg. von Friedrich Koldewey.

50. Martin Luther, Von der Winkelmesse u. Pfaffenweihe. (1533.)

51—52. Hans Sachs, Fastnachtspiele herausg. von Ed Goetze. 5.

53—54. M. Rinckhart, Der Eislebische christliche Ritter. (1613.)

55—56. Till Eulenspiegel. (1515.) Herausg. von Hermann Knust.

57—58. Chr. Reuter, Schelmuffsky. (1696. 1697.)

59. Chr. Reuter, Schelmuffsky. Abdruck der ersten Fassung 1696.

60—61. Hans Sachs, Fastnachtspiele herausg. von E. Goetze. 6.

62. Ein schöner Dialogus von Martino Luther und der geschickten Botschaft aus der Hölle. (1523).

63—64. Hans Sachs, Fastnachtspiele hg. von E. Goetze. 7. (Schluss.)

65—67. Johann Fischarts Geschichtklitterung (Gargantua). Herausg. von A. Alsleben. Erste Hälfte (Bogen 1—15).

Quellenschriften zur neueren deutschen Litteratur. Herausgegeben von **Alexander Bieling.** kl. 8.

Nr. 1. Gottscheds Reineke Fuchs. Abdruck der hochdeutschen Prosa-Uebersetzung vom Jahre 1752. 1886. ℊ 1,60.

Nr. 2. Lebens-Beschreibung des Herrn Gözens von Berlichingen. Abdruck der Original-Ausgabe von Steigerwald. Nürnberg 1731. 1886. ℊ 1,60.

Altdeutsche Textbibliothek. Herausgegeben von **Hermann Paul.** kl. 8.

Nr. 1. Die Gedichte Walther's von der Vogelweide. Herausgegeben von H. Paul. 1882. ℊ 1,80.

Nr. 2. Gregorius von Hartmann von Aue. Herausgegeben von H. Paul. 1882. ℊ 1,00.

Nr. 3. Der arme Heinrich von Hartmann von Aue. Herausgegeben von H. Paul. 1882. ℊ 0,40.

Nr. 4. Heliand. Herausg. von O. Behaghel. 1882. ℊ 2,40.

Nr. 5. Kudrun. Herausg. von B. Symons. 1883. ℊ 2,80.

Nr. 6. König Rother. Herausg. von K. v. Bahder. 1884. ℊ 1,50.

Nr. 7. Reinhart Fuchs. Herausg. von K. Reissenberger. 1886. ℊ 1,20.

Nr. 8. Reinke de vos. Herausg. von Fr. Prien. Mit 2 Holzschnitten. 1887. ℊ 4,00.

Altnordische Textbibliothek. Herausgegeben von **E. Mogk.** kl. 8.

Nr. 1. Gunnlaugssaga Ormstungu. Mit Einleitung und Glossar herausgegeben von E. Mogk. 1886. ℊ 1,60.